JULIA MARTIN DARE

DUBLIN, VIRGINIA USA

First Printing June 2023

This is a work of fiction. Names, characters, places and incidents are either the product of the author's imagination or are used fictitiously. Any resemblance to actual persons, living or dead, events, or locales is entirely coincidental.

Cover design by Autumn and Michael Morgera
Edited by RoMansa Hearts Publishing

Published by:
RoMansa Hearts Publishing
5245 Newbern Rd.
Dublin, VA 24084

https://sites.google.com/d/1_9YwDP9ObfxtcRjx-dc7AtMyxajsWvnh/p/1rClZuRcz9IR8B0ku2_I6ubli56gE3bKs

ISBN: 979-8-9883512-0-7 (paperback)

Printed in the United States of America.

This book is dedicated to my mom,
who has been telling me for years to write a book.
Well, Mom, here it is!
Thanks for believing in me!

ACKNOWLEDGMENTS

I'd like to thank several people for helping me with this book. First, my advance readers Pam Kimmel, Lynne Lewis and Karen Alderman. Thank you for your time, your encouragement, and your honesty. I'd also like to thank Lauren Sosik, BSN, RN, CCRN for helping with the hospital scenes, Chris Oliveira for sharing his knowledge of guns and Mike Garnett, NRP Extraordinaire. I love you guys. Finally, a huge thank you to Autumn and Michael Morgera for their editing expertise.

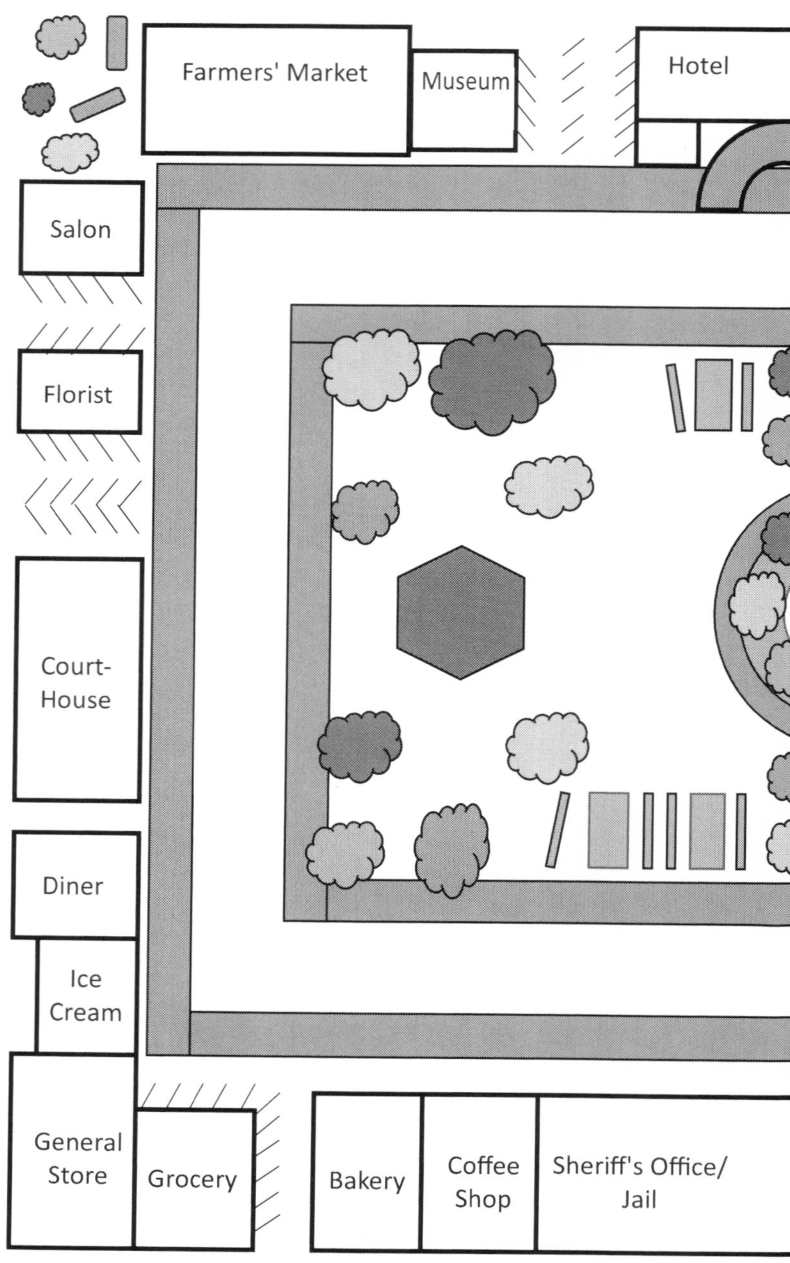
Farmers' Market
Museum
Hotel
Salon
Florist
Court-
House
Diner
Ice
Cream
General
Store
Grocery
Bakery
Coffee
Shop
Sheriff's Office/
Jail

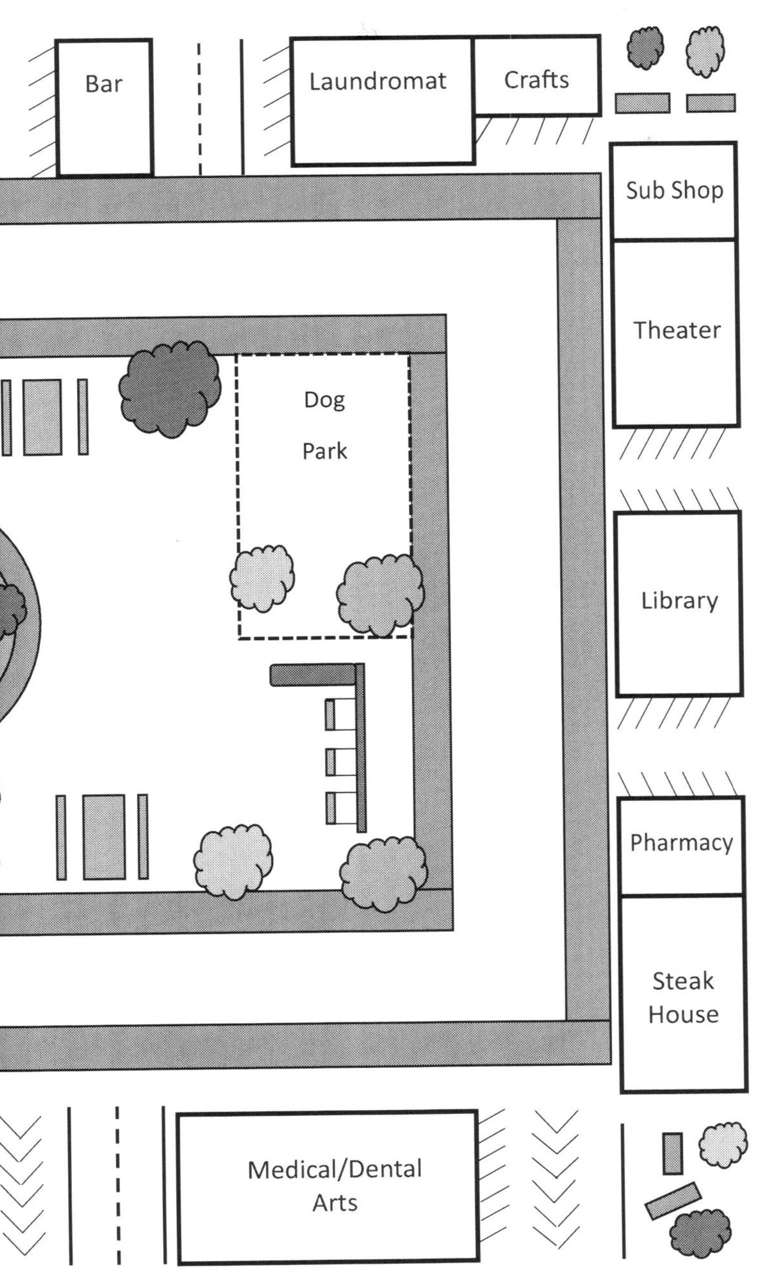
Bar
Laundromat
Crafts
Sub Shop
Theater
Dog
Park
Library
Pharmacy
Steak
House
Medical/Dental
Arts

THE SHERIFF'S STAR

I loved the silence of town just before dawn. It was my favorite time to jog.

Whirlwind was a great little town. I had passed through this town a long time ago and fallen in love with it, so when I needed somewhere to go where no one knew me and I could have some peace, this is where I chose. I loved the huge park that anchored downtown where I was currently jogging. The shops and businesses around the park gave the town a rural feel that I found myself craving despite having lived in Nashville my whole life.

So far no one seemed to have recognized me, and only my manager and personal assistant knew I was in Whirlwind. I wanted to blend in with the townsfolk, and with a ball cap, sunglasses and a brown rinse on my signature red locks, not to mention shorts and tank tops, I had been able to do it.

The melody in my head was repeating easily, but the words had been hard to come by. The label had finally agreed to let me record a couple of my own songs for the next album, so I needed the words to show up now! As I jogged, I looked up at the mountains that surrounded the town and saw the barest shimmer of sunlight against the tops. Sunrise. That word lit up my brain and other words started to flow.

Up ahead, out of the darkness I saw someone standing on the sidewalk. The hair on the back of my neck jumped to attention. The man, dressed in a ratty hoodie and torn jeans, stared intently at me and put his hand out as if to stop me. I swerved into the grass to pass him.

"Darci," he said. The sound of my stage name on this stranger's lips shook me since I was here incognito. I hadn't worn sunglasses, obviously, or put in my brown contacts, so I kept my head down. *Don't say anything. Don't say anything, just keep going.* I kept going.

I heard footsteps behind me. I shook my head and sped up. Thank God I could sprint with the best of them! The footsteps sounded louder as they ate up the pavement as I ran past the library. I put on more speed and turned the corner. The footsteps got closer and I suddenly felt hands on my arms and I flew up and landed in a heap on the sidewalk, road rash on my right arm and leg and my yoga pants torn. "What the hell, moron!" I cried.

He grinned like a demon on a mission, circling me with his phone in one hand and something glinting in his other. I dragged myself up off the ground, determined to get away from him and get rid of that video.

"Stop the video, jerk, and tell me what you want!" I said. I watched him fumble with his phone and whatever he had in his other hand, and while he was momentarily distracted, I grabbed his phone and took off. My wounds were throbbing in time with my racing heart.

"Darci, stop, you stupid bitch!" I heard him scream, but I kept running, headed for the Sheriff's Department down the street. The footsteps seemed to get further away, then I heard a car engine start somewhere behind me and tires squeal, so I headed directly across the street. I could see two deputies standing on the sidewalk outside the building and headed right for them.

The engine grew louder and I knew he was getting closer. I had almost reached the curb when suddenly a terrible pain exploded through my left side and I felt myself high in the air. My body flipped and I landed against the curb, my face in the storm drain. I heard yelling, squealing tires, my heart racing, the phone hitting the pavement, then nothing. Blackness surrounded me.

I couldn't believe what had just happened. My deputy had stopped me on my way out to ask a question about a report he had filed. We were just finishing when a woman in jogging clothes came running across the street with a cell phone out in front of her, and a black SUV close behind her.

I saw and heard the impact and immediately yelled for my deputy to call an ambulance. I managed to get the first few digits of the license plate but not all of it. The young woman had landed on her stomach with her left leg at an odd angle. Her ball cap had fallen off and her long hair spilled in the street.

I bent down and checked her pulse. It was racing and weak. She was unconscious and I could see scrapes and torn clothing on her right side, which was not impacted by the vehicle. What had happened to this woman?

I didn't recognize her, so I checked the right-hand pocket of her pants. I found a hotel key. At least that would give me a place to start. As I watched to see if she woke up, I used my cell phone to call Celeste at the hotel.

"Hello?" Celeste answered with a raspy voice. Shoot, I had woken her up.

"Hey, Celeste, this is Sheriff Leppard. Sorry to wake you. There was just an accident and one of your guests was involved. Can you tell me who is registered in room 206?" I heard sirens as she gasped.

"That sweet girl! Is she okay?"

"No, she's not, and I need some ID for the EMTs." Another gasp from Celeste. "Her name's Stacy Varner and she's from Nashville. Just visiting."

"Okay, thanks." I said. "After the ambulance leaves I'll need to get into her room. Be there soon."

"Alright, John. Take good care of her."

The ambulance arrived by the time I hung up. An EMT jumped out of the back of the ambulance loaded with equipment. As he applied a neck brace, the young woman groaned but didn't open her eyes.

I explained the incident to the Paramedic as she wrote the report. Ms. Varner was then carefully placed on a back board and loaded onto a stretcher. As the EMT took her vitals, the Paramedic palpated her stomach, which elicited another groan from the young woman. The Paramedic looked up and said, "We've got to go! Possible internal bleeding! I'm calling in the hospital's helicopter," she yelled. I turned to Deputy Long Cloud and instructed him to start the report while I got both ends of our section of Main Street closed off.

Once I'd done that, I returned to the ambulance. They had started an IV in Ms. Varner's arm and had a nasal canula in her nose. About 10 minutes later I heard the chopper in the distance. The Paramedic was on the radio advising them where to land.

As the chopper landed, I helped wheel the stretcher to the open door on the side. We loaded Ms. Varner in the chopper and the nurse on board took over.

I told her that I would be following shortly and that no one was to talk to Ms. Varner until I was there. She nodded and shut the door. We all stood back as the chopper lifted off. I thanked the Paramedic and the EMT and headed for the hotel as they headed back to the ambulance.

"Mornin', Celeste. Sorry again I woke you" I said as I entered the lobby.

"No worries. How's she doin'?" Celeste asked, wringing her hands.

"Not good," I replied as I headed for the stairs.

"Need any help?" Celeste yelled behind me.

"Nope," I said, waving her off. "I've got it."

THE SHERIFF'S STAR

I opened the door of room 206, not knowing what I expected to find. What I found was a neat room with a trashcan full of crumpled paper, an open laptop on the bed, post it notes on the walls, a guitar case on the bench at the end of the bed, and a giant stuffed sloth on the dresser. I searched the dresser first, finding only half the drawers in use, and nothing but clothes. The desk only yielded an assortment of pens and pencils in a rainbow of colors and several legal pads. I checked under the pillows and mattress but found nothing hidden.

The bathroom was surprisingly uncluttered. I found the usual – shampoo, facial cleanser, toothbrush, toothpaste, hairbrush and a hair tie. The medicine cabinet held only a contacts case and generic pain reliever. No dirty towels or trash in the trashcan.

I opened the guitar case, which was covered with stickers from all over the world. The guitar was obviously old and well-used, but that was all I found inside.

Last, I checked the nightstand and hit the jackpot. I found Ms. Varner's purse in the top drawer, and her wallet was inside. I also found a car rental receipt, a bottle of what appeared to be sleeping pills, and a contract of some kind with the name Darci Dorsette on it. Why did that name sound familiar? I couldn't place it, but why would Ms. Varner have this woman's contract? I put the contract in my shirt pocket.

Since I was going back to the hospital to speak with Ms. Varner, I decided to take a few things for her. I found a backpack in the closet and put the purse, toothbrush, toothpaste and her hairbrush inside. I took the contract with me to ask about, as well. Now it was time to go get some answers.

I arrived at the hospital about 30 minutes later and headed straight to the ER. I identified myself to the desk nurse and asked about Ms. Varner.

"Sorry, Sheriff. She's in emergency surgery right now. After that, she'll go to recovery and then a room. I don't know when you'll be able to talk to her. Tomorrow at the soonest," the nurse told me.

"Okay, I understand. But I'm having a deputy come over to stand guard, and no one is to see Ms. Varner except hospital personnel. Understood?" The nurse nodded solemnly and picked up her phone. I stepped outside and called the department.

"Sheriff's Department, Deputy Peters."

"Peters, it's Leppard. Who's on duty today?"

"Hey, Sheriff. Some excitement this morning, huh? We've got Sandoff, Rogetski and Thompson. What's up?" Peters asked.

"We need a deputy at the hospital with the hit-and-run victim. Send Rogetski and tell her to meet me in the ER. I'm waiting."

"Got it, Sheriff. Oh, we found a ball cap and broken phone outside. Figured they're hers. What do you want me to do with them?" He asked.

"Put the phone in an evidence bag and tag it and put both on my desk.

"Roger." Peters hung up.

About 30 minutes later, Rogetski met me in the ER. I told her about the accident and that she was to stand guard wherever the victim was since the attack appeared to have been intentional. "What time did your shift start?"

"Six a.m., Sheriff, so I'm good until 6 p.m."

"Okay," I said. "I'll have your replacement here by then. If Ms. Varner wakes up or gets a room, call me on my cell." I told Rogetski.

"Roger, Sheriff," she said as she nodded.

I left the hospital, taking the backpack with me. I wanted to talk to this Ms. Varner person before I turned over the belongings. I was still trying to place the name Darci Dorsette but not having any luck. On the way back to Whirlwind I called the hotel again.

"Whirlwind Hotel, how can I help you?"

"Celeste?" I asked.

"No, this is Bonnie. Who's this?"

"This is Sheriff Leppard. Can you tell me who stayed in room 206 before the current guest?"

"Well," Bonnie started, "That room was recently renovated and hadn't been rented in probably, oh, six months or more. I'd have to go through the records to find the last guest. What's going on?"

"Are the drawers checked whenever a guest checks out?" I asked.

"Yes, Sheriff, but all the furniture in 206 is brand new since the last guest." Bonnie replied.

"Huh," I said. Dead end. The contract had to have something to do with Ms. Stacy Varner.

"Alright, Bonnie. Thanks. Have Celeste give me a call when she gets a chance, will you?"

"Sure, Sheriff. Have a good day."

I parked behind the building and went in the back door straight to my office. The ball cap and phone were on my desk, but not the report of the accident.

"Peters!" I yelled toward the front of the building.

"Sheriff, I didn't know you were back," Peters said as he walked toward my office.

"Peters, do you know where Long Cloud put the accident report from this morning? I told him to start it."

"Well, no, Sir. He didn't say, but I'll check his desk. Just a sec." Peters turned and headed for the bull pen where the deputies' desks were. He returned a couple of minutes later with a small sheaf of papers.

"Hey, Sheriff. I think this is it." He put the papers on my desk. I looked at the top page.

"Thanks, Peters. You can go back up front."

"Okay," he said, turning to leave. He stopped and turned back toward me.

"Got an order for the diner, Sheriff? It's almost lunch time." He said.

"Turkey and avocado on whole wheat toast with fries," I said. "Thanks, Peters."

I sat at my desk and looked over Long Cloud's report. I made notations about my observations, added the partial plate I'd identified and set it aside for Long Cloud to finish. Then I picked up the damaged phone. The screen was shattered, but the body seemed to be intact. We'd have to get it to the IT guys in Bristol to see if they could recover any data from it.

With most of my deputies on patrol, I spent the rest of the morning going over reports and filing paperwork for the county. Around 11 a.m. I got a call from Deputy Rogetski at the hospital.

"Hey, Sheriff. Ms. Varner is out of surgery, but she is going to be in ICU for some time. She has a private room there, and I'm outside her door. The nurse also found a phone in Ms. Varner's pocket when they undressed her, and I have it now. It's been going off non-stop, someone named Romi. What do you want me to do, answer it?"

What? Another phone? Strange.

"No, don't answer it. Put it in Ms. Varner's room. What's that room number, Rogetski?" I asked.

"She's in bed 3 of the ICU, Sheriff."

"Okay" I said. "Your relief will be there in a few hours. Any changes, let me know immediately."

"Will do, Sir," she said and ended the call. I sat back in my chair, the springs squeaking in protest. I tried to make some sense of the few facts we had, but nothing made any sense. What was Ms. Varner doing in downtown before sunrise? Who was the driver of the vehicle that hit her and did she know him? Who was Darci Dorsette and what was her relationship, if any, with Ms. Varner? My brain was still going in circles when Peters came in with my lunch.

"Here you go, Sir. Mary down at the diner just delivered it. She said to say 'Hello'."

"Thanks, Peters. Did you get something for yourself?"

"Yes, Sir, got my usual."

"Alright, Peters. And advise all deputies to be on the lookout for any strange or unusual people around town and to keep looking for that vehicle."

"Will, do, Sheriff."

Pain. I slowly awoke to pain all over. Everything hurt. My head was throbbing, my gut felt like I'd been hit by a semi and I couldn't move my left foot. Then the noise started to sink in. Voices from far away, beeping…incessant beeping.

I tried to open my eyes, but I just wanted to sleep. Then I realized there was something in my throat choking me… I used my free hand to start grabbing at whatever it was, trying to pull it out. I felt like I couldn't swallow or breathe…

Suddenly there was a woman standing over me with her hand on mine, stopping me. I grunted at her and kept trying to pull at the thing in my throat. She looked at me calmly and said, "Stacy. Stacy, stop it. You're okay and can breathe. Just breathe for me." I stopped grabbing at my mouth. and looked up at the woman.

"My name's Joanie, and I'm your nurse today. You're in the County General hospital. You were hit by a car yesterday and had surgery. You've been intubated, which is why there's a tube in your throat. Hopefully that will come out in a day or so, but you can't pull at it. You'll hurt yourself. For now, blink once for 'yes' or 'okay', and twice for 'no' or 'not okay'. Alright?" she asked. I blinked once. She smiled.

"I came in to check your bandage and your cast but didn't expect to find you awake. I can bring in some paper and a pen if you want to communicate. I'm also gonna turn up your pain meds. I bet you're feeling pretty bad right now." I blinked hard once.

She adjusted the IV, then came over to my left side and pulled the blanket away. She lifted my gown and looked at something on my side. I felt the slight pull of something on my skin. Joanie pulled something from her pocket, and then I felt her pat something against me, lower my gown and cover me again.

I hated not knowing what was going on. I felt like I couldn't move. I tried to move my right leg, and that was fine. My right arm moved, as I already knew from trying to pull out my tube; my left arm seemed to be stuck though. I tried to lift it and the pain stopped me immediately. It was also bent, but I couldn't tell why. I tried to lift my left leg, but it was so heavy and hurt too badly. *When is the pain med going to kick in*, I wondered, just as I started to feel like I was floating. I wished I could roll over since I always slept on my right side, but I couldn't get my body to cooperate. I vaguely heard Joanie say something, but I just wanted to sleep…

I don't know what woke me up. Probably that damn beeping! I felt pain everywhere. I heard voices getting closer and tried to open my eyes. It was so hard, but I had to know what was going on so I kept trying.

Finally, I got my eyes partially open and tried to look around. I remembered not to move my head, which was throbbing anyway. I just moved my eyes around.

I could see a metal pole on my right with 3 IV bags. There was a TV in the front corner of the wall. A whiteboard was on the wall in front of my bed and listed my name and names of nurses—so I must be in a hospital. But why was I here? Oh, that's right. The nurse – what was her name? – had said I was hit by a car. *How long have I been here?*

The nurse came in the door.

"Hey, Stacy. Do you remember me? I'm Joanie. You slept for a while." I just stared at her.

"How are you feeling? Are you in a lot of pain right now?" she asked.

I blinked once. She nodded and came to the right side of my bed and checked the IV.

"I gave you a little more pain med. The lab will be by to get some blood. X-ray will also come to get some films of your leg to make sure it was set correctly. And Drs. Ranjeeb, and Michaelson, your surgeons, should be by soon," she said as she took readings from all the machines.

"They'll explain what's going on and what to expect in the next few days. If you need anything, just push the red but on this remote. The TV and bed buttons are also here." She set the remote near my right hand, then stopped to write on the whiteboard as she left.

The door opened a few minutes later and a man in blue scrubs came in carrying a plastic tray. He was average height with long dark blonde hair that reached his shoulders and was tucked behind his ears.

"Hello, Stacy. I'm Mike from the lab. Just need some blood today." He stuck a needle into the IV where it was attached to my arm and I saw blood flow into the tube. As Mike left, the door opened again and a short man with coffee-colored skin and thick white hair, and a tall man with salt and pepper hair came in. They wore ties and long white coats.

"Hello, Ms. Varner. I'm Doctor Ranjeeb, and this is Dr. Michaelson. You were in a terrible accident, very, very bad." He shook his head as he walked over to the right side of the bed. He took notice of the beeping machines and then looked back at me. "You have a dislocated left shoulder, a lacerated spleen, torn muscles in your upper left leg, both bones in your lower left leg are broken and you have a concussion. I performed surgery to remove your spleen, and Dr. Michaelson fixed the torn muscles, and set your leg and your shoulder. You will most likely be in ICU for a week or so. We'll keep the tube in until sometime tomorrow. Dr. Michaelson will tell you about your leg. Do you have someone to help you once you are released?" My mind struggled to keep up with what he was saying. That much damage? *I can't even remember the accident.*

I gave him a weak thumbs up, hoping Romi wouldn't kill me for volunteering him. He was going to have to come to me. I couldn't go back to Nashville like this. It would be a publicity nightmare.

Doctor Ranjeeb just nodded his head and said, "Very good. Very good." I loved the singsong cadence of his speech and his accent. He was adorable! He turned toward the door and said, "I'll be by tomorrow. Try to rest and stay calm." Dr. Michaelson reached down and squeezed the toes sticking out of my cast.

"How is your leg feeling, Ms Varner? Do you have much pain?" I blinked once and pointed to my upper leg.

"Yes, that kind of injury is especially painful and takes a long time to heal. We will start PT for your torn muscles and shoulder after we extubate you. I'll be by to check on you again. Do you have any questions?" I blinked twice and he smiled then left the room.

After he left, I lay there trying to remember the accident. I should have asked if it was normal to forget something that bad. I knew that Romi was probably freaking out since I hadn't talked to him in a while, maybe days.

I didn't know how long I had been here. Tom Montague, my manager, was probably going scorched earth trying to find me. I wish I knew where my phone was.

I realized the pain was lessening, and I started to get sleepy again. Sleeping was the only way to forget about this tube in my throat. Maybe a nap would help my brain start moving again and I would be able to remember something...

Next thing I knew, Joanie was back checking on my IV and taking my pulse. She told me the Sheriff of Whirlwind, where I had been staying, was here to see me. She asked if I felt like seeing him. I blinked once. She handed me a pad of paper and a pen. I took them in my right hand.

My eyes bugged out at the gorgeous man who walked into my room. He was tall, probably well over six feet, and very fit. He filled out his khakis extremely well. His shirt sleeves were tight around his biceps, and his hair was short on the sides but as he took off his hat, I saw that it was longer on the top.

A gold star glinted on his chest, and his utility belt held all sorts of dangerous-looking things, including a large gun. His skin was tan and firm, and his eyes were the color of dark chocolate. His eyelashes were full, as were his lips. I couldn't stop staring. My brain went further into hibernation.

"Ms. Varner, hello. I'm Sheriff John Leppard of the Whirlwind Sheriff's Department. I know you aren't feeling well and can't speak right now, but I do have some questions for you if you can handle it." I blinked once waved a hand for him to continue.

"The accident occurred yesterday at approximately 5:45 a.m. in Whirlwind. You appeared to be running toward the office with a phone when a black SUV ran you down. Do you remember any of this?" I blinked twice.

"Do you have any idea who might want to hurt you or whose phone you had?" Again, I blinked twice and my head started to hurt again.

"Does the name Darci Dorsette mean anything to you?" he continued.

I freaked. I blinked twice hard, hoping all the equipment hid the fear on my face.

"Hmm. Okay."

I closed and squinted my eyes against the light in the room. The sheriff stood.

"I think we'd best finish this later, Ms. Varner. I hope you feel better soon. There will be always a deputy on duty outside your room." He set a backpack I hadn't noticed in the chair by my bed.

He turned and left the room. Joanie came in to tell me x-ray was on the way up to check my leg. I hoped they hurried because I could feel myself falling asleep.

I was just dozing off when two young women in strange looking aprons wheeled a large machine into my room.

"Hello, Ms. Varner. I'm Chantell and this is Olivia. We're here to take a look at this broken leg of yours. You won't have to do any work, we'll handle it all. Just hold your breath when we tell you to and you'll be good."

They placed a slab under my cast and centered the window of the machine over my leg. After adjusting it a few times, they told me to hold my breath and I did. The machine made a whirring sound as Chantell pressed a button on the remote she held. They re-positioned the slab and told me to hold my breath again. The machine made its whirring noise, then they were done and heading out of the room with a polite goodbye.

As I felt myself falling asleep, my last thoughts were of the handsome sheriff and the lie I'd told him.

Surprisingly, when I woke it was the next morning. I was still in pain, but it was slightly less than yesterday. My head was not throbbing now, so I counted that as a win. I wiggled my left shoulder just a bit and still felt the pain there, so I didn't press it. My left upper leg was burning, though, and my side ached.

I felt around the bed with my right hand and found the remote. I held it up so I could see it and pushed the button for the nurse. A disembodied voice responded that someone would be in in a moment.

The door opened and Joanie stuck her head in. She smiled when she saw I was awake. She came in and came around to the right side of my bed.

"I wondered if you hit that button in your sleep, but I'm glad you're awake. How are you feeling today?" she asked.

I blinked twice for 'not okay', and she asked me to point to the areas that hurt. I pointed to my left side and my leg.

She smiled and said, "Well, that's better than before. So your head's not hurting today? I blinked twice for 'no'.

"Any dizziness?" she asked.

I blinked once for 'yes'.

"But, that's still improvement!" she said as she looked over the machines attached to me. She replaced one of the IV bags that had run low and came over to the left side to check my dressing. She seemed happy with what she saw because she didn't change it.

I grunted to get her attention and used my right hand to point to my tube.

She nodded in understanding. "Dr. Ranjeeb said we can remove it tomorrow morning if all looks good. Just a little while longer, okay?"

I blinked once for 'okay'. At least this damn tube had an expiry date on it. That was good news. And I needed all the good news I could get. I still wished I could call Romi. He was my best friend as well as my personal assistant, and I was sure he was worried about me. I never went this long without talking to him.

After Joanie left, I was bored. I was tired of lying on my back, tired of not being able to talk, and tired in general. I picked up the remote to look at it and found the button for the TV. I turned it on and went through the available channels but didn't find anything interesting. I shut off the TV and just laid there with my thoughts. *I really hate this damn tube. I hate all of this.*

I was supposed to be writing songs for my next album. I had music going through my head, but the lyrics were not coming. In the back of my mind it felt like there had been words, but I lost them in the fog of my concussion.

I decided a nap might revive my brain and had just dozed off when my door opened and the deputy stepped into the room. He took off his hat and stood at the foot of my bed.

"Ms. Varner, a Romi Mercado called our office to file a missing persons report on you. We told him what happened, and he said he'll be here as soon as he can get a flight. He wants to see you. When he comes, are you willing to see him?" he asked. I gave him my best thumbs up and he nodded in response and left.

I went to sleep hoping that Romi would be there when I woke up.

He wasn't there when I woke up. But I hadn't been awake long when I heard a commotion outside my door, and the door swung open wide. Romi rushed in with his arms ready to wrap me in a huge hug, but I put my hand up to stop him before he got all the way to me.

He stopped and looked at me closely, seemingly just noticing the tube in my mouth. He burst into tears and flopped down into the chair on the left side of my bed, throwing the backpack on the floor. I couldn't do anything but grunt to get his attention, then I made a slashing motion across my neck with my right hand. He gradually calmed himself and sat back in the chair and sighed. I tried to smile, but I probably failed miserably.

"What in God's name happened to you, Chica? I called you all day yesterday and couldn't get you, so finally I called the Sheriff's Office. If I hadn't, you'd still be here alone. Why didn't you call me?" he asked with a straight face.

I wished I could shake my head. I just pointed at the tube and looked at him.

He frowned at my response.

"Yeah, I get that you couldn't talk, but you still should have texted. Tom has been looking high and low for you, and when I called to tell him where you were, he swore. He actually swore! Have you ever heard him swear? No, you have not! It's not fun, let me tell you. So, when can you leave this place?" I just looked at him again. Sometimes his light bulb was just a little too dim.

I hung up the phone from talking with my deputy at the hospital. "Damn," I said as I slapped the top of my desk in frustration.

I was going nowhere fast in this case. Ms. Varner couldn't talk to me and she was my only witness, so we were still flyin' blind. I was gonna have to run that damaged phone over to Bristol since it was our only evidence.

I called to the deputy on duty up front.

"Sandoff, I'm headed to Bristol with this phone we found, so I'll be out of the area for a few hours. Anything going on I need to know about?"

"Not much, Sir. Celeste from the hotel said she's been getting calls for that Varner lady. She's just telling them that she is out of the hotel at the time and to call back. She also said that there have been no new customers at the hotel. We have shop owners keeping their eyes open for strangers. That's it for now."

"Okay. If anything changes or someone shows up, call me immediately. And make sure Thompson gets to the hospital in time to relieve Hastings."

"Will do, Sheriff."

As I left the office, I headed for the interstate. I was going over the few facts we had in my head when I decided to do some digging while I traveled and asked Siri, "Who is Darci Dorsette?"

Siri responded, *"From Wikipedia: Darci Dorcette is an American singer famous for her pop songs, including her biggest hit, 'Gone, Baby, Gone.' She was born June 21, 1998 and has no siblings. She currently lives in Nashville. She is famous for her long red hair and bright green eyes. She initially rose to fame when she won The Empire State Talent Show in New York while attending Juilliard. She has cut two albums with Meteor Records, both going platinum, and has just finished a world tour. It is rumored that she is being eyed for a role in an upcoming movie by director Wilbur Hart."*

I handed over the phone to the forensics evidence technician in Bristol and was told they should have some data within 3-5 days. I decided to have a late lunch while in town, so I looked for a parking spot near my favorite diner. I parked a few spaces down and went in.

"Well, how do, Sheriff? Haven't seen you in a minute!" said Naomi, the diner's oldest waitress.

"Hey, Naomi. It has been a while. How are you? How's Ben?"

"We're just a couple of old bodies living the dream!"

"Good for you. I'll have a burger, fries and a Coke." I said.

"Comin' right up," she said, turning toward the kitchen with my order.

I was sitting by the wall of windows in front of the diner, so I just people watched while I waited for my food.

I was smiling at couple of boys on the sidewalk with skateboards looking at a magazine when I noticed a man stop by my cruiser and look at it intently. He walked around the vehicle, then looked up the street then back at the diner. He was about six feet tall, skinny, wearing a worn-out hoodie and torn jeans. His brown hair was mussed like he hadn't brushed it in days. *I wonder what's so interesting about my car.*

He looked around furtively again, then started walking away from the diner. I contemplated following him but didn't have cause. I watched him until he vanished into a group of people down the block.

As I ate my lunch, I thought about Ms. Stacy Varner. She was undoubtedly beautiful, with long brownish hair, incredible bright green eyes and a smile that could knock me over. But she also had an air of mystery about her, and mystery always spelled trouble in my line of work.

I couldn't understand a young woman like her just shutting herself up in a small town to write songs. I mean, our town was great, but it was small, too. It seemed the questions never ended, and the answers never started. I would just have to try to talk to her again.

After I thanked Naomi for lunch and paid, I took off for home. I called the department on the way.

"Whirlwind Sheriff's Department. Deputy Rogetski."

"Rogetski, it's Sheriff Leppard. Do you know who's headed to the hospital to relieve Thompson?"

"Yes, Sir, Long Cloud is next up. He's leaving about 2:30 to head over."

"Okay. I'm headed back to the office. I'm about 40 minutes out."

"Yes, Sir, Sheriff."

There had been no sightings of the vehicle involved in the hit-an-run, but I just had a feeling it was still in our neck of the woods and would make sure my patrols were being extra vigilant. We had to find that vehicle and the crazy guy driving it.

It was Friday night, but I had no interest in going out. I couldn't stop thinking about that young woman alone in a hospital bed with tubes coming out of her, and what had driven someone, pun intended, to try to kill her. Because that is what they had been doing. No one drives a car directly at someone else unless they mean to kill them.

I headed home and took a shower. I sat down on my screened-in back porch with a beer and a sandwich and just listened to the quiet. I thought while I ate but didn't have an epiphany or anything. I was still stumped.

My thoughts wandered back to Ms. Varner. Stacy. She had told me she didn't know this Darci Dorsette, but she still had a contract with that name in her possession. I hoped that once she was able to talk again, she would have a better explanation.

After I finished my sandwich and beer, I leaned my head back on the cushion and dozed off. I woke up some time later and noticed the time on my watch. Time for bed. I got up and took my plate and bottle in the house and left them in the kitchen. I turned off the lights, turned on the alarm system and headed upstairs to bed.

Maybe the morning would bring answers.

Saturday dawned dark and stormy. But, yay! I was getting my tube out today! I was feeling slightly better. My head didn't hurt, and the dizziness was gone. The pain in my left side was still there but had faded to more of a dull ache. My leg still burned some, but even it was better. This was going to be a great day!

Not long after I woke up, Dr. Ranjeeb and a nurse I had never seen before came in. She introduced herself as Mallory. They had a tray of equipment with them.

Dr Ranjeeb spoke first. "Good morning, Ms. Varner. I hear you are doing very well. That is so good. We are going to take out your tube, but first we will give you a little something to make it not so uncomfortable." He gave me a shot in my IV.

He started talking again. "You will feel a little pain, but what I've given you will take the edge off. Your throat will be sore and raw for several days, but we can give you some spray for that. You will be able to eat and drink since we are removing the nasogastric tube, as well, but I would caution you not to eat or drink too much since your body is still healing. Do you have any questions?" he asked. I blinked twice for 'no'.

They set to work and I tried hard to stay relaxed as he advised, but it really was a surreal experience. I had been so focused on the tube in my throat that I hadn't even noticed the one in my nose before today. I could feel a slight tug as it came out, but it was a much smaller tube.

The extubation was a bigger production and harder, but Dr. Ranjeeb had been right; whatever he had given me made me not care about the pain. Once they finally had the tube out, I tried to take a deep breath, but that made me cough. Talk about pain! *No more coughing, Stacy.*

They asked if I'd like my bed raised, and I nodded, my throat too sore to say anything. Mallory offered me a cup of ice water with a straw, and I took a tiny sip. It felt good on my raw throat, but I could only take one sip. She left the cup on my bed tray, which she pulled closer to me.

Dr. Ranjeeb moved to the left side of my bed to check my wound dressing. He asked Mallory to change it since it was 'weeping,' and ordered an increase in my antibiotics. I hoped that wasn't a bad thing. I felt like I was finally on the right track and didn't want to backpedal.

After they left, taking the ventilator with them, I fell back to sleep. I was finally able to turn my head but not my body. Sleeping on my back for so long was getting uncomfortable, but it couldn't be helped.

I must have slept until lunch time because I woke to the smell of some kind of food in my room, and Romi sitting in the chair by my bed. I saw a lunch tray on my bed tray, but my stomach turned at the thought of food. I reached for my water cup instead. Most of the ice had melted, but it was still cold. I took a short sip, and when my stomach didn't revolt, I took another sip.

He came over and lifted the lid of my lunch tray.

"Beef broth and red jello," he said and put the lid back on the tray.

I tried to talk, but what came out was a cross between a grunt and a rasp. I swallowed and tried again. Same result. He just laughed. I pointed to the throat spray I spotted on the bed tray so he'd hand it to me. I also noticed my phone sitting there under a newspaper. The darn thing was probably dead.

Mallory came in just then, tall with her blond ponytail gleaming in the overhead lights. She went over and checked my lunch tray.

"I know the idea of food is unappealing right now, Stacy, but you need the fuel for your body. Please try to eat at least a little of the broth and some of the jello. You will be having PT after lunch. The therapist will come to you." She smiled at me and wrote something on the whiteboard and left.

Romi moved back over to my bed tray and lifted the lunch tray lid. He moved the tray closer to me and took the lid off the broth and the plastic from the jello. He handed me the spoon and waited. My stomach tried to rebel, but I forced down a spoonful of the broth, then I lied back and waited to see what would happen. When I kept it down, I tried another spoonful, then a bite of jello. Not a tasty combination, but it was better than nothing.

It took about 20 minutes, but I finally got about half the broth and most of the jello down before calling it quits. He moved the tray to the windowsill and handed me my water.

I felt full, which was weird because I could usually pack it away at a meal. I worked out and danced so much I usually burned off everything I ate, but now a little broth and jello and I was done.

Romi went back to the chair and started telling me about the comments on my social media accounts. There was speculation about where I was because I hadn't been spotted in Nashville for a while. He suggested he make a post for me telling everyone I was on vacation and what I was doing. I nodded and tried to answer. It came out a little better but was still not real words.

He showed me the post before he uploaded it:

> *Helloooo, Dorsetters! I hope y'all are doin' good! I'm having a little vacay and writin' some new songs for the upcomin' album! I'm havin' a wonderful time but miss y'all! I'll see ya soon! Stay fierce and keep listen'!*

I nodded my approval, and he uploaded the post. Hopefully that would make everyone happy.

Right then the door opened and a short woman, probably about 5'3" like me, with short blond hair in a pixie cut and in street clothes came in. She introduced herself as Paige, my physical therapist. She noticed Romi in the room and asked if it was okay with me if he stayed. I nodded and she put her clipboard on the end of my bed. She told me we would start with my shoulder, so she helped me out of the sling.

Forty-five minutes later I was beat. The left side of my body hurt and I was tired. Paige had worked my shoulder in all sorts of configurations, and she had helped me do leg lifts and seated squats for my quadriceps. Ugh. She had left, telling me she would see me on Monday. Great.

Romi looked at me sympathetically while seated comfortably in the chair by the bed. He had jumped up to help hold my cast up while Paige was helping me move it, but otherwise he had sat in his chair and smirked. Made me want to smack him.

Just as I was getting ready to send Romi back to the hotel so I could take a nap, Tom strode in the room. He was fully put together as usual in his bespoke suit, shined Italian loafers and silk tie, with his hair cut to the perfect length and styled neatly. He carried an expensive leather satchel with him. He looked at Romi then at me and shook his head.

"What have you done to yourself, Stacy?" he asked.

"Run over by a car." I said in a raspy voice. I coughed when I finished the sentence.

"The label is wondering where you are since you haven't been spotted out and about lately. I told them you were on vacation to write songs, and they want to see something soon. Have you got anything written yet?" he asked.

"Not yet, but it's right there," I rasped and pointed to my head. "Plus I have to get my voice back," I continued, then I coughed again.

"True. How long do you think that will take? So I know what to tell the execs?" he asked.

"They said my throat would be raw and sore for several days, so I'm not sure." I coughed from all the talking. "I think it's just a matter of resting my throat," I said, hinting that talking was not helping.

"Okay. I'll be at the hotel until tomorrow. I'll check on you before I leave town to head back to Nashville. Feel better, Stace," he said as he left the room.

"He's so emotional," Romi said sarcastically.

"Good thing he's not. Emotional managers get their clients in trouble," I said.

I asked Romi to get the deputy for me. When he came in, I wrote a note asking if someone could bring me some things from my hotel room, specifically pads of paper, pens and my contacts case. He said he would let the sheriff know and someone would bring them. I thanked him and shooed Romi out of the room so I could sleep. He promised to call later. I nodded and laid the bed down.

Sometime later I was awakened by someone knocking on my door. I told them to enter as best I could.

A female deputy came in with a bag of items and handed them to me. She apologized to me for waking me up. She asked if my backpack had everything else I needed. I hadn't even realized that was my backpack Romi found on the chair. I asked the deputy to hand it to me.

I looked inside and told her I had what I needed. I looked in the bag, too. All good. I thanked her for bringing it to me. She touched her hat and nodded as she left.

Yes! My contacts! I found my purse in the backpack and pulled out the little mirror I always kept there, as well as my contact solution. It was hard putting in my contacts with only one hand, but I made it work. I felt much better after putting them in. More in disguise.

I found the hairbrush and ran it carefully through my hair. I desperately wanted to brush my teeth, but that would have to wait. I raised the bed and put the backpack on the end of the bed between my feet. I pulled a pad of paper and pen out of the bag and set it next to the backpack.

I started thinking about my songs. A few lines seemed to be trying to get through, but the words were like brief glimpses in a mirror, there, then gone. I tried to focus, but they just weren't coming through clearly. This was frustrating.

THE SHERIFF'S STAR

I finally had my big chance to produce my own songs and the words just wouldn't come. *Damn. I need to write a song!*

I closed my eyes and thought about Whirlwind. I thought about the park, and the shops and the mountains. I thought about the people.I thought about the Sheriff and his beautiful eyes. His strong shoulders. His firm butt. His chiseled jaw. I thought about how sweet he was to pack things for me, and to send more items with his deputy.

Words started bouncing around my head like popcorn, nothing sticking, but they were great words. I opened my eyes and looked at the pad of paper. I wrote words in no special order. Mountains. Chocolate eyes. Tan skin. Firm. Sunrise. Glowing. Gilded. Love. Glory. Pretty soon I was scribbling madly, nothing making sense, but words coming at a rapid pace.

Suddenly I stopped and looked at the page. It was full of words, some repeated, some scratched out. It was overwhelming and fulfilling at the same time. I closed my eyes again and the words came more slowly. Then my pen dropped to the paper and I slept.

It was Sunday morning, and I was getting ready for church. Because the world was full of crazies, we tried to have a law enforcement presence at church every week, and this week was my turn.

I checked myself in the mirror, making sure my uniform was neat and my hair was cooperating today. As I looked in the mirror, she came to my mind again.

I had fallen asleep thinking of Stacy Varner and her incredible green eyes and had woken up still thinking of her. The dream I'd had during the night had left me hot and bothered, and I didn't know what to make of that.

She had been snuggled close to me, injury-free, rubbing her hand up and down my chest. She looked deeply into my eyes, and I swear I drowned in hers, like I was deep in a field of new grass, and I couldn't look away. Her lips were so full and pink, and I could just imagine how wonderful they would taste. As soon as that thought formed, she leaned closer and touched her lips to mine. She tasted of peaches and cream, of sunny days and clear, star-lit nights. I couldn't get enough. Just as I put my palm against her cheek, she moaned my name… and I woke up.

I was frustrated in so many ways. It had been so long since I had been with a woman, since I had even thought of being with a woman. I had also never had feelings for anyone I met in an official capacity, and knew that it was unethical, but the thoughts kept coming. I was dying to see her again and planned to visit the hospital after church to follow up on the accident. Hopefully she had remembered something.

I headed to the church and took a spot standing against the back wall. Many of the congregants said hello as they entered, used to seeing a deputy or myself in that spot. I let my eyes wonder the sanctuary, looking for anything suspicious or dangerous. Nothing ever happened, but it paid to be cautious.

Once the service started and everyone sat down, my thoughts started to wander to Stacy. I couldn't help but wonder why anyone would try to hurt that woman. What had she done, if anything, to make anyone so mad? Did she owe money? Had she insulted the wrong person? Had she stolen someone else's song? I had a hard time imagining her doing any of those things, but I had to remain objective and look at all possibilities until I had more information.

Before I knew it, everyone was standing for the benediction, then it was time to leave. After everyone had left, I headed back home to switch to my everyday uniform of a polo and khakis. I made a quick sandwich and ate standing over the sink before locking up and heading out.

When I arrived at the hospital, I entered the front lobby to find a group of security officers standing at the information desk and headed over to see what was happening. The hairs on the back of my neck stood up. "Good afternoon. What's going on? Do you need any help?" I asked.

One of the officers looked me over and answered, "No, thanks, Sheriff. Most of the excitement is over. Some weirdo came in screaming that he wanted to see Darci Dorsette, claiming he knew she was here and insisting we take him to her. He scared the desk clerk something awful and created quite the disturbance. Just as we got here, he took off out the front. We chased him through the parking lot but lost him one street over."

"Darci Dorsette, huh? Why would she be here?" I asked, concerned about the coincidence.

"No clue," replied the guard.

"All right, then. If you don't need me, I've got to see a patient. Y'all have a good day." I said and headed to the elevators. I did not like this at all. Darci Dorsette was becoming a common theme, and something told me this would not be the end of it. Could the disturbed man at the desk have had something to do with the hit-and-run? *Not crazy about the odds.*

When I got to the room, I instructed my deputy that she could go back to town and I would finish the shift. My deputies had been taking turns, so it seemed only right that I jump in, as well. I knocked on Stacy's door and was told to enter.

"Good afternoon, Ms. Varner," I said as I removed my hat. "I hope you're feeling better now. You certainly look like you do…" I looked more closely, and saw that she now had brown eyes? What the hell?

"Wait, didn't you have green eyes before?"

"W-well, yes, Sheriff, I did. I, uh, get a lot of comments on my green eyes, and it b-bothers me, so I wear these contacts. Sorry for the confusion," she said. She shrugged as if it wasn't a big deal, and I guess it wasn't.

"Well. I wondered if you had remembered anything about the accident yet. We don't have a lot to go on, so any new information would be helpful."

"Funny you should ask," she said. "I had what I thought was a nightmare last night, but as I've been thinking about it, I think it may actually be a memory," she said, looking like she was thinking hard.

"Go on," I said.

"Well, I dreamed that I was jogging before dawn, and a guy tried to grab me before I got to the library. He was scary looking, dressed in a dirty hoodie and torn jeans. I ran past him, but he followed me. The next thing I knew, I was on the ground all scraped up, and he was circling me with his phone out, like he was recording me. It gets a little hazy, but somehow, I grabbed his phone and started running harder. It gets hazy again, and the next thing in my dream was seeing you outside your office and running across the street. Then there was pain and the dream ended. Does any of that help?"

"It does if the phone we found on the sidewalk was his phone. Assuming the guys in Bristol can pull any data from it, we may be able to find this guy. I appreciate your help. This is good news," I said.

"I'd like to talk about Darci Dorsette again, now that you can explain things to me. How is it you have a contract with her name on it in your hotel room?"

"Oh, well, that's because she, um, s-she's a client of mine back home. Nothing nefarious there," I said, hoping he would drop this line of questioning.

"What do you do for a living in Nashville, Ms. Varner?" he asked with a skeptical look on his face.

"I'm a songwriter, Sheriff." *Well, I would be once I finished the two new songs for my album!*

"I see. What have you written? Something I might have heard?" His smirk was killing me. I was digging a big hole with a little shovel.

"The songs are going to be on an upcoming album, so you wouldn't have heard them yet, but you will."

"Oh. Okay. So what are you doing in Whirlwind? Celeste said you were just visiting. Do you have family around here?"

"No, Sheriff. No family. I just needed someplace quiet to get some writing done, and I had been through Whirlwind some time ago and fell in love with the place."

"Hmm. Alright. So there wasn't someone you were trying to avoid by leaving Nashville, was there? Someone who could have followed you?" He asked.

"No, Sheriff. I don't have a stalker out there. I'm just here to get away from the distractions of the big city and get some work done."

"So do you know what you were doing out before dawn on a Thursday in downtown? Kind of a strange time to hang out in the park," he asked.

"I was probably jogging. I like to jog before dawn since the humidity is lower and it's so peaceful. And I like jogging around the park." I smiled at him. *Nothing to see here, Sheriff.*

"Okay, I guess that explains everything," he said. "I'll be taking the watch today, so if anything else comes to mind, just let me know. I'll be outside the door, as usual." I started to leave, but she called my name.

THE SHERIFF'S STAR

"Sheriff Leppard, there's no need for you to sit outside the door. I'm kind of bored and could use the company. Why don't you sit with me and we can talk?" she asked. I shrugged, put my hat in the windowsill and pulled the chair closer to her bed.

"What would you like to talk about," I asked. She reached for a spray bottle on her bed tray and sprayed her throat. Her voice was rather raspy, I thought.

"Well, tell me about yourself. How long have you been the sheriff? Have you always lived in Whirlwind? Are you married? Do you have kids? That sort of thing," she said, coughing as she finished.

"Well, I'm not married, no kids, and yes, I've always lived in Whirlwind. I started as a deputy right out of college about 10 years ago and loved every minute of it. About three years ago, the previous sheriff had to retire suddenly for medical reasons, and I was elected to replace him.

"What about you? Did you always want to be a songwriter? Have you always lived in Nashville? Why come to Whirlwind to write your songs?"

"Yeah, I always wanted to write songs. I've done some singing, but never my own stuff. I love poetry and I love music, so songwriting just seemed the natural way to incorporate those two loves."

She stopped to clear her throat. "I don't have any brothers or sisters, just my parents. I've always lived in Nashville, but I travel a lot and meet tons of new people. Sometimes that gets to be too much."

She cleared her throat again. "When I wanted to start writing, I thought of Whirlwind. It's small, but not boxed in, and the people are so nice. I just needed some peace and quiet for writing, and to be where no one knows me. Just time to be me and see what words would come out," she said. She cast her eyes downward as though embarrassed.

"I can understand wanting to be somewhere you can be unknown. Growing up in a small town where everyone knows you and all your business, I get the desire to be alone. How's the writing coming? Got anything good yet?" I asked.

"Lots of words," she said, "but nothing put together. I wonder if the concussion is preventing me from writing."

"Possibly," I said, "But I doubt it. However, your body has been through one hell of a trauma, as has your brain, and that could just mean you need some time. Maybe once they spring you and you get back to Whirlwind and the fresh air, things will make more sense," I said.

"Speaking of getting sprung, will you need help getting around the hotel and Whirlwind?" I asked.

"No, I think I'll be alright. My, uh, friend, Romi, is in town, and he's going to go back to Whirlwind with me. He can help me maneuver and run errands for me. I do worry about those steps at the hotel, though. I don't see me getting up and down that steep staircase on crutches."

"If you'd like, I can let Celeste know that you'll need to be moved to the first floor. Your friend can move your things once you get back. Would that help?" I asked.

"Oh, that's wonderful! Yes! I can't believe I didn't think of it myself," she said. She looked at me for a moment, her eyes moving from my eyes to my lips and back again. She licked her lips and suddenly my pants got a little tighter.

Down, boy, I told myself. This is a professional visit and she's a victim, not someone you met at a bar. But still I found myself staring into her eyes, which seemed just as mesmerizing in brown as they were in green. I shook my head and blinked to reset my focus.

"No problem," I said. "When I get back to town I'll let Celeste know. She'll be happy to help. She's worried about you as it is."

"See? That's what I mean. The people in your town are so friendly!"

The door to her room opened and I stood. A nurse came in wearing a stethoscope around her neck. "Hello, Stacy." She looked at me a little longer than seemed necessary and said, "Hello, Sheriff. Stacy, time to check your wound."

I offered to step out of the room and Stacy smiled at me. "Thanks, Sheriff. But please, come back later." I just nodded and grabbed my hat from the windowsill.

After about 10 minutes, the nurse left the room and winked at me as she walked by. I shook my head and looked down at my phone. I was checking in at the department and didn't really want to encourage her.

According to my deputy, there was still no sighting of the vehicle we were looking for. The vehicle had to turn up somewhere. One interesting thing was a deputy had come across an abandoned hunting shack at the end of an old logging road and stopped to investigate.

He had found signs of a squatter, rather recent, too. Food cartons and newspapers where inside, and there were large tire tracks outside that were obviously recent, as well.

I instructed that all deputies make routine checks on the shack during every shift, hoping we could spot whoever was staying there. Tomorrow we could check the town's land records and see who owned the shack and find out what they knew.

I was just finishing up when a stranger walked up with a handful of balloons and made as if to go into Stacy's room. I stood up and intercepted him. "Who are you?" I demanded.

"Whoa. Wow, are you the new deputy?" The man asked.

"I'm Sheriff Leppard. Again, who are you?"

"I'm, um, Stacy's friend, Romi. She's expecting me. I was here yesterday, and the deputy let me in."

"Wait here," I instructed. I stuck my head in Stacy's room and asked if she was expecting anyone.

"Yes, Sheriff. Romi said he was coming by. It's okay," she said.

"Okay." I turned to the man behind me and stepped aside so he could enter.

Romi talked so loud in the room that I could hear every word.

"Wow, Chica! That's a tall, cooool drink of water right there! No wonder you like it in Whirlwind! Are there more like him? Hook a fella up!"

Stacy just laughed and shushed him. "Quiet, Romi! He'll hear you!"

I smiled and sat back down, shaking my head and chuckling to myself.

THE SHERIFF'S STAR

It was about three o'clock and Romi and I were still going over 'my' Instagram and Twitter accounts, responding to queries and trying to think of ways to post without letting anyone know about the accident or where I was.

Sheriff Leppard stuck his head in the door and said that Tom Montague was here. I smiled and asked him to let him in. The Sheriff nodded to me and opened the door. Tom came in fully decked out.

"Stacy, how are you? He asked, coming over to sit on the side of the bed and setting down his satchel. "How's your throat? Have they said how long you'll be in here? The label is making noises like they want to see you around town. I don't know what to tell them."

"Hey, Tom. I have no idea how long I'll be here. They're not even letting me out of bed yet."

"I have an idea," he said. "I'll go buy a piece of fabric somewhere, and we can put it behind you. Then you do your makeup and put on some different clothes, and we can post on the accounts. I think that would appease the execs at least for a while. How's that sound?" he asked.

Romi and I looked at each other. He had brought me a sparkly t-shirt that said 'Nashville' on it in swirly cursive writing, and a matching ball cap, along with some makeup.

"I guess so, Tom. But my voice is still not 100 percent. Think anyone will notice?" I asked.

"I hope not. Just do the best you can, Stace." He got up to go to the store, and Romi brought out the makeup and a lighted mirror from his messenger bag. After Tom left, Romi set up the mirror on the bed tray and pulled it closer to me. I set to work making magic.

I took out my brown contacts and he wrapped my hair up in the ball cap, letting a ponytail come through the hole in the back. I found a pair of earrings hiding in my purse, then had Romi help me take off the sling so I could put on the shirt. I didn't have a bra with me, but he had seen me naked so many times I wasn't embarrassed around him. He helped me dress and finish putting on my makeup. He could do it almost as well as I could.

Romi put away the mirror and brought a selfie light ring out of his messenger bag. He set it up on the bed tray and we waited. We talked and played a word game on his phone until Tom came back, carrying a piece of pretty floral fabric.

Tom helped me lean forward and put the fabric behind me. He helped me sit back and he raised the bed so I was fully sitting up. He turned on the light ring and stood at the foot of my bed while I made the post.

> *"Hellooooo, Dorsetters! How is everyone? I've missed all of you so much! I know I haven't been around much, but I'm just takin' a little vacay and writin' songs for the next album! So fun! I can't wait to be back in Nashville to start recording! I love readin' your comments and thank you for worryin' about me. I'm soooo good right now! Gotta go, but keep being wonderful, and keep listenin'!"*

Romi smiled and nodded, and I hit 'Post'. Hopefully that would buy me some time. The record label was so twitchy, even after two best-selling albums, so no one could find out about my accident. I had come too far to lose this chance.

He gave me some makeup remover wipes he pulled from his bottomless bag. He took back the lighting ring, then helped me take off the t-shirt while Tom turned his back. We got my gown and the sling back on and the bed lowered some, then Tom turned back around. Romi had folded the fabric and set it next to his bag, I guess to use another time.

Tom said he was happy with the post and thought it would make the execs happy before he said goodbye. He was flying back to Nashville this evening.

We went back to playing the word game on Romi's phone. It was then I thought to ask him if he had a phone charger with him. Of course, he pulled one out of his bag. He plugged my phone into an outlet next to me bed and left the phone on the bed tray.

About an hour later, the Sheriff stuck his head in to say he was leaving. He came in and handed me a card with his contact info on it. I set it on the bed tray to add the numbers to my phone.

"Call me anytime if you need anything," he said. He smiled at me, nodded at Romi and was gone.

"Girl, you better need something soon!" Romi said with a laugh. "He's about the handsomest thing I've seen in good long while!"

I just laughed at him. I picked up the card and looked at it. It felt important that Sheriff Leppard had given me his info. I don't know why, but I felt it.

I told Romi I was going to write for a while before dinner and sent him on his way.

I grabbed my pad off the bed tray and looked at the words I had written down in my free writing session last night. I looked at each of the words, but none of them seemed like the right ones. I started humming a new tune and turned to a clean sheet of paper. Words started to come together in a totally different way than I had imagined.

I have to leave today,
There's no reason to stay,
If you won't say
I love you

THE SHERIFF'S STAR

But I love you.
It's time to fly,
To say goodbye,
Since you won't say
I love you
But I love you.

Don't wanna leave,
Don't wanna grieve,
But you won't say
I love you.

I need to fly,
I'm gonna cry,
Since you can't say
I love you.

It's time to move on,
Make those mem'ries gone;
Out the window is a golden pyre,
Where the sun sets the clouds on fire;
I cast my love onto the blaze,
As tears fill my eyes with a smoky haze.

Don't wanna leave,
Don't wanna grieve,
But you won't say
I love you.

I need to fly,
I'm gonna cry,

Since you can't say
I love you.

The music always wins,
So I won't see you again,
It has to be okay,
'Cause you will never say
I love you
But I love you.

Don't wanna leave,
Don't wanna grieve,
But you won't say
I love you.

I need to fly,
I'm gonna cry,
Since you can't say
I love you.

Wow! Not what I expected, but not too shabby! It needed some work, but I felt like it was a really great start. And none of those words were on my list.

I was able to eat some more soup for dinner and spent the rest of the evening working on my song. I fell asleep with the pad of paper in my lap and the pen in my hand.

I had just opened my eyes and could see the sun peaking over the tops of the mountains in the distance when I heard the door open.

"Good morning, Ms. Varner," Doctor Ranjeeb said as he entered my room with Dr. Michaelson.

"How are you feeling today?"

"So far, so good," I said with a yawn.

"First off, let's check your dressing. He lifted my gown so he could check the surgical site.

"Very good, very good."

Dr. Michaelson spoke up. " I see that you started your physical therapy. How did that go?" He asked as he looked at my chart.

"Painful. Slow." I cringed as I thought about it.

"Well," he said. "That is to be expected. You'll have PT again today, but I think until then we should take the sling off your arm and try using it a little bit. Then put the sling on after PT. You're making a fantastic recovery," he said.

Dr. Ranjeeb said, "You'll only be here a few more days, then we can move you to a regular room for the remainder of your stay."

"Thanks, Dr. Ranjeeb, Dr. Michaelson," I said, disappointed that I wasn't being released sooner.

I picked up my phone and pulled up Twitter to see what my fans were saying about my post. Most of the comments were kind, excited about new music and the album. But there was a DM that sent the hair on the back of my neck straight up.

Darci. I know where you are. I failed last time. Not again.

I panicked and yelled for the deputy. He came into the room and asked what was wrong. I realized too late that I couldn't show him the threat because that would mean exposing myself. I had to make up something.

"I'm sorry. I saw this strange man walking on the sidewalk and he looked a little like the man who came after me, but it wasn't him. Sorry for the false alarm."

"It's alright, Ms. Varner. Better safe than sorry." He returned to his post, but my heart was still racing as I stared down at my phone. I realized now that in order to stay safe, I was going to have to reveal myself to the Sheriff. That was the only way this post could be investigated. I sighed. This was going to be a new nightmare.

THE SHERIFF'S STAR

My cell phone started ringing just as I got to my desk Monday morning. I looked at the screen and saw an unknown number and answered it. "Sheriff Leppard."

"S-Sheriff, this, um, this is Stacy… Stacy V-Varner."

"What can I do for you?" I asked.

"Well, Sheriff, I think I h-have some i-info for you about the case, but I'd like to discuss it with you in person, if that won't be too inconvenient. It's pretty important."

"I can come to the hospital in about an hour. Will that work?" I asked.

"Yes, Sheriff. Thank you so much." She ended the call.

"Sheriff! I think we got him!" cried Deputy Hastings from the front of the Office.

I ran up front. "Who are you talking about?" I asked, looking over the desk.

"The person who's been squatting in that old hunting shack at the end of the logging road. Rogetski just called it in. Said she pulled up to check the shack on her rounds and saw some guy walking into the shack. There is a black SUV parked around back. She attempted to make contact, but he apparently fled out a back window into the woods. She tried to chase him but lost him in the forest.

Thompson is on his way to back her up. Do you want them to keep searching?"

"Yes, I want them to keep searching! Who else is on patrol right now?"

"Long Cloud and Grey, Sir."

"Alright, send Long Cloud out to help with the search. Get that full plate number from them and start a DMV search. Maybe now we can get some answers. I'm headed out there now."

I ran back to my desk to get my hat and left by the back door. I sped out of town and down the old logging road into the mountains toward the shack. I pulled up to the shack and parked next to two other patrol cars. I called out for Rogetski.

"Yes, Sheriff," she called as she rounded the shack from the back. "We're back here looking for tracks into the woods."Thompson rounded the shack a few seconds later.

"We found tracks, Sheriff, but they stop when the underbrush gets too deep. There are broken branches in several directions, probably from deer going through the area, so that's no help to us. We just don't know which way he went. Rogetski says he's wearing a dark hoodie, so that will help camouflage him once the woods get denser. Do you want us to go back into the woods and try again?" Thompson asked.

"Rogetski, what do you think?" I asked.

"I think it's worth another look. He couldn't get too far ahead on foot, and he probably doesn't know these woods as well as the rest of us." She said.

"Alright. Long Cloud is on his way to help you. When he gets here, I want each of you to go about a half mile in a different direction to see if there is any sign of him. If there isn't, then go back on patrol, but continue drive-byes on the shack until further notice. Understood?"

"Yes, Sheriff," they replied.

"Okay. I'm gonna go check out the inside of the shack, then head to the hospital. Ms. Varner says she has important information for us.

"Rogetski, this is Hastings, do you read?" Squawked from the mikes on our shoulders.

"Yeah, Hastings, I read," she said. "What have you got?"

"That SUV you found is a stolen out of Nashville several days ago. No suspects, over."

"Hastings, this is the Sheriff. Call Nashville PD and let them know we have their stolen. Then call Henry's garage and get him to come tow the SUV behind the office. I want it gone over with a fine-tooth comb before the owner comes for it. "

"Roger, Sheriff."

"You two, start going over the SUV while we wait for Long Cloud. And make sure you give the grill a good going over. I want everything-- blood, hair, skin, cloth-- from that grill. I'm going inside."

I entered the shack and found a mess. There was an old sleeping bag up against one wall. Takeout containers littered the floor. I didn't recognize the name of the restaurant, so it must be in a different town. There were fan magazines in a pile by the sleeping bag. Whoever had been here was not concerned about his surroundings. I had to wonder how this person knew about this shack. I still needed to check the tax records to see who owned this place. There were no clothes or personal care items around. Someone had really been roughing it. I stepped back out into the sunlight.

"Don't forget to fingerprint those food cartons and magazines," I told my deputies. I saw that Long Cloud had arrived, and they were preparing to move out to search. "Everyone make sure you stay in contact and don't get lost. Once you get back here, Rogetski, go to the office and finish searching the SUV. Let me know the minute you find anything." I headed back to my cruiser to wait for Henry.

"Will do, Sheriff," they replied as they headed out.

About 30 minutes later, Henry came barreling down the road with his rig. I don't know how he got down that rutted excuse for a road with that big flatbed, but he did. We didn't have the keys to the SUV, so Henry had to turn and pull out to maneuver into position to pull the SUV onto the flatbed. It was a huge effort, and I told Henry how much I appreciated it.

"Just pull up behind the office and leave it there, Henry. We still need to go over it before the owner shows up to claim it. And please make sure it runs. I really appreciate you doing this. Send me the bill."

"You got it, Sheriff. Y'all have a good day, now." And he took off down the road the way he had come. I took off right behind him to head to the hospital.

I walked into the hospital about 20 minutes later than I had told Ms. Varner I'd be there. When I entered her room, Romi was there with her. I took off my hat and acknowledged both of them.

"Sorry to be late. We found some new evidence and I was scoping it out. So, what is this new information you have for me?" I asked, looking around at them.

"First of all…" Romi started.

"Romi, let me handle this, please." she said. "Sheriff, I need what I am about to tell you kept as confidential as possible, for lots of reasons, not the least of which is to protect your town. Alright?" She asked

I nodded.

"I'm Darci Dorsette," she said solemnly.

I tried to keep my face blank. This was a twist I did not see coming. I took my time answering.

"So you're not Stacy Varner?" I asked, trying to buy some time to think this through.

"Yes, Stacy Varner is my real, legal name. Darci Dorsette is just a stage name. I came to Whirlwind for the exact reasons I told you. For peace and quiet and to write. My label has agreed to let me record two of my own songs on my next album, and I have a deadline. No one can know where I am or about the accident. It would bring a media storm and negative publicity to your town that I don't want to be responsible for. But things have changed, I'm afraid. I found this DM today on one of my social media accounts." She held up the phone for me to see. I read the message.

"I agree that it seems like a threat," I said. "Who else knows you're in Whirlwind?" I asked.

"That's just it. No one except Romi and Tom know. Not even my agent knows. I don't have any idea how someone found me or why they want to kill me. None of it makes any sense!" Her eyes turned glassy with unshed tears, and I just wanted to grab her and hold her and keep her safe. But I stood my ground. Romi went over and hugged her. I saw a single tear fall from her eyes.

"That's why I have to recuperate in Whirlwind. If I go back to Nashville like this, all hell will break loose. I don't want anything bad said about Whirlwind."

"Well, we might have more leads as of this morning. We found the vehicle we think hit you. We're searching it for fingerprints and other evidence. Same with the shack where we found it. Hopefully the perp is in the system, and we can get a hit on the prints. But the fact remains, someone knew you were in Whirlwind. As long as that someone is out there, you're not safe anywhere."

"I'm safe here in the hospital, right? And it doesn't look like I'll be released soon. I'll worry about being safe in Whirlwind when I know I'm headed that way. Maybe Tom has some ideas," she said.

"I hope you're safe here, Ms. Varner. We can only do so much. We don't know how much this person knows about you or if they really know you're here. This is the only hospital for quite a ways, so it would be a good guess for someone if they knew you survived," I said.

"I'm really sorry, Sheriff. I didn't mean to bring all this down on you," she said, looking at her hands in her lap.

I put my hand on the end of her bed and looked at her until she lifted her head.

"This isn't your doing, so don't apologize. I appreciate you coming forward with the truth. I assume you've been in Whirlwind incognito since I hadn't heard of you until the accident. I'll keep sending deputies, and you keep your eyes open. If you spot anyone suspicious, call me. Any more electronic threats, call me. Let's keep each other in the loop," I said and put my hat on. I tipped it to both of them and headed out.

I stopped by the deputy on duty, Sandoff. I told him to make sure he was extra careful about who entered the room. He nodded that he understood.

I left the hospital and headed back home.

THE SHERIFF'S STAR

I woke up on Tuesday with a headache. Not a concussion-type headache, but a stress headache. I wanted to call Romi, but I knew he wouldn't be up this early. I had dreamed of a hidden pursuer chasing me all night so I hadn't slept well, but I was up now.

I was fed up with feeling less than. I hit the Nurse Call button on the remote.

"Yes, can I help you?" came the disembodied voice.

"Yes. I'd like a bowl of water and a cup of ice water, please," I said.

"What is it you'd like to do?" asked the voice.

"I want to brush my teeth," I said, getting huffy.

"Okay. We'll be there in just a few minutes," she said.

"Thank you," I answered.

A few minutes later, a tall man in blue scrubs with close-cropped dark brown hair came in with a bowl and a cup. He set them down on the bed tray and introduced himself as Chase, my day nurse.

I asked him to get my backpack for me, and he set it on the bed next to me. He offered to help me by putting toothpaste on my brush for me, which I appreciated. He watched as I brushed, then emptied the bowl of water in the bathroom and rinsed it out.

He then helped me take off the sling and get into a clean gown. He helped me get settled and I asked him to leave the backpack on the bed. I thanked him as he left.

I was just about to start working on my song when Paige came in. We worked for 45 minutes, and I was drained. I was also sweating, so I called the nurses' station to ask for a sponge bath. Or at least a wet washcloth. I felt gross.

After I got my bath, I was feeling refreshed enough to start working on my song. I had been at it for about an hour when Romi strolled in. His bag was bulging, so I knew he had brought a lot with him.

I told him good morning and went back to what I was doing. He would understand that I was in the zone. He came over and gave me a gentle hug on my right side and sat in the chair with his bag in his lap. He pulled out his laptop and got to work doing whatever needed doing. Probably answering emails.

We worked together for about two hours, until a cafeteria worker came in with my lunch.

I was able to eat for a change and sent him to the cafeteria to get something for himself. He came back about the time I finished my soup.

Romi pulled a bunch of books out of his bag. He had brought puzzle and trivia game books for me. I put down my pad of paper and picked up a crossword puzzle book. I asked him to do it with me.

We played for several hours until we both got bored.

He started to pack up and I asked where he was going. He said he'd met a man at the hotel bar, and they were having dinner tonight, and he wanted time to get ready. I laughed because I understood. It took him forever to get ready for his dates because he would try on every outfit available before deciding what to wear, then he'd redo his hair numerous times until it was just the way he wanted it to be. I sent him on his way and looked through the other books for something to do. I looked at my phone for the time and decided to call Tom to let him know I'd written a song.

He was glad to hear it and promised to let the execs know. I worked on a word search puzzle for a while, then I got bored again. I decided to take a nap until dinner.

I woke up to the sound of a tray being placed on my bed tray. The worker looked sorry for waking me, but I just smiled and waved.

I sat my bed up and was just settling in to eat more soup when my door opened again. The sheriff stepped in.

"Hey, Sheriff. You don't have to sit out there. I bet you get bored out of your skull." I said.

"A little," he said, "But it comes with the territory."

"Well, come in and sit for a while, Sheriff. Entertain me," I said as I laughed. He came in and set his hat back in the windowsill and sat in the chair.

"Well," he started, "What would entertain you?"

"Tell me more about yourself. Why is a man with a stable job like yourself still single? Where did you go to college? Did you go to college? What do you like to do in your spare time?" I asked, intrigued by this man beyond reason. I took a spoonful of soup.

"Well, I graduated from Virginia Commonwealth University with a degree in Criminal Justice. I always wanted to be in law enforcement, like my dad and grandfather. I was going to go into the service after college, but then a position opened up in the Sheriff's Office, so I went for it.

I don't have a lot of spare time, but I do like, um… well, um, Bingo. Don't laugh-" He looked at me as if to silence my mirth. My shoulders were shaking and I was trying to hold it inside, without much luck.

He shook his head. "I said, don't laugh. Bingo is lots of fun!"

I laughed out loud at that. A huge, built guy like him sitting among a bunch of old ladies at Bingo? I could not wait to see that! I slurped a spoonful of soup.

"Okay. So, um, Bingo. That's nice. What else do you like to do?" I asked, still chuckling.

"I like to hike, and play football with my friends, and go to the shooting range, and go bow hunting. What do you like to do?" He asked.

"Well, uh, I don't really know. I'm always so busy I rarely have time for hobbies. I do like to crochet while I'm traveling. And I listen to audiobooks while I work out. I like to go to little out-of-the way coffee shops and people watch. Stuff like that. Nothing as great as Bingo, though." I smiled.

"Funny. Not." He said with an answering smile of his own. "So, did you go to college?" He asked.

"Yeah. I went to Juilliard, but I didn't graduate. Decided to try things on my own, you know?" I told him about winning a talent show during my junior year that landed me a recording contract, and that's why I didn't finish.

"What did your parents think about you leaving school without graduating?"

"They were okay with it, said it was my decision. Plus, they didn't have to keep paying for it, right?" I said with a shrug of my shoulders. I winced at that move. My parents were thrilled with my decision when I bought them a new house in a suburb of Nashville.

"So, not to put a damper in all this happy talk, but have you noticed anyone following you, or have you had any strange phone calls or emails? Threats on social media beside the one you showed me? Anything that could explain why someone would deliberately run you down? Do you have any enemies or people you owe money to or who might think you stole their work?" Sheriff Leppard asked.

"No, Sheriff. I pay my debts, I haven't stolen anyone's work, and I try to be kind to everyone I meet. To my knowledge, this was random. I don't know what else to tell you." I said, looking down at my hands and pulling on a loose thread in the blanket. I reached over to take another spoonful of soup. I really did not know what to tell him.

He reached over and picked up the pile of books on my bed tray. He looked through them and asked, "Who brought these?"

"Romi. He knew I was getting bored, so he brought stuff to keep me occupied while he went on a date," I smiled as I told him.

"A date, hunh?" he said under his breath.

"Wanna do a crossword with me, Sheriff?" I asked.

"Sure," he said, selecting a book. "What kind of puzzle? Celebrities, animals,

TV, sports?"

"Celebrities, for sure," I said with a smirk.

He opened the book to a random page and started asking me the questions.

"Who is the Scottish actor who played King Leonidas in '300'? he asked.

"Oh, that's easy! I met him once. Gerard Butler!" I cried out.

"Okay. Butler. That fits. Next question..."

"Wait, Sheriff. Are you doing all one direction, or are you alternating directions?" I asked.

"All one direction. Why?" he asked, looking confused.

"Because alternating directions makes the puzzle easier, don't you think?" I looked at him innocently.

He just looked at me. "I, uh, didn't realize it made a difference," he replied.

"Oh, but it does. Just try it!" I said.

"Okay. Helena ___________ Carter," he called out.

"Bonham!" I cried.

We went back and forth like that for hours, completing one puzzle after another. He stayed until I started getting tired, then he put the book on top of the pile and moved my bed tray to the side of my bed.

"Goodnight, Ms. Varner," he said as he picked up his hat.

"Please, Sheriff, call me Stacy," I told him.

"Okay, Stacy. Call me John," he replied.

"Goodnight, John. Have a safe trip back to Whirlwind."

"Will do."

He turned and left the room.

The next day I was finally moved to a regular room. Dr. Ranjeeb had come in early that morning and told me he was very pleased with my progress, and he was releasing me from ICU. I was excited to get out of bed for a change. Even the ride in the wheelchair felt freeing.

THE SHERIFF'S STAR

I went to room 314 and called Romi to let him know I had moved. The nurse allowed me to sit up in a reclining chair for a while, which was a nice change of pace.

Romi arrived just as the nurse was helping me into the bathroom to have a more thorough sponge bath. I told him to wait for me in the room.

"I'll be here, Chica. I have news!" he said enthusiastically. Must be about his date, I thought.

It felt so good to be clean everywhere for a change. I was feeling very grungy up to this point. The nurse even helped me with dry shampoo for my hair. I was glad to get clean and into a clean gown. She rolled me back out to my room, and I sat on the bed feeling so much better. I even had on deodorant. Such simple things one takes for granted every day.

The nurse left and Romi started telling me about his date.

"His name's Brandon, and he's a banker here in town," he said. "He's about 6' 1", short blond hair, a light beard, and built like a basketball player – all long, lean muscles everywhere." He practically swooned as he said this.

"How do you know what his muscles look like?" I asked with a smirk, knowing the answer.

"You know, Chica. I don't kiss and tell," he said.

"Yeah, I know," I said as I laughed. I was happy for him. He had been alone and focused on me for so long, I knew he was lonely.

"I'm happy for you," I said.

"I'm happy for me too, Chica," he said. "Especially since he wants to see a movie with me tonight and take me to a jazz club after," he said.

"Wow! Two dates in a row! That's awesome!" I cried and I put my good arm out for a hug. I hadn't put my sling back on after my bath and didn't want to risk using it yet. He hugged me gently.

I was just about to ask him some more questions about Brandon when Paige came in with her trusty clipboard.

"Good morning, Stacy! I'm happy to see you've changed locations. Are you ready to work today?" she asked.

"I suppose," I said less than enthusiastically.

Romi moved his chair out of the way and went to work on his laptop while we did my exercises. We worked for closer to an hour this time, and I was worn out. But my shoulder felt better, looser. My leg was still burning, but that couldn't be helped.

I thanked Paige as she left and she smiled at me. Romi moved the chair closer to the bed and took his seat again. He told me he thought we needed another post for social media. I sighed because I was tired. I asked him if I could nap for a bit before we did that. He agreed and went back to work on his laptop while I dozed.

I dreamed of John. He was standing in front of me, protecting me from an unseen enemy. He had his gun out and was advancing on the enemy while I stayed close to him. I never saw the enemy, but John kept saying he'd keep me safe and not to worry. I woke with a start when I heard his gun go off. I looked over at Romi, and he looked at me sheepishly.

"Sorry, Chica. Didn't mean to wake you when I slammed my computer shut. It got away from me."

"'s okay," I said as I yawned and tried to stretch without too much pain. Romi got up to get his messenger bag and brought it over to me. He pulled out a bra, t-shirt and ball cap, as well as the makeup from the other day. He also pulled out a lighted mirror and a light ring, just like he had before. That bag really was bottomless.

I started on my makeup first. He helped me get the bra and shirt on, then helped me get my hair in the ball cap. He pulled out the fabric from the other day and put it on the bed behind me while I sat forward. It felt a little like 'Groundhog Day' around here. At the last minute I remembered to take out my contacts.

"Helloooo, Dorsetters! How are y'all? I'm doin' great here on vacay! I'm enjoyin' nature and sucking up the fresh air! I'm working hard on those songs and will be ready to record when I get back! I love y'all and appreciate all your comments! LOL! Y'all make me so happy! I'll see you soon, so keep bein' awesome and keep listenin'!"

I looked at him and he nodded, so I hit 'Post'. I immediately went to work wiping off the makeup before someone came in the room and saw me all done up. He brought me a wet washcloth to wipe my face after I was done.

He helped me get out of the t-shirt and bra and back into my gown. I put my contacts back in and instantly felt more normal. Then he went over some emails that needed my input.

I reached over on the bed tray and grabbed the puzzle books. I asked Romi to join me in a puzzle. He wasn't too into them but did one with me.

He left just as my lunch was delivered. He said he'd arranged for the mail to be forwarded to the hotel, and he wanted to be there to get it.

This time my soup had veggies in it. It'd been so long since I'd had solid food, I almost didn't know what to do. I got so excited I practically finished the bowl in 5 minutes. I also had crackers on my tray. I wolfed those down, too. I regretted it not long after, though, when my stomach revolted and I felt nauseous. I took a few deep breaths and managed to keep my food down, but I learned my lesson about eating too fast.

I spent about an hour working on puzzles, then decided to take a nap. I had been asleep for some time when I woke to a nurse I didn't recognize changing one of my IV bags. She saw my eyes open and introduced herself as Mollie. I smiled at her sleepily and closed my eyes again. I must have fallen back to sleep because the next time I woke, my dinner was sitting on my bed tray.

I used the remote I found to call the nurses' station for some help getting to the bathroom.

A few minutes later Mollie came in to help me into the wheelchair with my IV pole, and she rolled me into the bathroom. She helped me get situated then left to give me privacy.

When I was done, we rolled back into my room and I asked if I could eat while still in the chair. she agreed and lowered the bed tray so I could reach it, then told me to call when I was ready to get back into bed. I nodded.

I enjoyed my meal slowly this time. I turned on the TV and flipped through channels while I ate. I couldn't find anything to watch, so I turned off the TV and reached for my phone. I found my favorite Spotify playlist and put it on at a low volume.

I enjoyed sitting up and grabbed one of the puzzle books again. I worked through a puzzle, then another, before calling for help to get back into bed. My body must be working overtime to get better because I was so tired all the time.

Once I was back in bed, I reached for my phone and started checking 'my' social media accounts. No more DMs, thank goodness, but lots of comments on my posts. It seemed that everyone was buying the vacation story, at least for now. I really needed a change of scene for the next post, though, to keep people from getting suspicious.

As I was looking at my phone, I remembered I hadn't put John's info in yet. I put his work and cell numbers in my Contacts and had a crazy idea that I should text him goodnight. I thought about it some more but decided I might be overstepping by doing that, so I just told him goodnight in my head. I put my phone back on the bed tray, turned down the lights and went to sleep.

It was Wednesday, and that meant Bingo with Gram. I left work a little early and headed home to change. I took a shower and put on civilian clothes, then fried up a hamburger for dinner. I ate standing over the kitchen sink looking out the window at my property.

I was lucky enough to live in my family home on our acres and acres of pure, unspoiled land. It had never been cleared, except to build the house, and those trees had been used as building materials. It had never been farmed, either. It was just forest and woodland down to the creek on the back side. It was my family's legacy and would never be sold or destroyed.

I headed out to the church. Just as I pulled into a parking spot, I heard Gram's tires squeal as she raced into the lot. She pulled a fast turn into a spot next to me, almost taking me with her. I waited up against my truck until she was settled, then reached over to open the passenger door of Gram's bright red Nissan Versa for her best friend, Beverly.

Beverly gingerly got out, and when I said hello, she just grumbled under her breath. She was always scowling and grouchy, but she and Gram had been friends, or frenemies, for years. I shut her door and went around to help Gram. She had waited for me. I opened her door and put out a hand to help her stand up. She grinned at me and said hello.

"Hello, kid! How're they hangin'?" she cackled at her attempt at humor. I just shook my head.

"Low and full, as usual," I replied, much to her delight.

"Heard you had some excitement last week, kid! A helicopter and all!" she cried with enthusiasm.

"I've talked to you since then," I said as I helped her up the steps of the church. Beverly had gone ahead and was at the top of the stairs.

"Save us some seats," Gram yelled at her. Beverly just waved a hand behind her and kept walking.

"Yeah, you told me, kid, but I thought there might be more you haven't told anyone. Ya know I have to have the scoop. All the news goes through me!" she said as I held the door open.

I didn't say anything. We walked in, arm in arm, and found Beverly at a table with two empty seats. I led Gram to one of the chairs, and Beverly spoke up.

"Who said those are for you two?" she spat.

"No one else will sit with you since you pass gas every time you get a number, you old goat," Gram said as she sat down like a queen.

"I'll go get the cards and markers," I offered before they could get any feistier.

I came back to the table and Gram was just grinning while Beverly sat back in her chair with her arms folder over her chest, scowling like usual.

I handed out the cards and markers and took my seat. I looked around the room and saw all the familiar faces I usually saw at Bingo. The caller started the game, and I turned to my cards to play.

Two hours went by, and it was getting late. I told Gram she needed to head home since she wasn't allowed to drive at night. Good thing it was summer, and it stayed light longer.

She grumbled and kept marking her cards. I picked mine up and headed to the stage to return them, when I heard her call, Bingo! I also heard Beverly slam her fist on the table in frustration.

I walked the ladies out of the church and wished them safe travels. I headed home myself, ready to sit down and relax with a beer. But my thoughts strayed to Stacy. I thought about the accident and about her injuries. She really was badly hurt. I hated that and really wanted to find the man who had done this to her. It was also hard to believe that she was famous. She seemed so down to earth and almost fragile.

I pulled up at home and checked the cameras on my phone. I had an intricate security system because there were often poachers on my land, and I wanted to keep them out. All looked good, so I entered and locked up tight.

I went into the kitchen and got a beer, then headed out to the back porch and sat down. I leaned my head back on the cushion to think.

Bright green eyes filled my brain, and Stacy's face was in the forefront of my mind. She looked so small lying in that hospital bed yesterday. Every time that I saw her.

Something deep inside me wanted desperately to keep her safe forever. I'd never felt that need so acutely, not even with Gram. It didn't make sense since I hardly knew the woman, and only knew her as part of my job.

I thought about Stacy until I finished my beer, then headed inside for bed. I tried to turn my thoughts elsewhere, but Stacy still held the primary spot in my head. I got out of my clothes and lied down on the bed naked, as usual.

I put my hands behind my head and let my mind wander. I decided to go see Stacy tomorrow after work. I could relieve the deputy stationed there. Most of my deputies had families with kids, and I knew that whoever was on duty would be glad to get home early. At least, that's what I told myself as I drifted off to sleep.

I drove to the hospital the next evening after work. I had stopped by the diner for dinner first since I'd be at the hospital until midnight. My deputy was surprised to see me but happy to be released early. I knocked on Stacy's door and stuck my head in. Romi was with her, and they had their heads together looking at his laptop.

Stacy looked up and smiled brightly at me.

"Hey, John! Come on in! We're just looking over my social media accounts to see how the comments look after my post yesterday."

I had seen that post. I had taken to looking at Stacy's posts in the interest of the case, supposedly. I now subscribed to her Instagram and Twitter feeds and checked them periodically during the day.

"I saw that one," I said. "It looked pretty good, considering."

"Considering?" Stacy asked.

"Considering you were actually in a hospital bed, not on 'vacay' as you told everyone, and considering how badly you were injured just a week ago," I said with a smile to soften the words.

"Ah. I see what you mean," Stacy replied. Romi just looked up and seemed to disapprove of my comments.

"I was going to see if you wanted to do a puzzle, but you're busy. I'll be outside until midnight if you need anything," I said as I turned to leave.

"No, John, don't leave. Romi has a date and he's heading out now, anyway. Right?" she asked as she turned to look at him.

He just looked back at her then looked at me and shook his head.

"Yeah. Gotta go get ready for my date," he said as he closed the laptop and stood. He leaned down and kissed Stacy on the top of her head. He stuffed the laptop in his messenger bag and headed out without another word.

"I'm sorry. I didn't mean to interrupt," I told Stacy as I walked further into the room. I put my hat on the windowsill as usual and sat in the chair Romi had just vacated. Stacy was sitting in a wheelchair next to her bed.

"Oh, you didn't interrupt. We'd finished what we needed to do and were just messing around. I'm glad you're here, John," she said as she looked at me intently. I couldn't help staring back at her. Even brown, her eyes drew me in and held me captive. I couldn't look away. I finally had to shake my head to break the spell. I reached for the pile of books and pulled out the crossword puzzle book. I grabbed a pen from her bed tray and opened the book.

Stacy looked a little shell shocked, too. She looked down into her lap as I got the book ready.

"Okay, first question," I said, and we started the puzzle.

About two hours and three puzzles later, Stacy said she had to use the bathroom. She used the remote sitting on her bed to call the nurses' station for assistance. I thought about offering, but figured it was a little personal for a near-stranger to help with. I offered to wait outside until she was finished.

She was grateful. She asked me to come back once the nurse left. I nodded in agreement and grabbed my hat as I left.

The nurse arrived in just a few minutes. She left again about 15 minutes later and told me Stacy was ready for me to go back in.

I found Stacy sitting up in bed this time. She looked tired suddenly, and I felt like I was intruding.

"You look tired. I should let you get some sleep," I said as I entered the room and walked over to her bed.

"No, please don't leave. Why don't you tell me a story about your childhood or something. If I fall asleep, please don't be insulted, I just get so tired still," she said just as she yawned.

"Only if you're sure," I said as I put my hat down and sat in the chair again.

"I'm sure," she insisted.

I started telling her about the time I got hooked by a fishing lure when I was eight, then about the time I had climbed a tree and was afraid to climb down, and the fire department had to come get me. By the time I finished that story, Stacy was asleep. I meant to get up and go, but she looked so innocent lying there asleep, I couldn't help but just watch her for a bit.

Finally, I reached above her bed to turn down the lights and left.

THE SHERIFF'S STAR

By Saturday, we still had not heard from Bristol Forensics about the phone, so I called over there. I was told that they had a backlog on tech evidence, and it would be a few more days. I was even more frustrated because we still had no new evidence in the case. Stacy had been in the hospital for over a week and may be there a while longer. I felt like I was letting her down.

I still wanted to see her, though, so I called her phone and asked if she felt like having a visitor today. She sounded surprised to hear from me, but said she'd love it if I came by.

I stopped by the diner and picked up a quart of Mary's homemade chicken noodle soup since I knew Stacy was still not eating fully solid food yet. I got something for myself and headed over to the hospital.

Stacy was sitting in her wheelchair again as I entered. Romi was not there, so I sat the bag down on her bed tray and said hello.

"You look like you're feeling better today," I told her truthfully. She looked more awake, and her skin was brighter and she was smiling.

"They figured out a way for me to take a shower this morning, so I feel wonderful!" she said with an even brighter smile.

"Wow! I bet that felt amazing after all this time!" I said.

"You just don't even know," she replied.

I pointed to the bag. "I brought you some homemade chicken noodle soup from our diner. I thought it might be a nice change from hospital food," I told her.

"I really appreciate that, but I smell meatloaf!" she said.

"Sorry, that's for me, but if you eat your soup, I'll give you a bite of my meatloaf," I compromised.

"Deal!" she cheered.

I told her I'd be right back. I walked down to the nurses' station to get a small cup that I could put soup in for Stacy. I returned to the room with it, and served up the soup, and sat in the chair with my lunch.

We talked as we ate, mostly about nothing important, but about movies and the news and things like that. Once Stacy was done with her soup, I handed over my carryout container and let her have the last couple of bites of meatloaf. She moaned in appreciation and enjoyment. I enjoyed her enjoyment, and my pants suddenly got a little tighter. *How embarrassing.*

After she was done, I threw all the trash away and left the container with the rest of her soup on her bed tray. She asked if I wanted to do a puzzle, but I told her I'd like to hear about her childhood for a while first.

She told me all about the music lessons, singing lessons, talent shows and pageants as she grew up. She told me stories about going to school in New York City and being on her own so young.

We talked more about our childhoods and about things we liked and didn't like, and found we had a lot in common in some ways. Our childhoods had been very different, and our lives now were obviously very different, but who we were as people was very similar.

We held similar views on politics and people and animals and the environment. We both wanted to make the world a better place somehow. We both hated brussels sprouts but loved deviled eggs. We both voted for the current president but weren't sure it had been a good idea. We both wanted to try jumping from a plane but were too afraid to try. It was fun learning about the ways we meshed.

Several hours later I could tell that Stacy was trying to keep her eyes open. I stood up and told her that I had to go do some things at home, and I would be back on Monday.

She tried to get me to stay, but she was fading fast. I leaned over and kissed her on top of her head, which was the closest I dared get to her for fear of what I'd do. I wanted to kiss her in the worst way, but it was too soon, and maybe too much.

I smiled as I turned and walked out of her room. I wished I didn't have to go. I nodded to my deputy and left the hospital.

The days were running together. I saw John on Monday but he wouldn't be by today because it was Wednesday, Bingo night with his Gram. This morning had dawned dark and cloudy, looking like the heavens would open any second. I was just about to call for help getting out of bed when Dr. Ranjeeb came in the room.

"Good morning, Ms. Varner. How are you feeling today?" He asked.

"Tired. Didn't sleep well, but otherwise okay," I replied.

"Well, getting out of here and into your own space will probably help you sleep better," he said with his trademark singsong voice as he approached the bed. He motioned for me to pull up my shirt so he could check my surgical dressing.

I doubt it, I thought to myself, but said, "Yes, you're probably right."

"So, we'll be discharging you on Friday. I will be out of town tomorrow and Friday, so I wanted to talk to you today. I need you to make sure you continue your PT at an office close to home so we keep your muscles strong. You should be able to switch to crutches once your shoulder is healed.

"The nurse will give you discharge instructions, which will include an appointment to come back here for x-rays within four weeks, and possible cast removal. She will also have information on local PT offices near you. Do you have any questions for me?"

I shook my head. "No, Dr. Ranjeeb. Just thank you for everything. I owe you my life."

"Very, very good. I'm glad it all worked out. If you have questions or concerns, there will be contact information on the discharge papers. Don't hesitate to reach out. Goodbye, Ms. Varner." He turned and left the room.

I decided to take a shower and get dressed since it was too early to call Romi. I called the nurses' station for some assistance with wrapping my cast in plastic and taking a shower.

Thirty minutes later I was feeling more human. I kept the sling off and did some exercises on my shoulder. I was ready to get out of the wheelchair and start using crutches. After I ate breakfast I called Romi.

"Hey. They're letting me go on Friday, so get packed up," I said.

"Got it," he said. "Let me shower and dress and I'll head over. Have you told Tom yet?" He asked.

"No, I'll call him next." I said. "Bye."

I called Tom and let him know the plan. He stated he would book a flight and be in tomorrow.

"Understood," I replied.

Next, I called the Sheriff.

"Sheriff Leppard," he answered.

"Hello, John. This is Stacy. Just wanted to let you know that I'm going to be released on Friday, so if you could let the hotel know I would appreciate it."

"I can do that. How does it feel to know that you're about to be sprung?" he asked.

"Really good. I wish it was closer, but Friday isn't too far off. I'm sorry I'll miss you tonight," I said.

"Me, too, but it's a standing date with Gram, and one does not miss Bingo unless one is missing a body part. Even then, it's only a maybe," he said with humor in his voice.

"I think I would like your Gram," I said, smiling to myself.

"Everyone does," he said. "I'll try to come up tomorrow so we can discuss the plan going forward. I'll call Celeste and give her the heads up. Anything you need?" he asked.

"No, I'm good. My manager, Tom Montague, is coming in tomorrow, too, so we can all discuss the plans," I said.

"Okay. I'll be there around 2 p.m. then. Bye, Stacy."

"Bye, John."

When Romi got there, we decided to do a post in front of my window. There was nothing outside except a generic hill that would make a decent backdrop. I put on my makeup and took out my contacts, and put on the new shirt and hat Romi had brought. He helped me into the chair that he had set in front of the window.

> *"Helloooo, Dorsetters! Happy Hump Day! Hope your week's goin' as well as mine is. I'm workin' hard on those new songs, and can't wait to hit the studio! Then we've got the big tour comin', too! Send me a shout out of where you're from in the comments, and we'll send out some t-shirts to random fans! I can't wait to see all of you and to get back to work! Keep dreamin' and keep listenin'!" #HappyHumpDay #newsongscoming #livinthevacaylife*

Romi nodded and I hit 'Post'. Hopefully I wouldn't have to do another one of these for a while. I took the makeup remover cloth he handed me, and had just gotten my makeup off when the door opened and a nurse came in.

She introduced herself as Pam, and said she was checking to see if I needed anything. I told her I was set. She took her time checking the machines.

Romi helped me back into my gown, and I kept my eyes down while I put in my contacts. Pam kept looking at me, so I was anxious to get back into 'disguise'.

"So, Chica, Tom talked to the label and they seem satisfied that you are working on songs while on vacay..." I blinked hard and nodded toward the nurse as a gesture to shut up.

He blinked back at me and tilted his head to the side in confusion. I again gestured toward the nurse, who seemed to be hanging back longer than needed. Romi nodded.

Pam finally left, telling me to call if I needed anything.

"What were you doing?" I cried to Romi. "I'm trying to fly under the radar here, and you just blurt out my business in front of people. Geez!" I said anxiously.

"Sorry! I wasn't thinking! I was just trying to tell you that the execs seem to be buying the ruse, so that's good news," he said defensively.

"Yes, it's good news. Something we definitely need right now. Have you gone through all the mail yet? Anything from our stalker?" I asked.

"No, nothing in the mail or online, except for that one threat. Are you sure no one knows where you are? Do the folks in Whirlwind know who you are? Are they suspicious?" he asked.

"No, they don't seem to know. I have this brown rinse in my hair, wear my brown contacts, a ball cap and sunglasses all the time. I don't know how anyone could have found me. Are you sure you didn't tell anyone?" I asked.

"I didn't tell anyone. Even my roommate, Doug, who always asks about you, left on some weird business trip a few days ago and hasn't been around to ask me questions."

"Well, if the Sheriff still thinks I need protection, we're gonna have to work something out with Tom. The Sheriff's Office can't keep tying up its deputies to babysit me. it's not fair to them or the town," I said.

"When is Tom coming in?" he asked.

"He said he's flying in tomorrow, and the Sheriff said he'd be up here in the afternoon, so we can all talk about it together."

"Good. Tom will figure something out. I don't want you anywhere alone," he said.

"Oh! Speaking of getting out of here, I'm gonna need some clothes to wear. Can you please get me a pair of shorts, a tank top, a bra and panties? You know my sizes and preferences," I said.

"Okay, I'll hit the mall. Do you want designer?" he asked.

"The less designer, the better," I said. "Try Target."

"Target, here I come!" he laughed.

Tom showed up a little past one on Thursday. I told him of my concerns with security, and with relieving the Sheriff's Office of the responsibility.

"I can take care of security," Tom said. "We can hire a private company out of Bristol and have them take over. Does the Sheriff have any leads yet? We have to get this straightened out soon because you have to start recording in less than two months, then there is rehearsal for the tour, and the tour itself. And the talks with the production company. It's going to be extremely difficult to do all that with some nut case after you."

"That's what's so strange, Tom. Romi says there have been no rumblings on the internet, and no threats coming through him in the mail or online, except for one threatening DM. I have no clue who this could be, and there was not much info I could give the Sheriff." I put my arms around myself, feeling very vulnerable with all this talk of security and a nut job on the loose.

"Romi, Sheriff Leppard suggested having my room at the hotel changed to one on the first floor since there is no elevator, and I don't think crutches are going to work on their staircase. Would you make a reservation at the hotel and ask for a new room for me? When I get discharged, we can move my stuff to the new room," I said and I rocked on the bed.

Things had been quiet for a while so I had forgotten what had put me in the hospital in the first place, and what had been said in that DM. I had a funny feeling thinking about that message, so I checked the social media accounts while we waited for the Sheriff to arrive.

Sure enough, there was another one.

THE SHERIFF'S STAR

You won't get past me. I'll be wherever you are, then you'll be gone.

I held up my phone to show Tom and Romi, who squealed and covered his eyes. Tom simply shook his head.

Just then there was a knock on the door and John walked in, hat in hand. I just held up my phone toward him and grimaced.

He took my phone and I saw the line appear between his brows, and a thunderous look crossed his face. He handed the phone back to me and looked at Romi.

"Did you find this?" he asked Romi.

"No, I found it," I said. "Just now."

"Okay. I know we need to talk about the security setup in Whirlwind. I can have my deputies..."

"No need, Sheriff. I'm going to contract with a firm out of Bristol to have a protection detail on Stacy at all times. You can have your deputies back but thank you for all your hard work in keeping Stacy safe here," Tom interrupted.

"As I was about to say, my deputies and I are still on the lookout for this guy. Since we've taken away his place to stay and his vehicle, this person is going to be desperate, and that never leads to anything good. Have you considered how to minimize the gossip? Regular people are not surrounded by armed guards 24/7," John said. My face grew more horrified as he spoke, but these were real concerns that needed to be addressed.

"I hadn't thought..." I started, but Tom broke in.

"We'll say that she has a wealthy father, and since she left home, he wanted her to have security. Would that work, Sheriff?" he asked.

"I feel really bad about putting you in this position. I really just wanted a place to write. I never meant to bring this down on you." I sniffled and wiped my eyes. Romi handed me a tissue.

"I'm sure you didn't, Stacy. And my deputies and I will continue to investigate and do our best to protect you. I'll give Celeste at the hotel a heads up about the added guests and give her the story you came up with. I feel like she'll work with us. Just give me a call as soon as you're released, and we'll go from there. Mr. Montague. Mr. Mercado." He nodded at the men. "Stacy, I'll see you back in Whirlwind." He turned and left without another word. Hunh.

Tom stood up and picked up his briefcase.

"So, Stacy, how's the writing coming? The execs are going to want to see something soon."

"I've got the first song mapped out, but I need my guitar to get the music and lyrics lined up." I answered.

"Okay. Keep at it. This is your biggest break yet. If this album goes platinum with two of your own songs in it, you will be able to write your ticket at any label from now on. Sky's the limit. Try not to worry too much about extraneous stuff. Just get words down on paper," Tom said as he picked up his briefcase from the bed. "I'll talk to you soon." He said as he left.

"Bye," I said as the door closed. '*Extraneous stuff?*' I thought. A deranged would-be killer hardly seemed extraneous to me, but I guess I could see his point. I needed to get to work.

Romi sat back down and got busy on his laptop, and I pulled out my pad and pen and got busy myself. This song still needed some work on the words, and that was all I could do right now.

I was still upset about how John had left. He seemed upset, but I wasn't entirely sure why and that bothered me, probably more than it should.

I was furious, and I didn't even know why. The manager was going to arrange for private security for Stacy, which would free my deputies to go back to their normal duties. But I hated the idea of strangers being in control of Stacy's protection. Not that I was a long-time friend, but I felt like I had a stronger interest in keeping her safe.

This is why I didn't get involved with victims. Well, it would be if it had ever been a possibility before. I had never felt the desire to protect Old Man Gentry when someone stole his prized hog, or Scott Long when he rolled his car trying to tip a cow near a ditch, or Marge Thomas when someone shot her mailbox. No, this was new territory, and I didn't like it. At. All.

I called Celeste when I got back to my office. I told her that Ms. Varner would be back on Friday, and that she would need to be moved to a room downstairs. I also told her that there would be extra people coming that her father had hired to protect her, and they would need more rooms, but I wasn't sure how many. Celeste said she would take care of it and hung up.

I was frustrated and riled up, so I decided to take a shotgun, a rifle and my pistol to the range and get in a little target practice. I loaded up the weapons in my cruiser and headed to the range.

I was just setting up my station when who showed up but Gram. She sidled up to the spot next to mine and started to set up. She had brought two handguns and a shotgun, all of which I thought were too big for her, but she could shoot the antennae off a fly from 100 feet away, or so she claimed.

"What are you doing here, Gram?" I asked before putting on my ear protection.

"Heard you were on your way over, so I thought I'd get in a little practice with you, kid. What brings you here today?" she asked.

"Had to get rid of some pent-up energy, and this seemed the safest bet," I said. "And how did you hear I was headed here?" I asked in confusion.

"Colleen was taking the trash out behind the bakery and saw you load up the guns. She called me to see if something was going on. I figured out where you were headed since nothing came across my scanner," she said, all smug confidence.

I just shook my head. This woman always had her ear to the ground.

I put on my headset and sighted up my shotgun with the target. I fired, then reloaded and fired again. I kept it up for 15 straight minutes before setting down the gun. Gram had started with one of her handguns, and as she brought the target closer, I could see she had hit all her shots center mass, except one. That hit significantly lower than center mass. Gram was mad at someone, apparently.

She just grinned as she looked over the target. She pulled it down and folded it up and put it in her purse. She loaded another target and picked up a different gun.

I picked up my service weapon and put a target on the hanger and sent it flying down the course. I focused all my anger and frustration onto the target and sighted up my weapon. I fired quickly and emptied my clip. I brought the target in.

Fully center mass. Every shot. I felt a little better as I looked at the target. I knew I could take care of Stacy. I just hoped these hired guys could, too.

I emptied another clip into a clean target with the same results. I felt enough better to head back into town. I unloaded my weapons and took down my second target and threw it away. Gram was still shooting so I didn't interrupt her when I left.

I went back to the office, cleaned both guns and put away the shotgun and the rifle. I finished up some paperwork for the county and sat back in my chair, leaning far enough to set the springs to squealing. My thoughts turned back to Stacy. Maybe I had been a little abrupt when I left the hospital. Part of me wasn't sure how much about our new friendship she wanted to show the people in her life, and part of me was just angry that she was still in danger, and on my watch.

I didn't feel like cooking, so I headed to the diner for some dinner. As soon as I walked in, all conversation stopped. I wondered what that was all about. I looked around and nodded at a few people, then headed to the back to a quiet booth. People gradually started talking again. I looked up as Mariah came up to my table to get my drink order.

"Sweet tea, Mariah," I said before she could ask.

"Okay, Sheriff. Special's Roast Beef with Potatoes Au Gratin and broccoli. Want that or do you need a minute?" she asked.

"Just give me the special. And what was everyone talking about when I came in?" I asked her.

"Talkin' about how much you're goin' to the hospital, and about that hurt girl comin' back to Whirlwind," she told me.

"Tell everyone I said it's none of their business," I said.

"Will do, Sheriff."

She came back a few minutes later with my tea and then left me alone. I must have been putting out some kind of vibes because no one approached my table, and when Mariah dropped off my dinner, she scurried away as fast as she could.

That was fine. I didn't feel like making small talk anyway. I ate my dinner and left some cash on the table for the check. I decided that I didn't want to go home yet, so I got in my cruiser and made a couple passes around town, and even into the woods as far as the road would go. I also stopped by the logging shack we had found, but there was nothing new there.

After I'd procrastinated enough, I headed home. I checked the cameras but didn't find anything to worry about. I locked up and took a shower. I put on some pajama pants and headed back downstairs to have a beer. I put the sports channel on the TV but wasn't really watching it.

I wondered about this private security company Mr. Montague was hiring. I should have asked for their info, then I could have investigated them myself. I would have to keep an eye on them, but that would be hard to do and do my job at the same time. My duty was really to the people of Whirlwind, not just one visitor. So why was it so hard to focus on the many and not just the one?

Suddenly an alarm sounded on my phone. One of my camera triggers had been activated. I looked down at the app and saw a man moving around my property about 200 yards away in the woods. He had a shotgun in one arm and was wearing ratty clothing. I jumped up, grabbed some tennis shoes from by the front door, and got a shotgun out of the gun safe in my living room.

I headed out the back porch door into the night. I turned on the spotlight in the backyard from my phone and lit up the area. It didn't reach the area where I saw the man, but it covered a large enough area to get me started.

I ran as quietly as I could toward where I had seen him, and noticed some broken branches on my way. They could be from animals, but I wasn't ruling anything out.

I stopped and listened and heard sounds of movement ahead of me to the left. I headed in that direction but couldn't see anything. I had forgotten a flashlight. After a while I stopped again, listening. I no longer heard movement in front of me. I listened some more but didn't hear anything in any direction.

After several minutes of silence except for birds and insects, I headed back toward the house. Most likely a late-night poacher trying to get a deer. I had my property well-marked as private and no trespassing, but it didn't seem to stop everyone.

When I got home, I decided to leave the spotlight on for a while. I went in the house and locked up the shotgun, but kept my service weapon nearby. I tried to watch the game on TV, but was still too riled up from the chase. I decided to go into the basement and work out. I hadn't done that in a while and I was feeling it.

I went downstairs and connected my phone to the sound system and turned it up loud. I worked out for nearly an hour until I was sweating like crazy and tired. I went upstairs, locked all the doors and windows, then went up to my bedroom. I showered again and fell into bed, naked. I lied there with one arm behind my head and one arm lying on my stomach.

I started thinking of Stacy again. I thought of her long hair that curled at the ends. I thought of her bright green eyes, even though she usually had her contacts in.

I thought of how petite she was, but how strong she seemed to be on the inside. I thought of her laughter and her intellect. My hand moved lower until it was wrapped around my shaft. I was growing hard, and I pulled and stroked faster.

I thought of how serious Stacy was whenever we did puzzles together, or how silly she could be when we tried to make a word fit that didn't. I thought of the curves that he gowns only hinted at. I thought of the sight of her long, tanned leg and stroked harder.

I thought of how her nose scrunched up when she didn't like something. I got harder and hotter. I tightened my grip and thought more about her face, framed by that brownish red hair that always moved with her. I was stroking so hard now, my balls tightened and moved closer to my body. I could feel my orgasm gathering at the base of my spine and wanted it to happen.

I imagined the sounds she would make as I touched her and ran my tongue over her body. I pictured running my hands over her tiny breasts and plucking at her hard nipples. I went over the top, spilling my seed all over my stomach as I spasmed over and over. I groaned with how good it felt.

I lied there waiting for my heart to slow, then I got up to clean off. It had been so long since I had done that. Since I had anyone who inspired me to do that.

I felt worn out. I bet now I would sleep. Tomorrow was a big day. Stacy was coming home.

THE SHERIFF'S STAR

Friday dawned warm and sunny. This was it, the day I got to go back to Whirlwind! I was so excited I could hardly sleep. It was really early, but I was wide awake, so I called the nurses' station for help with a shower.

Next, I packed up the few belongings I had with me, put in my contacts, and put my hair up in my hat. To kill time, I checked my social media accounts. People were still speculating on where I could be. I made a quick post to wish my fans a wonderful day and hopefully assuring them I was fine.

Next, I called Romi. He was not an early riser.

"Hey! Today's the day! Get up and get packed!" I cried when he answered the phone.

"Chica, it's early. Tell them to wait. I need at least two hours." He hung up.

Ugh. Such drama!

I tried to kill time playing with my phone, but I was wired. I was so ready to go home! That's when it hit me that I thought of Whirlwind as 'home', not Nashville. That was strange.

I tried watching TV, but that didn't help either. Finally, they brought in my breakfast. I ate that, then called Tom. He was already up, of course, and said he and my bodyguard would be there within two hours, and not to leave without them. I agreed and hung up.

Romi finally showed up about an hour and 45 minutes later with his bag and a wheelchair.

"Okay, Chica, I'm here. Are you ready to go, yet?" He asked.

"No, still waiting for the nurse, and Tom and a bodyguard are on their way, as well. He said not to leave without them." I said. "Where'd you get the chair?" I asked.

"Rented it from a medical supply place," he said.

Romi and I went back over my social media accounts, I showed him the song I had written, and we talked about plans for Whirlwind. He helped me dress for the trip.

About 10 minutes later Tom came in with a very large, very scary-looking man with tan skin and short dark hair. He was a mountain! He wore a black polo shirt with a logo on the left breast, black cargo pants and heavy boots. He had a gun holster on his belt.

"Stacy, Romi, this is Malcolm. He will be on first watch and will go with us to Whirlwind. We will follow you in my car. I checked with the hotel this morning and they're ready for us. There will be two guards on duty at all times, one with you, Stacy, and one surveilling the perimeter of wherever you are. Are we ready to go?" He asked.

"Still waiting on the nurse," I said, just as the door opened again. The nurse stopped short when she saw Malcolm.

"S-Stacy, I h-have your discharge information here." She moved closer to the bed and showed me the stack of papers but kept glancing at Malcolm.

"Here are your wound care instructions. Just be on the lookout for infection near the surgery wound and keep your cast clean and dry. You should use the sling only as needed in order to return to normal function in your shoulder.

"On this page are some phone numbers in case you need to reach us for any reason. Any difficulty breathing, fever or unusual pain, come straight to the ER. Otherwise, call us with any other concerns. On the next page is your follow-up appointment for four weeks from now for your leg. You will be issued crutches at your choice of PT location. And here are your options for PT offices near Whirlwind. There are only two, but I'm sure one of them will work for you. Do you have any questions?" she asked.

"No, I think you've covered everything. Thank you so much for taking such good care of me." I reached out to shake her hand.

"No worries. Glad everything worked out for you. Be safe going home," she said.

"Thanks," I said.

After she left the room, I gathered my backpack and looked at the three men. "I guess we're good to go."

Romi guided my wheelchair out the door after Tom and Malcolm. I stopped to shake the deputy's hand and thank him for being there. He nodded and advised he would be following us back to Whirlwind. This was going to feel like a presidential motorcade.

When we got to the parking lot, Malcolm checked over Romi's car before letting us get in. I tossed my backpack on the back seat of the car and Romi helped me into the front seat. Malcolm stowed the wheelchair behind me and closed the back door. We were on our way, me and my band of merry men. Not.

I texted John that I was on my way.

The ride back to Whirlwind was quiet and uneventful. In other words, perfect. I was so happy to see the hotel come into view. Romi pulled up to the front door in the curved driveway, and Tom and Malcolm pulled up behind us. John was waiting for us at the door, along with another very large man in the same black uniform as Malcolm. Malcolm came over and got the wheelchair out of the car and helped me into it. He set my backpack on my lap and pushed me into the hotel lobby. I introduced John to Malcolm, and Malcolm introduced us to Barry, his counterpart. Malcolm advised that Barry would be walking the perimeter of the hotel. Malcolm pushed me up to the check-in desk where Celeste was waiting for us. Her eyes were wide as she took in the entourage, especially Malcolm and Barry.

"W-welcome back, Ms. Varner. I have moved you to room 108. Your friend will be in room 110, and your, ah, guards, will be in room 106. Would you like me to move your things from your old room?" She asked.

"Thanks, but Romi will move them. I appreciate your accommodating all of us on short notice. I promise we'll try to be as unobtrusive as possible." I said.

"No problem," she said. "I'm just glad you're going to be alright."

John handed Romi the key to my original room, and Malcolm pushed me in the direction of my new room. Tom followed as we rolled down the hall. "Are you staying here for a while, Tom?" I asked as we went into my room. I tossed my backpack on the bed and turned my head to him.

"No, I'm headed back to Nashville. There will be another pair of guards on duty after Malcolm and Barry. They will be staying in their room when off duty. I don't expect any trouble but keep me updated." He put his hand on my shoulder and squeezed. "I'll let you know when I get back to Nashville. Keep in touch." With that, he turned and left.

Romi entered right as Tom left. "I'm headed down to the diner to pick up lunch. What does everyone want? The special today is meatloaf, mashed potatoes and green beans." He said. I told him that the special was fine for me. Malcolm opted for a chicken Caesar salad, extra chicken. He took notes and left to find Barry.

As tired as I was of being in bed, it had been a long morning, and I had Malcolm help me onto the bed to rest while I waited for lunch. My mind was still spinning, but I must have dozed off. I woke to Romi shaking my shoulder, telling me lunch was here.

He had set up lunch at the table in my room, with two chairs pulled up for him and Malcolm, and space for my wheelchair. He helped me back into the chair and rolled me to the table. The smells were incredible, like when my grandma used to cook Sunday dinners. I took a sip of my soda and dug into my food. I noticed that Malcolm was sitting in such a way that he could see out the window and see the door to my room. He was eating quickly, I assumed so he could go back to sitting outside my room.

I told Romi my idea of making a video post to show people that I was alright. He agreed, and we decided to go out into the courtyard after lunch to video. I finished my lunch in record time, finally having my full appetite back.

After lunch, Malcolm texted Barry to let him know that Romi and I would be in the courtyard soon. I went into the bathroom to put on my makeup and change clothes. Romi had brought a couple of designer tops that I could wear in videos to maintain my signature look. I took out my contacts and made sure my hair was still covered by my ball cap.

We made our way outside and found a cute little bench surrounded by rosebushes that would make a lovely backdrop for the video. Romi helped me out of my wheelchair and onto the bench.

> *"Helloooo, Dorsetters! How are you, my lovelies? I am doin' great! As you can see, I'm surrounded by beauty, and lovin' every minute! I'm workin' hard on those songs I promised you and finished one already! I don't want anyone worryin' about me 'cause I'm better than ever. I feel wonderful and love bein' on vacay! Love y'all and keep listenin'!"*

Romi nodded his head and I hit 'Post.' Hopefully that would quell any worries people had about my being gone. He helped me back into the wheelchair and we decided to tour the courtyard for a bit. I could hear Barry behind us at a respectful distance. My shoulders relaxed and was able to enjoy the flowers and the sunshine that came through. We walked for about 20 minutes, then headed back inside.

I wheeled myself back to my room while Romi went upstairs to get my things out of my old room. I could not wait to get my hands on Mathilda, my guitar. She was named for my grandmother, who had given her to me for my ninth birthday.

I took off my makeup and put my contacts back in before changing into an old sweatshirt. My fingers were starting to move over invisible frets as I contemplated setting the new song to music. I managed to get myself into the armchair in my room in preparation for strumming.

THE SHERIFF'S STAR

Romi knocked once then entered carrying my guitar case and my suitcase. He set the suitcase by the closet and brought the guitar to me.

I pulled the guitar out of the case and rubbed my hand fondly along her curves. My fingers ran along the strings, and I felt like I was home. I had missed this so much.

I asked Romi to hand me my backpack. I dug through and found the pad of paper I had written the song on. I tuned the guitar and started strumming, no particular notes, just reading the words and moving my fingers. As I strummed, I looked down at my guitar case and saw a piece of paper in it that I didn't remember putting there.

"Hey, Romi. Can you reach that piece of paper for me?" I asked.

He came over from unpacking my suitcase and handed me the paper. I opened it with my guitar still in my lap and gasped.

I knew you'd be back. And so will I.

I screamed and Malcolm came running into the room. The paper fell to the floor and my guitar almost fell with it. I clenched the guitar neck and tears started falling from my eyes.

"Call the Sheriff," I told Romi. Malcolm picked up the note from the floor, holding only the very edges of the corners.

"Could this note have been in the case before your accident, Ms. Varner?" Malcolm asked.

"No," I said. "I would have seen it. There was nothing in there but some picks and my guitar."

"There's a deputy on their way over. Sheriff is over at the courthouse doing something and can't be here," Romi said.

We all just stayed where we were, and a few minutes later a deputy knocked at the door. Malcolm let her in.

"Ms. Varner, I'm Deputy Grey. I hear you found a note?" She asked. Malcolm handed over the note, and Deputy Grey immediately put it into an evidence bag before reading it. She read it and shook her head.

"Ma'am, do you have any idea how someone could have gotten into your previous room to leave this note? Did anyone else have a key?" She asked.

"No, I only ever had one key, and since my accident, the Sheriff has had it until this morning when we got back to the hotel. Then he gave it to Romi so he could get my stuff. "

Deputy Grey turned to Romi. "Mr. Mercado, correct?" She asked. He nodded, wariness covering his face.

"And before you ask, Deputy, I did not put that note in the case. It's my job to protect and assist Ms. Varner, not add to her distress." he harrumphed.

"Of course, not, Mr. Mercado, but did you notice anything unusual when you went to the room? Was it locked when you entered? Did any of Ms. Varner's belongings appear to be missing or out of place?"

He shook his head. "No, the door was locked and everything looked just as Stacy would keep it. I didn't notice anything out of place," he said. Then his head jerked up and he said, "Wait! Sloth wasn't there. Didn't you bring him, Stacy?"

Oh, no. Not Sloth. He was my emotional support stuffy. "Yes," I said, saddened. "I brought him. He was sitting on the dresser."

"Then something was missing, because Sloth was definitely not on the dresser. I wouldn't miss something that big." He cringed when he looked at me. "Sorry, Stace." He walked over and hugged my shoulders.

"Okay. I'm going to check the locks on the hotel and the room for possible tampering. I'll take this note and dust it for prints. Maybe we'll find some that don't belong. I'll let the Sheriff know what happened when he gets back from court. Do you have any questions, or any more info for me, Ma'am?" She asked.

"No. Thanks," I said, dejected.

"Good. I'll be off then. Keep your door locked and make sure your protection goes wherever you go." She turned and left the room. Malcolm nodded at me and left, as well.

I leaned over and put my guitar back into the case. The feeling of home was suddenly gone, replaced with repulsion and fear.

"I'm gonna lie down for a while, Romi. You can take some time and do something for yourself if you'd like. Go shopping or something," I said. I rolled over to the bed and was able to get in by myself.

"I think I will," he said. "I've never been to a General Store. I wonder what they carry?"

"Have fun," I said and laid down. I felt like my life was spiraling out of control and I just couldn't deal with it. Sleep pulled at me and I gave in.

"Court is adjourned."The judge brought her gavel down on the desk and we all rose. Once she left the courtroom, we all followed suit. I turned on my phone to see what I had missed. I had one missed call from an unknown number that I thought I recognized as Stacy's number. I listened to the voice mail message. It was from her friend, Romi.

> *"Sheriff, this is Romi Mercado. Stacy found a threatening note in her guitar case. Since you aren't answering, I'll call the station."*

I called the station immediately. "Sheriff's Office, Deputy Sandoff."

"This is Sheriff Leppard. Has anyone gone to the hotel to see about a threatening note Ms. Varner received?"

"Yes, Sheriff. Grey took the report and is dusting the note for prints right now. Do you want to talk to her?" He asked.

"Yeah, let me speak to her." I said.

"Hold one,"Torres said.

"Deputy Grey. Hello, Sheriff. How can I help you?" Grey asked.

"Bring me up to speed on the latest development." I said.

"Okay. Well, I've dusted the note and run the prints through NCIC. I'm waiting for results now. The note was found in Ms. Varner's guitar case, which has been locked in her old hotel room since the accident.

"I inspected and dusted the locks on the hotel and the room and found signs of a break-in on both the room door and a door at the side of the hotel. It is unknown when this occurred, and Celeste had no idea someone had broken in.

"Nothing else appears to have been disturbed in the hotel in general, but a large stuffed animal is missing from Ms. Varner's room. She's very upset, of course, but her protection detail is in place. Is there anything else you'd like me to do?" Grey finished.

"No, I think you've go it handled. I'll go by the hotel and see her before heading home. Have a good evening, Grey." I said.

I parked in the curved driveway in front of the hotel and entered the lobby. I nodded at Bonnie at the front desk and tilted my head down the first-floor hallway. She smiled and nodded. I got to Stacy's room and nodded at the bodyguard; I thought I remembered his name was Malcolm.

"Is Ms. Varner up for guests?" I asked.

"She was lying down earlier, but you can knock, Sheriff." Malcolm answered. I knocked quietly in case she was still sleeping. When I didn't get an answer, I knocked again a little louder.

"Come in," Came a muffled reply. I entered the dark room and waited for my eyes to adjust. Then a lamp came on by the bed, and there was Stacy, sitting up crookedly, her eyes puffy with sleep and her hair a tangled mess. But she was absolutely adorable. She looked so young.

"Oh, hi Sheriff. I thought you were Romi." She said.

"I'm sorry to disturb you, Stacy. I just wanted to check in after being briefed about the note. How are you holding up?" I asked.

"Truthfully, I don't think I'm holding up at all. I was just starting to feel settled and like things were getting back to normal, and this freak ruins everything. I don't know how much more I can stand! I just don't have the time to deal with all this and still get my songs done." She rubbed her eyes vigorously as if trying to prevent tears from falling. I pulled a chair over to her side of the bed and sat down with my hat on my knee.

"I can only imagine what must be going through your head, Stacy. I've never been in your shoes, but just know that everything that can be done is being done. We're here to help, and you have your protection detail. If it's at all possible, try to let us handle the scary stuff, and just concentrate on getting better and finishing your songs. I saw on your feed that you finished one, is that right?" I asked.

"You follow my feed?" Stacy asked me, incredulous.

"I do now," I said.

"Wow!" She said. "That's crazy cool!"

"Best way to stay on top of what's being said," I said.

"So," she said, more calmly. "What have you found out so far?"

"Well, so far no hits on the prints from the vehicle we found, but we did find food wrappers from restaurants in Watson, the next town over, so we're checking with those businesses to see if anyone remembers anything out of the ordinary.

"We also found fan mags in the shack, but they aren't carried at the General Store, so we aren't sure where they were purchased. Not a good lead at this point. The vehicle was stolen from Nashville, but the owner does not seem to have any relation to you or anyone you work with, so that was a dead end.

"We're running the prints from the note now and should know by tomorrow if there were any hits. We've also reached out to the administrators of the social media platforms to get info on the person who sent the threat, but that looks like it's going to take court orders to get us anywhere with them. Now you're up to speed on the investigation." I sighed. "I wish I had better news for you."

Stacy shrugged. "You can only do what you can do. I appreciate the effort, John," She said. She stared into my eyes with so much intensity I couldn't look away. Her eyes called to me and pulled me in.

I found myself leaning closer to her, and she moved in as well, then there was a knock on the door. We jumped apart and resumed our previous positions.

"Come in!" She called, glancing at the door then at me. My pants were getting tight, and it was hard to focus on who was at the door with Stacy still staring at me. The door opened and Romi ran in with the excitement of a 10-week-old pup.

"You'll never guess what I found at that General Store, Stacy! Look! He reached behind his back and brought forward a 3-foot-long stuffed cow, complete with udders. He shoved it at Stacy and grinned like crazy.

"Um, thanks, Romi. What is this for?"

"Until we find Sloth, this can be your emotional support stuffy! Isn't she darling?!" He really was so excited.

Stacy chuckled. "I suppose she could work. She is very soft." Stacy rubbed her hands over the cow, pretending to tickle the udders.

He seemed to finally notice me. "Oh, hello, Sheriff. News?"

"Not really, Mr. Mercado. Just updating Ms. Varner on the status of the investigation, but I think I 'll leave you two alone. If anything comes up, just give me a call. But try to wait until after Bingo, huh?" I grinned at Stacy and waved to them both as I turned and left the room.

I stopped and made sure Malcolm had my number in his phone and advised him to share it with his counterparts. He told me that another pair of guards would go on duty at 8 p.m., but that he and his partner would remain on the grounds 24/7. I thanked him and left.

Celeste stopped me on my way past the front desk.

"Sheriff, can I talk to you a minute, please?" She asked.

"Sure, Celeste. What's up?" I asked her.

"Well, I'm just not sure about Ms. Varner and her entourage being here. I mean, those men who are 'protecting' her? What's that about? Is she a princess or celebrity or something? Why does she need protection here?"

"Well, Celeste, as I told you, she comes from a wealthy family, and when she left home, her father was worried about her and the possibility of kidnapping. And he didn't want his daughter running around the country alone. Then there is the problem of the break-in that you apparently had where someone was in her old room and left a threatening note. Now, I don't think you or your workers are in any danger, but her family is not so sure about her, and they are willing to pay for the privilege of having security for her. I would think you'd be happy to have the added business during this slow season." I crossed my arms over my chest so she knew I was serious.

"Alright, Sheriff. If you think it's safe for me and my workers, and any other guests, I guess it's alright. But I've got my eyes on them. She's such a sweet thing, I never expected her to be this much trouble. But I guess she can't help it."

"Exactly. You have a good night, hear?" I said as I turned and walked out the door.

Tonight was a special night. The church was hosting a one-off Friday Bingo night to help raise money for the new playground. I went home after work and changed clothes, then made a salad for dinner. I finished my meal and tried to keep my thoughts on things other than Stacy. I rinsed my bowl and put it in the dishwasher and headed out the door. It was only a few blocks to the church, but I drove in case I got called out for some reason.

I arrived at the church just in time to see my grandmother pull into the lot with Beverly. I walked over to her little red car and helped her out. I bent down to place a kiss on her cheek. "Hi, Gram. How are you today? Ready to lose?" I smirked at her disgusted look.

"You'll never beat me, kid! Others have tried. All have failed. Right, Bev?" She asked, kissing me back on my cheek.

"Eh, she cheats. Of course she always wins!" Beverly said with a sneer. Gram slapped at Beverly's arm as the other woman walked past us.

"Save us some seats, Bev!" Gram yelled as I helped her up the steps to the front door.

"So, kid, what's new? I hear you have something going on at the hotel. What's that about? You know I have to be in the loop so the gossip gets to the right people," She said with a grin.

"Not much to know, Gram. A young woman got hit by a car, she's at the hotel recovering, and her parents sent in bodyguards to watch her. That's all. It's a slow gossip week."

"What's the girl's name, kid?"

"Stacy Varner. Why?" I asked.

"Just curious. Wanna get my facts straight," she said, cackling as I opened the heavy door for her.

"Just stay out of it, Gram. There's nothing to see there." I steered her toward the table where Beverly sat, two empty chairs on either side of the other woman.

"Who said I saved these for you, ya old bat?" Beverly said to Gram.

"Who else would you save them for, idiot? You sneeze every time you lose."

I just shook my head and went up front to get Bingo cards for all three of us, as well as Bingo markers. I was just sitting down when I heard Gram saying to the woman at the next table, "I just found out we've got a live one at the hotel. I'm gonna pay a call and see if she would be good for the kid. I bet she's pretty, ya know?"

I ran both hands through my hair because I could see where this was going. Nowhere good. On second thought, though, if Gram could get Stacy to go out with me under the guise of a busybody old lady, where could the harm be?

Two hours of Gram and Beverly bickering back and forth was about all I could take. I offered to clear the table and escort the ladies out, but they wanted to stay and keep playing. I reminded Gram that she was not allowed to drive at night, and they would need to leave within the next half hour or so. Gram just nodded distractedly and suddenly yelled "Bingo!" Beverly slammed her hand on the table and cursed like a sailor. I just laughed and shook my head as I left.

My mind had been occupied and thoughts of Stacy had faded, but as soon as I left the loud, stuffy church activity room, the thoughts returned with a vengeance.

I imagined Stacy in nothing but that faded, torn sweatshirt and lacy panties, waiting on my bed. I stopped at the car door and let the thoughts carry me away.

I laid down on the bed and crawled between her legs. I kept my weight on my forearms, and leaned in and kissed her slowly, running my tongue along her plump bottom lip, sucking it into my mouth and biting gently. I sat back on my heels and ran my hands under the sweatshirt to feel the warm, smooth skin beneath. I molded my hands to her bare breasts and rubbed her nipples with the pads of my fingers. I pushed up the sweatshirt until the bottom was above her breasts, then I laved at her nipples, one by one, until… a horn blared as a car sped past me. I shook my head several times to clear it before getting behind the wheel.

I was about halfway home when a call came out on the radio about a stolen vehicle. The vehicle apparently had been stolen from a campsite up in the mountains, and the owners had hiked down to town to report it. I made a U-turn and headed back toward the office.

Once inside, I headed up front to talk to the owners. "Hey, Peters. I heard about the stolen on the radio. Where are the owners?" I asked the deputy on duty.

"They headed to the diner once we got their statements. They've been hiking all day to get to town and were starved. Apparently, they had taken down their campsite and stowed all their gear in the truck, then decided to take one last hike.

"When they got back to the campsite, the truck and all their gear was gone. They were about halfway up the mountain, so it took almost all day to hike down. The truck is a 2016 Ford F150, blue, with personalized plates. I've sent the broadcast, but they have no way to get home."

I nodded as I looked at the statements. "Tell them to get a room at the hotel, then in the morning we can have a deputy drive them to the car rental agency in Watson. Sounds like you've got it handled, Peters. I'm gonna head home. Call me if you need me, but try not…"

"To need you. Got it, Sheriff. Have a good night."

"Thanks. You, too." I said as I turned and headed out the back door.

Once I got home, I headed for the shower to wash off the day. I stood under water that was as hot as I could stand it, and once again thoughts of Stacy raced through my mind.

As the thoughts came to me, I got harder and harder. I tried to ignore it until I thought I was going to explode if I didn't take care of it. I grabbed myself in one hand and jerked up and down my shaft, tightening and loosening and I pictured Stacy in her sweatshirt and nothing else, my breathing getting faster and faster as

I moaned in pleasure. Just when I thought I couldn't take any more, I exploded against the wall of the shower, and found it hard to catch my breath.

My body continued to shake as I washed off, and I felt little prickles of electricity along my spine as I dried off. Geez. If this is what it was like just imagining her, what would happen if I ever got the chance to really be with her? I had to sit on the side of the bed while I pondered that.

Finally, I threw the towel on the floor and lied down on my bed, still warm from the shower and what I'd done in there. I stared at the ceiling sure I wouldn't be able to sleep. I kept picturing Stacy when she laughed, when she cried, when she was scared and when she was brave. Eventually, I fell into a deep, dreamless sleep.

I dreamed about him all night. I dreamed he was chasing an invisible bad guy up and down the mountains to keep me safe. I dreamed he raced in front of the car that hit me in order to protect me. I even dreamed he was riding my stuffed sloth.

Then I dreamed about his full lips, coming closer to me and kissing me, pulling me into his body, running his tongue around my whole mouth, biting my lips, rubbing them with his tongue. He ran his tongue from my clavicle to my ear, then kissed around my jaw and back to my mouth. It was spectacular, and I never wanted the dream to end. But it did.

I woke up to a sunny morning with birds singing outside my window. I felt the need to make some music of my own, so I got up and into the wheelchair, then went over to the window and got my guitar out of the case on the table. I just started strumming chords and notes, trying to imitate what the birds sounded like.

Then a melody started coming together. I looked at the song I had written on the pad and started trying to match up the melody to the lyrics. I hummed along with the guitar, and soon I started to sing, as well.

I reached for my phone to bring up the recording app. Once it started, I sang the song with the new melody. I was just starting the playback when there was a knock on my door. Since I wasn't dressed for company, I asked them to wait.

I put my guitar away and rolled back to the dresser to pull on a pair of shorts. Once decent, I invited the person to come in.

It was Romi, of course. "What are you doing up so early?" I asked him.

"I got a message from Tom. The label wants a Zoom meeting with you to verify that you're alright. They apparently got wind of that threatening DM on IG, and want proof of life, or some such thing. Then the production company wants a Zoom meeting to talk about the movie and your potential role in it. Again, proof of life. I figured you'd want time to get ready. It's all hands on deck today, Chica."

"I was afraid it would come to this," I said. "Okay. Let's get some breakfast and then I'll transform myself for the big guys."

We called for room service, and the new guard brought our breakfast in about 20 minutes later. He was another huge man dressed all in black, but his skin was darker than Malcolm's, and he had a scar running through his left eyebrow. He introduced himself as Eduardo and advised that his partner outside was Martin. I thanked him and sat down to eat. The scrambled eggs and corn muffins were divine, and the fresh fruit smelled like a summer day. We ate everything on our plates, and Romi took the empty plates out into the hallway.

"Okay, Chica, time to change. I picked up a couple more shirts for you while you were in the hospital. See what you think." The first one was a beautiful teal silk, with crystal cowboy designs on the shoulders and buttons. The other was pink crepe, with a cowl neckline and flowing sleeves. It had crystals scattered over the shoulders.

"I think I feel pink today, Romi. Can you get it steamed somehow while I put on my face?" I asked.

"Yeah. Let me check with the front desk to see if they have a steamer." He left the room and I headed for the bathroom. It was hard to see into the mirror while in the wheelchair, so I had to stand on my good foot to put on my makeup.

After I was done, I heard the door open and figured Romi was back. I started curling my long hair, hoping the lighting would hide the fact that it was not red. When I finished I went back into the bedroom and found him steaming my blouse over by the closet. I went to my suitcase and found a pair of large crystal chandelier earrings to put on. Once Romi was done, I went into the bathroom to change my shirt. When I came out, he had changed as well into a button-down shirt and a tie. He looked so different I did a double-take.

"What's with the grown-up clothes?" I asked, smiling.

"Tom told me to look like an adult on these calls, so I had to grab what I could find at the General Store. Don't give me grief. I hate this." He pouted like the good little man-child he was. He went over to the table in my room and closed the curtains to cut any glare and put up a selfie light to give us better lighting.

I told Romi that I needed to have my pad and guitar ready because the label execs were probably going to want proof that I had been working on songs. He made sure the guitar was where I could reach it and the pad was on the table in front of me.

I had just finished straightening myself when the call connected, and I was suddenly staring at a table full of middle-aged men in dark suits. "Good morning, y'all," I greeted them, on-camera persona in place.

"Good morning, Ms. Dorsette, or should I say Ms. Varner?" The man in the center of the table asked with a forced chuckle.

"I answer to either, so all's good," I said.

"As your manager has probably made you aware, Ms. Varner, we had some concerns about your well being given some of the comments on your social media; however, you appear to be alive and healthy. How has the songwriting been going?" He asked with a blank face.

"Thank y'all so much for worrying about me! That's so sweet! The songwriting is going really well. In fact, I just set the first song to music this morning. Would you like to hear it?" I asked, smiling my fakest smile.

"Well, um, sure, we can listen to it. I don't imagine it will sound like a real song yet given the surroundings, but yes, we'd, um, like to hear it.

"Okay. Let's do this." I said, and started playing the intro. Once I'd gotten through the song, the men all looked at each other instead of looking at me.

Time to move this along. "Well, guys, what did you think?" I asked, again with my fakest smile.

The man in the middle looked at me and nodded. "Very nice, Ms. Varner. We'd like to hear a recorded version with all the um, extras, before giving a final opinion, however," He said, blank face still in place.

"I understand. All those 'extras' make the difference, don't they?" I asked sarcastically.

Romi was shaking his head at me, knowing I was about to lose my cool.

"Yes. Well, thank you for letting us talk to you today, Ms. Varner. Enjoy the rest of your vacation and we'll talk to you soon." He said before ending the call.

I put my guitar back in the case and closed the laptop. I slid down in the chair and let out a huge sigh. Why couldn't it be easy, just once?

Romi spoke up, putting a hand on my shoulder. "Don't let it get you down, Chica. They're just suits, what do they know about music?"

"Yeah, but they have the power to not let me record my songs. That's what they know."

"Well, we've got about an hour and a half before the next call. I know you don't want to go outside with your face on, so why don't you just hang out here and work on the song, and I'll work on the social media, okay?" he asked.

"Maybe for a while," I said. All the fun had just been leeched out of music for the day. But I followed Romi's advice and worked on the lyrics and music for about 45 minutes until I got bored. Then I hounded him into playing a couple of hands of Rummy with me. Then we decided to make a quick video talking about the songs to keep the label happy.

> *"Helloooo, Dorsetters! Happy Hump Day! Just wanted to let you know that the new song has been set to music, and it sounds awesome! I really hope y'all will love it! I'm still on vacay and writin' away, but no worries! I'll be seeing y'all soon and I really miss y'all! Keep dreamin' and keep listenin'!"*

#newsongscoming *#vacayrocks #HappyHumpDay*

Soon it was time for the call with the movie production company. Tom was joining this call, as was my agent, Anna Lindstrom, so we had to wait for all the parties to come online. Once they did, I was surprised to see the director, Wilbur Hart, on the call. Normally it would just be studio reps.

"Good morning, everyone," Tom said by way of greeting. I smiled and said good morning in my best stage voice, and Mr. Hart just said, "Mornin'."

"So, Mr. Hart, what did you want to talk about today?" Anna asked.

"The movie, of course. Is Ms. Dorsette still interested in the role?" He asked curtly.

"Of course," she answered. "What sort of role did you have in mind, Sir?"

"She's a small-town girl who goes off to seek her fortune in the music biz, and meets this guy in a band, and they go cross-country getting into trouble. The usual. We also want her to do the soundtrack along with the male lead. We haven't decided on him yet, but he'll be a musician, too. Can she do that?"

I wanted to scream *I'm right here, douche bag! Ask me yourself!* Romi put a hand on my knee to keep me calm. Tom even looked over at me on the screen as if to say, "Don't do it."

"That sounds good," Tom said, "But when would you need her? She's writing some new songs right now, then has to record an album."

"We need to start shooting in 3 months. Does that give her enough time?" Mr. Hart asked Tom, again ignoring me completely.

Tom looked at me. I shrugged. I felt like I could do it if the label cooperated.

"She can do it," Tom said. "Anna will call the studio and get started on the contracts. Do you have anything to say to Stacy?" Tom asked

"Just to get her tail here in 3 months." He disconnected.

"Do I really want to work with someone like that?" I asked no one in particular.

Romi grinned. Tom shook his head, as did Anna.

"It's the beginning of a whole new career for you," Anna said. "I hear he's a wonderful director, and sometimes that also means no personality. I think you'll do well. He can't ignore you on set, after all." The corner of her mouth went up slightly and Tom nodded.

"Let's just hope I get out of this cast in four weeks like I'm supposed to. Romi, we need to set up PT so I can be in fighting shape in time for filming. Tom, any trouble with the label over this movie?" I asked. Romi was on his phone looking up the PT locations. Tom was looking down at something in his hand.

"No, we should be good as long as you can get this album done in time. I'll get the songs they have lined up and send them to you so you can start learning them. It looks like filming will take about a month, then there will be a short publicity tour. That means we will have to start rehearsal for the album tour as soon as that tour is done. You're going to be really busy the rest of the year, kid." Tom said.

"Okay, we're set to start PT tomorrow in Watson. And we can go as often as three times a week. Does that sound okay, Chica?" Romi asked.

"Sure. We need all the help we can get," I said.

"Alright," Tom said, "Anna, you call the studio and get started on contract negotiations. Let me know how it goes. Stacy, make sure you're focused on the songs and on PT. Those are your jobs right now. You've got this." Tom ended his part of the call.

Anna looked at me in all seriousness and said, "This is a big, big break, kid. I know it's all a bit overwhelming, but we're all here to help you. Just get better and get that other song written. Talk soon. Kisses." And she was gone, too.

I let out a huge sigh and got back into the wheelchair. I rolled into the bathroom to take off the makeup and put my contacts back in. I stuffed my hair under my ball cap and changed back into the sweatshirt.

I rolled back into the room and told Romi I felt like going to the courtyard for a while to work on the other song. I grabbed my pad and a pencil and let him lead me out of the room. Eduardo called Martin to let him know we were coming.

I rolled myself, which felt like a win. It meant my shoulder was getting better, and hopefully I could be using crutches soon. I rolled over to my favorite bench in the middle of the roses and scooted out of the chair.

I sat back on the bench and he sat with me. I looked out over the roses and smiled at the bees looking for honey. I listened to the birds all around us. I felt words trying to come out, but they made no sense. My mind kept drifting back to John, and what I hoped would happen the next time I saw him.

I wanted to taste him, to feel him close to me. He always made me feel safer when he was around, and never more so than when his arms were around me.

Then the calls from earlier came back to me. I was going to be so busy in the coming months, when would I have a chance to be with John? I would be traveling between Nashville and The Coast, then around the country, and then around the world.

There just wouldn't be any time. And we weren't close enough yet for me to ask him to come with me. For goodness' sake, we hadn't even kissed yet! My brain was on overload and about to spin out! I needed to breathe, to calm down and get my focus back on my career. I just didn't have time for love. I mean lust.

I spent the rest of the day tooling around on my guitar and hanging around the hotel. I was getting cabin fever seeing the same walls all day long. I decided I wanted to go to the diner for dinner. Their food was to die for, and I needed a change of scene.

Barry was not a fan of the idea. He didn't want me straying too far from the hotel, and he was my personal shadow this afternoon. I stomped my foot, figuratively, and told him I was going with him or without him. Romi just looked on as we stared each other down. Barry finally agreed after conferring with Malcolm, who agreed to stay at the hotel and continue walking the perimeter.

Our gay little troupe headed out of the hotel and down the sidewalk to the right, past the museum, the farmers' market, the beauty salon and the florist. The courthouse was an imposing building built of stone and brick, standing in the middle of the block. I was slightly out of breath from rolling myself, but it felt good to exert myself.

We entered the diner and all conversation stopped. People looked at us and whispered among themselves. The hostess led us to a booth in the back, away from prying eyes and the large picture windows.

Barry took a table next to us and sat so that he could see both the back of the restaurant and the front windows. I sat with my back to the rest of the restaurant, so no one got a really good view of me. Romi sat across from me and snickered.

"It never gets old watching you enter a room, Chica." He said, grinning.

"Oh, it gets old, dear friend, believe me. I didn't realize how obtrusive the three of us would look."

"Hello, my name's Angela. The special tonight is fried pork chops, sweet potato casserole and turnip greens. What can I get you to drink?" Angela asked as she looked at me. She looked down at my cast, then at the wheelchair, then back at me. "I'll have tea, Angela. Thank you." She looked at Romi next.

"I'll have a diet soda, please." He said. Angela then walked over to Barry and repeated the special. He ordered water, of course.

When Angela came back with our drinks, we ordered our dinners, and made small talk while we waited. As predicted, the food was wonderful. I was going to have to start exercising soon or I would balloon up fast.

Once we had finished and I had paid the bills, we headed out for a leisurely stroll back to the hotel. Romi was pushing me since it was slightly uphill, and Barry was behind us. The street was quiet as most businesses had closed for the night and most everyone was home now.

Just as we reached the museum, there was a loud bang and the front window of the museum disintegrated beside us. Romi let go of the wheelchair and crouched down between me and the museum, so I started rolling backward.

Barry grabbed the wheelchair and raced me into the parking lot between the hotel and the museum and just as we passed the corner of the building, another shot rang out and large chunks of brick exploded above my head. Several landed in my lap. Barry hid me behind a large pick-up truck and Romi raced in behind us and crouched down low. Barry had his gun in one hand and his phone in the other, looking out of the parking lot toward the park across the street. He was probably talking to Malcolm. Then I heard him tell Malcolm to come around front and go into the park since the shot seemed to come from the northeast corner.

Then Barry called 9-1-1. He told them we'd been shot at and that the shots seemed to come from the corner of the park, and another protection agent was in pursuit. After a minute or two I heard sirens and people had started to gather at the entrance to the parking lot, looking at the museum's window and speculating on what had happened.

A patrol car screeched to a stop in front of the parking lot, and two deputies got out. One went toward the museum, telling people to move away from the damaged window and broken glass. The other, who I recognized as Deputy Rogetski, came into the parking lot and met Barry. She asked Barry to holster his gun, which he did.

She came over to me and asked me what had happened. I told her what I knew, that we were walking by the museum window when it suddenly shattered into a million pieces right next to me, then Barry whisked me into the parking lot.

Romi had much the same story, but a little more dramatic. Barry confirmed everything since he was behind us and had a bird's eye view. He gave the deputy his opinion on where the shots had come from, and she nodded her head.

"We've got deputies combing the park right now. Hopefully they'll turn up something." Suddenly Barry looked at his phone. "It's my partner, Deputy." She nodded that he should answer the phone.

"What did you find, Malcolm?" Barry asked. He listened, nodding his head, then handed the phone to the deputy. "He's got news, Deputy." He said.

Rogetski listened, occasionally saying, "Uh, huh," and nodding. She finally thanked Malcolm and handed the phone back to Barry. He walked a few steps away, still listening to Malcolm.

Deputy Rogetski used the mike on her shoulder to request the Sheriff be called in. She also offered to call an ambulance for me, but I declined. Except for some pieces of brick in my lap and hair, I felt fine. She drew my attention to the bits of blood on my left arm and the side of my face that I hadn't even noticed, probably due to adrenaline coursing through my body. I ran my right hand down my arm and didn't feel any pieces of glass there or on my face, so I again declined, saying I could clean up in my room.

I felt numb, like nothing was bothering me and my body was floating, but that felt wrong. I should be upset. I looked down at Romi, and saw blood on his arm, too. I reached my hand down and ran it over his arm. He looked up at me with a blank stare and didn't acknowledge me at all.

I suddenly started shaking uncontrollably and Deputy Rogetski ran to her car and returned with two blankets for Romi and me. Even with the blanket I felt cold all over, but just sat in my chair waiting for what came next.

That was John. I saw his cruiser pull up behind Rogetski's patrol car and him get out. He raced over and when he saw me, he dropped down to the balls of his feet next to me and put his arm around me. He pulled the blanket tighter and asked me how I was doing. My teeth were chattering when I answered.

"S-s-so c-cold," I said.

"You're in shock. You should probably go to the hospital, Stacy."

"No. J-just take m-m-me back to my r-room, p-please." I said. I looked down at Romi, who was now sitting on the pavement, rocking back and forth with the blanket around him.

"And him, t-too." I said.

"Barry, you can come with us. We can get the rest of your statement later. Where is your partner, the one who pursued?" John asked Barry.

"He's back at the hotel, Sheriff. He's waiting in the lobby." Barry said.

"Okay. We'll head in the back fence to the hotel. I don't want Stacy on the street if we can help it." We walked through the parking lot and to a back fence I hadn't noticed before. It led into the courtyard behind the hotel.

We walked in a back door and down the hallway to my room. We all entered my room and Romi crawled onto the bed and lied down on the side I never used. I got into the other side and curled up with the blanket still around me. The shaking had subsided somewhat, but I still felt cold and numb. John leaned down and pulled the covers up over me, too.

He sat down in a chair across the room and looked at Barry with thunder in his eyes.

"What the hell were y'all doing out on the street, walking to the diner and back? Is that how you protect your charge, Barry? What the hell were you thinking?!" John shouted.

"I didn't have much choice, Sheriff. Ms. Varner insisted on going to the diner, with me or without me. She's not a prisoner, so I can't keep her locked in her room."

"He's r-right, J-John," I interrupted.

Barry continued. "I followed protocols and did my best to keep her safe. How in the hell did someone end up shooting at us, anyway?" He asked, his voice slightly raised.

"From what your partner says, when he ran into the park, he saw someone jump out of a tree near the duck pond carrying what looked like a rifle. He gave chase, and chased the person out of the park, around the steakhouse, and into the back alley, where the person jumped into a pick-up truck with plates that match a stolen from yesterday. He didn't get a good description of the person.

"Since the truck was full of camping gear, including two shot guns and a rifle, when it was stolen, this person can be hiding anywhere in the mountains. I don't think this is the safest place for Stacy anymore. What do you think Barry?" He asked.

Barry nodded. "I agree. But where are we going to take her?" Just then Barry's phone vibrated and he looked at the screen. "It's her manager."

Barry stepped out of the room to take the call. John came over to my side of the bed and sat on the edge.

"What are we going to do with you, Stacy? How are we going to keep you safe?" He asked in a soft voice, almost as if talking to himself. He leaned down and kissed my forehead so softly. He pushed the hair out of my eyes and cupped the side of my face in his hand.

I could feel the callouses and the warmth of his skin and curled into it. My eyes closed and I fell asleep, feeling warmer and safer than I had all night.

I watched as Stacy fell asleep, my hand still curled around her cheek. I waited as her breathing evened out and relaxed, and I gently pulled my hand away. I turned off the lamp on her nightstand and left the room to talk to my deputies.

As I left the room, I saw Celeste talking with one of my deputies and Barry and went over to join them. Celeste was wringing her hands and had fear written on her face.

"You said my workers and I would be safe, Sheriff, but look what happened? What am I supposed to do now? I can't have all this going on in the hotel!"

"Celeste, this didn't happen in the hotel, or even on hotel property. What do you want me to do that we aren't already doing? We're investigating, we've put plywood up over the museum window, we're searching for whoever took pot shots. What else do you want?"

"I want her out of here. I just can't have this. She's nice and all, but this is just too much, Sheriff!"

"Alright. We're trying to find a place to move her, but let's let her stay tonight. She's had a rough night, and she's already asleep. I'll keep looking for somewhere else. Okay?"

"Okay, but she has to be gone tomorrow, Sheriff. At the latest." Celeste said, shaking her head and pulling on her fingers. She turned and went into her office. I turned to Barry.

"I think I have an idea, but it's a little crazy. I live just outside of town in my family's house. It has four guest rooms and a huge basement. I think we should move all of you out there. It would be farther from town, easier to guard, and we'd be able to keep Stacy in one place much easier. What do you think?"

Barry looked at me curiously. "You really want all these extra people in your house, Sheriff? That seems like above and beyond the call, right there. Is this really just to protect Ms. Varner?" He asked as he continued to stare at me.

I looked him in the eye, too. "I don't know of anywhere else to take her where she won't be found out. And it's the safest place I can think of. I have weapons and a top-notch security system in place. Unless you have a better idea?" I cocked my head. slightly to the right and raised my eyebrows, as if to say, *Well, let's hear it*.

"Alright, Sheriff, we'll do this your way. I'll let the others know, and we can get her moved over after she goes to PT tomorrow. I just hope you know what you're doing," Barry said and turned to go down the hall to Stacy's room. I really wanted to go with him, just to see Stacy once more, but instead I turned and left the hotel. I was off the next day, so I would be driving Stacy to Watson. And no one could stop me.

After I checked in again with my deputies doing clean-up on the glass and brick shards, I headed home. I cleaned the house from top to bottom, although I was seldom home long enough to really get it dirty.

I did all the dishes and put them away, vacuumed the whole house, cleaned the bathrooms, changed the sheets and towels and washed the dirty ones. I straightened up the magazines on my coffee table, which were there courtesy of Gram, and dusted every surface. I opened some windows to air out the place since it had been closed up so long. Again, I was hardly ever here for more than sleeping and eating, and the place smelled stale. I wished I had some of that spray that would make it smell like flowers or something. Once I folded the clean sheets and towels, I jumped in the shower to rinse off and fell into bed.

A strange feeling of dread washed over me as I thought of the events of the evening. This phantom causing all the problems was getting bolder, and that wasn't good. He seemed to have a real vendetta against Stacy, but I couldn't figure out why. Of course, crazy was sometimes just that, crazy, with no real reason. I hated that for her. I could still picture her shaking, with shards of glass and brick in her lap, and the cuts on her arm and face. Barry was right. She wasn't a prisoner, but we had to keep her safe, and that meant keeping her out of public view. That made my house the perfect location. It was away from downtown, on a private road, with a complete security system that included multiple monitors and cameras around the property.

I would need to pick up groceries in the morning before picking Stacy up for PT. I would also pick up a couple of air mattresses to put in the basement in case we needed them. I had plenty of firewood outside, and a freezer full of deer meat, in addition to tanks of propane. We could be totally self-sufficient if we needed to be in order to keep Stacy's presence under wraps.

I closed my eyes and tried to sleep. I couldn't stop picturing the fear on Stacy's face when I had gotten to the scene. No one should ever have that look on their face, especially not her. I had just wanted to kiss her and make it all better, but that wouldn't have been appropriate. As long as she needed my help, I didn't want lines getting blurred. I didn't want anyone questioning my motives or actions in relation to Stacy, for her own good.

I finally fell into a fitful sleep, full of nightmares about gunshots and blood, and Stacy's frightened face. Morning came too soon.

By 6 a.m. I gave up on sleep and got up. I made some breakfast and ate it at the breakfast bar in the kitchen. I drank two cups of coffee to try to wake up, then took a cold shower in my room. I went back through the house once more to make sure it was ready for guests and was out the door headed to the grocery store.

I arrived just as they were opening up at 7 a.m. I grabbed double the amount of the same items I usually got, like milk, eggs, bread, bacon, cereal, vegetables, coffee, creamer and toilet paper. I also got a can of spray to make the house smell good, then I picked out some sweets from the bakery case because I thought they might make Stacy feel better. I loaded up my car and headed back to my house to unload. Gram's car was in the driveway when I rolled up. *Oh, brother*.

Gram got out of the car as I stopped next to her. I rushed over to help her.

"Good mornin', Gram. What are you doing here?" I asked, kissing her cheek as we walked toward the steps.

"Heard you were laying in some serious supplies, and thought I'd come see what was going on. This used to be my house, you know, kid. So what's the story?"

"There's no story. I'm just going to have guests for a while and needed supplies. End of story. Would you like to wait in the house while I unload everything?" I asked her as we stepped in the house.

"Of course I would," she said. "I need another cup of coffee this morning. Does that fancy machine of yours make black coffee?" She asked with snark in her voice. She was referring to my Keurig.

"Yes, Gram, it does, very well, too," I grinned at her. I sat her down at the breakfast bar and made her a cup of coffee, then headed back out to the car for a load.

When I came back, she was wondering through the house, sniffing.

"Smells stale, kid. Did you buy something to make it smell good?" Gram asked as I set the bags down on the kitchen counter.

"Yes, Gram, I did," I said as I headed back outside. I needed to get moving or I'd be late picking up Stacy.

I brought the rest of the bags in the house and started putting the cold items away in the fridge. I figured the rest could wait until we got back here and got settled. Gram was in the bedroom spraying.

"Gram, come on, I have to go!" I called as she moved to another room, still spraying.

"You go ahead, kid. I'll just finish this up and head out. Call me later and tell me about these guests of yours, got it?" She asked.

"Yes, Gram. Be careful going down the stairs, please. And go slowly down the road. The last rain left ruts in some places." I yelled as I headed out the door. I was going to have to air out the house again after she got done spraying.

I pulled up to the front of the hotel 15 minutes later and went straight to Stacy's room. Eduardo was at the door, and I knocked.

"Come in," Stacy said.

I went in the room and found her dressed in shorts and a short-sleeved shirt, with her hair up in a ponytail and her contacts in. She was just putting her ball cap on when I entered.

"John! Good morning! What are you doing here?" She asked.

"I'm your chauffeur today. I'm taking you to your PT," I said, looking her over from head to toe and smiling.

"Oh. I thought Eduardo was taking me, but this is a nice surprise. Why are you taking me?" She asked as she picked up her phone and looked at it.

"Oh, shoot. I must have turned off the ringer last night and forgotten. I've got several missed calls. Just give me a minute, please. She dialed her voicemail and listened. Her face suddenly got pale and that fear crept back into her eyes. She dropped the phone on the bed and looked up at me.

I went over to her and sat on the bed with her.

"What is it, bad news?" I asked.

"N-no. I-It's someone I-I don't…" She started shaking again. I put my arm around her and asked her to pull up the voicemail again so I could listen.

It was a strange, stilted voice saying, "Darci… Darci," and nothing else. I pulled away from Stacy and put a hand on each of her arms to look her in the eye.

"Who has your phone number, Stacy?"

"R-Romi, Tom, A-Anna, my a-agent, some f-family, but that's it. And they all know me as Stacy. They would never call me D-Darci." She was still shaking, but looked like she was trying to fight it.

"Let me listen to the rest of the voice mails, Stacy. See if there are any more," I said as I handed her the phone back. She pulled up the voicemail app again and I listened. Two more of the messages were the same thing, and one message was from her agent. I passed that message along, then called my office and instigated a tap on Stacy's phone.

Just as I finished my call, Stacy's phone rang. She looked at me with fear still in her eyes, and I told her to answer and put it on speaker.

"Hello, this is Lieutenant James Stacy from Nashville Police Department. May I speak with Stacy Varner, please?"The man said.

"Uh, this, uh, this is Stacy V-Varner. H-How can I help you?"

"Ma'am, I'm sorry to call so early, but your apartment was burglarized within the last couple of days, and we need you here to go over the apartment and make a statement. Can you come into town today?"

"Well, n-no, Lieutenant. I was hit by a car last week, and my injuries make traveling such a distance difficult." She looked at me for guidance. I mouthed 'Romi' at her.

"But my personal assistant, who, uh, has an office in my apartment and knows everything in the apartment, could drive there and look everything over and give you an inventory of what's missing. How, um, how did you find out about the burglary?"

"Two nights ago one of your neighbors reported loud noises in your apartment to the management. One of the desk clerks was trying to leave a notice on your door today and found it open. He called us, and we came right over. We finally got your contact info from the building management. I'm sorry to hear about your accident. Where are you right now and how long have you been there, Ms. Varner?"

I looked at Stacy and shook my head. I took the phone from Stacy.

"Lieutenant, this is Sheriff John Leppard of the Whirlwind Sheriff's Office. Ms. Varner has been under a protective detail since she was released from the hospital on Tuesday of this week. She was in a hit-and-run accident Thursday two weeks ago here in Whirlwind and was hospitalized immediately. She has been in Whirlwind for about three weeks. Can you tell me how much damage there is?" I asked.

"It appears to be pretty extensive. All the furniture has basically been destroyed, ripped apart, even turned over and the bottoms ripped out. Can you tell me if she was out of the country in the last few months?"The Lieutenant asked.

I looked at Stacy. She nodded mouthed that she was on tour until a month ago.

"Yes, Lieutenant. She was out of the country until about a month ago. Why? Do you think it's related?" John asked.

"Well, it certainly looks like someone was looking for something they thought would be hidden. That's why we need a statement from Ms. Varner."

I looked at Stacy again. "Ms. Varner has a medical appointment to get to, but we can have her assistant on the road within the half hour to meet up with you at the apartment, and I will have her call you from my office to give an official statement, if that works for you, Lieutenant." I said. I looked at Stacy and smiled.

The Lieutenant was silent for a moment. Then he said, "I suppose that will work. But please have her call today and make her statement. How long will it take the assistant to get here?"

"About three hours," John said. "His name is Romi Mercado. I'll give him your number and have him call you when he gets close."

"Thank you, Sheriff. Ms. Varner," and he hung up.

"I don't think I'm his favorite person right now," Stacy said with a sad smile on her face.

"I don't think I am, either," I said. "But the reason I'm here is Celeste does not feel safe with you here anymore, and we need to get you out of the public eye as much as possible, so you and your team are coming to stay at my house outside of town…"

"No! We can't stay with you! Why would you even do that for me?"

"Yes, you can, and it's the best way to keep you safe. Someone obviously knows you're here, and the protection detail hasn't been completely successful. So, the best place for you is at my house where I have a security system, and we will be out of downtown away from prying eyes. I was going to have Romi pack your stuff, but we need to get him on the road. Call him and get him in here, please." I said, placing a hand on her face.

She looked up at me, concern in her eyes, either for me or for herself, I didn't know which. She slowly put the phone to her ear and called Romi.

"Romi, I need you here right now," she said and hung up. I leaned down and pulled her to me in a hug, trying to tell her without words that it would be all right. She hugged me back, but pulled away just as the door flew open and a very disheveled Romi came running in.

"Oh, my God, what's wrong?! What's happened?" he cried and he collapsed on the bed in footie pajamas. In spite of the circumstances, I had to stifle a laugh.

"Two things," I said. "First, we have to leave the hotel and move to my house for security reasons. We need to leave by the time Stacy and I get back from PT. Second, Stacy's apartment was burglarized, and the police need you to go to Nashville to make an inventory of whatever might be missing and of the damage. You'll need to leave within the next 20 minutes or so. I'll text you the Lieutenant's number, and you need to call him when you get close to Nashville so he can meet you at the apartment. I'll also text you my address so you can come to my place when you get back. Go!" I said as he just stood there looking between me and Stacy.

"Oh, my God!" he cried again as he turned and ran out the door.

"Okay. We have to go. We're going to be pushing it to be on time as it is," I said to Stacy wheeled her toward the door.

"I just can't believe all this is happening," she said with a stunned look on her face. I stopped to tell Eduardo that we were moving locations and to give him my address. I told him that as soon as we got back from PT and Stacy packed, we would hit the road. He nodded and said he would pass the word to the others.

As we left the hotel, we passed Celeste at the front desk. She wouldn't look Stacy in the eye, but I told her the plan and that we would be relocating later that morning. She just nodded and went back to what she was doing.

Stacy and I headed out for Watson in my old truck. She was pensive and kept her eyes on the view outside her window. I reached over and took her hand in mine. It felt cool and clammy, and I knew she was scared. I rubbed my thumb over the back of her hand, trying to calm her the best I could. Her hand eventually started to warm up, and she looked over at me with a small smile before returning her gaze out the window. I took that as a small sign that she was feeling somewhat better.

We arrived at the PT office with only a couple of minutes to spare. I wheeled Stacy into the office and took a seat next to her in the waiting room while she filled out paperwork. She only spoke to ask me what to answer for the question about whether the injury was due to a car accident. I advised her to write 'hit-and-run' so they would know that the driver's insurance was not covering the cost. She nodded and finished filling out the form. I walked it back up to the desk for her when she finished. Other than to say, "Thank you," she remained silent. When the physical therapist arrived to take Stacy back to the exam room, Stacy smiled at me before turning her attention to the front.

I went back out to the truck to call my office.

"Sheriff's Office, Deputy Long Cloud."

"Long Cloud, this is the Sheriff. I need someone to run a trace on some phone calls to Ms. Varner's phone. Here's the number." I read it off to him. "She got several harassing phone calls sometime between last night and this morning. I want the originating number and to know who owns it. I already called for a tap for future calls. See what we can find out." I said.

"Sure thing, Sheriff. I'll run the trace myself. Oh, I ran into Celeste at the diner this morning and she said all those folks are leaving the hotel today, is that true?" he asked.

"Yep. I'm moving them to a safer location once I get back into town. I'm in Watson, by the way, with Ms. Varner at PT if anyone needs me. We'll probably by back within the next two hours." I said.

I couldn't make sense of the facts that we had. First the stalker, because let's face it, that's what he was, was in Whirlwind, hunkered down in the shack. Then I think he went to the hospital and tried to see Stacy.

Then he was back in Whirlwind stealing a truck and camping gear and shooting at Stacy; but now he was in Nashville trashing her place looking for I don't know what. Maybe nothing, maybe he was just mad and frustrated. But why was he traveling between Whirlwind and Nashville at all when he obviously knew where she was.

None of it made any sense. And we still didn't know who we were looking for or why he was after Stacy.

My phone rang about an hour later with Stacy's number.

"Hello," I answered.

"Hey," she said. "I'm finished." She sounded tired.

"Be right in," I told her and went into the building. She looked really wrung out, almost sleepy, when I got inside. I smiled at her and started pushing her out the door. She slid a small card into her purse. I asked if she had another appointment scheduled.

"Yeah," she said. "Tomorrow morning, to work on my leg. We worked mostly on my shoulder today." She leaned her head against the passenger side window and promptly fell asleep. I took her left hand in mine like I had on the trip down and wished her pleasant dreams in my head.

PT was the ninth level of hell. Well, maybe just the seventh. But it hurt. A lot. I hadn't hurt this much since right after the accident. I needed some Ibuprofen and a glass of wine, then a nap. That was my last thought until we arrived back at the hotel.

When we arrived, John offered to leave me in the truck and pack my things for me, but I felt like I wanted to do it myself. He helped me into the wheelchair and wheeled me inside. Eduardo, Martin, Barry and Malcolm were all in the lobby. Apparently, John had called to tell them we were close. John wheeled me to my room and left me by the dresser. He brought my suitcase over close to me so I could throw clothes in as I went. He grabbed my backpack and guitar case and set them on the bed while I packed.

After I got all the clothes out of the dresser, I rolled myself into the bathroom to get everything else. John helped me by getting my shampoo and conditioner out of the shower since I couldn't reach them. I threw all the personal care stuff into my backpack and told John I was ready. I looked back at the bed and saw the cow. I couldn't leave the cow behind, either. Romi would be heartbroken.

I still hadn't said much to John. I didn't want to impose on him, but I didn't know what else we could do. I'd been kicked out of the hotel, and I couldn't go back to Nashville until I got my cast off. I suppose we could have gone to a hotel in Watson, but I really didn't want to leave John. He made me feel safe, even more than my protection detail. What I needed to do was straighten up and be appreciative of him, not shut him out.

I turned to John before he could open the door.

"John, I want to say how thankful I am that you're letting us stay at your home. I know it's an imposition, especially with so many people, but thank you. Really." I put my arms out for a hug. He walked over and put the suitcase on the floor. He leaned over and lifted me out of the chair. He wrapped one arm around my shoulders and the other around my waist and pulled me close. I hung on for dear life with my arms wrapped around his waist, never wanting to let go. He smelled so good, like leather and the outdoors. I squeezed harder, trying to tell him how much he already meant to me.

He pulled me even tighter and I moaned at how good it felt. He slowly released his hold and I released him, too. We looked at each other for long seconds, then I reached up and kissed his jaw. Then I moved my lips along his jaw to his mouth and ran my tongue along his bottom lip. He groaned and opened his mouth and I went all in. We pulled each other closer again and our mouths took over. His tongue searched my mouth and licked my lips. My tongue mated with his as I moved my mouth over his. It was everything and not enough all at once.

There was a knock on the door. Martin said, "Celeste is giving us the stink eye. I think we need to go, guys," through the door. John and I slowly separated, our lips full and bruised and tasting of one another. With one more long look, I grabbed my backpack, cow and purse, and John opened the door and he asked Martin to grab the suitcase and guitar case, and we left the room.

The protection guys were following us in their rental. John kept his eyes glued behind us, looking for anyone following behind the second car. He seemed satisfied that no one was following us because he looked at me and smiled.

"I want you to know what we're doing to get this figured out. I have one of my deputies running a trace on that unknown number that called you. He's going to try to get the number, then find out where it was bought and who bought it.

You're going to want to get a new number, but I'd wait until we get more info on this guy." He looked at me again, then turned his eyes back to the road.

"My house has four bedrooms and four baths. You can choose your room. I also have air mattresses to put in the basement if we need more space. You're welcome to anything in the kitchen or in the house, for that matter. There's a screened-in porch in the back you're welcome to use. I'd offer the hot tub, but it might be hard with that cast. I have cameras all around the property and in the house, but not in the bedrooms or bathrooms. I can monitor all of them from either my office or my phone, and I'll give the guys access, as well. You'll be safe at my place. Make yourself at home."

Just then we pulled up in front of a beautiful gray wood-sided house with white shutters and a red front door. It was surrounded by woods on three sides, with the driveway and front porch being open spaces. The house was two stories tall with a stone chimney on each side. I was in love with it already. Then I noticed the little red Nissan Versa parked next to the porch. Hmm, I thought John lived alone.

John must have seen the car too, because he smacked his hand on the steering wheel and shouted, "Shit!"

"What is it?" I asked.

"My Gram is still here. I thought she would be gone by now. No one is supposed to know you're here and she is gossip central. Damn!" He hit the steering wheel again. "Stay here, Stacy. Let me see if I can get rid of her quietly. Though I doubt it."

He got out of the truck and ran up the porch stairs two at a time.

I could hear him holler "Gram!" from in the truck.

I saw a short little woman with gray hair poke her head out of the front door.

"Don't come into this house shouting like a mad man, kid! I can hear you just fine." She stepped out onto the porch and John towered over her. He leaned down and put his hands on her shoulders carefully and spoke more quietly. I couldn't hear what he said to her, but she turned and looked right at me. The men had not yet gotten out of the other car, but she tilted to the side to get a look at them, too.

She turned toward the steps and John put her hand in his elbow and helped her down. He stopped next to the red car, but she kept going, coming right to my window. I rolled the window all the way down.

"Hello," I said.

"Hello, there, Girlie. You plannin' on stayin' with my grandson are ya?"

"Yes, Ma'am, if that's alright with you, of course." I said with a smile. John came up behind her.

"Sure, and it's fine, as long as you marry the kid!" Gram cackled so loud she startled birds in the trees.

"Gram," John groaned. "Listen, like I told you, this is for Stacy's protection. And no one can know she's here, so you CANNOT tell anyone, not even Beverly. Do you understand me?"

"I understand, I understand. But I've got my eyes on you two. Don't you forget it!" She cackled again and turned toward the other car. She walked up to the passenger window and whistled through her teeth.

"Whew-wee," she said, "That's a lotta man in that car! One of you big boys come help me to my car!" Martin stepped out of the vehicle and offered Gram his arm with a half-smile. Gram grabbed his bicep and marched back toward her car with him in tow. John just shook his head. I could hear the other protection guys laughing behind us.

Martin helped Gram into her car and she tore out of there like the hounds of hell were chasing her. John opened my door and gave me a self-deprecating grin. He lifted me out of the cab of the truck bridal style and walked up the steps. Once inside he set me on a charming floral sofa and put my cast up on the coffee table.

"You stay here and we'll bring everything in," John said as Martin came in with my wheelchair.

The rest of the protection guys came in with duffel bags while John went back out for my stuff. Once everything was inside, John offered to make lunch for everyone. He made quick work of subs and chips, and we all sat down at the scarred dining table that could easily seat 12 people. Lunch was quiet until John started telling the men about the latest developments in my case. I didn't really want to rehash it all, so when I finished my sub, I wheeled myself back into the living room.

I found a bunch of magazines on the coffee table, so I picked one and started reading. I didn't picture John being a fan of People Magazine and had to wonder if this was Gram's contribution. As usual, it felt a little surreal to see blurbs about me in the magazine, so I skipped over those. Didn't care what they said.

I looked at my watch. Nearly one o'clock. Romi would almost be to Nashville by now. I wanted to know how bad the damage was, but then again, I didn't want to know. Good thing was that it could be cleaned up before I got back there and I'd never have to see it. But I would always wonder.

The men had cleaned up from lunch and reconvened in the living room. John offered to show everyone the house and let us choose our rooms. He carried me upstairs and I leaned against a wall in the hallway.

"Here's my room and office," he said, pointing to the room at the end of the hall. He walked into the room next to it and laughed.

"I think Gram picked your room, Stacy. There are flowers on every surface in here." He smiled.

"I guess that's my room then." I smiled back. He picked me up and carried me into the room and set me on a soft, blanket-covered chair near a window. He was right. There were bouquets of wildflowers everywhere. We would need to distribute them around the house or I would come down with hay fever.

John took the men to the other rooms and showed them the rest of the upstairs, including his office where the security monitors were set up.

One of the rooms apparently had two sets of bunk beds, because I heard the men laughing about it. I could hear John saying, "But they're extra long since my brothers and cousins are so tall. You could totally fit in them!" More laughing.

They picked a room for Romi and one for two of the men. The other two men were going to sleep on the air mattresses in the living room, not the basement. That way both the first and second floors were protected during the night.

John also showed them the gun safe and gave them the combination. This was starting to feel very real. I suddenly felt very tired and the pain was returning. I hopped over to the bed and laid down. John must have heard me hopping because he came back up the stairs and into my room.

"Hey, getting tired?" he asked.

"Yeah. And I hurt all over from this morning. Think I'm gonna take a nap. Could I get some Ibuprofen?" I asked

"Sure. There's some in the bathroom, which, by the way, we share, so don't hog it." He smiled then headed toward the bathroom. He came back with Ibuprofen and a glass of water in his hands.

"Here ya go," he said, handing them to me. I sat up and took the pills and a big swallow of water. "Thanks," I said, and laid down again. There was a blanket folded at the foot of the bed, and he pulled it up to cover me.

"You rest, and when you get up we'll have dinner and watch some TV or something. Okay?" he asked.

"Okay," I said as my eyes closed.

Several hours later I woke up to near darkness, and the most delicious smell. I rubbed my eyes and sat up. I ran my hands through my hair, which I was sure was a rat's nest mess. I started to get out of bed and realized my wheelchair was still downstairs. God, I hated being dependent on that thing! I decided to hop to the bathroom on my own.

Once I finished my business and had made myself somewhat presentable, I hopped to the bedroom door and opened it. There was an empty chair, and I heard the sound of TV from downstairs, but didn't see anyone around. I called out and Malcolm answered, coming to the bottom of the stairs.

"Hang on, Ms. Varner, I'll come get you." I didn't want to be in anyone's arms but John's, so I declined.

"No, I can do it. Just be ready to catch me if I fall," I said. I sat down on the top step and went down step-by-step on my bottom. It was slow going, but I did it on my own, which felt great. When I got to the bottom, Malcolm helped me up into the wheelchair.

"Where is everyone else," I asked Malcolm.

"They're outside grilling with the Sheriff. Do you want to go onto the back porch and sit?" he asked.

"Sure. Why not?" I wheeled myself out to the screened-in porch and looked out into the back yard. Malcolm stayed in the doorway behind me. All the other men were standing around a large black grilling station, complete with counter space and a small, built-in refrigerator. This man took his grilling seriously!

I called out, "Hello, everyone. What's for dinner?" All eyes turned toward me. Barry, Eduardo and Martin all nodded and issued various greetings to 'Ms. Varner'. John looked at me and smiled that delicious half-smile of his.

"Please, all of you call me Stacy. 'Ms. Varner' makes me feel very old," I told them. I turned around to include Malcolm in my statement.

"Okay." "Yes, Ma'am." "Alright." "Will do." Came from the men. John came up onto the porch and opened the door, still holding the grilling tongs in his hand.

"How did you sleep, Stacy?" he asked, looking at me like I was dinner, his eyes darker than usual.

"Pretty well, I guess. It was a long day. Thanks for letting me rest," I said, holding his gaze just as intently. I wished we were alone right now. I could really use a kiss. It really felt like the world fell away in that moment, like we were the only ones there.

John suddenly shook his head as if to shake off the heaviness of the moment, and said, "Glad it helped. We're grilling steaks, and I made a salad and French bread to go with them. How does that sound?"

"Sounds and smells delicious. Is there anything I can do to help?" I asked.

"Nope. Steaks will be done in about five minutes. Table's already set. Just hang tight." He smiled again and turned to leave the porch. I wanted to stop him but couldn't think of a good reason to. I just sighed and wheeled myself back into the house.

Malcolm was setting water glasses at all the place settings. I asked if there was anything I could do, but he shook his head and thanked me for offering. I wheeled into the living room and saw that the news was on. My phone rang in my pocket.

I pulled it out, half afraid it would be my mysterious caller, but it was Romi. I also noticed I had missed a call from him during my nap. I answered.

"How bad is it, Romi?"

"Oh, my God, it's bad. So bad, Chica. I'm sorry," he cried. "All the furniture, I mean all the furniture, is ruined. There isn't one piece that can be saved. Fortunately, I have all the order forms from when you first bought everything, so it can all be replaced just like new. What's worse is there are holes in some of the walls, your art was destroyed, and he even broke into my file cabinet in the office and went through all my paperwork, like your bills and invoices. It doesn't make any sense." He sighed into the phone.

"My God. I can't believe it," I said. "Who would do this, and why?" I asked, not expecting an answer. Something suddenly struck me.

"Hey, Romi, where my phone bills in those files, too?" I asked.

"Yeah," he said, "All your bills were. Why?" he asked.

"Because that could explain who someone got my phone number without me giving it to them. It's on all the phone bills, right?" I heard paper shuffling on the other end.

"Yep, you're right. It's right here on the bill," he said. "Son of a bitch!"

"At least," I replied. "But that's one question answered. Can you get the cleanup set up and then head back here? I need you. You can have the mail forwarded to the Sheriff's house and handle all the bill payments and things from here. Let's not order new furniture just yet. I may decide to go a different way. I just can't think about it right now."

"Alright. I'll call around and get a company in here tomorrow to get rid of everything. The maintenance crew can handle the physical damage on the apartment. I can be there in a day or two. I need to check my apartment while I'm here. I've been trying to reach Doug for days, but now his phone says it's no longer in service, and I don't know what I'll find at my place. I'll let you know when I can leave town, okay?" he asked.

"Stacy, dinner's ready!" I heard John call from the kitchen.

"Yeah, that's fine. I hope everything's alright at your place. Let me know," I said.

"Will do," Romi replied and hung up.

I put my phone back into my pocket and wheeled myself into the dining room. They'd left room for me at the end of the table. In the center of the table was a large wooden salad bowl full of fresh vegetables, and a basket of warm French bread wrapped in a tea towel. There was also a plate piled high with steaks. John grabbed the plate of steaks and held it while I took one and put it on my plate. He then took one and passed it on. He did the same with the salad and bread, and soon my plate was full.

Once everyone was served we all started eating. There was no talking, just sounds of us all enjoying our food.

After I had eaten my fill, I turned to John. I needed to tell him what Romi had said.

"So, I just talked to Romi," I started. "He said the apartment is demolished and all the furniture has to be trashed. There is also damage to the walls. But the most interesting thing was that the person got into his filing cabinet and went through all the files, including my phone bills, which all have my phone number on them. I think that's how someone got my phone number." I said.

John seemed to mull that over. He looked around at the other guys and they all nodded in agreement with my idea. "I think we need to send the fingerprints we got from the vehicle to Nashville and see if they match any they might have found in your apartment. It sounds like this may all be the same person," he said.

"Let's get you a burner phone to use for business and leave your current phone for this weirdo. That way it will be easier to trace any calls from him. When we go to PT in the morning, we'll stop at Walmart and get you one," John said.

I just nodded, hating that my life was being so easily manipulated up by this guy. Who was he and why was he after me? What could I have done to anyone to deserve this? Nothing, I told myself. I didn't deserve this and it wasn't on me that this was happening.

I told the guys I was going to help clear the table and took the salad bowl and bread basket and set them on my lap to take into the kitchen. I went back for some of the guys' plates, again stacked in my lap. Barry brought in the rest, and we worked on rinsing dishes and loading the dishwasher.

I felt a sense of accomplishment, which I hadn't had for a while. I rolled into the living room and found Eduardo and Malcolm playing a video game, while Martin read the paper on the couch. John was sitting in his easy chair looking at his phone, and Barry sat on the love seat and took out his own phone.

I rolled over next to the armchair and my phone chose that moment to ring. I pulled it out and looked at it apprehensively, but it was Romi.

"Hello, Romi," I said.

"What the hell?!" he shouted into the phone. I pulled mine away from my ear to save my hearing.

"What's wrong? And calm down. You're going to make me deaf," I said.

"My room's been ransacked! It's a total wreck, almost as bad as your apartment!" he cried.

"What are you talking about? Where's Doug? Does he know anything about this?" I asked.

"I don't know where he is. I haven't seen him since a few days before I went to Whirlwind. I told you he said he had some business out of town. His room just looks like he packed in a hurry but isn't damaged. Just my room. It sure as hell didn't look like this when I left! Now his phone says it's no longer in service, like I told you, and I don't know where he is!"

"Call the police and file a report," I said. "They can look for Doug. Is there any sign he came back while you were here?" I asked.

"No," he said. "The mail was all piled up in the vestibule because it would no longer fit in the mailbox. I don't see any sign that he was here," he said.

John motioned for the phone. I handed it over and he put it on speaker.

"Romi, this is Sheriff Leppard. Call the police and be sure to let them know about Stacy's apartment, too, in case these cases are related. I don't see how they could be, but there's too much at stake not to take every precaution. Then I would advise you to have your mail held and come back here as soon as you can."

"S-Sheriff, do you really think these cases might be re-related?" Romi asked, sounding really scared.

"I just don't know, but I don't want to risk information getting lost either way. Just get back here as soon as you can," John said, and handed the phone back to me. I noticed all the other guys had stopped what they were doing and were looking at John and me. Then they looked at each other.

I took the phone back from John and took it off speaker.

"Romi, just do what John said and come back to Whirlwind. Let the police handle Nashville and we'll handle everything else here. Okay?"

"Okay," he said. "I'll call as soon as I'm on the road," he said.

"Okay. Be safe. Bye," I said.

"Bye." I looked at John, sure that the fear I was feeling was showing in my face.

"Why would anyone trash Romi's room, but not Doug's, or the rest of the apartment?" I asked.

"How well do you know this Doug?" John asked.

"Well, I met him two or three times with Romi, but they didn't really hang out much together. Doug is some kind of software engineer or something, I think. He and Romi don't have much in common that I'm aware of. Why?" I asked.

"Not sure, but like you said, why would his room be the only place in the apartment that was searched?" John asked rhetorically.

I couldn't think of anything to say to that, so I sat in my chair, just thinking about everything that had gone on in the last two weeks.

I hated feeling afraid and out of control. So much of my regular life was controlled by other people, like Romi and Tom and Anna, but I still had input and knew what was coming, but with this situation, no one was in control but the crazy guy stalking me. I just didn't know how much more I could handle.

I decided to take a hot bath. Maybe that would help to relax me. I turned to John and asked him to help me wrap up my cast and carry me upstairs.

He stood and wheeled me into the kitchen. He reached into a bag holder on the wall and took out a couple of plastic shopping bags and stuck my foot in them. Then he reached into a drawer in the counter and took out some cling wrap and wrapped that from the tops of the bags to the top of my cast.

Once I was sufficiently covered, he wheeled me back to the stairs, picked me up and carried me up to the bathroom. He set me on the closed toilet seat and shut the connecting door to his room and locked it from the bathroom side.

He knelt down in front of me so we were almost level with one another. He looked into my eyes, placing his right hand on my knee, and wrapping his left hand around my jaw. He smiled gently as he looked at me.

"It's going to be alright," he said with a rasp in his voice. "We're all here to protect you, and nothing is going to happen to you, or Romi," John said. "I personally will do everything in my power to keep you safe. I have plans for you, ya know?" His smile turned wicked and he chuckled.

"Really? Plans for me? What kind of plans," I asked in a sexy whisper.

"Plans that I think you'll like," John said as his lips found mine. I opened my mouth to his kiss and savored the tastes and feelings his mouth gave me.

His tongue tangled with mine playfully, and I sucked on his bottom lip. I used my tongue to map his mouth, to learn all the hills and valleys inside, then I ran my tongue along both his top and bottom lip, relishing the taste. John groaned with pleasure and pulled me closer to him.

He put both my hands around his neck, then ran his hands up my sides from my hips to my breasts. His left hand found my breast and fondled it through my clothes. He ran his finger across my nipple and it hardened to an excited peak. I moaned in response and pushed against his hand to increase the pressure.

His other hand came up to my other breast and started the same motions. He rubbed the nipple, causing it to harden, then he pulled off my lips and sucked my nipple through my clothes. He bit down gently and I moaned even louder. He lavished the same treatment on my left breast, then rejoined my lips with an intensity I had never experienced before. He was trying to own me through that kiss, and I wanted him to.

I gave as good as I got, running my tongue in a frenzy against his. I couldn't get enough of him, and moved one of my hands down the front of his pants to the erection that was waiting there. I ran my hand up and down over the warm hardness and started reaching for the button at the top of his fly.

John gently pulled back from my lips and pulled my hand away from him. He rested his forehead on mine and sighed.

"Now isn't the right time for all my plans," he said. "You need to relax and soak in the tub, and I need to go over some things with the guys, set up schedules and such," he said as he pulled back slightly to look me in the eye.

"But," he continued, "I want you to think about this, and make sure it's what you want. If it is, then we can move ahead, but if it's not, if you have any doubts, then I'll keep my hands to myself and leave you alone. Can you promise me to think about it?" he asked seriously.

"Yes, I'll think about it, but I already know what I want, John." I said, just as seriously. He nodded and stood up, adjusting himself in his pants.

"Enjoy your bath, Stacy," he said and left the room, shutting the door behind him. I waited until I heard the bedroom door shut, then got undressed and ran the water as hot as I could stand it. I sat on the side of the tub, facing away from the faucet, and with some acrobatics, used the bar on the wall to stand and turn and gently lower myself into the water with my cast resting on the ledge by the wall.

The water felt so good, and as I lay there I could feel my muscles relaxing. John had been right, I needed this, especially after PT today. God, had that just been this morning? It seemed like it had been a week.

Then I started thinking about John and that kiss from before. I started running my fingers over my breasts, feeling the peaks get hard and pop up out of the water. Soon my hand was headed toward my mound, and I ran a finger over my clit. I shuddered at the feeling, loving how turned I was just from remembering John's kiss.

I circled my clit several times, loving the feel of it swelling and the flow of my juices. I slipped a finger inside and started moving in and out. I remembered John's hands on my breasts and moved faster and faster. I remembered how his tongue took over my mouth and I felt the orgasm rising in my body, the tingles moving from my toes up toward my rapidly moving finger and moving from my breasts downward.

Soon I called out John's name and the orgasm rushed through me, my muscles tensing and releasing quickly and the warmth engulfing me. I now felt even more relaxed.

I must have dozed because the next thing I knew, John was knocking on the door on my side, and calling my name.

"Stacy, are you alright?"

I jerked awake and splashed water over the side of the tub.

"Y-yes, I'm fine. I'm getting out now," I said.

"Do you, um, need any help?" he asked.

"No, no, I think I can handle it. Thanks, though," I replied. I sat up, pulled the plug, then got my good leg under me and stood. Then I sat on the side of the tub and turned around. I grabbed the towel and dried off as best I could, then stood on my good leg and hopped to the door with the towel wrapped around me.

When I opened the door, John was still standing in my room. I stopped and looked at him and blushed as he stared at me with wide eyes.

"I, uh, forgot to unlock your door so you might want to do that before you go to bed," I said standing there by the door.

"Um, yeah, okay," he said, then scooted past me quickly and entered the bathroom. I hopped to the dresser to grab a sleep shirt. Crap, I should have brushed my teeth and taken out my contacts while I was in there. I slid the shirt over the towel, then pulled the towel off and tossed it toward the hamper. I missed, of course.

John came back out of the bathroom and looked at me, then turned his head as if he couldn't look any more. I smiled to myself. He's too cute, I thought to myself.

"Goodnight, John. See you bright and early," I said, waiting for him to move or say something.

He turned and walked toward me. When he reached me, he put his hands on my shoulders and kissed me gently.

"Goodnight, Stacy. Sweet dreams." He turned and left the room, closing the door behind him.

Sweet dreams, for sure.

I had turned the ringer off on my phone so any calls would not disturb Stacy in the next room, so when the call came in at 4:28 a.m., I heard the phone vibrating on my nightstand.

"Sheriff Leppard," I said groggily.

"Sheriff, it's Thompson. We had a break-in at the General Store, and Hastings took a hit to the head in the process. The ambulance is on its way, but figured I'd better give you a call."

"Okay. Who else is there with you?" I asked.

"Hudson is here now, and Long Cloud is on his way."

"Okay, give me 20 minutes and I'll be there," I said, already out of bed and headed for the closet.

"Right, Sheriff," Thompson said then hung up. I got dressed and was about to leave my room when I decided to check on Stacy before I left. I stepped into her room and found her sound asleep. I closed the bathroom door and went back to my room to grab my gun and phone from the nightstand. When I got downstairs, Malcolm was on the couch watching something on TV. I told him what had happened and suggested he get one of the other guys so someone could watch the cameras. He agreed and headed downstairs to get Barry, who was working out in the basement.

I raced out to my cruiser and headed toward town, making the 15-minute trip in about seven minutes. I pulled up behind the General Store and spotted the ambulance and Thompson. I went to the ambulance and looked inside. Hastings was lying on a stretcher with his eyes closed. I looked at the EMT and asked, "Is he going to be okay?"

"I think so, Sir," he answered. "He took a good hit to the side of the head from the front, so we need to screen him at the hospital, but he was semi-alert when we got here. We're headed out now," he said.

"Okay. Make sure someone from the hospital keeps me updated. Do you have my phone number?" I asked.

"Yes, Sir, the other deputy gave it to us."

I nodded at the EMT and headed over to Thompson.

"So, tell me what we know, Thompson," I said, looking at the back door of the building on the grocery side.

"Well, Sheriff, according to the log, Hastings was making his rounds and got back here about 4:10 and spotted a truck at this back door, and the door was open. He hit his lights and called for backup. We know that for sure. It also looks like he got out of his vehicle and approached the perpetrator. I doubt he let the perp walk up to his car and hit him without fighting back. Hudson and I did a sweep of the store and we found signs of robbery in the grocery and main sections of the store. Hudson is dusting the shelves for prints, and I called the manager down to do a quick inventory to give us some idea of what is missing. She's in the store now, as well."

"What time did you get here, Thompson?" I asked. He looked down at his notebook.

"4:16 Sheriff. I was down by the river when the call came in."

"Okay. Did Hastings say anything when you got here? Was he conscious?" I asked.

"He was semi-conscious, Sir, but didn't make a lot of sense. I did hear him call in a want/warrant on a blue Ford F150 with a plate. It sounds like the one that those campers reported stolen the other day."

"So now we need to find out why he didn't wait for back-up before confronting the perp, if that's what he did. Let me go take a look around and talk to the manager. Why don't you head to the hospital and let me know what happens with Hastings," I instructed Thompson.

"Will do, Sheriff," he said before turning back to his patrol car. As he sped off behind the ambulance, I walked into the store, looking closely at the damaged back door. It looked like someone used a crowbar on the door first due to the dings and creases in the metal, then jimmied the lock to get in.

As I walked into the grocery section, I was astonished at the amount of damage done. Foods were knocked onto the floor, shelves were hanging crookedly from their backs, there were divots in the floor. Someone came in mad.

I walked up to the cash register and found it destroyed, but the cash drawer was still secured inside the machine. I tried to open it, but it was stuck. I felt sure there had not been any cash in there at the end of the night, but I would have to clarify with the manager.

Speaking of whom, I went in search of her on the general side of the store. I found her in the Men's Clothing area.

"Mornin', Ms. Kramer. Sure am sorry we had to get you up for something like this, Ma'am." I said as I approached her.

She shook her head. "I don't know what is going on in this town, Sheriff. First the hit-and-run, then the shooting, now this. How are you going to stop whatever this is, Sheriff?" she looked at me intently with a clipboard in her hand.

"We're doing our very best, Ms. Kramer. I'm still sorry this happened to your store." I said.

She sighed. "How's that deputy doing? Is he going to be alright?" she asked.

"The EMT seemed to think so. They took him in for some tests just to be sure," I told her as I turned around. "Does anything seem to be missing?" I asked her.

"According to my printouts, I'd say a couple of pairs of jeans and three or four flannel shirts. I haven't finished looking, though," she answered.

"Okay. We're gonna have to close the store for most of the day, at least while we finish collecting evidence, but we'll get it done as fast as possible. Sorry for the inconvenience." It felt less than sincere enough, but I didn't know what else to say. She just shook her head again and went back to her work.

As I walked back out of the store, I spotted Hudson putting up the crime scene tap around the building. I jumped in to help him since it was a big job.

Once we finished, I left Hudson to finish the dusting and evidence collection, and Long Cloud showed up just as I was leaving. I instructed him to help Hudson with evidence collection.

I called the hardware store owner to arrange for a new door to be ordered and for plywood to be put in place until the new door showed up.

I drove back home, tired but wide awake at the same time. I called dispatch on my radio as I drove and asked if the plate Hastings had called in was the same as our stolen. It was. So the perp who stole the truck had stayed in the area. That was so odd. Why wouldn't he head out immediately to lessen his chances of being caught red-handed?

It was now close to six a.m., so I decided I'd better try to get a little more sleep before I had to take Stacy to PT and to buy a phone. When I walked into the house, Barry was on the couch watching the early news. He told me that Malcolm was watching the cameras upstairs.

I went into my room and told Malcolm he could stand down since I was home. He nodded and headed back down the hall to his own room. I stripped off my clothes except for my boxers and took a few minutes to look over the camera feeds. It all looked quiet, but something felt off. I couldn't pinpoint what exactly, just something didn't feel right. Since nothing looked suspicious outside, and the inside was covered, I decided to sleep on it and see if anything gelled in my mind.

My alarm went off a eight a.m. I yawned and stretched and listened for sounds from the bathroom. I didn't hear any noise, so I knocked gently on the door to see if Stacy was in there. I got no response, so I opened the door a crack. The room was empty, so I went in and took a shower. I was just finishing drying off when a knock sounded from Stacy's side.

"I'll be out in just a few minutes," I called.

"Okay. Just checking," she replied.

I shaved as quickly as possible and brushed my teeth, then called to Stacy that the bathroom was free.

"Thanks," she called back.

I went back into my room and put my street clothes on, then locked my gun in my nightstand and put my phone in my back pocket. When I got downstairs, Eduardo was in the kitchen cooking something that smelled amazing.

"I didn't know you could cook, Eduardo. What are you making this mornin'?" I asked as I headed for the Keurig.

"French toast with fried plantains," he said. I scrunched up my face in confusion.

"Did I buy plantains without realizing it?" I asked.

He laughed. "No, I found this little shop in Watson that carries exotic foods and picked some up. You'll love it, trust me," he said with a smile.

"I usually love anything that someone else fixes," I joked. I heard some thumping and rushed into the other room. I found Stacy making her way down the stairs on her butt. I just shook my head and laughed. She glared back at me as she continued her journey.

"Not funny," she said with fake anger.

"Sure it is. I just hate to think of that cute little butt getting all bruised like that. Such a waste." I smirked as I said it.

"You could just kiss it and make it better," she said with a naughty smile on her lips. I walked up to where she sat on the second to bottom step, put my hands on either railing, and leaned into her. I looked at her lips, then into her eyes, and I kissed her softly, knowing we could be seen at any moment. Speaking of which, I heard a door opening upstairs and pulled away. I helped her up and into her wheelchair.

"Eduardo's cooking this morning," I said as I wheeled her into the dining room. "Would you like some coffee?" I asked her, trying not to stare.

"Yes, please, with some flavored creamer, if you have it," she said.

"Peppermint Mocha or French Vanilla?" I offered.

"Ooo, Peppermint Mocha, please. Thanks," she replied. I nodded and headed into the kitchen to fix the coffee and grab my mug.

As I was headed out of the kitchen, Martin and Barry came in.

"Good mornin'," I said to them.

"Mornin'," they said in unison as they headed to the coffee maker. I set Stacy's coffee down on the table and sat next to her.

"Heard you had to leave pretty early this morning, Sheriff. What happened?" asked Barry. I felt rather than saw Stacy turn her head in my direction.

"You left?" she asked.

"Yeah. Had a break in at the General Store during the night. One of my deputies was hit on the side of the head when he ran into the perp and is in the hospital. I've got to drive over and see him after we get back from PT this morning," I said, not looking at Stacy.

"What? That's awful!" Stacy cried. I finally turned toward her and told her, "It appears to be the same person who stole that truck from the campsite the other day. At least the plates match, so we know the perp is still in the area. But I don't want you to worry, Stacy. No one knows you're here, and you are well protected.'

I hoped I was right that no one knew she was here. That meant that Gram had not jumped on the gossip train, and that was always a good thing. I hadn't heard from her or from anyone else wanting info, so hopefully that was the end of it.

Eduardo slid two plates full of French toast across the breakfast bar, and I got up and handed one to Stacy and one to Martin. When he slid two more plates over, I handed on to Barry and kept the second for myself. Eduardo had just sat down with his own plate when I heard a car in the driveway. I jumped up, as did the other guys, and ran to the front window.

Speak of the devil, I thought. Gram was here.

I opened the front door for her with a glare on my face. "What are you doing here, Gram?" I asked impatiently.

"I just came to check up on things and make sure you're treatin' that young lady right. Don't get your nose out of joint, kid," she said as she hobbled into the house. One of the other guys had dragged another chair to the table, and Eduardo fixed up another plate of breakfast.

"Here ya go, Ma'am," Eduardo said as he took Gram's arm and led her to her chair.

"Why, thank you, young man! Kid, this is how you treat a lady!" Gram cried with glee as she looked at me. Everyone around the table laughed, except me.

I sat back down and started eating, not giving Gram my attention.

Stacy must have noticed my inattention because she tried to engage Gram in conversation.

"So, what brings you by, Mrs. uh, Mrs. Leppard?" she asked.

"Lottie Leppard, little lady. Sorry the kid here has forgotten his manners. I hear your name's Stacy. What about these handsome fellas?" she asked with rapt attention. The guys went around the table introducing themselves.

"Well, you are one lucky lady livin' here with all these gorgeous men. The testosterone must be suffocatin'! I'd be happy to move in and help level it out..." I put my hand down on the table.

"Gram! I told you no one can know Stacy is here. If you move in, Beverly will want to know why, then it will be all over town within minutes, and someone somewhere will figure out that she's here. You can't stay here!" I was getting frustrated with Gram always trying to be in the thick of things.

"You don't have to yell at me, kid! I can hear just fine! I was just offerin', tryin' to be neighborly. Ease up, kid," Gram frowned at me and went back to eating her food. I just shook my head and drank my lukewarm coffee. I could see grin on Stacy's face and her shoulders shake as she tried to hold back a laugh.

"Stacy, we've got to head out for PT. Gram, you can walk out with us. Eduardo, thanks for breakfast, man," I said as I stood up. Stacy pushed back from the table and thanked Eduardo, as well. I carried our dishes out to the sink and rinsed them, waiting for Gram to get the hint. I loaded the dishes in the dishwasher, then went back into the dining room for Gram.

"Come on, Gram. Play time's over. Time to go." I slid her chair back and helped her stand up. As she hobbled back to the front door, mumbling under her breath, Stacy grabbed her purse from the end table and rolled toward the foyer. I told her to wait a minute while I helped Gram down the stairs. Once Gram was in the car, I went back in for Stacy. I carried her to the truck while Martin carried the wheelchair down.

Once Gram had headed down the drive, I started after her and headed away from town toward Watson. As we headed down the road, Stacy started laughing uncontrollably. She laughed so hard she had tears rolling down her face.

"What's so funny?" I asked, looking over at her quickly.

"I-I d-don't know!" she cried through the laughter. "I just c-can't s-stop!" She was using both hands to wipe her eyes now. I reached over to the glove compartment while keeping my eyes on the road and handed her some napkins I had in there. She thanked me but kept laughing.

"I think this might be a delayed reaction to everything that's going on now," I said, trying to calm her down. I looked over at her again, and she was taking deep breaths and trying to control her laughter. When she was calmer, just chuckling now and then, I reached over and took her hand in mine.

She looked at me and grinned. "I don't know," she said. "It might have something to do with your grandmother and her love of hunky men," she continued. She laughed again but didn't go crazy.

I couldn't help but grin, too. It was kinda funny, Gram always going after the guys. But I still had to keep her away to keep her safe, too. I let go of Stacy's hand to turn on the radio, keeping the volume down low. I took her hand again and brought her knuckles to my lips. She looked at me and smiled softly.

I wanted to talk but didn't know what to say. This wasn't a good time to talk about all the things I was feeling, that I most definitely should not be feeling and I didn't want to talk about the other stuff going on because clearly, it was getting to her. So I just held her hand and sang along with the radio under my breath. Then I heard it.

Stacy started singing along with the radio. It was soft and beautiful and like nothing I'd ever heard before. She had her eyes closed and was relaxed into the seat, singing the song like it was a part of her. I no longer had to worry about what to say because I was speechless.

She sang the rest of the way to Watson, and I just sat back and let the words she sang seep deep into me like sunlight on warm earth.

We finally pulled up to the physical therapy office. I got the wheelchair out and rolled Stacy inside. I tried to be as unobtrusive as possible as I looked around for anything or anyone suspicious but didn't find anything to worry about.

I left once the physical therapist had collected Stacy and went back to my truck. I'd gotten a text from Thompson about Hastings but wanted to call the hospital for more info. I called and asked for Hastings' room. It rang four times before a groggy voice answered it, then it sounded like the phone was dropped several times before someone spoke again. I almost didn't recognize Hastings' voice.

"'Ello?" he answered.

"Hastings? This is Sheriff Leppard. How are you feeling?" I asked.

"Sheriff?" he asked.

"Yes, how are you?" I asked again.

"Oh. Okay. Except my vision's blurry and they don't know how long that will last. They said they'll keep me another day or two and see how it does. After that I don't know," he sighed.

"Okay. Well let me know what's going on. We'll send someone to pick you up so your wife doesn't have to leave the kids to do it, alright?"

"Thanks, Sheriff. I'll let you know what the doc says." He hung up. I called the office then.

"Whirlwind Sheriff's Office, Deputy Peters," came the answer.

"Hey, Peters, it's Sheriff Leppard."

"Yeah, Sheriff. What's up? Have you talked to Hastings?" he asked.

"Yes, I just spoke with him. I need you to call the florist and order a bouquet of flowers, something masculine, to be delivered today to the hospital. Have them bill the office. Did the manager of the General Store ever get a final inventory of missing merchandise to us?" I asked.

"Yes, Sir. Looks to be about $300 worth of food and clothes. The damage comes to about $3500, not counting the new back door, which will be around $2300. That was some burglary," Peters finished.

I whistled. Such a waste. "Alright. Check in with her and make sure the hardware store sent over the plywood and got it up and in place of that door. Also, check with the other businesses on that street. I know at least two of them have cameras in the back. I want to see if this clusterfuck was caught on camera. If so, I want the tapes today. And have the digital logs downloaded so I can review them when I get in this afternoon," I instructed Peters.

"Yes, Sheriff. Will do," he said and I hung up.

I sat back and started going over everything from day one. Stacy remembers they guy who hit her tried to grab her first. He then ran her over with a stolen truck from Nashville. Then someone got into her hotel room and left a note in her guitar case. Someone also showed up at the hospital trying to see her but ran away. Then someone stole a truck from a campsite and took shots at Stacy when she got back from the hospital. Then the phone calls started.

Just around the time that happened, someone broke into Stacy's apartment and demolished it, and probably got her phone number, and then someone trashed Romi's room, but not the rest of his apartment.

Finally, someone using the same stolen pick-up broke into the General Store and left an unholy mess. And let's not forget Romi's missing roommate. I needed to get more info on him. I'd have to ask Stacy for details. Just then my phone buzzed with a text.

I'm ready and have a surprise!

I wonder what her surprise could be. I got out and went back into the office, only to find Stacy on crutches. She looked so excited to finally be out of the wheelchair.

"Wow! Look at you up on crutches! You'll be a speed demon now." I laughed and grabbed the folded wheelchair to carry out. "We'll be able to take this back to the rental place at your check-up in a couple of weeks," I said. I held the door for Stacy to go through. I raced ahead and put the wheelchair in the backseat, then had to help Stacy into the truck. I put my hands on her waist and stood there for a moment, just looking at her. Then I hoisted her into her seat and patted her knee. I took the crutches and put them in the backseat before closing the door. I went around to my side and heard her phone ring.

She answered it as I got in the truck. I saw her face blanch and her eyes get wide. I took the phone out of her hand and heard an odd voice saying, "Darci. I know where you are. You will never be safe until you're dead," and the line went dead.

I dropped the phone into the cup holder and reached across the seat to wrap her in my arms. She was shaking, and I ran my hands up and down her back trying to warm her. Her shoulders started shaking and I could feel warm wetness on my shirt. Shit, she was crying. *Damn!* I screamed in my head. *This has got to end now!*

We sat like that for what seemed like hours but was probably only 10 minutes. Stacy had stopped shaking, and the sniffling was leveling off. I pulled away from her and got some more napkins out of the glove box and handed them to her. I used one to wipe away her tears after she blew her nose.

I didn't know what to say, once again. I felt like promising to fix it would only sound like a platitude, and that wouldn't sound sincere. I ended up saying nothing, just pulling her seat belt across her chest and clicking it closed, then scooting back to my seat and starting up the truck.

"We really need to get you that new phone now," I said. "We can use my card so it doesn't come back to you," I finished.

"That's not necessary," she said. "I have a prepaid card that is not registered anywhere that Romi makes me carry in case I want to buy something personal. I can use that," she said, still sniffing.

"Alright."

We drove about five minutes to Walmart and Stacy wanted to use her crutches. I encouraged her to buy some small hand towels to wrap around the tops once we got home, and she picked out a couple of them.

Then we headed slowly back to the electronics department. After a few minutes, she picked out a phone she thought she would like, a case and a pop-up thing to put on the back. She made her purchase and we headed out of the store.

I could tell she was getting tired, not being used to crutches. I wanted to have her wait by the front of the store so I could just pick her up but didn't dare leave her alone. Instead I had her drape a hand towel over each rubber top, and that seemed to help a little.

On the drive home, Stacy called to set up her new phone and get her phone number. I handed her my phone and had her input the number.

I suggested she text the other people she wanted to have the number since they might not respond to an unknown number if she called. She did that and was dozing against the side window by the time we pulled up in front of the house.

I walked around to the other side of the truck and lifted Stacy out of the truck. She barely even registered the change of location. I carried her inside and up to her room with the phone and packaging still in her lap. I laid her on the bed and moved the other items to the bed beside her. I pulled the blanket up over her and kissed her forehead.

I went back out to the truck and got the crutches and her old phone from the cup holder. I took all the used napkins in as well and threw them away. I left the phone on the counter downstairs and took the crutches up to her room and left them next to the bed.

I went back downstairs and found all the guys in the living room either reading on their phones or playing video games. I told them about the phone call and made sure they all had Stacy's new number. I then called the station again and left instructions for a trace to be run on the call. We were still waiting for info on the number and who owned it but could still run another trace. I had to get to the office and advised the guys that they would be on duty until close to midnight. I didn't like leaving without telling Stacy, but I didn't think it was wise to wake her after her busy morning.

I went upstairs to my room and changed into my uniform, unlocked my nightstand and took out my gun. As I left the house, I asked the guys to monitor the cameras, and to have Stacy silence her old phone and put it in a drawer when she got up. They all nodded and Eduardo headed upstairs to take camera duty.

I arrived at the office about 20 minutes later and parked in back. I went straight to my office and sat down. There was a report on my desk that the date and time of the phone purchase had been determined, and that it had been bought at the Watson Walmart. I dialed the Sheriff of Watson.

"Sheriff Landry," he answered.

"Hey, Sheriff, this is Sheriff Leppard in Whirlwind. How's it goin' over there?"

"Not a crazy as it is over there from what I hear. Got a real crime spree in Whirlwind sounds like," he laughed.

Not funny, I wanted to say. But what I said was, "Yeah, I guess you're right. That's sort of what I wanted to talk to you about. We've got a stalker situation over here, and he's making calls to his victim from a burner phone he bought at your Walmart this past Wednesday at 3:48 p.m. I'd like your help in looking at the video footage of that time to see if we can put a face on him. Can you help me?"

"I don't think that'll be a problem, Son. How about you come over whenever you're ready and we'll see what we can see?" he said.

"Great. I can be there about 4 p.m. today if that works for you," I said.

"Sure. Let me call over there and get them started on the review. Which register was it, do you know?" he asked.

"I don't know for sure, but I think you have to pay for them in electronics, so I'd start there," I replied.

"Alright. Will do. See you in a while," and he ended the call.

Well, at least we were making some kind of progress.

I woke up to yelling. Martin was outside John's door yelling that someone was coming up the drive, and I heard thundering footsteps going down the stairs.

I grabbed my new phone and my crutches and made my way to the door and opened it. I went out into the hallway and looked down the stairs. Barry was in the kitchen looking around the corner to the foyer with his gun in his hand. Martin was in the foyer with his gun out, and Malcolm was standing by the large picture window, holding the curtain back with his gun. Suddenly the doorbell rang.

I could see Martin ease into the foyer and up to the door. He looked through the peephole and nodded back to the others. I saw him put his gun behind his back and slowly open the door.

I heard someone say, "Delivery for Ms. Varner." Martin didn't reach for the package, but asked, "Who's it from?"

"It says Tom Montague," the driver replied. I stepped forward toward the top step and said, "I was expecting a package from Tom, Martin." I sat on the top step and slid down the stairs holding my crutches in one hand and my phone in the other. About halfway down Martin put up a hand to stop me from coming any closer.

"Okay," he said to the driver, who then handed the large manila packet to

Martin and turned to leave.

Martin stood in the open door until the driver returned to his car and took off down the driveway. He then closed the door and brought the packet to me.

"Open it and make sure it's what you were expecting," Martin told me.

I opened the packet and found a stack of music sheets and lyrics. Just what I was looking for.

"All good," I said, and put my phone in my pocket and the envelope in the front of my shorts before climbing back up the stairs on my knees, pulling my crutches behind me. Once I got to the top, I stood up on my good leg and grabbed my crutches.

I went back into my bedroom and sat down in the chair by the window. I took the packet out of my shorts and put it on the end table and grabbed my guitar case. I was a little leery as I opened it, half expecting another note, but only found my guitar and picks.

I set the case back down and pulled the first song from the packet. It was called 'Love in a Honky-Tonk'. It was more country than I usually do, so I was not a fan at first. I played the music, getting a feel for the rhythm and melody. I ran through that a few times, then started adding the words.

After a few run-throughs it was actually kind of a fun song with a bubbly rhythm that would play well on stage. I couldn't wait to hear it with the full band.

Once I felt I had a good grip on that song, I moved on to the next one. This one was called 'The Longest Mile' and was more of a pop tune. It wasn't necessarily sad, but it was slower than I was used to.

Just from these two songs, it seemed like the label had me all over the place on this album, and I wasn't sure how I felt about that. My fan base was used to a certain sound from me, and changing things up too much might not play well, especially with only two albums under my belt.

I decided two new songs was enough for one day. I put the music and lyrics away and put my guitar back in the case. I pulled my phone out of my pocket and saw three missed text messages from Romi, Tom and Anna, all acknowledging the new number.

I called Romi to find out when he was headed back. He answered on the third ring.

"Hello, Chica. What's up?" he asked.

"Just wanted to check on you and see when you're headed back here. I'm getting bored without you," I said.

"I'm actually in an Uber headed to the airport right now. I should touch down in Blountville in about two hours, and be back with you an hour after that," he said, sighing.

"What did you decide to do about your apartment?" I asked him.

"I cleaned up what I could and packed some stuff. I don't think I'm going to stay in that place when we get back to Nashville. I can't afford it without out Doug, and at this point, I don't want to see him again. He's basically ghosted me. But he left his stuff behind. Weird," Romi said.

"You can always stay with me," I said. "I have that extra room, and you wouldn't have to worry about the commute."

"Yeah, but then I would really be at your beck and call. I'd never have a life!" he laughed.

I laughed, too. "Boundaries, my friend, make some. Besides, I won't be around much between the studio and tour practices, and I'll be gone a month or more for the movie work. You'd pretty much have the place to yourself."

"That's true! I hadn't thought of that! You've got yourself a roommate, Chica!" He sounded so relieved, I felt good about making the offer.

"Well, I'll let you go so you can catch that plane. I'll see you soon!" I said.

"See you!" he answered.

I was about to head back downstairs for some company when a call came in from an unknown number. I briefly panicked, then remembered that I had not transferred any numbers into this phone. I answered hesitantly.

"Hello," I said.

"Hello, Stacy, it's John. I'm texting you a picture of a person and I'd like to know if you recognize him."

I heard the signal on my phone and looked down at it. The picture was grainy, but it showed a man with scruffy facial hair, unkempt hair, in jeans and a t-shirt buying what looked like a phone.

I studied the picture but could not place the man. He didn't look familiar. I put the phone back up to my ear and told John that I didn't recognize the man. He sighed.

I suggested we show it to Romi when he got in later that evening to see if he could recognize him. John agreed and said he needed to go. I stuck my phone back into my pocket and grabbed my crutches.

I headed back downstairs and sat on the couch, on the opposite side from Barry. Apparently, Eduardo and Martin were sleeping to get ready for the night shift. Malcolm was sitting in the armchair looking at his phone. Barry was focused on the documentary on TV. I wasn't interested in WWII, so I pulled out my phone to play a game.

Suddenly, I heard a strange noise coming from the kitchen. It sounded like something rattling around in a drawer. I got up to check it out, but Barry beat me to it. He pulled open the drawer at the end of the counter and took out my old phone. I could barely hear the vibration now, but by the look on Barry's face, I could tell it was not a call I wanted to take.

He made note of the time on a pad of paper I hadn't noticed on the counter. I was sure John would have a trace run when he got home. I headed over to the counter and saw two other times listed on the paper. So, I was still getting calls. Not good news.

I checked my new phone and saw that it was getting close to dinner time. I walked to the fridge to see what I could fix. I found some chicken breasts and some carrots, as well as Italian dressing. In the pantry I found a bag of red potatoes and onions.

I carefully turned and set the chicken breasts and carrots on the counter, then went back to the pantry for the other vegetables. Holding the bags while on crutches was a little tough, but I managed. Barry came into the kitchen to see what all the noise was.

"I'm fixing dinner," I said. He smiled and offered to help. I let him work on cutting the potatoes, onions and carrots since that took two hands. I searched the drawers until I found a mallet and set about tenderizing and flattening the breasts. Once that was done, I searched the cabinets until I found a deep roasting pan.

I set the chicken in the pan and drizzled the dressing over the breasts. Barry added the vegetables around the edges and I covered the pan with foil. Barry put the pan in the oven after it preheated, and we each washed our hands.

"You did that pretty well for someone with a handicap," Barry said with a grin.

"I loved the challenge," I replied, grinning too.

We headed back into the living room, and I resumed my spot on the couch. I started playing my game again when I got another call from John. I had remembered to save his number last time he called.

"Hey, Stacy. I have to run to the hospital and look in on my deputy. I'll be a little late getting home. Can you save me some dinner?" he asked, sounding tired.

"Sure. I made chicken and vegetables, so I'll leave a plate in the oven. Anything else going on today?" I asked him curiously.

"Not too much. A couple of people reported seeing the pick-up outside of town, but we were not able to locate it. The fingerprints still haven't come back yet but should be back soon. I'll see you when I get home. Be safe," he said then ended the call. I hated how frustrated he sounded. It was my fault, but there was nothing I could do to make it better. Great. Now I was frustrated.

I had played my game for about an hour when Barry got up to check on the chicken. It was done, so we all sat down to eat. We had been at the table for about 15 minutes when a loud alarm started to sound. Martin ran upstairs, I guess to the cameras. Barry ran into the living room and entered the combination in the gun safe, took out a shotgun and loaded it.

He called up to Martin to see which direction he needed to check. Malcolm stayed with me, putting his hand on my shoulder and guiding me back into the kitchen. He advised me to sit down in there to stay safe.

Martin yelled down that he saw movement in the back yard, so Barry headed that way. Eduardo came running down the stairs in sweatpants and a t-shirt with his gun drawn. He and Barry headed out the back door onto the porch, then lit up the yard with the spotlight.

They each went a different direction, calling back to each other about any sounds or sightings. Barry reported finding two cigarette butts near a broken branch. Eduardo reported no sightings and moved back to meet up with Barry. He had apparently put the butts in a plastic baggie to give to John later.

Both men continued to search the yard and surrounding forest while Malcolm stayed with me. About 20 minutes later both men came back into the house.

Barry took the shotgun back to the gun safe and unloaded it before putting it back. Eduardo put his gun on the breakfast bar and went in the kitchen to make a plate. Malcolm helped me up off the floor, and I went into the dining room to finish my meal. It was surreal how normal something like this felt. Barry was on the phone with John, from the sound of it. I suddenly remembered to let them know that Romi would be here in the next hour or so, just so no one would freak out. Which they totally would anyway.

I fixed two plates and left them in the oven for John and Romi. Then Barry helped me put the leftovers in the fridge. I wiped down the counters and stove top, then went over to the sink to start rinsing dishes. Barry loaded the dishwasher as I handed him the dishes.

After I finished I washed off my hands and dried them. Barry followed me back into the living room. I wanted to wait for Romi to get there and make sure nothing crazy happened when he arrived.

I sat on the couch and logged into my social media accounts for the first time in days. The comments seemed more upbeat, and people seemed to be talking up the new album. I typed a post updating my fans.

> *Helloooo, Dorsetters! How's it goin'? I'm busy with new songs for the album and getting' ready for movie makin' magic! I can't wait for you to hear this new album and see this new film! Lots of great things are happenin', Dorsetters, and I can't wait for you to follow me on this journey! Mention where you're from in the comments because we are plannin' the tour now! We'd love to see you live and in person! Five random*

fans will receive a free tour t-shirt when they come out, so keep watchin' and keep listenin'! Love y'all!

I checked emails and responded to those that couldn't wait. I skipped the rest. I ended up playing a new game I found online. I checked the time and saw that Romi was due any minute. Just as I had that thought, I heard tires on the gravel outside. I looked to the other guys and no one was making a move, so I assumed they thought it was him as well.

I moved to the window, but that got the guys moving. Malcolm asked me to sit down on the couch while they checked the door. Barry walked to the front door and checked the peephole with his gun at his side. Malcolm stood at the window with his gun, as well. I saw Barry tuck his gun into his waistband just as the doorbell rang. He opened the door and Romi stumbled in with two huge suitcases in his hands.

I got up and headed slowly over to the foyer. He tossed down the suitcases when he saw me on crutches and raced to give me a hug. I almost fell over from his exuberance but just managed to stay upright. He grinned widely and yelled, "Crutches! Girl!" and hugged me again. I think he was happier about them than I was.

I turned around and headed to the stairs to climb up on my knees to show Romi to his room. Malcolm, who had put his gun down on the coffee table, came over and put his hand on my arm to stop me.

"I'll show him his room. You don't need to go back upstairs," he said.

"Okay, thanks, Malcolm. It is kinda hard on my knees." Malcolm took one of Romi's suitcases and started up the stairs. Romi followed him with the other one. I heard Malcolm giving him a tour of the upstairs as they headed to his room.

I was feeling antsy. I was bored and tired of being stuck in the house. I hobbled over to the back porch and stepped out to an outdoor couch. I reached out and lit the fire pit that sat in front of the couch.

I sat back and closed my eyes to listen to the sounds of the night. I heard frogs and crickets and a howling deep in the woods. I could hear the trees gently sway in the soft breeze that wafted over my skin. I felt myself start to relax and my muscles release their tension.

I heard the door open and the air swirled around me. Romi stepped out onto the porch with his plate in hand. He sat on the other end of the couch and started eating.

"How was your trip?" I asked him.

"Quick, once I got on the plane. It sucked before that. I'm just so angry about everything that has happened to us," he answered.

"I know," I said. It's been a rough couple of weeks, and it doesn't look like it's going to be ending any time soon," I said, dejected.

"Hopefully John can get us some answers. Speaking of John…" he dropped off as the door opened again and John stepped out onto the porch. He smiled at me tiredly and said hello to Romi. He sat down on the chair that sat perpendicular to the couch next to him.

"Hey. Sorry to interrupt your dinner, but I have a photo I need you to look at. He opened the screen on his phone and showed him the pic he had sent me earlier.

Romi took the phone in his hand and held it up to his face. "I don't know, it looks kinda –" His face blanched and he stood up, taking the phone with him as he headed into the house. I looked at John, stunned, and he just looked back at me and shook his head.

Only about 2 minutes elapsed until he came back onto the porch. His face was pale and his mouth was open. He moved back to his seat and handed John his phone back. John looked at him, not saying anything.

"It-it's D-Doug," he said softly.

"Doug?" I asked. "Your roommate, Doug?" I asked again.

"Yep. He looks like hell, but it's him. I'd bet on it." he said.

"So this guy is your missing roommate?" John asked.

"Yeah." Romi just shook his head.

"What's his last name?" John continued.

"Meznu. Doug Meznu. He's a software engineer for a company in California but works remotely. I just d-don't understand this," he muttered.

THE SHERIFF'S STAR

I looked at John in a panic. Why would Romi's roommate be after me? I didn't even really know him, certainly never did anything to him to warrant his attention.

I felt the hair on the back of my neck perk up and looked around at the forest surrounding the house, looking for hidden eyes in the dark. John seemed to sense my discomfort and started staring out into the night, as well. I could see his eyes move back and forth along the tree line. Neither of us found anything to explain the sensation of being watched.

Romi was sitting so still and quiet I was worried about him. He didn't handle drama well, even though he often created it on his own. I reached down and took his hand in mine.

"It will be alright. We'll get to the bottom of all this. Won't we, John?" I prompted.

"Sure, we will," John said. He stood up and took Romi's plate back into the house with him. I nudged Romi until he stood up and I joined him. I led the way to the door, but he held it open for me. I saw John in the kitchen eating his dinner at the sink. I told him that we would be in my room. He nodded as he chewed.

I started climbing the stairs on my knees and Romi carried my crutches. We went into my room, and I sat in the chair by the window. I pulled my guitar from the case and pulled out the music I had practiced before. I started playing the music and looked at him. He was looking at the ground as he sat on my bed.

"Hey, listen to this new song and tell me what you think," I said as I strummed. I started singing the song and he slowly turned his head toward me. I finished the song and looked at him again, one of my brows raised in question.

"Why do they have you singing a country song?" he asked.

"I don't know, but it's kind of growing on me," I answered.

"I can see that. It does have a nice beat. I bet the choreography will be awesome," he said.

"That's what I thought, too," I said.

I shuffled the papers until I found the other song I had practiced. I played that one, and Romi looked confused.

"That's, um, not quite you, is it?" he asked.

I shrugged my shoulders and said, "Not really, but it depends on what the other songs sound like. If they're going to have me singing too many styles, it won't work at all. My fans will not buy that. I guess I'll have to wait and see," I said.

I put the guitar back into the case and put the papers back in the envelope. I went over and sat on the bed next to Romi. I put my arm around his shoulders and pulled him closer to me in a side hug. He rested his head on my shoulder and sighed.

"So, Doug, hunh?" I said. It was just so weird.

"Doug. I don't know what he could be thinking. He's always asked me tons of questions about you, but there's no way he could have found out where you were. The only place I wrote it down was on a post-it that I stuck on my nightstand…Oh, my God! It's my fault! That post-it was missing when I was at the apartment! Oh, Stacy, I'm so sorry!" he buried his head in my chest and cried like a baby.

I head a soft knock on my door and saw John standing there. I motioned him in with my free hand.

"Romi knows how Doug found out where I am," I said. "He had it written on a post-it in his room, and when he went back to the apartment, the post-it was gone. He said Doug asked about me all the time. I guess we know who we're looking for now," I finished.

John nodded and put his hand on my shoulder. He looked at me intently and I had the strongest urge to kiss him but couldn't with my other arm full of a sobbing Romi. I smiled at him and reached up to touch his hand. He leaned down and kissed mine. His other hand scrubbed his face, and I knew he was exhausted. I pulled his hand off my shoulder and pushed it away.

"Go to bed, Sheriff. We need you in top form tomorrow," I told him gently. He smiled and shook his head.

"Goodnight, Stacy. I hope he stops crying soon, for your sake," he said and turned to leave the room through the bathroom door.

I shook my shoulders to dislodge Romi. "Hey, that's enough. You're going to dehydrate at this rate, dude." I sat up farther and he fell over onto the bed, but he stopped crying.

"Ugh! Snap out of it! What's done is done, although I don't know why you'd have my location written down at home. What were you thinking?" I asked, anger suddenly coursing through me.

"I don't know," he wailed. "I just don't know!"

I picked up a pillow and hit him with it repeatedly. "You stupid ass!" I yelled at him.

Romi squealed and covered his head with his arms. I kept hitting him because it made me feel better.

He finally sat up and grabbed the pillow out of my hand. He held it to his chest and turned so it was out of my reach.

I sat there pouting, still feeling angry and hurt.

"I'm so sorry, Chica. I really didn't mean to hurt you," he whispered to me. I looked at my feet, not at him. He slid off the bed and landed on his knees in front of me. He leaned up and put a hand on my face so I would look at him.

"I'm sorry. I really am. You know I love you."

"I love you too, you big dog turd. Geez, you've got me so mad I can't even curse like a grown up!" I said, trying to hold in a laugh and remain serious.

Romi stood up and wrapped his arms around me. He kissed my forehead and turned to leave the room.

"I'll see you in the morning, Chica," he blew me a kiss as he walked out.

I fell back on the bed and blew out a huge breath. God, I was tired.

It was Sunday, and not my day at church, which meant I could sleep in. So why was I lying here, wide awake at 6:15 a.m.? I sighed and just looked at the ceiling. I tried to relax my heartbeat which was going faster than it should be for a man laying in bed. All the events of the past few weeks kept running through my head, making it impossible to calm down.

I just wish I could shake the feeling that we wouldn't be able to keep Stacy safe.

I turned toward the nightstand and grabbed my phone to check the camera feed. None of the alarms had gone off, so I was sure I would find it quiet around the house, but I checked anyway. I was going through the cameras when my blood suddenly went cold. Out in the farthest reaches of my property, near an old deer stand, was a man. He had a shotgun laying across his arm, and he stood still, seemingly staring right into the camera.

I jumped up and grabbed some sweatpants and a t-shirt, and my gun, and ran down the stairs. I headed to the gun safe, and Eduardo jumped up off the couch when he saw me. I grabbed two shotguns from the safe and loaded them, then tossed one to him. I told him our guy was on the property and headed right out the back door with him following me. He had his phone to his ear, probably calling the other guys to wake them up.

I headed straight for the deer stand, trying to make as little noise as possible. Eduardo was about 10 yards away to my right side. We could almost make out the stand when we heard gunshots go off. We both hit the dirt and lined up our shots. I shot toward the stand, then heard branches breaking off to the left side, headed away from us. I got up and gave chase.

Eduardo was right behind me, talking into his phone again. I could see the man about 40 yards in front of me, running with his shotgun in his hand.

I picked up speed and closed the distance to about 20 yards, but he got to a truck and jumped in and took off before I could reach him. I spotted the tags and saw that it was our stolen.

Eduardo came up next to me, telling the person on the other end of the call that we had lost him when he escaped in a truck. He hung up the phone and put it back in his pocket.

I shook my head. The pieces were coming together, but we still couldn't catch this guy. Now I had to figure out how he had outmaneuvered my alarm system.

I turned back the way we had come and started walking to the deer stand. Eduardo followed me. Once I got there, I put my shotgun down on the ground and started looking at the stand carefully.

I found a few cigarette butts and picked them up. They looked like the ones Barry had given me last night. I put them in my pocket until I could get home and put them in a baggie.

I walked around the perimeter of the stand until I found the alarm trigger. It had been cut. How had he seen it? It was hidden in a hollow tree, and no one should have thought to look for it in the first place. I would have go to the hardware store and get a new one to replace it. This guy was something else. I smacked the tree and growled in frustration. Eduardo just stood back and watched me from a distance.

I finished my walk around the stand without finding any other evidence. I returned to Eduardo and nodded my head toward the house. He nodded in response, and we headed back.

Once back at the house, we found Martin downstairs by the window with his gun drawn. When he saw us, he holstered his gun and turned from the window. I took both shotguns back to the gun safe, unloaded them, and put them back in their slots. I closed and locked the safe. Martin advised that Malcolm was monitoring the cameras and Barry was with Stacy and Romi. I told him that the alarm trigger had been cut and that I would have to replace it.

I headed into the kitchen to get a baggie for the cigarette butts. I laid the bag down next to the other bag to take into the office today. We would have to get them to the forensics office in Bristol to have DNA tests done on them. Even though we knew who we were dealing with, DNA would only cinch the case for us.

I left Eduardo and Malcolm downstairs and headed up the stairs two at a time. I went to my room first and let Martin know I was back and he could stand down. Then I headed to Stacy's room and knocked, identifying myself. Barry answered the door, and I found Romi and Stacy sitting in the bathroom looking at me. Barry nodded at me and headed downstairs. "I'll fix breakfast," he said as he left and I nodded.

Romi helped Stacy get on her crutches and leave the bathroom. I couldn't help myself; I had to hug her, just feel that she was alive and well. I wrapped my arms around her, crutches and all, and hugged her hard. She somehow managed to free her arms enough to wrap them around my waist, and we just stood there, holding each other. I didn't care who saw us, I was just glad she was alright.

I don't know how long we stood there, but eventually he cleared his throat to remind us that we were not alone. I slowly released Stacy, making sure she was steady on her crutches before letting her go completely. She looked up and me and smiled, and the world was back on its axis. I smiled back at her, hoping she saw in my eyes how glad I was to see her.

Stacy walked over to the chair by the window, her favorite place to sit. I sat in the chair across from her, and Romi sat on the bench at the end of the bed. Stacy started asking questions.

"So, what happened? I was sound asleep then Barry was knocking on my door telling me we were going on lock down and he and Romi barged in. Then he told us to go into the bathroom and stay there," she said.

"I was looking at my cameras this morning and saw a man down by an old deer stand at the edge of my property. He had a shotgun with him. I took off after him with Eduardo. We got withing 20 yards of him on chase, but he had his truck nearby and got away. I'm sorry if you were scared, but Barry was just following protocol. Are you okay?" I asked her.

"I think so," she replied.

"Hell no," Romi said at the same time. He was biting his nails as we spoke. Stacy noticed and snapped her fingers in his direction to stop him. He put his hands in his lap. He looked at me and asked, "What are we gonna do? He's getting bolder and closer than ever."

"We're gonna keep doing what we've been doing. I'm going to head to the station and check on the fingerprint results, then I'm going to take the cigarette butts to Bristol to the forensics office. While there I'll check on the results from his phone. I should have heard something already. You guys hang out here where it's safe –" he raised an eyebrow in Romi's direction – "and keep each other occupied. I shouldn't be long," I said.

Stacy reached across the side table and touched my hand. She looked concerned, so I turned my hand over and laced my fingers through hers. "What's wrong, Stacy?" I asked.

"I'm just worried about you being out there alone. He's coming for all of us now," she replied.

"I'm never alone, sweetheart. My deputies are out there, too. I'll be careful," I said as I squeezed her hand in mine. She gave a gentle squeeze back. I let her hand go and stood up.

"I'm gonna get dressed and head out now, before it gets any later. I won't be long, then we'll have the day together." I leaned down and kissed her forehead before turning to leave via the bathroom.

"So, what's up with you and the lawman, Stace?" I heard Romi ask Stacy as I walked into my room. I put on my uniform and headed downstairs.

I told the other guys that I was headed to the station as I grabbed the baggies off the counter. I also grabbed the piece of paper with the times of the most recent calls to Stacy's old phone. May as well kill two birds with one stone, I thought to myself.

I headed to my cruiser and drove down the driveway headed for the main road.

I had only been on the main road for about 5 minutes when I noticed a vehicle coming up behind me very fast. I sped up a little, but he kept up and seemed to go faster, too. It was a blue truck, and the thought crossed my mind that it could be our perp. I pulled to the side a bit to let him pass, but he didn't. We were headed up a slight incline, which slowed our speed somewhat.

Once we crested the hill, however, headed toward the bridge over the river, the grade was steeper and the truck sped up. He hit my rear end hard and I jerked the wheel unintentionally. I reached for the radio to call this in. Just as I started my transmission, he hit me hard again, and the cruiser pulled to the side. I hit the brake pedal, but the brakes were slow to engage.

I was driving dangerously close to the edge of the shoulder, which was a steep drop into the river. He hit me again, and I tried once more to brake, but nothing happened. I kept pumping the brakes but my cruiser kept picking up speed, not slowing down.

I was trying so hard to keep my cruiser on the road that I forgot about making the transmission. I tried to steer the vehicle back onto the hardtop, but the truck hit me again, this time from the driver side rear, so that it pushed me toward the shoulder. My brakes still would not engage, and I was going faster and faster.

I tried once again to steer toward the road, but he hit me once again, and this time stayed on my bumper. I could only hope that if I went over the side, he would go with me. We were just about to hit the bridge when I saw red out of the corner of my eye, then I hit the abutment and was flying out over the water.

I opened my eyes and saw a deflated airbag. My head, face and nose hurt, but it didn't feel like anything was broken. I reached for the radio to transmit my location, but the radio was dead. I used both hands to push the airbag out of the way and tried to unbuckle my seat belt.

Water was starting to enter the cab around my feet, but the seat belt would not come undone. I also knew that I would not be able to get the window down since it was electric and the car was partially submerged. I reached into the glove box for the special tool I had for just such emergencies. I used it to cut the seat belt, then used the other end to break the window. Water started pouring in, and I struggled to get out of my seat and out the window.

In the distance I could hear sirens. My sides were torn up from squeezing through the window that was too small for my large frame, but I had to get completely out now, or be drowned in the vehicle.

I finally pushed the rest of the way out and got my head above water, struggling for breath in the cold. I could see the riverbank not too far away and started swimming toward it. My vehicle was being dragged away by the current and I couldn't help but be very thankful that I was no longer in the cruiser.

I swam until I was almost too tired to go on, but finally felt my feet hit the bottom of the river near the bank. I barely managed to pull myself up onto the muddy bank when I heard people calling my name. Then nothing.

I woke up to the sound of beeping. I tried to turn my head to see what was making the noise, but it hurt too much. I could tell that my face hurt, my shoulders and back were sore, and I felt burning on my sides. Then it started to come back to me. The truck behind me, hitting me, then pushing me into the river. My escape from the car, then landing on the riverbank and collapsing. I sighed. Which really hurt.

I heard a door open and saw Gram come into the room. She smiled when she saw me awake.

"Good! I wondered how long it would take you to wake up, kid! How're ya feeling?" she asked gleefully.

"Like horse shit, quite frankly, but glad to be alive. How did I get here?" I asked her.

"I was headed to your place and saw that truck hit you and saw you fly into the river. I stopped and called 9-1-1, and by the time I was off the phone, that jackass had turned around and raced back the other way. When the deputies got there, I sent one to your house to let them know what had happened so they could be on the lookout. Did I do good?" she asked.

"You did very good, Gram. Thanks." I looked down and noticed I was in a hospital gown.

"Where are my clothes, Gram?" I asked her.

"I told them to toss them. They were full of river water and mud and crap. I know you can get another uniform, and I'll go out to your place to get you some clothes to wear home. They're gonna keep you overnight, so I'll be back in the morning with the goods, kid," she said, smiling like a Cheshire Cat.

"I don't know what you've got up your sleeve, Gram, but don't. Just don't." I told her.

Damn. Now I needed a new cruiser and a new uniform, on top of everything else. I could drive to Watson for the uniform, but insurance would probably take forever to get the cruiser replaced.

"Oh, by the way, your police car got caught on the bank about 2 miles downriver and Henry was able to tow it back to his shop. I called Mike Callaghan at the insurance office and told him to get over there tout suite and get the insurance moving so you can get a new truck. He headed right over," she said, looking quite pleased with herself.

I laughed, which hurt, but I couldn't help it. Gram was a force to be reckoned with when she put her mind to something. I heard her phone ring with a pop song ringtone. I moved my eyes to look at her questioningly. She answered on the third ring without acknowledging me.

"Hello, dear. What's up?" she asked into the phone.

"No, dear, you can't do that. Why? It's not safe for you. Well you can talk to him, he's right here." She handed me the phone.

"Hello," I answered.

"John! Oh, my God! Are you alright? I'm coming over there. I'll steal a car if I have to. What happened? Are you okay?" Stacy cried.

"Stacy, calm down. I'll be okay. No major damage except to my cruiser. I'll be home tomorrow, and you CANNOT come into town, especially now. Stay at the house with the guys where you're safer. There's nothing you can do here, anyway," I said.

"But I could be with you. Touch you and know for sure that you're alright," she said, sounding sad and frustrated.

"I love that you want to be here, sweetheart, but you're better off at home right now. I'll be there soon, okay?" I asked.

"Well, okay. If you say so. I just don't like the idea of you being there all alone when this monster just tried to take you out," she said.

"I'll be fine. He won't bother me here. Too many people around. And it's really you he wants, so I should be good for the night. You just get some sleep tonight and I'll see you late tomorrow morning, okay? Oh, you'll have to get one of the other guys to take you to PT. Don't forget about it," I told her.

"I'd already forgotten about it," she said sheepishly. "I'll tell them now. I'll miss you. Be safe, John," she said, then hung up. I handed the phone back to Gram. I tried turning my head again, very slowly, so I could look at her. Next thing I knew, there was a flash and she was cackling as her gnarled fingers raced over her phone.

"What the hell was that?" I asked, outraged.

"I'm just sending proof to Stacy so she calms down and doesn't do anything stupid," Gram said.

"Oh, brother, Gram," I sighed.

She put her phone back in her purse and stood up, slightly unsteadily. I tried to reach for her out of reflex and groaned as I fell back onto the bed. She just laughed.

"I've got to head out, kid," she said. "Bev's trying her hand at quilting again, and I have to go supervise," she cackled again.

"You mean nit-pick, don't you, Gram?" I asked.

"Tomato, Tom-ah-to," she said as she headed for the door. "I'll see you in the morning, kid. Be good to the nurses!" she said as she left the room.

I saw the bed tray near my feet and tried to use my foot to pull it closer. I finally had to raise the bed and pull it by hand, which was not fun.

I reached for my wallet laying there, and started to sort through what was damaged and what had survived being dunked in the river. I knew my phone was toast, but most of the important stuff in my wallet, like my badge, driver's license, credit cards, appeared to be okay.

I took them out and laid them in neat rows on the bed tray to dry. I wished I had a way to get online and order a new phone to be over-nighted, but I'd have to wait until I got home.

My door opened again and Deputy Hastings walked in with a nurse by his side with her hand in his arm. "Sheriff!" he called as he entered the room. I greeted him and asked how he was doing.

"My vision's still blurry, so they're running more tests. I get to go home today, but my wife is going to have to lead me around like a blind man," he said, shaking his head. "Heard about the accident, Sheriff. How are you?" he asked.

"Just bumps and bruises for the most part, but I don't recommend climbing out a car window that's smaller than you," I laughed.

He laughed, too. "I wouldn't think that was fun, but at least you made it out alive. That's half the battle," he said. We both fell silent.

"So, what do they say about your eyes, Hastings?" I asked, cringing a little at the question. But I was his boss, I needed to know what we were up against.

"They suspect damage to the optic nerve but aren't sure how long it will last. It hasn't changed much in the last day or two. I may have to go out on leave if it keeps up. I can't even walk by myself, let alone drive or use a gun. I'm not much good to anyone right now," he said, looking down at the ground. The nurse shifted uncomfortably next to him.

"Well, you know we have your back, yours and Kelsey's. we'll be around to help with the kids or whatever you need. Keep me updated so we can let HR know what's going on," I said, trying to look confident.

"Thanks, Sheriff. I guess we should let you get back to resting. Are they keeping you overnight?" he asked.

"Yeah. Just a precaution, but I should be home tomorrow morning late," I said, feeling bad that he was still stuck here.

"Okay, well I guess I'll see you around, or not, depending on my eyes," he said morosely as he and the nurse turned to leave.

"Take care, Hastings. Tell Kelsey to let us know what you need and we'll get it taken care of," I said to their backs. Hastings just lifted an arm and waved over his shoulder as he left.

I laid there and tried to think, but my mind was running as though still slogging through water. Everything was still a little foggy, and I eventually gave up and fell asleep.

I woke up sometime after lunch, apparently, because there was a lunch tray sitting on my bed tray, and my drying cards had been stacked neatly to the side. My phone was sitting in a bowl of dry rice next to the stack. I pulled the bed tray closer and looked under the lid of the lunch tray. It looked to be some kind of stew with a biscuit and a pat of butter. It was not even lukewarm, so it had been there a while. I was about to call a nurse to see if they would warm it up for me, when the door opened and amazing smells came in.

Deputies Thompson and Grey came in carrying a to-go bag from the diner in town. It smelled like meatloaf and mashed potatoes. My favorite. They came in smiling, saying hello.

"Hey, thanks, guys! I was just facing the prospect of cold stew. What did you bring me?" I asked with a smile on my face.

"Hey, Sheriff! You look pretty good for a guy who went flying over the bridge! Mary sent meatloaf, mashed potatoes, and green beans when she heard about the accident. It isn't even meatloaf day at the diner!" Thompson said in his booming voice, "And we had some info for you, but knew your phone was out of commission, so we came in person," Grey added.

Grey walked up to the bed tray and took the lunch tray away and placed it in the windowsill. She opened the diner bag and pulled out a Styrofoam container. She slid the bed tray in my direction and encouraged me to eat while they talked.

"We finally got the results on the fingerprints we sent to NCIC and some data from that phone you took to Bristol. They had to go back a lot of years on the prints, but finally gave us a name." She pulled out her notebook and looked at it.

"The name's Douglas James Meznu, Sheriff. The phone belongs to him. He's got a rap sheet for being a Peeping Tom when he was 15, and for stalking and assault when he was 17. Seems he got himself together before he hit 18, because there have been no other charges since. Guess he didn't want to get tried as an adult. He was listed as a person-of-interest in another stalking case about 5 years ago, but no charges were ever filed. That woman was an actress of some sort, but after the stalking claims, she quit the business and has never been seen in public since. "

"Why do you think he's after Ms. Varner? Is he the one who ran you off the road?" Thompson asked.

"I saw the license plate before he tapped me the first time, and it was the stolen those campers reported. I think it's this Meznu guy, but as to why he would be after her, I don't know. I want an APB out on him immediately and I will tell you something, but it has to stay between us". Both deputies nodded in agreement.

"Ms. Varner is a singer who goes by the name Darci Dorsette. Have you heard of her?" I asked.

"Hell, yes, I've heard of her!" Thompson cried. "My daughter's got her posters all over her room and her songs play in our house all the time. Why is she in Whirlwind, Sheriff?" Thompson asked.

"She's writing some new songs, and since the accident, she can't show up in Nashville in a cast, so no one can know about the accident. She's trying to keep a low profile, and no one can know she's still here. She has a protective detail and they're all staying at my house. We've had some issues with someone getting on my property and cutting my alarms. I need to get out of here and head to the hardware store to replace them," I said, my brow furrowed as I remembered the cut alarm wires near the deer stand.

"We're off duty, Sheriff. We can fix the cut alarm for you if you tell me where it is," Grey offered.

"It's about 100 yards from the back porch, in a hollow tree behind the old deer stand. You may have to look hard. I know he was somewhere else on the property earlier as well, but you'd have to ask Barry, on the protection detail, where they found the cigarette butts he left behind. I hadn't had a chance to check on it yet. And the cigarette butts I was going to take to the forensics office in Bristol just floated downriver with my cruiser," I said, frustrated again.

"Alright, Sheriff. We'd best be going so we can get this done in daylight. We still have to stop in and see Hastings before we go. Have you seen him?" Thompson asked.

"Yeah, he came by earlier today. Sounds like he's going to be out for a while. We're gonna have to take care of things for him and Kelsey," I said, shaking my head.

"Man, I hate that for him," Thompson said.

"Me, too, Thompson. Me, too." I said.

"We'll see you back in town, Sheriff," Grey said as they headed out.

I sat back and took the take-out container with me to finish my food. It was mostly cold now, but even so, it tasted like heaven. I thought as I chewed, mostly about Hastings and what his future held. I couldn't believe that he wouldn't fully recover. I had to think positively. His family needed him whole. That got me thinking about Stacy again. I wanted her to be whole, with her life out in front of her, not cowered in a bathroom every time someone moved in the woods.

I was gonna find this guy, and he was going to pay for what he'd done to Stacy, and what he might have done to Hastings, and for what he'd done to me.

I would end this.

It was about 10:30 the next morning, and I was pacing my room on my crutches, waiting for John to get home. He had left the hospital with his Gram around 9:45 and should be here any minute. But time kept passing, and I kept pacing. Finally, around 11:00, I stopped my pacing, grabbed my hair in both hands and yelled into the room. Was I overreacting? Possibly. Probably. But someone had tried to kill John because of me, and I wanted him here, in front of me, alive and well. NOW!

Romi looked up from where he was checking in on my social media accounts and said, "Why don't you just text him and see where he is?"

"I don't want to hover," I said, exasperated.

"I don't want you wearing a hole in the floor or in your underarms by pacing on crutches. Just text him.'

So I did.

Hey, where are you? Are you okay?

He answered almost immediately.

Sorry to worry you. We stopped at the station so Gram and I could write our statements about the accident. One of my deputies will follow us home, so we'll be safe. We'll be there soon. Thanks for worrying. Heart emoji.

He even used a heart emoji. I smiled to myself and sent a heart emoji back to him.

"So, what did he say," Romi asked.

"They're at the station writing their statements. They'll be home soon with an escort." I sat in my favorite chair and grabbed my guitar out of the case on the floor. I started strumming and humming to the song in my head. I had been noodling with a song but didn't think it would be commercial enough. I really needed to focus I writing the second song I wanted to use on the album, but this song just stuck in my head.

He's a small town lawman
The long arm of the law
With deep chocolate eyes
And a firm chiseled jaw
He's the walking, talking arm of the law

He keeps his town safe with
The strength of his hand
And the heart beating in his chest
No danger's too great to protect his land
With his star and heart and hand

He's a small town lawman
With a pistol on his hip
He's sworn to defend us all
With a promise on his lips

He never hides
He never lies
In every place and every way
He saves the town every day

THE SHERIFF'S STAR

He's a pistol-packin' peacekeeper
Patrolling all our streets
With a tip of his hat or a small hello
For everyone he meets

The power of his office and
The star upon his chest
Bring us safety and security
And keep out lawlessness

He's a small town lawman
With a pistol on his hip
He's sworn to defend us all
With a promise on his lips

He never hides
He never lies
In every place and every way
He saves the town every day.

It was just a silly song, but I dabbled with setting this to music so I could present it to John as a gift. Finally, about an hour later, I heard Eduardo call downstairs from his post at the cameras.

"Sheriff's coming up the drive."

I put my guitar away and grabbed my crutches to head downstairs. Romi got up and followed me. I made my way down with Romi behind me carrying the crutches.

Once I got to the bottom, I grabbed the crutches and practically bounced in anticipation. Martin headed toward the door and waited in the doorway for John and Gram to come inside.

I guess John must have been having trouble, because Martin went out and helped Gram up the stairs so John didn't have to try. I waited in the doorway, stepping aside so Gram and Martin could come in. Gram stopped to kiss me on the cheek as she went past.

I waited for John. When he got close to me, he stopped and we just looked at each other, realizing that things could have turned out so differently and we might not have seen each other again.

I couldn't resist. I grabbed him by the front of his shirt and pulled him toward me. I kissed him hard, so grateful that he was back with me in one piece. His lips didn't move at first, then he wrapped his arms around me and opened to me. His tongue found mine and we explored each other for several minutes.

I moved my arms around his neck and my crutches fell to the ground. I hopped closer still, never wanting to let him go. Our kiss softened, and soon we were just tasting one another, our lips licking and planting gentle kisses around each other's faces.

Gradually I let go of John, pulling my hands from around his neck and wrapping them around his waist in a hug. He wrapped his arms around my shoulders and hugged me back.

"Stacy," he groaned into my ear.

"I'm so glad you're safe, John," I said breathlessly. We pulled apart and turned to find everyone in the house gathered around the foyer watching us.

When we turned, they scattered like dust bunnies on a breeze. I laughed and John joined me. He bent over slowly to grab my crutches and I felt bad that he was in pain.

I took them and turned to go into the living room while he closed the door. He walked behind me very slowly, holding his side as he went.

The others had left the armchair free for him, and I sat on the coffee table in front of him. He sat down very carefully and sighed as he settled in the chair. Eduardo came out of the kitchen holding two beers in his hand.

"Beer, Sheriff?" he asked.

"Sure. Thanks," John said as he took one of them from Eduardo's hand.

"Where's Gram?" he asked after taking his first long drink.

"She's in the kitchen making lunch," Eduardo answered.

"So what exactly happened, Sheriff, and is there anything we can do?" asked Malcolm from over by the picture window, his favorite place to lean.

As John began telling the story, I decided to go into the kitchen to see if Gram wanted any help. I didn't think I could handle the whole story right now. I got to the kitchen as Gram was dredging chicken thighs and breasts through a flour mixture to make fried chicken. I could hear the oil starting to pop in the cast iron skillet on the stove.

"Hey, Gram, need any help?" I asked her as I hopped onto a bar stool at the breakfast bar.

"Sure. You can get the beans ready for me." She handed me a plastic bag of fresh green beans to snap, and a large bowl to put them in. I started snapping in silence, listening to the low drone of voices from the living room, and the pop and sizzle of the oil as Gram added pieces of chicken to the pan.

"So, how are you doing with all this, Girlie?" Gram asked me after a few minutes of silence. I continued snapping beans and looking down at the pile. I didn't quite know how to answer. I thought for a minute, then looked up at her.

"I don't really know, Gram. I mean, it was bad enough when someone was just after me, but now they've targeted Romi and John, and I find it really hard to bear that. It was just notes and phone calls before, but now it's gunshots and running people off the road into rivers to kill them. I just don't know what to think or feel anymore." I looked back down at the beans and went back to snapping them.

Gram nodded and stirred a pot of boiling potatoes that I hadn't noticed before.

"I can understand your concern, but the kid can handle himself. Hell, I saw him go into the river and I knew he would save himself! This crazy guy, whoever he is, has picked on the wrong guy and gal, if you know what I'm saying. The kid will get 'im, and you'll be able to go back to your fancy life in Nashville and won't have to worry again. You'll see." She used tongs to turn the chicken in the skillet, then turned off the burner below the potatoes and hefted that big pot over to the sink to drain them.

I watched as she put the pot on the counter, added milk, butter and sour cream, and started mashing them by hand. After a few minutes, she stopped, and went back to the stove to remove the chicken onto a wire rack set on top of paper towels. Once she had removed all the pieces and set them to drain, she added more pieces to the skillet, and it popped and sizzled loudly. She then went back to the potatoes.

"Better finish them beans. They still need to be cooked before we can eat." I started snapping again, going as fast as I could. I could still hear the drone of voices in the living room, but they were even quieter now. Probably planning something.

I finished the pile of beans and pushed to bowl toward the other side of the bar. Gram stopped mashing the potatoes and took another skillet out of the cabinet by the oven. She pulled over a small mason jar of something white and scooped some of it into the skillet. She turned on the burner, and while it was heating, I asked her what that was she put in the pan.

"Bacon grease," she said. "I save all my grease in this here jar, then I have it when I need it," she said.

I nodded and just watched, fascinated at how she worked so gracefully and methodically. While the grease was melting, she went back to the potatoes.

"If you want, Gram, you can hand me the potatoes and I'll mash while you do your thing," I said.

"Alright, here ya go." She handed the large pot to me with the masher inside. I started mashing with all my might. Gram looked at me and laughed.

"Go easy, Girlie. All it takes is a little elbow grease and a lot of love. Those aren't rocks you're tryin' to juice. Just potatoes. Don't strain yourself."

I smiled and looked down at the potatoes, feeling like an idiot. I'd never mashed potatoes before, so what did I know? But I went more softly this time, pushing and mashing, and waiting for John to come in the kitchen so I could see him again. It was silly, really, how much I just wanted my eyes on him.

Gram added the beans to the grease a little at a time and turned them using the same tongs she used for the chicken. She alternated turning the chicken and the beans for a while. Then she moved the drained chicken onto a large serving plate, and moved the cooked chicken onto the draining rack. She took a large serving bowl out of a cabinet overhead and placed the beans in as they cooked.

I thought I had finished the potatoes and had her check them. She pronounced them done and took the bowl of beans to the dining room table. She called for one of the guys to come set the table and one to get drinks.

I stayed at the bar out of the way as Gram finished the food, and it was carried into the dining room. The rest of the guys came in, with John coming in last. I hopped down from the bar and made my way to the table. I sat on John's right side, and Gram sat on his left. We all ate in silence, except for the moans and groans of how good the food was. Gram was one heck of a cook, that's for sure.

After lunch was over and the dishes had been loaded into the dishwasher, we all headed into the living room to watch TV. I lowered myself to the floor next to John's chair, just to be close to him. He reached down and ran his hand surreptitiously from the top of my head down to the base of my neck, over my hair. I looked up at him and smiled. He gently squeezed my neck and kept his hand there.

We wound up watching a rerun of Jeopardy, with all of us yelling out answers at once. That ran into another rerun and another, and pretty soon the afternoon was fading into night.

John told Gram she needed to leave before dark settled in, and she hesitantly got up from her spot on the couch. Malcolm stood up as well to walk her to her car. He told us he would follow her home to make sure she got there safely. I could tell John was relieved by the big sigh he let out. Gram leaned down to kiss his cheek, then patted me on the head as she left.

Eduardo and Martin got up to fix dinner before heading to bed. They would be coming back on duty at midnight, so they had to get some sleep. They made sandwiches for everyone since we'd had such a big lunch. We all sat at the dining room table and ate while waiting for Malcolm to come back. He arrived about 20 minutes later, reporting he had checked Gram's house before she went in, and all was well. John thanked him for his help.

John got up from the table and announced he was going to take a hot bath to soothe his sore muscles. He leaned down and said in my ear, "I'll need someone to put new bandages on my scrapes when I'm done, if you're interested."

I looked up at him and smiled and nodded. I waited a few minutes until he was upstairs, then went up myself, ostensibly to work on my songs. Romi followed me but went into his room. He had been really quiet since he got back from Nashville, and I felt like he just needed time to resolve what had happened to the both of us. I wished him goodnight and went into my room.

I knocked on the bathroom door and told John I was there whenever he was ready. He just moaned and said okay.

I pulled out the songs I had learned already and started to practice them again. Once I'd gone through each one twice, I pulled out a new song to practice. This one was called 'All I Ever Wanted,' and was a ballad. I didn't do many of those but had two under my belt. I started with the music, as usual, and as I got comfortable with that, I added the lyrics. As I learned the lyrics, I thought of John all through the song. I sang from the heart.

After about the fifth time through, I thought I heard humming coming from the bathroom. I stopped strumming my guitar and just sang the words, and yep, John was humming along.

I put my guitar back in the case and picked up my crutches and went over next to the bathroom door. I kept singing and John kept humming. We were well-matched pitch wise, and I felt so close to him, sharing such a pretty love song. I let the last note linger, then softly knocked on the door.

"John, are you finished with your bath yet?" I asked.

"Yeah," he said. "I'll be out in a few minutes." I heard gentle splashing like he was moving around a little. Then a moan that sounded like my name. Then the splashing got a little stronger and there was another moan, then nothing.

Oh, my God. Was he... I think he was!

I stepped away from the door as quickly as my crutches would allow and headed over to the bed. I sat on the bed with my back against the headboard, turned on the lamp and waited. I was so embarrassed to have heard that. That was something private. But I was flattered at the same time.

The bathroom door opened and John stepped out dressed only in some gray flannel pajama pants. I gasped audibly and John grinned at me. I had never seen him bare-chested before, and he was something to see. Despite the bruises and scrapes, he was beautifully built. He had strong pecs, and his six-pack abs were things of beauty.

I was at a loss for another word. His biceps were huge and his forearms were porn-worthy. He walked over to the bed and I could see the Adonis v that led down below the waist of his pants. Swoon! I licked my lips and blew out a breath as he sat on the bed with his left side facing me. He handed me the first aid supplies he had brought.

I set the supplies down on the bed and lightly ran my hand over the large bruise covering his side.

"What caused this bruise?" I asked gently.

"Climbing out a window that was smaller than me," he said quietly, almost like the news would break me.

I sucked in another breath and looked more closely at the scrapes within the bruise. I unrolled the gauze and cut several strips. I taped the gauze over the worst of the scrapes so they wouldn't catch on his clothes. After I finished, he turned fully around and sat on the bed so I could reach his right side. It looked much the same as the left, with a large bruise covering most of his side and scrapes within the bruise. I added more gauze swatches to the scrapes, then bent over to gently kiss the bruise.

I felt so much for this man, good, warm feelings. But the anger over what had happened to him was beginning to override the good feelings, and I started to get anxious and nervous. My good leg started bouncing up and down at a frantic pace, and I felt a little out of control.

John put his hand on my bouncing leg and the bouncing stopped. He looked deeply into my eyes and I saw pain there, but it didn't seem to be pain that he was feeling. It seemed he was pulling my pain into himself.

John maneuvered himself so he was sitting between my legs with his legs on either side of mine. He put his hand on the back of my head and pulled me close. His lips lightly grazed mine, not really kissing but calming me. He ran his tongue over my lips, tasting me, bringing my focus to him and not the anger boiling in my belly. I opened my mouth and his tongue lightly teased mine, exploring inside my mouth softly, intentionally.

With my eyes closed I focused on his mouth and nothing else, until I ran a hand up his chest, across his nipple and up to his shoulder. His skin was warm, likely from the bath, and with just a smattering of hair. His shoulder was like a rock, hard and strong and big. He must either work out a lot or do a lot of work outdoors to get a body like this, I thought.

I brought my other hand up and ran it through his hair, loving how the strands felt on my fingers. I moved closer to him, wanting to feel more of him near me. I moaned into his mouth and tugged a little harder on his hair. I ran my other hand back down his chest to his abs and felt every ridge there. I moved my hand a little lower and found the waistband of his pants. I kept moving my hand down until I felt his ridge, hard and warm and excited.

He moaned as I touched him and deepened the kiss. I rubbed my hand up and down his hardness, wanting so much to see and feel him without the clothes between us.

I pulled myself up onto my knees and pushed him back on the bed so I could taste him better. I pulled my mouth away from his and moved to his abs. I ran my tongue along each ridge, including the strong ridge leading into his pants.

I moved up and licked up to his pecs, circling his nipple with my tongue, sucking the hard point with my mouth, then biting it gently. He groaned as I did that, so I repeated the motion. I continued to move up his body until I reached his neck. I gently sucked the spot where his neck and shoulder met, then licked the area.

I kissed along his jaw and ended up back at his mouth. He reached both hands around me and moved me so that I lay on top of him, his hardness lining up perfectly with the tingling part of me. He bent his knees, locking me in place.

"Stacy, I need you so badly," he said quietly.

"I need you, too," I said, breathless from my exploration.

"Tell me you want this, that I can have you. I don't care who knows. I just need you right now," he said with a groan as I licked his chin.

"I want this. I want you. Now, John," I said, wrapping my arms around his neck.

He gently unwrapped my arms and set me to the side and got up off the bed. He reached down and picked me up from the bed bridal style and carried me through the bathroom into his room. He locked both his bedroom door and the bathroom door on his side.

I was his tonight. Maybe forever.

I woke up from the best sleep I'd had in years. I didn't open my eyes but could feel Stacy's warm body beneath my arm. I was on my stomach with my left arm across her torso.

My mind raced over the memories of last night and I smiled. I heard her make a soft noise in her sleep and felt her wiggle against my side. I could not be happier. I gently squeezed her with my arm and leaned over to place a kiss on her cheek. I was hoping to wake her gently so we could make love one more time before the world broke in on us, but there was a knock Stacy's door.

I wasn't sure what to do since she was still asleep, so I quietly climbed out of bed and put on my pajama pants. I opened my door and found Romi at Stacy's door, waiting impatiently.

I leaned my head out and greeted him.

"Good mornin', Romi. What's up?" I asked

He walked over toward me and said, "Stacy got a DM on her Instagram account. Another threat." He held his phone up to me so I could read it.

He can't protect you. I will be back.

I read the message three times. This wasn't good. I shook my head and ran my hand through my hair. I was so sick of this.

"She's still sleeping. I'll tell her about this when she gets up. We have PT again this morning, so she'll be up soon." Romi just looked at me and shook his head.

"You realize she'll be leaving here soon, and she'll be too busy to have a relationship, right? She's got a movie to film, an album to record and a tour to prepare for and work. I mean, I like you, and I like the two of you together, but I don't want to see either of you get hurt. She has a huge heart, but her focus has to be on her career right now, you know?" He looked at me intently. I scrubbed my hand over my face.

"I hear what you're saying and I would never stand in her way. I know there is an expiration date for us. I just want to enjoy the time I have with her while it's here. And to keep her safe, too," I said.

"Okay," he said and turned to head downstairs. I checked my watch and knew that I had to wake Stacy. I went back into my room and found her sitting up in bed with the sheet around her chest.

"Good mornin', Sunshine," I said, trying to smile like nothing was wrong, even though Romi's words kept running through my head.

"Mornin'. What did Romi want?" she asked.

"I hate to give you bad news first thing," I said, "But there was a DM on your IG account and he showed it to me. It was another threat." I walked over and sat next to her on the bed. I ran my hand up and down her leg in a soothing motion. I leaned over and kissed her gently on the side of her face.

She sighed and hugged the sheet tighter to her. I ran my hand over the other side of her face and cupped it. I looked deeply into her eyes and smiled for real.

"I loved last night. I've never been happier and I hope we get to repeat it again and again."

She met my stare and smiled, too. "I'm happier than ever, too. Last night was amazing."

I sat up and took her hand in mine. "We have to get moving if we're going to get to PT on time," I said.

She sighed again agreed. I got up off the bed so she could swing her legs to the side and get up. I reached down and handed her clothes to her. I headed into the bathroom while she dressed and brushed my teeth and used the toilet. She knocked on the door when she was done dressing, and I opened the door to pick her up. I carried her to her room and set her by the bed. I handed her crutches to her and kissed her deeply before heading back to my room to dress.

Once I was dressed, I headed downstairs to get some breakfast. No one had cooked so it looked like I was on deck this morning. I got eggs and bacon from the fridge, and some bread for toast.

As I was cooking the bacon in a skillet, Stacy and Romi came to the breakfast bar and sat down. They just watched me silently, probably thinking about that message, which I was sure he had shown Stacy by now.

As I was pulling bacon from the skillet to drain, I heard Barry and Malcolm coming into the kitchen. Barry grabbed the orange juice from the fridge and a glass from the cabinet while Malcolm started making coffee for everyone, one cup at a time at the Keurig.

Malcolm set a cup of coffee next to the stove for me and I nodded my thanks. I told him we had PT today, and he told me that one of the guys would follow us in their car. I didn't think it was necessary, but they disagreed.

Apparently, they had updated Tom Montague on the recent events and had been told to up their protective duties for Stacy. He told me that two more protective agents would be arriving and staying at the hotel, and one would be patrolling the property at all times.

I could understand Tom's concern, but more people would definitely be noticed, especially at the hotel. I sighed. I finished scrambling the eggs and put them into a large bowl. Barry carried the bacon and toast into the dining room, and I grabbed the eggs, butter and jam.

Martin and Eduardo were sleeping since they had the overnight duty, so it was just Stacy, Romi, Barry, Malcolm and myself for breakfast. It was a quiet affair.

Once we finished and cleared the table, I announced it was time to leave for Watson. Barry and Malcolm discussed it briefly and decided that Barry would follow us. I had to admit, having someone on my tail did make me feel a little better. Being alone on that open road was intimidating after my accident, but I'd never admit that.

We left shortly after the discussion, me and Stacy in my truck in the lead and Barry behind us. I still kept a close eye behind us for anyone else, but it was a quiet drive to Watson. Stacy and I walked into the office and I did my usual scan of the area.

Once she was taken back into the room, I headed back outside and stood by Barry's car talking to him. We discussed plans for the new guys patrolling the property, and how we would handle Stacy's PT going forward, because I would not be able to accompany her every time. I had to start spending some time at the station, especially so we could finally catch this guy.

Time passed quickly and soon I had a text from Stacy that she was ready to go. I went into the office to get her, and we headed home. I asked her how it went and she said it was fine. I could tell, though that something was bothering her.

"What's up?" I asked. "I can tell something's bothering you."

"I'm just tired of being cooped up in the house," she said with a deep sigh.

"I can understand that, but it's the safest place for you, recent events notwithstanding. I tell you what, how about we stop for coffee at the coffee shop. I think we can pull that off and it will give you a break," I said.

Her eyes lit up and she smiled brightly. "I'd love that! Could we drink it in the park?" she asked.

"I'll have to ask Barry what he thinks. It might be safer to stay in the coffee shop." I looked behind us but did not see anyone following us beside Barry. I told Stacy to call Barry and let him know we planned to stop at the coffee shop in town. She dialed his number and put it on speaker.

"Barry, we're gonna stop for coffee at the coffee shop in town. Can we please go to the park?" she asked.

"Sheriff, I know you're there. Do you really think this is a good idea?" he asked me.

"I haven't seen anyone following us, and Stacy has cabin fever pretty bad. I think as long as we're on high alert, we should be fine. The park should be fairly busy this time of day, so I think we will be okay for a short time." I looked at Stacy. She just smiled.

"Okay, Sheriff. I really don't like this. But I get it," he said.

"We'll see you there," I said and motioned to Stacy to hang up.

About 20 minutes later we pulled into the parking area by the coffee shop. I told Stacy to wait until Barry pulled in next to us before she got out of the truck. Barry did a sweep of the front of the parking lot and coffee shop before coming back and motioning us to follow.

We started to enter the shop, but Stacy stopped in the doorway to take in the interior. I placed a hand on her back to move her along since I didn't feel safe standing in the doorway. She looked around with her mouth hanging open.

The shop was cute, I guess. It was painted a bright yellow with white curtains in the windows. In the back, there was a cluster of tables and chairs set up, with bookcases lining those walls.

There was a glass case full of bakery items on the left just inside the door, and on the wall opposite and in front of the window were softly used couches and easy chairs for people to sit and stay a while.

I followed Stacy to the bakery case and Barry stayed behind me. She looked over the baked goods with a huge smile on her face. She finally settled on a vanilla bean cupcake and an iced mocha to drink. I settled for black coffee as did Barry behind me. Stacy insisted on paying, and she led us to a couch near the back while I carried the drinks and cupcake.

"I thought you wanted to sit in the park," I said as she sat down and put her crutches next to the couch.

"I did, but I know how worried that made you guys, so we can just sit here. It's still a change of pace," she said, still smiling.

I could hear Barry's sigh of relief. He and I were sitting between Stacy and the door, in the best possible scenario for being out of the house. Stacy was really enjoying her cupcake, licking the icing and taking small bites. She wound up with frosting on her nose. I wiped it off and put the frosting in my mouth.

"Yum," I said with a wicked smile.

"Definitely yum," she said, winking at me.

I sipped my coffee and looked around at the people in the shop. I recognized most of them but not all. No one else had entered the shop after us, so I felt relatively safe with Stacy in here.

As soon as she finished her drink and cupcake, though, I recommended that we head out. Stacy looked disappointed but didn't say anything as she rose and grabbed her crutches.

I grabbed the trash and put it into a can on the way out. Barry headed out first to do another sweep. Stacy and I waited by the door in the shop until he came back with the all-clear. We went to the parking lot and headed for home.

Romi was standing in the doorway when we got back to the house. He had a thunderous look on his face as we pulled up. He stalked down to my truck and pulled Stacy's door open.

"What the hell were you thinking taking her out for coffee?" he yelled at me from across the truck. I just looked at him, then at Stacy. She shook her head and gave Romi her hand to help her down.

"It wasn't their fault. I insisted on going somewhere to get a change of scene. They did their best to protect me, and we all made it back home in one piece. Relax," she said.

I had to admit, it felt good hearing her call my house 'home'. I got out of the truck and headed for the steps. I heard Stacy's crutches, so I knew she was following me, and I also knew that Barry was behind her. Suddenly there was a blast of shotgun fire and the picture window of my living room exploded all over the front porch.

Barry had Stacy down on the ground in front of the truck, and I grabbed Romi and pulled him there, too. Another shotgun blast sounded, and it hit Barry's rental car right in the engine compartment. One more blast sounded that hit the back end of my truck and sent metal shrapnel flying all over the yard.

I reached for my phone and called 9-1-1. Barry was on his phone talking to Malcolm. It sounded as though Malcolm was hit. I advised the operator to send an ambulance as well as deputies. I heard the front door open, and Eduardo and Martin came running out with shotguns in their hands.

"Behind us down the drive to my right," I shouted to them. They took off running toward the gunman. One more shot came at us, hitting my rear tires and making the truck tilt backward. I knew we had to get Stacy in the house and somewhere safe, Romi as well.

I told him to get up and I shielded his body with mine as we ran for the house. Barry was right behind me carrying Stacy bridal style to keep himself between her and the shooter. We entered the house and shut the door. I sent Romi into the kitchen, and Barry carried Stacy in there, too.

I ran over to Malcolm to check his wounds. I could hear sirens in the distance and knew they'd be here soon. Malcolm had blood all over his left side. It looked as though he took the hit right in his torso. I took off my shirt and held it to his wound while we waited for the ambulance.

Barry came over and looked out the window carefully. There were no signs of the protective detail or the shooter, and no more shots had been fired. I knew the shooter could not have been too far away since he used a shotgun. I needed to review the tapes of my cameras.

I heard gravel flying as vehicles came down the road, and Barry told me that two patrol cars had arrived, and the ambulance was right behind them. He went to meet the deputies and EMTs at the door. Deputies Peters and Hudson came through the front door, followed by an EMT and Paramedic with a stretcher and boxes of equipment.

I moved aside so they could assess Malcolm. I told Barry to call his home office about the incident since we would need a replacement for Malcolm as soon as possible. I also told him to call Tom Montague to apprise him of the situation.

Malcolm was strapped to a back board, and an IV had been started in his arm. The EMT was holding a bandage to the wound as he helped the Paramedic roll the stretcher out of the house. Barry followed behind them as he talked to his office. I knew he would be going to the hospital with Malcolm.

I called Eduardo and asked if they'd found the shooter. He said they had seen him, but he'd gotten to his truck before they could catch him or fire on him. I slammed my fist into my leg. Damn! This could not keep happening!

I told Eduardo that he and Martin needed to return to the house since both Malcolm and Barry were gone.

I turned to my deputies. They were looking out the opening of the living room window at my truck and Barry's car. Now we had no transportation and were stuck here.

I told the deputies to stay with Stacy and Romi while I went out to my shed to get some plywood to put over the window. While I was walking, I called my insurance agent to let him know what had happened, and to arrange for a rental and window replacement.

I got the plywood and headed to the house. I grabbed screws and my electric screwdriver from the back porch and went to work putting up the plywood. Once that was done, I told Stacy and Romi they could come out of the kitchen.

Stacy took one look at the plywood and burst into tears. Romi put his arm around her and led her to the couch. I handed her a tissue from the box on the side table and sat on her other side.

"Okay. Let's get these statements done," I said to the deputies. They went over the events that occurred once we got home, taking copious notes. None of us had seen the shooter, so we could only say what we had heard and felt. I looked over at Stacy. She was still hiccupping a little but had stopped crying while talking to the deputies. Romi was trying to be stoic, but I could see the fear in his eyes as he looked at me. Eduardo and Martin walked in just then.

After we'd given our statements, I followed the deputies outside to look at the property damage more closely.

Both of my rear tires were flat, and there was a hole in my tailgate. The glass in the back of the cab was also mostly gone. Barry's whole engine was ruined. The shot had not only taken out my window, but a good portion of the siding around the window.

Now I wanted to know why no one saw the shooter on my property before all hell broke loose. There should have been someone on the cameras since I was not home and an alarm should have gone off.

Now that Eduardo and Martin were back, I asked Peters to take me to the rental car company in Watson and told Hudson to stay at the house. I sat back down next to Stacy before heading out.

"I know I promised to keep you safe, and I meant it," I said into her ear so only she could hear me. She just nodded but kept looking straight ahead. Romi gave me a questioning look, but I didn't have any answers for him.

I stood and told them we'd be back in about an hour and a half, and to stay away from windows when at all possible. I nodded to Hudson as Peters and I headed out. While Peters drove down the driveway, I kept looking to see if I could see anyone in the forest. If he was still there, he was doing a damned good job of hiding.

We got to the rental office in good time. They gave me an SUV to drive and Peters whistled in appreciation for the new-looking vehicle.

"That's a pretty one, Sheriff! Don't let anything happen to it!" he laughed. I just looked at him without amusement and shook my head.

"Too soon, Peters," I said.

"Sorry, Sheriff," he replied.

We headed back home. Once there, I saw Henry hooking my truck to his tow truck. There was another truck from a different towing company, probably one sent by the rental agency, hooking up Barry's car.

I waited outside until the other tow company had gone, then told Henry to just worry about the tires and any damage that affected the safety of the truck, but not so much about the hole in the tailgate. That could wait. He nodded and spit a wad of chewing tobacco toward the side of the parking area. He climbed in his truck and rumbled off.

I went back inside and told Peters and Hudson they could leave, but I needed one of them to go to the county hospital to pick up Barry. Hudson said he'd go and they left. I called Barry and told him that Hudson would be there within a half hour. He told me that a representative of their company was flying in and would be at the hospital by the time Malcolm got out of surgery. Apparently the shot had missed all the vital organs, but there was still damage to be repaired. I thanked him and hung up.

Eduardo told me that Romi and Stacy were in her room upstairs. I nodded and headed into the kitchen for a beer. I took it out on the back porch and just sat, listening to the quiet. I knew I shouldn't be outside alone but could not resist the silence. I didn't even hear any crickets right now. I just needed to unwind. I laid my head back on the seat and sat with the beer in my hand on the arm of the chair.

Sometime later I heard the screen door open and the sound of crutches coming onto the porch. I didn't open my eyes but could almost feel Stacy sit down on the couch next to my chair. She took the beer out of my hand and took a drink, setting the bottle on the table when she was done. She put her hand on my arm that still sat on the arm of the chair and rubbed up and down while she leaned forward with her other arm on her knee.

"I know you're doing your best, John," she said. "I know you care and want to help, but now you're a target, and your property is a target, and I can't stand all this. I think I need to leave. I don't know where I can go, but I can't keep putting you in the line of fire." She hung her head and stopped rubbing my arm, leaving her hand just sitting there.

"There's nowhere you can go, and I don't want you anywhere else. I need to know you're okay and I need you with me. I guess that sounds selfish, but I don't care. I have to keep you safe. Please stay," I pleaded with her.

I could hear quiet sobs coming from her, and her body was shaking as she cried. I stood and picked her up and sat on the couch with her in my lap.

She curled into my chest, and I could feel my shirt getting wet from her tears. I hated the man who was causing all this pain. I wanted him dead, as bad as that sounded. I wanted to be sure he could never hurt Stacy again. I didn't care for my sake. I would heal. My property would get repaired. But the damage he was doing to Stacy was irredeemable. I would make him pay, I vowed to myself, and to her.

The next few days passed in relative peace. It reminded me of that old song by Simon & Garfunkel, 'The Sound of Silence'. The silence here really was so loud it was deafening. Overwhelming. Frightening. I felt as though I was waiting for the next shoe to drop and I was in a constant state of readiness. There was always a sense of electricity buzzing just under my skin and it was hard to concentrate. But I tried. I still had another song to write and I had nothing.

I spent my days learning new songs. The packet had included another country song and ballad, but the rest were mostly pop songs that would work well for me. I also strummed absentmindedly, waiting for my own words to show up. Still nothing.

The nights were a different story, though. Spent with John in his bed, my time within those four walls was a haven, a piece of heaven right here on earth. We talked and laughed and made love, but we didn't make any plans or talk about the future. It still weighed on my mind that I would have to leave in a couple of weeks, and it would be hard to find time to see him. My feelings were growing stronger every day and it was getting harder to keep them in check.

John spent his downtime with Eduardo putting up new cameras closer to the main road. They also walked his property to make sure the existing triggers were still in place. The new men had arrived and were patrolling the area constantly, too.

Things were quiet for about three days. Then the package came.

Murphy had found a package leaning against the mailbox and brought it up to the house. It was addressed to Darci with no return address. I knew it wasn't anything good.

John put on gloves and took the brown paper off the box and folded it. Then he carefully took the lid off, touching only the edges of the lid. I gasped as I saw the contents.

Inside was a Darci Dorsette doll. Her head had been ripped off and the hair cut off. Her eyes were gouged out, and there was a red substance all over the clothes. The jacket was unzipped, and a huge gash was in the chest where a heart would be.

I slumped down to the floor. I didn't pass out, but felt like I could. I didn't say anything to anyone as John helped me back to my feet. I just went upstairs. No one followed me.

I closed my door and the door to the bathroom and sat on my bed. I leaned against the headboard and started crying. I cried until my head was stuffed up and my face was puffy and my eyes were almost swollen shut. I realized I didn't have any tissues handy, so I got up to go to the bathroom. I could hear the drone of male voices coming from John's room, and figured it was him and Long Cloud working on the camera system.

I left the bathroom, shutting my door again, and headed back to bed. I heard a soft knock on my bathroom door, and called for John to come in. I felt bad that he would see me looking like this, but I couldn't help it.

He came in and sat on the edge of my bed next to my legs. He ran his hand from my foot up my leg as far as he could reach, and just looked at me. I lowered my head to try to hide from him, but he reached over and put his hand under my chin to raise my head. I raised my eyes to his and tried to make a small smile, but feared I failed miserably. He ran his hand down the side of my face and then rubbed his thumb across my lower lip.

"John, I don't blame you at all. I just wish I hadn't brought all this to your doorstep," I replied.

He gave me a soft smile and leaned over to touch his lips to mine. Not really a kiss, just an acknowledgment of feelings. He patted my leg and got up and went back into his room through the bathroom.

I decided to take a bath. It was still fairly early, but the hot water would ease some of the tension I was carrying in my body. I grabbed a sweatshirt and shorts and headed into the bathroom. I locked the door on John's side and ran the bathwater. I found some bubble bath under the bathroom sink and poured it in. Wonder what he was doing with bubble bath. It must have been Gram's contribution.

Once the tub was about three-quarters full, I undressed and climbed in. The water felt incredible, and I sank as far as I could, until only my head was above the water. I closed my eyes and let my mind wander, trying to clear it of all the bad things and fill it with words that would make a song. I found myself humming one of the new songs I had learned but made myself stop since I needed to write a song of my own.

Safe harbor. Warmth. Loving you. Feelings. Too early but I know. Safe harbor. Safe harbor. Loving you. Feelings. Warmth. The words kept going round and round in my head and I started to doze off. I must have slept for a few minutes when a knock on John's door startled me.

"Yes?" I asked.

"Stacy, Eduardo and I are going back outside to make some adjustments to the camera triggers. All the other guys will be here with you, though. Okay?" he asked.

"Okay. Thanks," I said.

I went back to dozing in the tub until the water started to get cold, then I got out and pulled on my comfy clothes and climbed into bed to take a real nap. I found Romi asleep on the other side of my bed on top of the covers and just left him there as I climbed under the covers. Sometimes you just needed someone nearby to feel safer.

THE SHERIFF'S STAR

I slept several hours and woke up around three o'clock. Romi was no longer on the bed. I got up and grabbed my crutches to head downstairs. Just then he came out of the bathroom drying his hands.

"How'd you sleep," he asked me.

"Good. Guess I needed the extra sleep. How'd you sleep?" I asked him.

"Okay, I guess," he said.

"Look, I know this has been a lot to handle. If you feel like you can't stay with me, I'll understand. I don't know how I'd get along without you, but no hard feelings if you want to bail," I told him in all seriousness.

Romi sat down on the bed. "Are you kidding me, Chica?" he cried. "I could never leave you. I just don't know what to do right now. I mean, if even the guys who are supposed to know how to handle all this can't get it to stop, what can I do? I don't want anything to happen to you, or to me," he said dramatically.

"I know. But they're doing their best, and we have to let them handle it. I just need you to keep me focused on my writing and handle the bills and other detritus that surrounds me. Hey, look at me using big words!" I laughed, trying to lighten the mood.

"Yeah, you're a walking thesaurus, Chica," he said with a slight smile. I'd take that as a win.

"Come on. Let's go downstairs and see if anyone left us some lunch," I said.

Romi stood up and followed me.

We got downstairs and found two sandwiches sitting on the breakfast bar with a big bag of chips next to them. He got us some drinks from the fridge, and we sat down to eat. I looked around and found no one in the living room. I got up and looked on the back porch, but didn't see anyone there, either. I walked over to the living room window and looked outside and caught sight of Martin as he rounded the side of the house.

Hmmm. Barry and Murphy must be sleeping. I knew Eduardo was with

John somewhere out on the property. I went back over and sat down at the breakfast bar. I took a few bites of my sandwich then turned to Romi.

"Does it feel strange to you that suddenly we're practically alone in the house?" I asked.

"Creepy. It feels like the protective detail is dropping like flies," he answered.

Just then John came in the back door, followed by Eduardo. John was carrying a toolbox that he set on the dining room table. He waked over and grabbed two sodas from the fridge.

He handed one to Eduardo and took a seat at the table, breathing a little hard. They both were, for that matter.

"Well, I think we've fixed at least part of the problem," John said. "I had my triggers set up higher because I was trying to catch humans that didn't belong, not animals, so it was easy for Doug to stay low under them. We've lowered all of them so it should be harder to avoid them from now on. We also added cameras and triggers around the house," he said. "And Long Cloud has added some software doodads that should let us know if Doug is trying to sabotage my system"

"Well, that's good news, John," I said with a smile. I could tell he felt better now that he had actually done something that felt like it mattered. I finished my sandwich and opened the bag of chips. I held it up to the guys to see if they wanted any. They all just shook their heads. I grabbed a handful of chips and put them on my plate.

After we finished, Romi got up and took our plates over to the sink to rinse them, then put them in the dishwasher. He turned and leaned against the kitchen counter looking at all of us. John stood up and said that he was going to the grocery store to pick up some things for Hastings' family and then deliver them. I offered to go with him, but he declined, saying I was better off at the house with protection. I worried about him driving that road alone, but he was the Sheriff and I had to believe that he could take care of himself.

He went upstairs to clean up, and Romi and I settled on the couch to watch a movie. At least I tried to settle, but my leg kept jumping, and the flashes of electricity kept running through my body. I knew I was just nervous about John being on that road, but I had to calm down, if for no other reason than to stop from transmitting my nerves to Romi.

John came back downstairs in a clean shirt and jeans. He came over to the couch and leaned over to kiss me goodbye. Romi just stared, and Eduardo pretended to look somewhere else. I smiled at John and told him to be careful, trying very hard to appear calm. I don't think he bought it for a minute because he very surreptitiously put his hand on my jumping leg to calm it. I just kept smiling like I had no idea.

Once he left we started streaming the movie and I tried to follow the plot. I just kept thinking about John on that road where he had almost died just a few days ago. I felt my phone vibrate and found a text from John.

Got to the grocery store okay.

Awww. He was just too much! He knew I needed to know that and wanted to make me feel better. I settled deeper into the couch and focused on the movie.

Just as the movie ended I got another text from John.

Headed home, it said, with a heart emoji.

I smiled and texted back three heart emojis.

I stayed on the couch with Romi, watching an old sitcom, waiting for John to get home. Martin stopped in to make sure all was well before he resumed his rounds outside.

About 20 minutes later we heard tires on the gravel outside, and Eduardo took up Malcolm's favorite position by the living room window. I could see his shoulders ease when John drove up. His truck was followed by Gram's cute red Versa. I got up and stood at the window as John got out of his truck and went to help Gram from her car. I could see resignation on his face, and thought it was cute. His Gram was the kind of comic relief we needed.

I smiled as they came through the door. Gram was already cackling in her raspy voice.

"Hey, Girlie! How's kicks?" she asked as she looked at me. John just rolled his eyes from behind her. "Hey, boy. Don't look so glum!" she said as she looked at Romi. I saw him fight a smile at her words.

"Heard about the excitement over here today," she said. John just shrugged and walked into the kitchen. Gram came over and sat next to me on the couch. Eduardo followed John in to the kitchen, out of the line of fire, I'd bet.

"I don't know what to do, Gram. I just keep piling more trouble on John without meaning to."

Gram just cackled again.

"Girlie, he needs someone to liven up the place. He's been alone too long, just coasting along in life, never taking chances or living on the edge. It's just plain boring and such a shame!" she said. "You're just what he needs," she finished.

"But I have to leave soon, Gram," I said. "I have to get back to work and I'll be traveling a lot, too. I can't be here for him," I said.

"Nonsense. When you find the one, I mean THE ONE, you find a way to be together. It won't always be moonshine and barbecue, but it'll be worth it every day," she said, sounding uncharacteristically serious.

The One. I felt like it was way too soon to be saying that, but I couldn't deny my feelings. But what would happen once the danger was gone?

I knew that John made me feel safe, but what if all the feelings went away once I was really safe and all this was over? How did I know these feelings were real? I mean, John and I had talked, a lot, about ourselves and our lives and our opinions on everything from movies to politics to religion to music.

I felt like I knew him almost as well as I knew anyone, even Romi. But Romi and I had been friends and colleagues for years and had been through a lot together. I had only known John a matter of a couple of weeks. How could I know him so well?

I felt like I needed some time alone, so I told Romi and Gram I was going upstairs to do some work. Gram still didn't know who I was, so I couldn't be specific about what kind of work I would be doing.

I climbed the stairs and went into my room. I sat in my favorite chair and stared out the window. I saw Martin pass by on his patrol. I pulled my guitar from its case and started strumming nothing in particular. As I strummed and thought about John, and what it meant to be leaving him while I was making a movie and on tour, words started filling my brain. I grabbed my pad and a pen and just started writing.

It was a sad song about being out on tour and missing the one I loved. I wasn't completely happy with it, but it was a good start, and more than I had a while ago. I wasn't sure how the label execs would take to it. I was surprised to find that it was exactly how I felt about this upcoming tour. We would be on the road for six months or longer, not counting the weeks of tour prep beforehand. No matter how real or not real my feelings were, the thought of being away from John for that long was eating at me.

I heard a soft knock at my door and called for whoever it was to enter. It was Gram.

She came over and sat in the other chair at the table. She just looked at me and grinned like the cat who'd eaten the canary.

"I knew I was right. It's you. You're Darci Dorsette! I have one of your songs for your ringtone on my phone. As soon as I heard you singing I knew I was right!" she shouted with glee.

I sighed and tried to calm her down. "That's great, Gram, but I'm incognito for a reason, so no one can know. I don't know if the protection detail even knows. Please keep this between us. If John knows that you know, that will be even more stress on him, so don't tell him. Or anyone. Please, Gram?" I pleaded.

"Don't worry, Girlie. I'll keep this to myself until just the right time, after you're gone, and spring it on the town. I don't want to give the kid anythin' else to worry about," she said.

"Good. Glad we're on the same page," I said, patting her knobby knee.

"So, workin' on a new song, sounds like. Is it for the new album I've heard about?" she asked.

"Yes, it is. It's the second one I've written myself, and I hope it goes well. Do you listen to my music a lot?" I asked her.

"Of course! Got you playin' in my car all the time! Drives Bev nuts because she likes that old school country stuff, but I like something with a better beat that I can move to!" she exclaimed, and I laughed out loud at her enthusiasm.

"Well, I'll make sure you get a signed copy of the new album, and a t-shirt," I said, and she jumped up and hugged me. Well, not jumped, exactly.

"I gotta head out, Girlie, before it gets dark. You and the kid work it out between you. I know there's a way. I'll check in on you in a day or two." She hugged me again and headed out into the hallway. I heard Martin call up the stairs for her to wait for him to help her. I wondered where John was.

I put my guitar back in the case and headed downstairs myself. I hadn't realized how long I'd been upstairs. I didn't see John in the living room or the kitchen, so I checked the back porch. I found him sitting on the couch, head back, with a beer in his hand that was draped over his knee. I made my way around the fire pit and sat down next to him. He didn't stir except to turn his head to look at me.

"Did you and Gram have a nice talk?" he asked me with a smirk. I had a feeling he knew what Gram and I had talked about, but I was not about to address the elephant in the room.

"We did. We understand each other," I said by way of explanation. He just nodded. I grabbed the beer out of his hand, took a drink, and set the bottle on the unlit fire pit. I scooted over closer to him, picked up his arm and draped it over my shoulders and settled in next to him. He groaned a little under his breath and I smiled. He tightened his arm around me. This felt like home.

The lights on the porch were off, so I could see the outline of the trees in the distance and could hear the sounds of crickets and frogs. I was startled by the sound of footsteps but made out Eduardo walking past on his rounds. He and Martin must have switched off. I settled back down into the cocoon of John's arm. Ahhh.

"I've been thinking about when you leave," John suddenly said.

"Don't," I said. "I don't want to think about that. But I have been wondering if all this, with us, is just because of the situation, or if it could be, well, real?" I posed it as a question but didn't expect an answer.

"What I feel is real. I want to take you out on a real date. I want to go grocery shopping with you, plant flowers out front with you, take showers with you, and grow old and sit in rocking chairs with you on this porch. I think we met due to the situation, but I really believe my feelings are real. But if you doubt yours, I can understand and respect that. We don't have to talk about it anymore," he said.

"But I don't mind talking about it," I said. "I want to know the truth. I have very strong feelings for you, but we've never done the regular dating things. I want so badly to spend time with you outside of danger and the unknown," I cried, desperate for answers.

"Tell you what. How about after PT tomorrow, we go on a date. We can get some lunch, go to a movie, and just spend time together. Of course, we'll have bodyguards with us, but we can still be together," he said, looking hopeful.

"Do you think that's safe?" I asked. It sounded wonderful, but I didn't want to put anymore strain on him and the protection detail than I had already.

"I think it will be as safe as we can make it, but if it makes you uncomfortable, then we won't do it," he said.

"No, I think I'd like to try it. It would be so good to just have a day to have fun and spend time together," I said, looking up at him. He leaned down and kissed me, not deeply, but softly. A promise of what was to come later tonight.

"Okay. Let me go brief the guys and set up a plan," he said before kissing me again, more deeply this time. I brought my arm around behind his neck and pulled him closer. He wrapped his free arm around my waist and pulled me up closer. I opened my mouth and let him in, and he took charge.

His tongue felt along the inside of my mouth and tangled with my tongue. He then ran his tongue along my bottom lip and sucked my lip into his mouth before kissing me again. I loved kissing John. It never got old and was always fantastic.

Finally, he let me go and got up. He picked up the beer bottle to take inside. He glanced at me one more time before going into the house. I just smiled back at him.

I was sure this idea was not going to go over well, but I wasn't prepared for Romi's reaction. I entered the living room and found him there with Martin. I called Eduardo and asked him to come in from outside so we could talk. Once he came in, I laid out the plan.

I wasn't sure how to start, so I just jumped in.

"Stacy and I want to spend some time together, so after PT tomorrow, we want to go out to lunch then to a movie." I stopped and looked around.

Romi's face turned bright red and he jumped up and lunged at me. Martin grabbed him to hold him as I took a step back.

"Are you freakin' crazy?" he yelled. "How can you think about putting her in such danger just to get your rocks off? There's a crazed killer after her and you want to have a date?!" he screamed.

I heard Stacy come up behind me and put her hand on my shoulder. She stared at him without blinking. She moved her arm around my waist and continued to stare at him. She finally blinked.

"Romi. We know this is a lot to ask, but we just need some time away from here together. My time here is getting short, and we want to spend whatever time we have together. Surely you can understand that?" she asked him.

"But it's too dangerous!" he yelled. She held up her hand.

"It may be, but if we work together, we can hopefully minimize the danger to everyone. John has a plan if you'd just listen."

He seemed to fold into himself and turned back toward the couch. Stacy went over and sat next to him with her arm around his shoulders.

I looked at Martin and Eduardo. "I think if two of you guys follow us in the rental, and we head to Bergen after PT, then we should be good. No one will expect us to go there, and we can make sure we aren't followed. With you guys shadowing us and me with Stacy, there will be plenty of coverage," I said. Martin and Eduardo looked at each other, then at me. I could tell they were against the plan, but they knew it was going to happen anyway.

"I'm going with you," Romi burst out.

"I can understand your concerns. If you have to come, please stay with the guys, okay?" I asked.

"Fine," He spat out, still clearly upset.

"Where is Bergen?" Stacy asked.

"It's the next town over from Watson," I answered. "It's a little bigger than Watson. Most people from Whirlwind don't venture that far away, but it's a nice city," I told her.

"Oh, okay," she replied. I smiled at her and winked.

Eduardo headed back outside to continue his patrol and Martin went into the kitchen to start dinner. I sat in my easy chair and looked over at Stacy and Romi. He was glaring at me still, and Stacy was whispering something to him. He turned to look at her and she smiled at him. He just shook his head and stood up. He headed for the stairs but stopped at my chair. He looked down at me and said, "it's on you if she gets hurt," and headed up the stairs.

I stood up and headed to the couch next to Stacy. I pulled her into my lap and nuzzled my nose in her neck, enjoying the smell of orange blossoms and vanilla that I would forever associate with her. She giggled and rubbed her head against mine in return. I whispered to her, "I'm crazy for you, ya know?" She laughed and said, "I know. I'm crazier for you."

"Not possible," I responded, nuzzling further down her neck. She giggled again. My girl was ticklish, it seemed.

She pulled herself a little away from me and found my lips with her own. She kissed me like she hadn't seen me in a month, and I let her do it. I opened my mouth, and my tongue invited her in. She ran her tongue along my bottom lip, nipping and sucking as she went. She put her tongue in my mouth and rubbed against my tongue, twisting and tangling in a delightful dance. I would never forget her taste and the Good Lord willing, I would never be without it!

We sat like that for what seemed like seconds but must have been much longer. A throat clearing from the direction of the kitchen broke us apart.

"Dinner's ready," Martin said. He called upstairs to Romi, as well.

I helped Stacy up from the couch and we walked to the dining room together. Romi came down the stairs at the same time. He still wouldn't look at me without shooting daggers, but at least he was quiet and calm.

After we had eaten and put the dishes in the dishwasher, Martin headed outside to relieve Eduardo so he could come inside and eat. Suddenly an alarm went off on my phone. We all stopped what we were doing and I pulled my phone out of my back pocket.

I pulled up my cameras and was pleasantly surprised to see that a family of deer had set off one of the newly lowered triggers. We all watched as they wandered away from the camera into the woods.

"Wow! I think my heart stopped for a minute, there!" Stacy said. We all laughed, even Romi.

Stacy said she had to work on her songs for a while, so I followed her upstairs to her room. I just wanted to sit and be with her for a while. She took her guitar out of its case and pulled some music sheets out of a manila envelope on the table in her room.

She looked at the first song and started playing while she sang. I could only watch her in awe. She actually seemed to glow while she sang. She closed her eyes and settled further into the chair and seemed to let her body feel the music. She sang and played beautifully, but I knew that the full performance version of the song would be incredible.

She went through four songs, then said she would play her newest song for me, one she'd written.

As she played and sang the words, I felt tears prick the back of my eyes. It was a sad song and one I could tell came from the heart. I made my heart hurt at the thought of her being gone for months at a time on tour, of not being able to be with her or see her or feel her.

I felt a tear roll down my cheek as she finished the song. She put her guitar back in the case and just sat back in the chair.

"I don't know that the album execs will accept that song," she said. "It may not be commercial enough for them, and it's obviously a sad song," she said, and I could see tears in her eyes, as well.

I stood up and held out my hand. I helped her up and we just stood there, holding one another and swaying to music only our hearts could hear. I put one hand on the back of her head and one arm around her waist and held her close, telling myself that we would find a way to be together. I just hoped the date tomorrow was a success.

I pulled back slightly and looked into her face. I bent down and handed her the crutches and said, "Let's go to bed." She nodded and followed me to my room.

The next morning I woke up before Stacy, as usual. I took a shower and put on one of my nicer shirts and my good jeans. I put on cologne and made sure my hair was in good shape before heading downstairs to grab some coffee.

Barry was in the kitchen when I entered, sipping a cup of coffee and looking out the kitchen window. He and Murphy had been on night duty, and he would be heading to bed soon.

"Heard about the big date," he said without looking at me.

"Yep. Looking forward to it," I said.

"Don't think it's a great idea, but I get it," he said. "Just be on the lookout for anyone following you or taking too much of an interest in you," he said, turning to look at me.

"Will do. That's why I suggested heading to Bergen rather than stay in Watson. Hardly anyone in Bergen knows me, and it's big enough we can blend in," I told him.

I grabbed my mug when the Keurig finished and headed upstairs to wake Stacy. When I got to my room, though, the bed was empty, and I heard the shower running. I headed back downstairs to sit on the porch while I waited for her to come down.

I'd been on the porch for about 20 minutes when Barry yelled that breakfast was ready. I headed inside but Stacy was not yet downstairs. I sat down at the breakfast table and Barry brought me a plate with what looked like a frittata on it. Full of peppers, onions, mushrooms and broccoli, it looked wonderful. I hoped Stacy got down here in time to eat.

Just as I had that thought, I heard the distinctive sound of Stacy coming down the stairs. I looked over my shoulder and saw her with her crutches and her backpack hitting the bottom stair.

"Just in time for breakfast, sweetheart," I said quietly to her.

She just smiled and came over to the table. She set her backpack on the seat next to her. Barry brought her a plate and she thanked him.

We ate in companionable silence while we waited for the others to come down. Martin came down first, saying Eduardo would be down shortly. Stacy and I finished our breakfast and headed to the living room to wait. Romi came down the stairs next, looking half asleep. He passed on the offer of breakfast but made himself a cup of coffee instead.

Finally, Eduardo came down and sat down for breakfast. Barry also made him a cup of coffee to save time. Romi came into the living room and sat down next to Stacy. We were watching the morning news when Romi suddenly looked up at Stacy.

"Hey, Chica, we need to get the interior designer going on fixing up the apartment. I don't know how long it will take, but if we want it done by the time we leave here, it should be started in the next day or two," he said.

"Fine," she said. "Tell them I want Boho Chic with pale gray walls and white trim. I want big fluffy furniture that you can sink into. I'm thinking teal and fuchsia as the primary colors," she added.

"Okay. I'll get on it while you're at PT. Do you want to use the same decorator as before?" he asked.

"If she's available," Stacy said.

"Okay." Romi started messing around on his phone. Eduardo came into the living room saying he was ready.

I went over and conferred with Barry just as Murphy came in the house. I had installed my camera system on their phones a few days before so they would have easier access to the cameras. Murphy said he'd gotten a call and the new men had shown up in Whirlwind and were headed out to the house to monitor while Barry and Murphy slept. The guys would stay up until the new guys arrived.

The rest of us headed out. Romi went with Martin and Eduardo to their rental car, and Stacy and I headed for my rental. I threw her backpack and crutches into the back seat and helped Stacy into the front. She leaned over and kissed me just before I closed the door. I smiled at her.

The drive to Watson was uneventful. No one seemed to be following us which helped ease my fears somewhat. I walked Stacy into the office, making my usual visual sweep of the area and other people inside. Everything seemed in order, so I went back to the truck. I needed to check in with the station while I was waiting.

Hastings had called in stating that his forward vision was clearing somewhat, but that he was developing tunnel vision now. I advised the deputy on duty to call Hastings and have him get with HR about long-term disability. Nothing else was going on at the station.

I then called Malcolm in the hospital to see how he was doing.

"Hello," he answered.

"Malcolm, hello. This is Sheriff Leppard. How are ya doing, man? Ready to come back to work?" I laughed.

"I wish. Better food. But I'll be here for another day or so, then headed home to rehab. I have a nice chunk missing from my side, but that idiot missed all the vital stuff, so I'm very lucky," he said.

"Well, I'm glad you're going to recover. The company just sent two new men to replace you."

"Barry said he would come by once you guys were settled back at the house today, though."

"Oh. Okay. He should be getting to bed right about now, so it will probably be later this afternoon before he gets out there," I told him.

"Yeah, I figured," he said.

"Okay, I'll let you go. Behave for the nurses and let us know how you're doing, alright?" I asked.

"Will do, Sheriff. Take care."

I hung up and walked over to the rental car. Romi was doing something on his phone, but Martin and Eduardo were doing visual sweeps of the area on either side of the parking lot. I pulled up theaters in Bergen and asked what everyone wanted to see. We all decided on the latest action film and made plans for the trip. Romi looked up and put in a request for chocolate covered raisins with his popcorn. I just smiled and shook my head at him. He was really just a big kid, a very organized, detail-oriented big kid who took care of Stacy's life.

I looked down at my watch and saw that Stacy had been inside longer than usual. I typed out a text to see where she was.

Where are you? Are you done yet?

She answered almost immediately.

Just sprucing up for our date. Be out in a minute or two. Heart emoji.

I smiled to myself. She wanted to look pretty for our date. Well, she was always pretty, but I liked that she was making an effort to do something different. I felt the occasion warranted it.

When she came out of the building, my jaw dropped. She had changed into a beautiful sundress with pretty little daisies all over it on a yellow background. The dress had what the ladies called a halter top that wrapped around her neck leaving her shoulders bare.

Her hair was pulled up in the front, and the back hung down to her ass. I'd never seen her hair down like that and it was a sight to behold. I just wanted to grab it in my fist and... *Cool it. The date's just beginning, man.*

I walked around her since I couldn't spin her around. I whistled through my teeth and smiled as big as I ever had. Boy, had she made an effort!

"You look absolutely gorgeous!" I said.

She made a partial curtsey on her crutches and grinned back at me.

"I figured I was entitled to look as good as possible for our date. I see you made an effort, too."

I grinned, humbled. I walked her to the SUV and helped her in after stowing her crutches and backpack.

We drove about 45 minutes to Bergen, a city to the east of Whirlwind. I headed straight for the movie theater and parked a little way off from the building where there weren't so many cars. The guys pulled in next to me.

"What are we seeing?" asked Stacy.

"The general consensus was for the new action flick that just came out," I told her.

She grumbled under her breath, but I just laughed and told her she was out-voted.

Stacy insisted on paying for all the tickets, and Romi's snack buffet. We got seated with our chaperones one row behind us and spent the next two hours studiously ignoring the film.

Our date was wonderful! We had so much fun during the movie acting like randy teenagers on our first real date. Sometimes our eyes were on the screen while our hands roamed each other's bodies; other times we were kissing like we were the only ones in the theater, which we practically were. Going to the first showing of the day meant the theater was almost empty, but our chaperones were still in the row behind us. Whenever I would take my eyes off John and look behind us, they guys' eyes were focused on the screen but I didn't care what they were looking at. I didn't know when I'd get another chance like this one, and I was taking full advantage.

John kept his right arm around me the whole movie, while his left hand was busy exploring me under the cover of darkness. He fondled my breasts over my dress, then would move his hand to my thigh, where he would slowly move my dress up higher and higher until he could touch my panties. Then he rubbed me over the panties until I felt like I was going to combust, then he'd stop and move on to someplace else. He was a menace to my heart rate. I was so worked up by the end of the movie that I almost pulled him into the empty bathroom to find release, but he just smiled and looked at me with promises in his eyes.

When the movie finally ended, we all paraded out and into the sunshine to go to lunch. My eyes took some time adjusting from the darkness of the theater to the beautiful day in front of me. I wanted to hold John's hand while we walked but couldn't because of the crutches. So, I settled for holding his hand while we drove to the restaurant.

The one John had chosen had a beautiful back patio, but we couldn't sit out there for safety reasons. The view from inside was very pretty though, looking out onto a wide expanse of green grass and wildflowers in the park behind the restaurant. We sat at our own table while the guys and Romi sat two tables away from us. It actually felt like we had some privacy. Our waitress was a pretty young lady with short blonde hair and piercings up both ears. John only gave her a passing glance, keeping his eyes on me.

I let her know that the other table where the guys were sitting was also on our tab. John and I held hands from the time we sat down. After we placed our orders, we focused on one another. We talked about the movie, which we had apparently paid some attention to. We talked about how good it felt to be out of the house. We talked about my songs and when I would get my cast off. We talked about everything and nothing, never once talking about all the troubling events of the past weeks. It was a splendid relief.

Lunch passed in a blur. I couldn't tell you what I ate because all I could do was look at John and listen to him talk. I felt like I had to store all these memories up for the day when I wouldn't have him near me. I looked once at the table where the other guys were sitting. Martin and Eduardo were constantly looking around the room, but Romi just looked at us. I smiled at him and went back to listening to John tell me the story of a hunting trip he and his brothers had gone on long ago.

When we were finished eating, John helped me up and we walked ahead of the guys back outside. We walked slowly back to where we had parked, almost like we didn't want the day to end. Which I didn't.

John and I didn't really talk on the way home, just held hands, occasionally kissing the other's knuckles. He would look at me every so often and I would smile to let him know I was happy. When we got back home and parked, I was just about to open my door, when John put a hand on my arm to stop me. He was staring at the front porch. I could see what looked like a white box on the porch and hoped like hell that nothing was going to happen to bring a bad end to such a good day.

Martin exited their car and walked slowly up to the porch. I could see his head swivel as he looked around the area carefully. He bent down and looked through the box, then stood up and called John forward. He walked up and joined Martin on the porch as they looked at the box and its contents. John finally gave the all-clear and we all got out of our vehicles.

As I made my way to the steps, John called to me, saying it appeared to be my mail. Oh! I'd forgotten I had Romi forward the mail here! He ran ahead of me and grabbed the box like his life depended on it. He bounced on his feet while Martin unlocked the door. I had never seen him so glad to get my fan mail.

John came down the steps and carried me and my crutches up so I didn't have to sit on the steps in my dress. I thanked him with a kiss and went inside in search of Romi. I found him at the dining room table with the box in front of him, going through the letters. He was making one stack of letters addressed to Darci Dorsette, and one stack of letters addressed to me.

I took the first letter off the stack for Darci and opened it. It was a request for a signed picture. I set that aside to start a new pile of requests for photos. I opened the next letter and it was a fan writing about how much my songs meant to her, and how much she loved me. I set that in its own pile of letters that would get a form letter.

Romi was going through the mail for me, such as bills and other correspondence. He had several stacks going as well.

He and I spent two hours going through the mail. He had gone up to his room to get his tablet and was making notations regarding what had come.

I had received several invitations to various parties and events in the next few weeks that he had to send regrets for, as well as a copy of my contract with the picture studio. As I read it, I looked over at John, who was sitting with Martin and Eduardo in the living room watching a sports show.

I didn't know if I could do this. If I could leave. I left Romi to the mail and went into the living room to sit on the end of the couch closest to John's chair.

John held out his hand for mine. I grasped his like a lifeline across the distance between our seats. I knew I needed to get upstairs and work on my songs, but I didn't want to leave this spot. I wished it was just us in the house so we could wrap ourselves up in a blanket and lie on the couch watching a movie, or just enjoy the feel of each other.

Romi called me over. I must have missed him going upstairs again because he had retrieved his home mail system, photos and a sharpie, and sat me down to sign photos. He usually did that for me, but I knew he was trying to keep me focused on work.

I spent an hour signing photos and letters until John came up behind me and put his hands on my shoulders. He asked if I'd like something to drink. I was glad for the distraction since I had a cramp in my hand and my writing was getting bad.

I sat there and let him rub my shoulders as I asked for a soda. He leaned down and kissed my cheek then went into the kitchen. He came out a few minutes later with sodas for me and Romi, and a beer for himself.

I drank some of my soda and went back to signing things. Romi was keeping his head down and not looking at me, until I heard his tablet ping with an incoming message. He jumped up and showed me the tablet screen. On it were pictures of sofas and chairs of varying colors.

"It's the designer," he said, excited. "She sent pics of some of the items she's chosen for the apartment!" He was more excited than I was. I didn't want to think about going back to Nashville alone.

"That's great. Why don't you work with her on selecting the items since you know my style and what colors I like," I said.

"But Chica, this is your apartment, where you live. Don't you want some say in what goes in it?" he asked.

"Like I said, it'll be almost a year before I get to spend any real time there, so it'll be just you. You should have just as much say as me," I answered.

"Yeah, I guess you're right," he said, losing some of his exuberance. He packed up the photos and letters, and the mail system, and went upstairs with his tablet to play with furniture.

I decided I would make dinner tonight, so I went into the kitchen to see what I could come up with. I found some ground deer meat thawed in the fridge and decided to make a comfort food casserole. While I was looking for ingredients, I heard John's phone ring, and stopped to listen. It sounded like it was Gram, so I kept working on dinner.

I browned the meat in a skillet that I had found sitting on the stove, then had one of the guys drain the meat in the sink.

I found a stock pot in the cabinet next to the stove and got it out. I boiled water and put in two boxes of shell pasta I found in the pantry. Once that was boiled and drained, I added shredded cheddar and Swiss cheese, sour cream, milk and the meat and stirred it.

Then I took baby carrots out of the fridge and cut them in halves. I boiled them until they were soft, then drained them and returned them to the pan. I added brown sugar, honey and butter to the pan and let the carrots simmer in that mixture for a few minutes. Then I called everyone for dinner.

John made up plates for everyone and carried them to the table for me. Barry and Murphy had just gotten up, so we had a full table. There were compliments all around for the simple but filling food.

After we'd eaten and the guys had cleared the table, I went up to my room to work on my songs. I still had a few new ones to learn and wanted to work on my own songs some more. I sat in my favorite chair and did nothing for a few minutes. Just thought. Then I picked up my guitar and pulled a new song out of the envelope.

This was a catchy tune, one that would play well on the radio and be very commercially successful. I smiled just looking at the music before I even started playing the notes. I had just added the lyrics when my door opened quietly and John came in. He closed the door and came over to sit in the other chair. I continued playing and singing, and he started tapping his fingers on his leg in time with the music. I thought that was a good sign.

Once I felt I had a good grip on that song, I pulled out the last new song from the envelope. This one was also catchy, and I enjoyed learning it. Overall, it didn't seem like the album was going to be that different in style from my previous two, which was good. After a while, I started playing the first song I wrote. John listened and looked at me, confused. When I finished the song, I asked him what was wrong.

"Why are both the songs you wrote so sad?" he asked.

"I don't know. I hadn't thought of it, but you're right. I wrote them both after I got here and met you, so they should be happy, shouldn't they?" I asked him back.

"Are you really unhappy here, Stacy?" he asked.

"Not at all. Except for the reason I'm here. But being here with you is wonderful. I guess maybe my subconscious worries about leaving are coming through. I should probably work on a happier song," I said.

John just looked at me intently. Then he stood up, picked me up off the chair, and sat back down in his chair with me on his lap.

"I don't want you to worry, Stacy. If you decide that you want to continue this relationship we seem to be building once you leave, I will figure out a way. I know your career is going to be the most important thing in your life, and you're going to be uber busy for the next long while, but I will find a way to make it work," he said with so much feeling that tears pooled in my eyes. As I looked at him through my tears, I knew that I loved him.

"I don't think my career is the most important thing anymore," I said as I leaned over to kiss him.

The next week fell into a routine. John would go to the Sheriff's Office in the morning, and one of the protection detail guys would take me to PT.

Then I would come back from PT and help Romi with the mail. He had an order of Darci Dorsette t-shirts sent to John's house, so now we were sending those out, as well. I was signing photos and letters right and left and getting a permanent cramp in my hand.

John would come home for lunch some days, and he and I would sit on the back porch to eat. He'd go back to work, and I would work on the songs. The script for the movie had also been delivered, so Romi started helping me learn lines. I hadn't told John about that yet because it seemed to be just another reminder that I would be leaving soon. Two more weeks until I could get my cast off, then more PT to get my leg working again.

Tom came to visit one day, bringing news of Nashville, none of which I was particularly interested in. I don't know for sure, but I think Romi told Tom about John and myself. Tom kept giving me strange looks but didn't say anything about it.

Malcolm was finally released from the hospital and went home. He sent us a message that he got there just fine and was starting his PT so he could get back to work.

Alarms continued to go off when deer crossed the path of the triggers, so we got kind of lax about security.

Everything seemed quiet until one night I was sitting on the back porch, when suddenly what looked like a very large man can running up toward the porch. I heard the alarm go off on John's phone and I screamed.

John came running out onto the porch with a shotgun in his hand and stared outside. Then he started laughing and told me to go into the house. I didn't think it was funny and didn't want to leave him out there alone. Murphy came over and led me into the living room and went back out onto the porch with John.

They both came back in several minutes later shaking their heads and chuckling.

"What's so funny, you two?" I yelled at them.

"It was just a bear, sweetheart. Nothin' but a bear," John said as he put the shotgun away in the gun safe.

"Well, it looked like a man, and was running straight for me!" I cried as I plopped down on the couch and crossed my arms angrily across my chest.

"Of course, it looked like a man," John said trying to cajole me out of my anger. "But it was just looking for food. He was being nosy, not homicidal," John finished with smile. I was not amused.

All of a sudden, the alarm sounded again on John's phone, and his phone rang at the same time.

It was Barry, who was on patrol outside. He'd seen a man, not a bear, trying to get near the house. He was in pursuit.

Murphy grabbed a shotgun from the gun safe and took off out the front door to assist. John sent me and Romi upstairs to hide in my bathroom. As I climbed the stairs I saw him grab a pistol from the gun safe and sit at the dining room table so he could see both the front and back doors.

Once I got to the bathroom, I heard footsteps headed downstairs and knew that Martin and Eduardo were up now, too.

About 20 minutes later I heard the front door open and Barry and Murphy came in. Apparently, the bear had gotten into the pursuit, so Barry and Murphy had to split up to avoid the bear, and lost the man.

Romi and I came out of the bathroom and went back downstairs. Barry was headed back outside and Martin and Eduardo were headed back to bed. Murphy sat on the couch watching some news show, so I sat on the other end of the couch to play with my phone. That's when I realized I hadn't done a video for my social media in almost a week. I decided to do a quick post to keep everyone engaged, then I would have to do a video tomorrow.

> *Helloooo, Dorsetters! It's been a while, but I'm doin' great! Saw a real bear for the first time up close and personal here! Nature's all around me! I'm workin' on lots of new songs for the album and will be shootin' a movie in just a few weeks. I can't wait to take you along on this amazin' journey with me! Keep bein' wonderful and keep listenin'!*

There. Hopefully that would forestall any rumors about what I was doing. I looked over and saw John and Murphy sitting at the dining room table talking in low voices. About the man, no doubt. I knew it had been too quiet.

My phone suddenly rang, and I saw that it was Gram. John looked over at me and I just smiled as I answered.

"Hello, Gram, how are you?" I asked.

"Good, Girlie, real good. My spidey senses were tingling so I thought I would call and make sure you were all right. John's with you, right?" she asked.

"Yep, he's here. We're fine. Had a bear come snooping around a few minutes ago, but that's about it." I deliberately didn't tell her about the man running around the woods. Didn't want her to worry.

"Well, okay. Just wanted to be sure. Tell John to call me sometime. I haven't even seen him at Bingo in a while. Guess he's got better people to spend his time with," she cackled as she hung up.

Then it hit me. She was right. John had been at home every night for the last couple of weeks and hadn't gone to Bingo. And tomorrow night was Bingo night.

"Hey, John, I think Gram misses you. I want you to go to Bingo tomorrow night. It's been weeks since you've been," I said across the room.

"I'll think about it. Gram doesn't need me at Bingo. She cheats no matter who's there," he said with a small smile.

"Go. Make your grandma happy," I said.

"Fine, I'll go if it will make you happy," he answered.

"I'll be thrilled beyond belief," I answered sarcastically. He just laughed and went back to his conversation with Murphy.

I decided to head upstairs. I wasn't interested in whatever was on TV, and Romi had gone up after dinner and not come back. I went up and knocked on his door. He called for me to come in and I entered. He was sitting in a chair in the corner with his tablet on the table in front of him. I walked over and took the other chair at the table. I reached for his tablet and saw that he was looking at fabric swatches. He was really getting into this interior design project.

"So, what's been up with you lately. You're hardly talking, and you're entirely focused on redecorating my house. Have I done something wrong or pissed you off?" I asked earnestly as I pushed the tablet back over to him.

"No, you haven't pissed me off. It just seems like things are changing. You're spending most of your time with John now, and I have to force you to do work stuff. You used to love signing photos and sending letters and t-shirts, but now it's a struggle to get you to do it.

I know you have feelings for John, but we'll be leaving soon and heading to LA, and I just need you focused on getting ready for that. I don't want you brokenhearted when your career is really taking off.

I'm supposed to be your best friend and confidante, but it feels like you haven't told me anything recently."

"I'm sorry you're feeling left out. You are my best friend, Romi, but now John's my friend, too. I have a different relationship with him and don't want to leave him behind when we go. But we are going, for sure. I think I love him and that makes him important to me, and to you, I hope. And I hate to tell you, but I've always hated signing pics and letters, but I never had anything else to do with my time so it was easier to focus. But we are moving forward with the movie and the tour, so don't look so down. I will be sad, but not brokenhearted because John swears there's a way for us to be together. I just don't know his plan yet."

He got up and came over to hug me. I hoped that meant things would return to normal. I challenged him to a game of Rummy and let him beat me. That seemed to make him feel better. Rummy was something we could do no matter where we were or what was going on around us. It was our game.

After three more games I headed to my room. I didn't know if John had come up yet, but his bedroom light wasn't on so I guessed he was still downstairs.

I took out my contacts and put on some pajamas and got into bed. I knew John would come in once he got upstairs. I fell asleep while playing a game on my phone.

When I woke up, sunlight was streaming in my room, and John was asleep on the bed next to me. I hadn't even heard him come in last night. My phone was laying on the mattress next to my pillow and looked like it was dead. I put it on the charger on the nightstand and turned back over to just look at John. He looked so peaceful asleep. He was usually up before me so I never got this chance to look my fill. I checked my watch and saw that it was just after 6 a.m. He still had time to sleep, so I just snuggled down into the covers and watched him. Soon my eyes closed and I fell back to sleep.

I was awakened by a kiss on the forehead. Then a kiss to my cheek. Finally a kiss on my lips. I slowly opened my eyes and smiled at John. He grinned back and asked if I had enjoyed watching him sleep.

"How did you know?!" I cried. "You were sound asleep!"

"Was I?" he asked with a Cheshire Cat grin.

"You dog!" I said and hit him in the arm. He just wrapped both arms around me and pulled me so I was lying on top of him.

"How did you sleep, sweetheart?" he asked once he finished kissing me.

"Really well. I didn't even hear you come in. What time did you come to bed?" I asked.

"Must have been 1 a.m." he said.

"Wow. You and Murphy were having a great talk, then, I take it?" I said.

"Yes, and now I have a plan, but I'm not going to tell it to you yet, so don't ask," he told me.

"What?" I screeched. "That's not fair!"

"You'll know when the time is right. For now, just know that I'm all in," he told me as he kissed me again, probably to distract me. Which it did.

"I'm all in, too," I said. "Or at least as far as I can be given my work obligations."

"That's good," he said. "What are your plans for today?"

"Just more of the same, I guess. Signing things and working on my songs. I've got to have them memorized before I leave here," I said. "What are your plans?" I asked him.

"I've been training Rogetski – you remember her, right? – to take over if I ever have to be gone. We're working on teaching her the county way of doing things right now. More of the same, like you said."

"Hmmm," I said.

"Okay, sweetheart. I have to get up and get ready for work. You stay here and rest a while." He tucked the covers around me, basically trapping me in the bed. He jumped up and headed into the bathroom with his phone, wearing nothing but pajama bottoms. Oh, my, what a view.

Rogetski was catching on quickly. I had given her a book about forensic procedure, and she was acing every question I threw at her. She was already great at evidence collection and interviews, so now we were working on the requirements of the county and state. I wanted her to be prepared if I had to leave for any reason.

I had even ordered a passport, just to be on the safe side. I really did have a plan, but I didn't want Stacy to know about it just yet. It was only if she decided she wanted me to come with her.

I didn't want to be a distraction, or someone else for her to worry about. I just didn't want to be without her and as soon as I knew she felt the same way, I would put my plan into action. I just didn't want to take for granted that she wanted me to follow her.

We'd had no further sightings of the stolen pickup, so that meant Meznu was hiding somewhere. With the limited number of deputies I had and all the other things to be done in town, we just didn't have the time or resources to search too often for him.

I had promised Stacy before I left that morning that I would go to Bingo with Gram tonight, so after work I headed to the diner to get some dinner and called Stacy.

"Hello," she answered.

"Hey, sweetheart? Whatcha doin'?" I asked her.

"Just taking a break from working on my songs and playing some Rummy with Romi," she said.

"That sounds like fun," I told her with a smile on my face.

"Only when I let him win," she whispered into the phone.

"Ah, I see," I said, laughing.

"What are you doing now?" she asked me.

"Just came to the diner to get some food before Bingo," I answered.

"What are you having?" she asked.

"Chicken fried steak with mashed potatoes smothered in gravy, and collard greens," I told her.

"Yum, that sounds so good, but so bad for my waist," she laughed.

"Good thing you're not eatin' it, then, right?" I snickered..

"You're mean," she said.

"Nah, just speakin' truth," I told her.

"Well, Romi is dealing the cards so I guess we're playing another round. Go have fun with Gram, and give her a kiss for me," Stacy said.

"Will do, darlin'. Have a good night and I'll see you in a bit."

"Bye, John," she said before hanging up.

Dinner was really good, but like Stacy said, I shouldn't have been eating it. Too much fat. And my workouts in my home gym were few and far between lately. I would have to step up my workouts to make up for this meal.

I headed over to the church but didn't see Gram's car yet. I waited out front until I heard her tires squeal as she pulled into the lot. I gritted my teeth and bit back the lecture that would fall on deaf ears. I walked over to help her out of her car and said hello to Beverly.

"Crazy bat," was all Beverly said as she walked by.

"Beats walkin'!" Gram yelled at Bev's back.

"Hey, kid! How's things?" Gram asked me as she took my arm and I helped her up the steps.

"So far, so good," I said noncommittally.

"Good, good. How's the girl? She come 'round yet?" Gram asked me with a smirk on her face.

"Come around to what?" I asked her.

"To stayin' here with you, of course," she said and slapped my arm with her other hand.

We had just reached the top of the stairs and I let go of her arm and turned her to face me. I put my hands on her shoulders.

"Gram, she can't stay here. She has to get back to work as soon as her cast comes off in a couple of weeks. We want to be together, but we don't know how that is going to look yet, so please, just let it go," I said sincerely, hoping she would get the message.

She just harrumphed and went into the church. We found Beverly at a table with two seats saved for us. I went to the front and got Bingo cards and markers, as usual. I sat down next to Gram, and she organized her cards. She wouldn't look at me, but that was okay. She'd eventually get the picture that she couldn't create an outcome out of the sheer force of her will, although it was mighty.

We played for several hours before I told Gram it was time to leave. It was getting close to dark, and she needed to be off the road by then. She and Beverly stacked their cards on the table, and I took them and the markers back to the front then met the ladies at the door.

As soon as we got outside, I knew something was wrong. My SUV was sitting lower than it should be. I walked over and looked at it carefully. All four tires had been slashed and were flat. I swore out loud. I told Gram and Beverly to go on ahead and I would call for someone to pick me up.

I called Eduardo, who I knew was on duty. I told him what happened, and he promised to send someone to pick me up. Then I called the car rental agency and reported the damage. They promised to have a tow truck pick up the SUV as soon as possible. "Shit!" I screamed into the air. "Not freakin' again!"

About 20 minutes later Martin pulled up in their rental to get me. He got out and looked over the car.

"Looks like a pretty big knife, Sheriff," he said. I concurred. I would have to file a report in the morning, but there was no reason to bother my deputies with this tonight. Nothing could be done. My insurance would certainly take a hit, though.

When we got home, Stacy was waiting in the foyer for me. She moved as fast as she could to give me a hug when I came in the door.

"John, are you alright? Is Gram okay?" she asked.

"Yes, we're both okay. It was only the car that took the hit," I said.

"Well, I'm glad," she said with her arms wrapped around my waist.

"I'll call Henry in the morning and tell him I need my truck back, new tailgate or not," I told her.

"We'll call it a battle scar," she said with some snark.

"I'm gonna run up and take a shower," I told her as I took her arms from around my waist and set her away from me. I just needed a moment to breathe and realize we were all still okay. She looked confused as I headed up the stairs, but I couldn't help that.

I stood in the shower, set as hot as I could stand it, and just thought. Things had been going so well that I'd forgotten the danger was still out there. This was just a reminder, I'm sure, that he could hit any one of us at any time.

I stayed in the shower for a long time, long enough for the water to get cold. I hoped no one else wanted a hot shower tonight. I heard movement in Stacy's room, and after I dried off and wrapped the towel around my waist, I opened her door to the bathroom. She was sitting on her bed looking bewildered.

I knocked on the door even though it was already open, and she looked up. I tilted my head slightly, silently asking to come in. She just shrugged.

I walked over to the bed and sat down in front of her. I tucked a loose strand of hair behind her ear, then left my hand cupped around her face.

"You know, babe, there are going to be times when one or both of us need some space, some time to think alone. It doesn't mean anything is wrong, or we're over, or anything like that. It just means that we need some time. And that's okay. Okay?" I asked.

I could see in her eyes the moment she realized I had referenced the future, and she smiled. I leaned my forehead to meet hers, and asked, "Okay?"

"Okay," she said.

I called Henry first thing the next morning and asked him to bring my truck to me. He told me that the tailgate was on order and would take another two weeks to come in.

"Just slap some plywood over the hole, Henry. I need my truck back today," I said.

"Okay, okay, calm down, Sheriff. I'll have it ready in about two hours," he said.

"Fine. Just bring it to the station. I'll have one of my deputies pick me up." I ended the call somewhat abruptly.

I called the station and asked the deputy on duty to send someone to get me. He was curious why I needed a ride, but I wasn't in the mood to have to explain it multiple times, so I decided it could wait until I got to the station for one big reveal.

After I drank my coffee, I went upstairs to say goodbye to Stacy. She was already sitting up in bed, her hair a mess and her eyes a little puffy. She looked warm and safe, and I wanted to climb back into bed with her immediately. She looked up at me and blinked several times. She looked dazed.

"Good morning, Sweetheart," I said as I walked over to the bed and sat down. She smiled at me sleepily.

"Good morning to you, too," she said. She reached out her hand to run it along my jaw line.

"You look a little out of it today," I told her, trying to hide a chuckle.

"Well, you should know why. You kept me very busy last night and I loved every minute!" she laughed out loud.

"Some of my best work, actually," I laughed with her.

"Yes, it was. Are you headed out to work?" she asked.

"Yep. One of the deputies is coming to get me. Henry is going to drop off my truck at the station later this morning so I'll have transportation. What are your plans today?" I asked.

"Same old, same old. Working on songs. Probably a couple of rounds of Rummy. Those make Romi happy, for some reason."

"He does seem happier this last day or so. What's causing that?"

"Redecorating my apartment," she said. "He's really working hard with the designer to get it finished, and I think it's going to be in his taste instead of mine, but I won't be seeing much of it for a while, so it doesn't really matter," she said, looking down.

I put a finger under her chin to bring her face up. "Hey, don't get sad talking about the future. Like I said, I have a plan I'm working on."

"Sheriff, your ride's here," Romi called up from downstairs.

"Okay. I have to go but keep that chin up. I expect nothing but smiles when I get home tonight, got it?" I asked with a smile.

"Okay," she answered with a lift of her lips. I placed a soft kiss on her lips and got up to leave. I heard her moving around and looked back. She was getting out of bed and I had to stop and look at the long expanse of leg showing under her sleep shirt. She was one beautiful woman, indeed. I shook my head with a smile and headed downstairs.

Deputy Rogetski was in the living room talking to Barry and Murphy when I came back down.

"Heard you needed a ride, Sheriff. What's wrong with the rental?" She asked.

"I'll tell you all about it at the station," I told her and grabbed my hat. She just smiled and headed for the door.

On the ride to the station I quizzed her about policies and procedures that we had been going over. She was coming along well.

Once we got to the station, I called all the deputies in the office over to let them know what had happened to my rental and to remind them to be on the lookout for that stolen pickup. There had been one or two more sightings, but nothing concrete that would get us any closer to catching this sicko.

I went out on patrol with Rogetski for the day to observe her doing her job. We had just decided to head back to the office when we spotted Gram's Versa in a ditch on the side of the road. She hadn't even fully stopped the car when I jumped out and ran to the little red vehicle.

I opened the driver's side door and found Gram slumped to the side with blood all over her face. I yelled at her to call an ambulance and Henry.

I pulled Gram upright and checked over the parts of her body I could get to. She was wearing her seat belt, but there was a bruise forming on her forehead, so she must have glanced off the steering wheel, probably because she drove sitting so close to it. Her arms and legs looked okay and she didn't appear to be trapped.

I heard Rogetski yell that the ambulance was on its way, and Henry was about 10 minutes out.

I tapped Gram on the cheek to try to rouse her. She groaned but didn't regain consciousness. I heard the siren getting closer. I tried to rouse her again, but she just groaned. Then I saw her eyelids flutter like she was trying to wake up. I tried talking to her.

"Gram. Gram, wake up. This is what you get for speeding everywhere you go," I told her.

Still no response.

"Come on, Gram. I think you're faking it, hoping for a really good looking EMT to carry you out of here. Wake up and stop fooling around!"

That got her eyelids moving faster. I knew it. Always the drama with this one.

The ambulance pulled up, along with another deputy. The EMTs wheeled the stretcher over to the car, and I told them that she had been unconscious and unresponsive when I got there, but she was showing signs of waking up.

One EMT reached over and unbuckled her seat belt. He put his arms around her shoulders and under her legs and lifted her from the car. I saw her eyes open. Ham.

The EMT laid her out on the stretcher on a back board and put a neck brace on her. The other EMT asked me for information about her and I told him everything. I looked down at Gram and could have sworn she was trying not to grin. I just shook my head. They loaded Gram in the ambulance and left for the hospital. I hoped she was having a good time.

Rogetski and the other deputy were looking over the car when I turned back around. I started looking, too, trying to find out why she was in that ditch. It was a straight stretch of clear road, not known for animals crossing, so I couldn't figure out what had happened. Until I noticed her driver's side front tire. It had what was obviously a bullet hole in it. Not a very big hole, but enough to force her off the road.

I had a bad feeling about this. I told Rogetski to put out a call for all hunters in the area in the last few hours today to see if maybe someone had a legitimate excuse for shooting Gram's car, but I doubted it. It seemed like our sicko had a new target.

I sent Rogetski and the other deputy back to the office, and I waited for Henry. I searched the floorboards and found Gram's purse. I would have to drive to the hospital to give it to her.

Henry showed up about 10 minutes later. I helped him hook up Gram's car, and told him to replace the tire, but to keep this one as evidence. I also asked him to make sure nothing else had been damaged. He offered to drop me off at the station to pick up my truck and I accepted.

"So. You wanna tell me about the bullet hole in your Gram's tire, Son?" he asked.

"I don't think so, Henry. Let's just keep this between us for now, alright? No sense scaring people that a crazed maniac is shooting cars off the road outside of town," I told him.

"If you say so, Son, but word does tend to get around, especially when your Gram's using them. Best not let her know if you're wantin' to keep this a secret," he said.

He was right about that. Gram would have this spread far and wide as quickly as possible for the attention it would get her.

"You're right, Henry. I won't tell her."

He just nodded and continued driving. I thanked him when he let me off in front of the station about 10 minutes later. I took Gram's purse and got in my truck to head to the hospital.

When I got to the ER, I asked for Gram and was lead to a small exam bay with a curtain around it. I found Gram lying on a gurney in a hospital gown with her eyes closed.

"Gram?" I whispered. "Are you awake?"

"Of course I'm awake, but these damn lights are too bright and my head's throbbin' something fierce. I reached over her head and turned one of the lights off. She held her hand over her eyes and opened them.

"That's better. Thanks, kid." She smiled at me. Someone had cleaned the blood off her face and forehead, and the bruise was really starting to show up on her pale skin.

"Besides your head, how are you feeling, Gram?" I asked her.

"Well, got a big bruise across my boobs, but no one's gonna see that; my neck hurts and I've got a spasm in my back, but otherwise I'm good."

"Are they planning on keeping you overnight, did they say?" I asked.

"Haven't seen the doc yet, but the nurse mentioned something about that. Guess since I hit my head they wanna make sure all my sense is still rolling around in there somewhere," she cackled, then moaned when that hurt her head.

"Well, Henry is gonna fix your car and get it back to you soon. It'll be waiting for you when you get out of here," I said. "I've gotta head home, but call me and let me know what the doc says tonight, okay? I brought your purse." I set it on the little table next to her bed.

"Thanks, kid. I'll be out before you know it!" she said.

I just laughed and shook my head as I headed out. I dialed Stacy's number as I left the hospital.

"Hello," she answered.

"Hey, Sweetheart. How're you doin'?" I asked her.

"Okay. Bored. But still here. Are you on your way home?" she asked.

"Yeah. Gram had a minor car accident this afternoon, and I just left her at the hospital. She's gonna be fine, but I wanted to check on her," I said.

"OMG! What happened?" she cried.

"Just a small blowout that landed her in a ditch. She bumped her head on the steering wheel, so I think they're keeping her overnight for observation. She'll be fine." I was NOT going to tell Stacy my suspicions about the cause of the blowout.

"Oh, okay. I'm glad she's going to be alright. So we'll see you soon?" she asked.

"Yep. Just a little while," I said.

"See you soon, babe," she said and hung up. Hey, she'd called me 'babe'. That was the first time she used a nickname for me. I kinda liked it.

I walked into the house 40 minutes later and Stacy met me in the foyer with a very enthusiastic hug. I hugged her back and kissed the top of her head. She leaned the top of her body back and looked up at me with a smile.

"I missed you today," she said.

"I missed you, too, Sweetheart. How are the songs coming?" I asked her.

"The ones I was sent are coming along fine. The ones I wrote, though, are a little tougher. I need to change up the second one and it's just not happening," she told me.

"Well, I have faith in you. Maybe you just need some inspiration," I said and leaned down to kiss her properly. She immediately opened her mouth to invite me in. I ran my tongue over her entire mouth, then licked her lips. She moaned quietly to let me know how much she enjoyed what I was doing to her mouth. She tangled her tongue with mine, and now I was moaning.

I pulled back a little, placing soft, fluttery kisses around her mouth. Her head fell back with another moan and I couldn't help but kiss the exposed neck she presented. I smiled at the look on her face.

I stepped back and asked if dinner was ready. She told me my plate was in the oven.

"You go eat," she said. "I'm gonna go take a hot bath and think about all that inspiration you give me," she said with a devious grin on her face. Now my head fell back with a moan at the image she planted in my mind.

"Vixen," I said to her as she turned and headed for the stairs. I didn't see

Romi anywhere downstairs, so once Stacy was safely in her room, I went into the living room to brief the protective detail guys. All four guys were in the room since it was nearly time for two of them to go off duty.

"Guys, I don't know if Stacy told you, but my Gram had a car accident this afternoon."They murmured that they had heard.

"The thing is, it wasn't an accident. There's a bullet hole in her tire."This caught them off guard. "This guy is now targeting anyone we know. Since we've had Stacy undercover here, there shouldn't be anyone else in danger, but this has gone too far. I think we need to step up our patrols, including checking our vehicles before driving them. That includes the new guys. One of them is outside, right?" I asked.

Murphy nodded. "Yeah. Kelvin is outside on patrol. Devon will come on at midnight," he said.

"Okay. We need to pass the word to them, too, so they're prepared. I don't even trust that their vehicle is safe at the hotel now. I think this guy has gotten hold of another gun, because the hole in Gram's tire is not from a shot gun. He's just upped the ante," I said.

The men all nodded in agreement with me. Murphy went outside to locate Kelvin to fill him in.

I walked into the kitchen to get my plate and a beer. I sat down at the dining room table to eat and think.

Murphy came over and sat down next to me.

"About what we talked about a few days ago," he started. I nodded.

"I talked to my boss about your idea. He said he has no problem with you going through our training, but we aren't Stacy's usual security company. Working with us wouldn't keep you close to Stacy," he said.

"I know. It was just an idea I had as part of a plan for when this is all over. Thanks for checking. I'll let you know what I decide." He nodded and left the room.

I finished my meal and put my dishes in the dishwasher and set it to run. I headed upstairs to see how Stacy was coming along with her inspirational thoughts in the bathtub.

THE SHERIFF'S STAR

I was stuck. That's the only way to say it. I could not use the second song I wrote. It made me so sad to sing it that there was no way I could sing it all through the tour. I needed another song and quick. I tried thinking of John, but that only distracted me. I tried to think about the nature outside, but that only put me to sleep. I wasn't even dreaming these days, so I couldn't even look to the sandman for inspiration.

It was being in this house all the time, only leaving for PT, and being surrounded by the same very nice men all the time, that made me feel stuck. I needed a change of scene, but I knew that wasn't going to happen any time soon. But I could try.

I went downstairs and found Romi and Eduardo on the couch in the living room. I walked up and stood in front of Eduardo and said, "I need to get out of the house. Can we please go to the park?" He just looked at me, and I could see Romi's jaw drop in my peripheral vision.

"I'm trying to write songs," I said, "But I can't get inspired if I'm staring a these same four walls all day every day, with the same people. I know it might be a teensy bit dangerous, but please, can we go?" I batted my eyelashes even though I knew it wasn't going to work. But I had to give it my best shot.

"I'll call the Sheriff," Eduardo said.

"No!" cried Romi. "It's too dangerous to be on that road! Are you crazy, Stacy? Putting yourself and others in danger just for a change of scenery?" Romi sounded disgusted with me, but I couldn't help it.

"Sheriff, Stacy wants to go to the park. She says she needs a change of scene so she can write."

He looked over at me as he listened to John on the other end, even moving the phone away from his ear slightly. I held out my hand for the phone.

"John. John, stop yelling. I'm telling you, I need to get out of this house. I've never been this still before and I need to see something different. I know it's dangerous, but I can't help it." Romi was shaking his head vigorously in the negative. What did he know that I didn't?

"Okay, Stacy. I'll come home for lunch, then we can all drive in together. But you will be surrounded by those same people in the park that you're with every day. There's no way around that. Let me talk to Eduardo," John sounded frustrated and resigned. That was my fault.

Eduardo got off the phone then went to find Martin. This was one time I was glad I wasn't a fly on the wall for that conversation.

I hid in my room the rest of the morning. Romi was not talking to me, just muttering about shootings and tires and being wrapped around someone's finger. I knew he was referring to me.

I put on my sundress, the only one I had with me, and put my hair up in my ball cap. I made sure my contacts were in and grabbed my backpack. I loaded it with paper and pens and sunglasses in case inspiration struck while we were there. I grabbed the blanket at the end of the bed to take, as well.

When it was time for lunch I dragged my supplies with me down the stairs. Romi was nowhere to be seen, so I just set everything down near the foyer.

I went into the kitchen to check on lunch, and Martin gave me a side eye with a raised eyebrow. He wasn't happy with the plan, apparently. He had made sandwiches for everyone, so I grabbed the big bag of chips and headed into the dining room.

Martin carried in a big plate covered with the sandwiches and yelled upstairs that lunch was ready. He stuck his head outside and called Kelvin, too.

When Kelvin came in, Martin headed outside to relieve him. I picked a sandwich from the plate and took a handful of chips. I was halfway through my food when Romi showed up. He wouldn't look at me and took a seat as far away from me as he could get. He nodded to Kelvin, who was busy chewing and nodded back.

Once Kelvin finished his food, he said goodbye to me and headed back outside. Martin came back in, and Eduardo came upstairs from the basement. He must have been working out. He gave me a look that let me know he was not amused and sat down to eat.

I finished my meal and took my plate into the kitchen. Then I went into the living room and sat on the couch to play a game on my phone. I was getting twitchy. When was John coming home? He'd said lunch time, so where was he? I was about to text him when I heard his truck on the gravel drive.

I heard more than one voice, so I got up and looked out the window. Gram was with him and he was helping her up the steps. Their voices were raised.

"I'm tellin' you, kid, I want my car back today! I have things to do and people to annoy!" Gram yelled at him.

"And I'm telling you that Henry had to order a new tire from Bergen since your car's so small no one around here had one! It'll take a day to get here. You'll live a lot longer without driving, anyway," he yelled back. "You drive like a crazy woman!"

John stopped when he saw all the people looking at him and Gram. He murmured an apology under his breath and headed for the kitchen. I half expected him to come back with a beer, but he had lemonade in a glass. He sat down at the table and motioned for Gram to do the same. She sat down and looked at Martin and Eduardo.

"Hello, boys! Guess I'm with you, today," Gram said.

"No, you're not. I'm dropping you at home on my way back into town after lunch. You need to take it easy today with that head wound," John said as he helped himself to a sandwich. Gram just shook her head as he offered her one. He shook some chips onto his plate and dug in.

Martin got up and asked Gram if she would like a drink.

"Beer," she answered.

"Lemonade," John countered.

"Beer, kid!" Gram said loudly.

"Lemonade, Gram. Doctor said no alcohol today," John said in a steady voice.

Gram folded her arms across her chest and refused to look at John. Martin came back in with a glass of lemonade. Gram thanked him but ignored the glass. John just sighed and kept eating.

My leg started bouncing up and down as I watched the scene play out. I was anxious to get moving. Romi finally looked at me and shook his head. He knew my tells and knew that I was working up to something.

"Gram, are you going to eat so we can go?" I asked. Everyone in the room stopped what they were doing and turned to look at me, including Gram.

"In a hurry, Girlie? I hear you're going to the park. Maybe I'll just go with you and enjoy this sunny day." She looked at John like she was daring him to disagree with her. He just sighed again and resumed eating.

"I just really want to be at the park," I said.

"Um-hmm," Gram muttered and grabbed a sandwich from the plate. I just sighed and resumed my leg shaking.

About 20 minutes later everyone finally finished eating. It was decided that Eduardo and Martin would follow us in their car, and Kelvin would stay at the house since Barry and Murphy were sleeping. We all piled into our respective vehicles, Romi riding with Martin and Eduardo. I was so excited I could hardly stand it. My leg was bouncing like crazy and I couldn't think what to do with my hands. A buzz of energy was running through me. I felt my creative juices flowing even though we weren't at the park yet.

John and Gram didn't say anything on the ride over. I knew John was upset with me, but I hoped he would see how happy this little trip was going to make me, and maybe that would cheer him up.

THE SHERIFF'S STAR

John parked next to the Sheriff's Office, and Eduardo parked next to him. John told me to wait while Martin and Eduardo made a sweep of the area. Once the all-clear was given, Romi got out of their car and John, Gram and I got out of his truck. The men surrounded me, Gram and Romi as we crossed the street to the park.

I felt alive again! The air was warm from the sun, and the humidity was relatively low today so it was comfortable to breath. The grass smelled so sweet, and the flowering trees surrounding the duck pond were beautiful to look at.

Gram and I discussed our options and decided on a spot near a swing set. She helped me put the blanket down and I set my backpack on one of the corners. The wind was light, but I didn't want to risk the blanket blowing up.

John helped me and Gram to sit on the blanket, then he took a seat with us. Romi sat at a picnic table nearby with Eduardo and Martin, who were searching the area with their eyes constantly. I laid down on the blanket on my back, just listening to the sounds of the park and smelling the air. I closed my eyes and just let myself be. I felt John take one of my hands in his, but he didn't say anything. Gram sat back on her hands with her legs spread out in front of her. She seemed content to be quiet for a change.

After a while I decided to get up and go swing, something I hadn't done since I was a child. John looked at me curiously but handed me my crutches. I told him I was going to swing and he followed me. I picked a swing and sat down, putting my crutches on the ground near my feet. I was about to push myself back when John moved behind me and pulled on my waist. He lifted me up and let me go with a good push.

We didn't talk, just enjoyed the time, me flying freely and him pushing me. I could feel the smile on his face even though I couldn't see him and felt like that justified this trip.

I eventually signaled to him to let me slow down, and finally came to a stop. I was grinning from ear to ear and turned to thank him. He was smiling just as big and leaned down to kiss me. I felt completely buzzed and leaned into the kiss. His hand moved behind my head to pull me in closer just as I heard a small voice next to me.

"Hey, lady, can I have this swing? It's my favorite," said a little girl with brown pigtails and a gingham dress on.

"Of course, you can," I said as I pulled away from John and reached down for my crutches. I smiled at her and John and I returned to the blanket as she pushed off.

Once I was seated again, I noticed that Gram appeared to be dozing on the blanket. I asked John quietly to hand me my backpack. I pulled out a pad and pen and started writing. I felt a new song in my heart and wanted to get it down on paper.

About an hour later Romi jumped up and ran to John with his phone out. He stopped in front of John with his brows furrowed and his face getting red. I leaned over to see what was upsetting him. It was a DM on my IG account.

I see you in the park. I could reach you so easily. Soon.

I immediately started looking around us. John got up and went over to Martin and Eduardo with the news. I leaned over and shook Gram's shoulder to wake her. I knew we would be leaving right away. She jerked awake and I told her we had to leave. She stood up and helped me up, too. We worked on folding the blanket but John came over and just grabbed it up in a ball. He took Gram's arm and Romi came over beside me. Martin and Eduardo walked on either side of us and we all crossed the street.

John told the guys that he had to drop Gram off at home on our way back to his house. They nodded and got into their car. Romi went with them once I was in the truck. John looked over at me with thunderclouds in his eyes. He didn't say anything, but he didn't need to. I knew he was mad.

Gram wanted to know what was wrong, so I told her about the message. She just hissed through her teeth and swore.

"Damn sumbitch! Really knows how to ruin a good nap!" she said, a little too loudly for the interior of a vehicle. I just nodded. We pulled up to Gram's house and John helped her from the truck. Martin came and stood next to me as John walked Gram up to the house and saw her inside. She turned and waved at me and I waved back.

John came back to the truck and Martin got back in his car. We all headed home in silence. I was not going to let the sudden end of our trip ruin what had been a wonderful time, so I headed upstairs to continue working on my song.

A few hours later I heard Martin yell up the stairs that dinner was ready. I put down my pen and looked at my pad. I was happy with the way the song was coming along. It would be a great replacement for the second, sad song I had written.

I headed downstairs and found everyone but John at the table. Barry and Murphy were already awake and ready to go on duty. It was almost dark outside, so I knew I had been working for a long time. I asked the table where John was. Martin answered that he had gone back to the station to do some paperwork.

My spirits fell a little bit. Why hadn't he told me? He could have at least texted me. I pulled out my phone and saw that it was on silent, and John had texted me to say he was feeling antsy so he'd gone back to the office for a while.

I felt a little better and managed to enjoy my dinner. Martin and Eduardo had grilled salmon and served it over wild rice with asparagus on the side. Very yummy.

I decided to take a bubble bath since I didn't know when John would be back. I got my cast wrapped in plastic and headed upstairs to relax. I enjoyed the hot water until it wasn't hot anymore, then got out of the tub. It was getting late but I hadn't heard anything more from John, so I texted to see when he would be home.

While I waited for a response, I put on some night clothes and climbed into his bed. I set my phone on the bed beside the pillow so I'd hear when he texted me back. I eventually fell asleep waiting for his text.

I heard the click as soon as I sat in my truck.

It was nearly 10 o'clock and I was just leaving the office. I had wanted to catch up on some paperwork and get things ready for Rogetski's trial run this coming week. I was going to let her act as Sheriff to see how she did.

I had parked at the very back of the lot next to the office, and there was only one other vehicle in the lot, which I knew belonged to the deputy on duty inside. I didn't dare call using my cell phone, so I sent him a text that there was a pressure switch in my truck and to call the bomb squad. I knew I'd be waiting for a while, so I tried to stay calm.

I couldn't believe Meznu. The balls it took to plant a bomb on a vehicle in the Sheriff's Office parking lot were huge. At least it wasn't the middle of the day and the lot was almost empty. The deputy came out and approached the truck. I told him to stop so he wouldn't come too close.

"The bomb squad is on its way, Sheriff. They said not to move at all if you can help it."

"Get your car out of the lot, Deputy," I told him. I didn't want any collateral damage it if could be helped. He jumped in his car and headed left, probably to park next to the bakery a few doors down.

My phone dinged and I tried not to jump. It was a message from Stacy. I didn't dare try to send another text, so I couldn't answer her.

My deputy came running back into the parking lot. He told me he was going inside to let the deputies on patrol know what was going on. I told him to let them know not to come back to the office until they received the all-clear. He nodded and headed to the back door.

I could feel eyes on me but didn't dare even turn my head to look around. I'd always heard that when you are about to die, your life flashes before you. Mine didn't. All my thoughts were of Stacy and our short time together. I hoped that this all worked out, but if it didn't, I knew Stacy would blame herself, and that bothered me almost more than the prospect of dying. I decided that if I got out of this in one piece, I was going to tell her how I felt, pride be damned.

Time passed slowly, and I was starting to sweat. I didn't dare move a muscle, not even a finger, so I was starting to cramp up. I was just contemplating the risk of stretching my legs when I heard the rumble of a heavy truck turning into the parking lot. The heavily armored vehicle pulled to a stop about 50 feet away from my truck and parked.

Two men got out and went to the back. I watched as they pulled on various pieces of padding and protective gear. They also brought out what looked like a large military-type duffel bag that looked to be heavy. They set the bag down near the truck and went back to their vehicle. Two men got out of the back of the vehicle and started lining up sandbags about 10 feet from me. They lined up four rows of sandbags on top of each other, making a wall about as long as my truck. Those two men took up positions on the other side of the bomb unit truck.

One of the padded men came up to me and introduced himself. I told him that I had heard the click of the pressure plate as soon as I sat down. He had a long metal pole with a mirror on the end and started searching under my truck. After he was done, he used a large flashlight to search under my seat. He said he could see the pressure plate and the bomb.

He told me that they were going to try to replace my body weight with their sandbag "dummy," which was the bag I had seen. He said as soon as I was out of the seat to run to the other side of the wall they had built and cover my head in case the bomb detonated. I told him I understood, not willing to risk nodding.

They had me lean forward very slowly as he and his partner lowered the dummy behind me. I scooted inch by inch off the seat as the dummy added more weight to the seat. As soon as I could clear the cab I ran for the wall and tossed myself to the ground. So far, no explosion.

The bomb techs came over and told me to head into the building. They said that due to the configuration of the bomb and pressure plate, the safest course of action was to detonate the bomb rather than try to remove it. My insurance man was not going to be happy about this. I could only laugh because I could feel myself going into shock. I was starting to shake and felt very cold. I thanked them for getting me out of the truck and headed into my office to find a blanket.

About 20 minutes later there was a loud explosion that rattled the windows, and the phone started ringing in the office. I went up to the front and told the deputy to tell people that the explosion had been due to a vehicle fire, so there would not be a mass panic. I also told him to send a broadcast to the deputies on patrol not to park in the lot, but on the street in front of the office since the lot would be covered in debris.

I grabbed some baggies and went outside to start collecting debris for evidence. My truck was demolished from the front end to halfway down the bed. All the tires were destroyed, and the only thing still intact was my tailgate with the piece of plywood screwed into it.

I placed a call to Henry, who had been awakened by the explosion and asked him to come over with his flatbed. He said he was on his way. I thought about texting Stacy but figured she would be asleep by now, so I didn't. I did call Barry and tell him what had happened. They hadn't heard the explosion, which was good. They were far enough away.

Gram lived closer, though, so I called her to reassure her. She sounded wide awake when she answered.

"What the hell was that, kid? Sounded like downtown blew up!" she yelled.

"Just a vehicle fire that got out of control. Didn't want you to worry," I said.

"Why would I worry, kid? I'm not downtown!" she cackled.

"Well, okay. Get some sleep, Gram. I'll talk to you tomorrow."

I got back to collecting evidence. The bomb tech came over and said I would need to fill out a report for them and handed me a clipboard. I walked over and leaned against the wall to complete it. I was sick to death of filing these reports.

All of a sudden, my hand holding the clipboard fell to my side, and I punched the wall with the side of my other fist. "That rat bastard blew up my truck!" I screamed. "Shit!" No one even looked at my tantrum. I guess it was a normal response to almost dying.

I scrubbed my free hand over my face and settled back into the report. When I was finished, I walked it back over to the bomb tech I had first talked to and handed him the clipboard. He thanked me and walked back over to his truck.

I suddenly realized that they would be the ones collecting evidence, not me. I was still rattled from the whole experience. Instead, I got the deputy from inside and had him help me tape off the parking lot so no one would park there until the evidence collection was done. Then we'd have to clean the area of any remaining debris.

Henry was just pulling in when I looked up. He stopped near the entrance of the parking lot and his jaw hit the ground, sort of. He turned and looked at me and just stared. Then he looked over the remains of my truck, saw the tailgate, and burst out laughing. I couldn't help but join in.

He stopped laughing, though, when I told him that the remains had to be driven to Bristol as evidence. He just shook his head, and he and I got busy loading the biggest parts onto the flatbed and strapping them down. I was going to owe him big time for this.

By the time Henry left and the techs had collected every piece of the bomb they could find, it was almost 2 a.m. I asked one of my deputies to come take me home and collapsed at my desk while I waited. This was so bad.

There was no way I could spin this that Stacy wouldn't feel responsible. The vehicle fire story wouldn't work because she'd still be suspicious of how my engine mysteriously caught fire, and that would lead her to think of Meznu. The truth was even worse. God, my head hurt.

The deputy I had called knocked on the door frame of my office.

"Sheriff, ready to go home?" he asked.

"Yeah. Guess so."

I dragged myself out of my chair and followed him out the front door. I was silent as we drove, but still watched the side mirror to see if we were followed. No one else was on the road. That bastard was probably still watching the parking lot, enjoying his handiwork.

When we pulled up to my house, the only light was from the TV in the living room. I thanked the deputy and walked up the steps and into the house. I heard the car turn and head back down the driveway.

I found Barry on the couch watching another one of the documentaries that he loved. I just stood there, not sure what to do. Barry got up and went into the kitchen and came back with a beer that he handed me. I nodded in thanks and dropped into my armchair.

I heard a door open upstairs and the sound of crutches in the hall. Stacy called softly down the stairs.

"John, is that you?" she asked.

I looked up and saw her looking down at me with concern.

"Yeah. Just having a beer then I'll be up," I said.

Still staring, she said, "Okay," and headed back to bed.

I laid my head back on my chair and drank some of the beer.

"This is so bad," I said to Barry as Murphy came up from the basement where he'd been checking doors and windows.

"Yep," Barry said. He looked at me for a long moment and just shook his head. Murphy just looked at me as he headed over to join Barry on the couch.

"She's gonna go ballistic," Murphy said.

"Yep," I said. I finished my beer and took the bottle out to the kitchen. I leaned over and put my hands on the counter as I hung my head. This was so bad.

I stood up and left the kitchen. I said goodnight to the guys and trudged up the stairs. I started undressing as soon as I hit the upstairs hallway and entered the bathroom from Stacy's side so I didn't disturb her. I took a quick shower to wash the smell of smoke and burned rubber off me, then wrapped the towel around me and brushed my teeth.

I grabbed my clothes and threw them toward the hamper in the bedroom, then dropped my towel and got into bed. Stacy was sleeping on her side so I slid in behind her, big spoon to her little spoon, and scooped her up next to me. She wriggled a bit then settled down and gave a soft moan. I smiled despite my exhaustion. She was so cute. I kissed the top of her head and fell asleep.

When I woke, the sun was up and Stacy was not in bed. I heard noises coming from her room, so I put on a pair of pajama bottoms and wandered over there.

She was frantically throwing clothes into her suitcase and her backpack and guitar case were on the bed. I stood and stared for a moment, then went over to her. I walked up behind her and put my hands on her arms. I must have startled her because she turned around swinging.

"Stacy, what are you doing?" I asked, trying to stay calm.

"I'm leaving, obviously!" she yelled.

"I see that, but why? And where are you going?" I asked her, starting to panic.

"Anywhere away from you, your Gram and this town! Maybe to Bergen. Maybe a hotel near the hospital so I'll be close when it's time to get my cast off. Just away from here!" she screeched. I took a deep breath and used my arms to lead her to the bed and set her down.

"Why are you leaving?" I asked.

"I was about to head downstairs for breakfast when I heard Barry talking to Murphy about how YOUR TRUCK ALMOST BLEW UP WITH YOU IN IT! WHY DIDN'T YOU TELL ME?!" she screamed and started trying to beat my chest with her tiny fists. I backed away and grabbed her fists and held them between us.

"First of all, you were sleeping when I came home. Second of all, I didn't know how to tell you because I knew you'd act just this way and try to leave. You can't go. You're not going to be any safer anywhere else," I said.

"Maybe not," she said with her head hanging low, "But you and Gram will be."

I let go of her fists and grabbed her in a bear hug.

"I'm gonna be fine, and so is Gram. And so are you if we stay together. I can't be where I'm not with you, Stace. I have to be able to lay eyes on you and know that you're safe," I told her with all the emotions I was feeling on display. I felt tears building up behind my eyes. I loved this woman, I realized. This wasn't the time to tell her, when emotions were high on both sides, but I would tell her soon. I'd learned my lesson last night. There were no guarantees about tomorrow.

I could feel her tears on my chest, and she hiccupped. I rubbed my hands around on her back and she did the same to me.

Suddenly I needed her like never before. I pulled back and looked down in her eyes, puffy from crying. I leaned down and kissed her softly. She ran her hands up into my hair and kissed me back with fervor. I opened my mouth against her lips, and she welcomed me home. I learned the inside of her mouth with my tongue and brought my hands around to her sides so I could run them up and down alongside the sides of her breasts. She moaned and leaned back, pulling me with her.

I pulled away just long enough to put her backpack and guitar case on the floor, then I resumed my exploration of her mouth and body. This was why I was alive. This woman.

We were curled up in bed together with the blanket over us some time later when there was a knock at the door.

"Who is it?" Stacy asked.

"Romi. Tom called and is coming here today. He'll be here in about an hour."

I groaned, knowing another difficult conversation was about to take place.

I kissed Stacy and rolled out of bed. I put my pajama pants back on and headed to the bathroom.

"Better get up, sweetie and gird your loins. This is not going to be fun," I said as I left.

Stacy was in the shower when I left my room dressed for the day. I had put on old clothes because I was going to join the cleanup crew down at the office once this conversation was done.

Stacy came downstairs while I was drinking my coffee, wearing shorts and a tank top. I offered her a cup of coffee and she accepted. While it was brewing, I asked her what she thought Tom would say.

"About us, or about this nut job?" she asked.

"About any of it," I answered.

"I don't know, John. I really don't know."

We sat down at the dining room table to drink our coffee, neither of us in the mood for food. Just as we finished, I got an alarm on my phone that a car was coming up the drive. I checked the cameras and saw it was a BMW SUV. I showed Stacy and she nodded. It was Tom. She headed for the foyer to wait for him, and I headed to the armchair. Figured I'd at least be comfortable for this.

I greeted Tom at the door and offered a hug. He didn't take me up on it. He looked mad. I led him to the living room where John, Romi, Barry and Murphy were already seated. I introduced Tom to Murphy and told him to have a seat. Someone had brought over a couple of dining room chairs to add to the seating.

I sat on the arm of John's chair, staking my claim from the get-go. I wasn't going to hide my relationship from Tom. He needed to deal with it.

"So, what Romi told me is true. You and the Sheriff are a thing," Tom said with disapproval evident on his face.

John took my hand in his.

"Yes, Sir, it's true. Stacy and I are together for as long as she's here." Wait. What? I didn't like that qualifier. That's certainly not where I was going with this. I was looking at forever, not 'here, now'.

Tom cleared his throat and continued. "The label wants to see more work done on the song you gave them. They don't think it's completely commercial yet. They also want you back in Nashville, like yesterday. I realize you don't get the cast off for another few days, and you may not be weight-bearing right away, but as soon as you can walk on that leg, you need to come back. We can tell people you got a bad sprain on a hike or something. I don't know, but we need you back to your usual schedule."

I didn't say anything. Leaving was too painful to think about. John didn't say anything, either. He just looked at Tom, then looked at me. I shrugged at him. I didn't know what to say.

Tom just kept looking at both of us, then he held up his finger like he'd had an idea.

"I'm going to tell the execs that you fell while hiking and broke your leg, and that you're recuperating away from Nashville to stave off any negative publicity. I'll tell them you're undergoing PT and will be able to go on tour as scheduled. That should get them off your back some and buy you a little time." He smiled at his own idea.

"Do you think they'll be okay with it?" I asked.

"They'll have to be, otherwise there will be too much speculation about your health and about the tour being delayed. They'll want to avoid that at all costs," he said.

I looked at John and he just looked at his hands in his lap. I guess he didn't feel like he had a say in any of this, but that couldn't be further from the truth. But Tom was right, we had to tell the execs to explain my long absence and to get them off my back about going back to Nashville.

"Okay, Tom. You're the expert. I'll leave it to you. I'll have to call you after I see the doc and tell you what the updated timeline is."

"Got it. I need to take Romi with me to the hotel. We have to start making plans for LA and for the tour. We've got scheduling and travel to start working on. The label gave me a list of the cities they want you to perform in, and we have a lot of work to do. The tour is going to take more than 6 months," Tom said.

I just sighed. It was going to be so much work. And what about John? I couldn't imagine going six, or more like eight, months without him! We had to figure something out! John kept saying he had a plan, but he never told me what it was, so I didn't know if he really had one at all.

I got up and headed into the kitchen to look out the window. I didn't dare go out on the back porch anymore. I propped my crutches against the counter and leaned on the sink as I stared out. I was watching a squirrel digging for nuts when I heard soft footsteps behind me, and a strong arm wrapped around my shoulders. John reached down and nuzzled the skin where my neck met my shoulder, and I shivered in pleasure. But I kept silent. The ball was basically in John's court right now.

I heard the front door shut and figured Romi and Tom had left. John pressed fairy type kisses along the sensitive area of my neck, and I just melted into his chest. He wrapped his other arm around my waist, and I was cocooned in his warmth.

I heard the basement door open and close. Barry and Murphy must have gone down to work out.

I turned my head up, searching for John's lips. He met me and licked my lips to open them. I opened to him and let him lead me where he wanted to go.

Suddenly, I was in his arms, and he was carrying me up the stairs. He took me into his room and closed the door with his foot. He set me gently on the bed and leaned over me. He continued the kiss I had started in the kitchen, and he consumed me. he started to push my shirt up my chest, and I sat up so he could remove it.

He released my lips long enough to pull the shirt off over my head, then he laid me back down and ran his hands slowly over my lace-covered breasts. He reached under me to undo the hooks and slid the bra straps down my arms until the bra was off and tossed it over the side of the bed.

He looked down at my naked breasts and smiled before latching onto one hardened nipple and sucking. My back arched and I moaned with such intense pleasure I wasn't sure I'd survive it. His fingers plucked and fondled my other breast, and he pulled the nipple until it was as hard as the other one. He moved his mouth to love on my other breast and his hand reached down for the button on my shorts.

I reached my hands up and ran them over his chest and his biceps. I wanted to see him like he was seeing me, so I pushed at his t-shirt to try to remove it.

He pulled his hands from me and grabbed his shirt from behind and pulled it off. He tossed it somewhere across the bed, but I didn't care. He was spectacular to look at. His pecs moved as he ran his hands over me, and his abs were works of art. He obviously worked hard on his body to be in shape for his job.

I ran my fingers over the Adonis belt that ran into his pants and pulled at the waistband. I wanted to see all of him now. I ran my hands down his forearms and pushed his hands to his pants. I undid the zipper on my shorts, and wiggled to get them off. John took the hint and pushed his pants down and stepped out of them.

He crawled onto the bed and hovered over me with his arms on either side of my head. I knew that this time would be different, that this was more than sex. This was making love. I wanted to tell him how I felt.

"John, I, um, I l-love you," I said, nervous of his reaction.

He smiled down at me and leaned in for a kiss.

"That's good, Stace, because I love you, too."

I wrapped my arms around him and pulled him down to rest on my body. I didn't care about the weight, I just wanted to hold him, all of him. And I wanted to hear those words again. And I did, over and over that afternoon.

We stayed in bed talking and making love until about dinner time. John had called into the office to let them know that he wouldn't be coming in after all but was told that several of the townsfolk had shown up to clean the parking lot, and it was almost back to normal, so John wasn't needed. He was encouraged to take the day off. So he did.

We headed downstairs to take our turn fixing dinner, only to find that Eduardo had jumped in and started cooking already. John and I stayed in the kitchen to help, and unfortunately, talk between the men turned to my stalker.

John and Eduardo were debating about where he could be hiding out, and what he could be up to next. John reached into the kitchen drawer where he had put my old phone and pulled it out. He tried to turn it on, but it was obviously dead. He dug around in the drawer until he found a charger and plugged the charger and my phone into the wall outlet.

When he could turn the phone one, he pulled up my missed messages. There were 73 unknown caller messages. He showed the phone to Eduardo, who just shook his head. Doug was still trying to reach me on that phone. But at least he hadn't found my new number. John turned off the phone and left it to charge.

I was pouring lemonade into glasses when an alarm sounded on John's phone. He looked at it and said that it was Romi and Tom coming back. Barry and Murphy both came into the kitchen to confirm with John. Soon I heard a knock on the front door and Barry went to open it and let them in.

Murphy started setting the table for all of us. I pulled down two more glasses and poured more lemonade. Romi came in and gave me a hug. He whispered in my ear, "You smell like good lovin' , Chica."

Ew, gross. I should have showered, I guess. But I didn't really hate the idea that I smelled like John loving me all afternoon. I didn't want to forget those hours.

Tom was sitting in the living room talking sports with Barry, Murphy and Martin. I went in and sat in John's armchair. I looked at the TV but didn't see it. My mind was elsewhere.

I was trying to picture how John would fit into my life. I knew he loved his job and his town and didn't know what he'd say about leaving all this to follow me on the road.

I could ask him to move in with me, but we would still be living out of suitcases for a long time. Would he get bored? What would he do to fill his time while I was working? And I'd be working and rehearsing until all hours.

That wouldn't be fair to John, to ask him to leave his world to live in mine with nothing to do. And what about Gram? Would he be able to leave her? Would he be willing to leave her?

The more questions I had, the fewer answers came and the more depressed I got. When they called us in to dinner, I mostly moved food around on my plate and didn't eat much. I had been so happy earlier, but now reality was taking a bite out of my day, and it sucked.

After dinner I left the table without saying anything and headed up to my room to work on my "not commercial enough" song. I had a few ideas, and since I hadn't worked this afternoon, I was behind.

I had been working for about an hour when there was a knock on my door. I called out for whoever it was to enter.

John came in, looking sheepish. He stopped just inside the doorway and waited for me to say something.

"You can come in, John. I need a break anyway," I said as I put my guitar back in the case. He walked over and sat down across from me.

"What's on your mind, John," I asked him.

"I was going to ask you the same question," he said. "You hardly ate any dinner and left without saying anything. Did I do something wrong? Did I tell you how I felt too soon?" he asked.

"No. Nothing like that. I just started thinking about how unfair it would be to ask you to come with me when I leave. I would feel terrible asking you to give up your job and your town and your Gram to come on the road with me where you wouldn't have anything to do. I want to ask you to come, but how can I?" I felt tears running down my face and I started sniffling. I wiped my nose but couldn't look at John after my word vomit. I had assumed a lot, and now I was embarrassed.

John got up and came over to me, sitting on his knees with my hands in his.

"I bet you're embarrassed after saying all that, but please don't be. I've been trying to figure out how to invite myself along when you leave. I've thought about leaving here to go with you. I'm even training Rogetski to take over for me so I can take vacations, or even a leave of absence, if needed. Don't be embarrassed for asking or thinking of asking. I want to be with you as much as it sounds like you want to be with me." He reached over with one hand and tucked some hair behind my ear.

I reached up with one hand and cupped his face. He was so sweet and thoughtful. But I still didn't want to drag him away from his life here into a life of boredom. This would require some thinking.

I didn't have a sofa in my room, so the only place we could sit together was on the bed. We made our way there and sat with our backs against the headboard.

I told John exactly what my schedule would be like for the coming months so he'd know what my concerns were about how he could spend his time.

He pondered the idea of getting a job with Nashville PD, but then he wouldn't be able to take time off right away, or take a leave of absence. And I got the idea that he wasn't thinking of leaving Whirlwind permanently, anyway. Just time away. That would be better than nothing.

Eventually, Romi knocked on the door and said Tom was leaving. John and I headed downstairs to see Tom off. After he left, we all sat down to watch a movie with Martin and Eduardo. I fell asleep halfway through the movie, and John woke me to go to bed. We headed upstairs and into John's room for the night.

The next morning, John hitched a ride into town with Devon, who had been on duty patrolling the outside of the house last night. He didn't have a rental yet, and I could only imagine how that conversation with his insurance agent was going to go, especially after the first two claims he'd filed.

I spent the day working on the new songs and Romi was shut up with Tom working on the trip to LA and the tour. John texted around lunch to let me know that since he didn't have a car, he would be staying in town for lunch today. I sent back a few heart emojis and went back to work.

A short time later I heard an alarm go off, and Barry hollered downstairs that it looked like John's grandmother's car coming up the drive. I went to the top of the stairs and waited to see if it was her. I couldn't think why she'd be coming by when John wasn't here. I hoped nothing was wrong in town.

Barry confirmed that it was her car and went outside to greet her and help her in. She was grinning like a loon with her arm in his when they came into the house.

"Hey, Gram! What brings you out here today?" I asked as I hugged her.

"Came to see how you're doin', Girlie. All that excitement the other night could have just sent you to packin'. Wanted to make sure you were still here with the kid!" she said.

We walked into the living room and she sat down in John's armchair. I sat on the couch close to her. I wondered how she knew so much about how I reacted. I doubt John told her. She seemed to have the inside track on everyone, including me.

"What makes you think the bomb would have sent me packing, Gram? As you can see, I'm still here."

"I know all that, but I know how you think, and you'd think that this was all your fault and would want to get out of town to protect us, especially me and John. That's what would have sent you packin'. Tell me I'm wrong!" she cackled as she spoke.

I ignored that challenge.

"What makes you think you know me so well, Gram? We've known each other only a few weeks and have only seen each other a handful of times. What makes me so easy to read?" I asked, genuinely curious.

"Love," she said succinctly. "Love makes you want to protect those around you, and I've seen how you and the kid look at each other. There's love there."

I just smiled at her. I couldn't fault her logic.

Gram got up and went into the kitchen. She came back with two glasses of sweet tea in her hands. I grabbed one from her so I could help her sit down.

She asked about my new album and the songs I would be singing. We talked about celebrity news and compared gossip. We passed most of the afternoon this way, and it was lots of fun. It also kept my mind off things for a while.

John got home around dinner time. He invited the deputy who brought him home in for dinner. I headed into the kitchen to start working on dinner. Gram came in and helped me. John went upstairs to change clothes. The deputy sat in the living room with Barry and Murphy.

Gram helped me fix country fried steak for everyone, with roasted red potatoes and broccoli. It was fun to cook with Gram because she never took anything seriously, and never used a recipe. She kept me laughing the whole time.

We called everyone to dinner and fixed a plate for Kelvin, who was patrolling outside. Once we sat down, Gram kept us laughing with stories of

John from his childhood, like the time he went frog giggin' and fell in the pond head first, or the time he tried to make fire using a magnifying glass in the sun and set fire to his jeans. Not so funny at the time, but hilarious now.

An alarm went off, and John checked his phone. Barry got up and looked at John, who just shook his head and said that Tom and Romi were coming up the drive. Barry went to the front door to greet them and make sure they got in alright.

They both came into the dining room and sat down. I asked if they wanted to eat, but they'd eaten at the diner earlier. I went back to my food when Tom spoke up.

"I have some strange news," he said.

"What?" I asked.

"The company that usually provides security for you has been closed down by the government. Apparently, the protection details were gaining access to clients' accounts and stealing them blind. Now the owners are in jail, and the company is kaput. Romi and I have been going over your accounts all day and they all seem to be okay, no signs of theft. But that means we need new coverage starting when you leave here."

"Why don't we hire the company all these guys work for?" I asked. "I mean, I know these guys are probably tired of me, but surely they have others?"

I looked at John and saw him look over at Murphy and smile. I wondered what that was about.

"I've got a call in to the head office already to see what we can work out. From what I've gathered, most of their business has been within the US, so it would be something different for them to work outside the country. It'll take some planning, for sure." Tom said.

I just nodded, sure Tom would work it out. Gram looked around the table and cackled for no apparent reason, and I laughed with her.

Tom just shook his head at us and stood up. He said his goodbyes and left the house. Barry followed him to the front door to lock up.

John clapped his hands with news. He looked at me and smiled.

"My new cruiser will be here tomorrow, so I'll have transportation again," he said proudly.

"That's awesome," I cried and wrapped one arm around him. "How did it happen so soon? I thought for sure that the insurance would dicker around for a while to avoid the expense." I said.

"Apparently, Mike down at the insurance office told them that it was a line-of-duty vehicle, and it was totaled in the line of duty, so they had better get on the stick. I wasn't expecting it this fast, either, but I'm glad, especially since now I'm down a personal vehicle," John said. I grimaced at the reminder. John leaned over and put his arm around my shoulders. He whispered in my ear, "I love you."

I smiled and leaned in to whisper the same thing back to him. Gram watched us closely and grinned like a maniac.

John walked Gram out after dinner. She waved at me as I watched from the window. I still wasn't comfortable outside, so I stayed in the house.

John came back in saying he'd forgotten to get the mail, so he was going to ride to the end of the drive with Gram, then walk back. Murphy nixed that idea and a look passed between them. He tossed John the keys to their rental so John could drive down and back, which was much safer.

Or so I thought. When John came back home, he looked ready to kill. He held out a letter to me.

"This was in the mailbox, but wasn't mailed," he said. It was addressed to Darci.

Murphy stepped up and put out his hand as though asking for the letter. I handed it to him. He told us he would take it outside and open it on the porch to make sure nothing had been put in the envelope. Again, a look passed between him and John.

We watched out the window as Murphy used his multipurpose tool to open the letter, then set it down on the porch railing. When nothing happened, he shook the letter, open end down, to see if any substance came out. Nothing did. Murphy held the letter up to the porch light and seemed satisfied that there was nothing dangerous in the envelope. He brought the letter back in to me, and I pulled out the sheet of paper inside, touching as little of it as possible.

The message was made with letters cut from various sources, like magazines and newspapers. It was very clear that I was still in danger.

> *I know what you're doing with him.You should be dead right now. If I can't have you, then the world can't have you.You will die very soon, and so will he.*

I dropped the letter and fell to the floor after it. My crutches fell too, making a loud clattering sound on the floor. I cringed at the sound but felt numb all over.

I saw John squat down next to me but didn't acknowledge him. My mind went to a very dark place. I had to get out of here, I had to run, but where? I had nowhere to go and was an easy target for this guy. I had to run, I had to run...

I started to get up, shaking all over and screaming in my head, but by the look on John's face, I was screaming out loud and he grabbed for me as I tried to turn and run without my crutches. He had a hand on each of my arms and was saying something to me I couldn't hear for all the noise in my head. He pulled me into him and wrapped his arms around me tightly.

I continued shaking and had the fleeting thought that I was in shock again. I couldn't understand how John could see that note and not be shaking too. Then I realized he was. I felt myself get cold, and I wrapped my arms around John's waist. I held on to him as much to hold him up as he was holding me up. I felt tears start to fall from my face and soak into his shirt. Then I felt wetness in the hair on top of my head. He was crying, too.

Gradually the shaking subsided, and we both pulled away slightly to look at each other. We were a mess of tears and shock. I looked down at where the letter lay crumpled on the floor between us.

The numbness had faded, and I suddenly felt warm all over, but not in a good way. I pulled away fully from John, and leaned back until I fell into the armchair sideways with my feet hanging over the side. I looked up at John. He looked grim, as I'm sure I did.

He bent down and retrieved my crutches and leaned them against the armchair for me. He bent down again and picked up the letter by one corner and headed into the kitchen, probably to get a baggie.

I looked around at all the big, scary men around me, and knew by the looks on their faces they were worried. I didn't see Romi anywhere, but suddenly heard him coming down the stairs. He stopped at the bottom and looked around. He walked toward me and stopped in front of the armchair.

"What happened now?" he asked with a resigned look on his face.

"Threatening letter left in the mailbox," I said.

"Where is it?" he asked in a monotone.

"John has it in the kitchen," I told him and pointed in that direction.

He headed for the kitchen, and I could tell by the shriek that he saw the letter. He raced back into the living room and tried to drag me out of the chair by my hands. I just relaxed into the chair and stayed put.

"We have to get out of here now," he screamed at me, still pulling at my hands.

"And go where, Romi? This guy, your roommate, knows where I go and who I'm with. There is nowhere else to go," I said, trying to be calm so he would relax.

"How can you be so calm?" he screeched.

"I'm not calm, but there is no use in getting excited. We're at his mercy until he's caught, and everyone is trying their best. Getting upset and making stupid decisions will only make things easier for him. I don't intend to do that. If I'm going down, I'm going down standing tall and facing it head on," I said, then turned to sit in the chair the right way.

John must have heard what I said, because he came to stand in front of me and said, "We really are doing our best, Stace." He turned and went upstairs. I knew he was feeling like he'd let me down again. I also knew he needed some time to himself, so I went upstairs with Romi to hang out in his room for a while to calm him down.

I sat with him for a couple of hours and we played Rummy, then we did a crossword puzzle from one of the books he had brought me in the hospital. All the books had ended up in his room somehow.

By then, I figured John had had enough time to stew, and I got up and went to my room. I went in the bathroom and knocked on his door. He wrenched the door open and grabbed me in a huge bear hug.

"I love you; I know you're doing your best," I said into his neck as he held me.

"I love you, Stace. I'd lay down my life if it meant getting you out of this," he said.

"Don't say that. I want us both to come through this." I rubbed my hands up and down his sides and could still feel some of the scabs from when he was run into the river. I shivered at the memory and hugged him tight.

"Come on," he said, pulling me into his room. "Let's go to bed."

I laid awake most of the night, waiting for an alarm to go off or something else to happen. It really pissed me off that this guy was still running around my town, and I hadn't been able to stop him. This was what I trained for, and he was still getting the best of all of us. I couldn't wait to get even more training when I put my plan into motion, but until then, I had to keep moving forward as best I could. Which wasn't good enough. Stacy was still being terrorized.

I tried not to toss and turn and disturb Stacy, but it seemed she wasn't sleeping well, either. She kept mumbling in her sleep and twitching her arms and legs. I hated that even her sleep was being impacted negatively by this asshole.

Eventually I got out of bed, careful to not wake Stacy. I put on some athletic shorts and a t-shirt and headed down to the basement to work out. Maybe I could tire myself out.

I found Martin in the home gym when I got there. He was just finishing on the treadmill, and I asked him to spot me on some weights. He said yes and we got started.

We took turns lifting, and he could out-lift me by nearly 75 pounds. That meant I had some serious work to do to catch up. After we finished lifting, I jumped on the treadmill and ran 7 miles. I was getting tired and headed upstairs again.

I took a quick shower to rinse off, then climbed back into bed. Stacy seemed to settle down once I was in the bed again, and I wrapped her in my arms and pulled her into my chest. She sighed in her sleep and snuggled against me. That made me feel like a man, like I was her protector, even in sleep. I finally drifted off, but my sleep was fitful.

I woke up to an empty bed. I heard the water running in the bathtub and Stacy humming in the bathroom. I smiled to myself and rolled over to go back to sleep. I heard the water turn off and Stacy moving around.

I was just about back to sleep when I heard a loud yelp and a big splash. I rushed into the bathroom naked and found Stacy, all of her, sitting in the bathtub with a derisive look on her face. Then I realized that her cast was in the water, too.

"What happened, sweetheart?" I asked her.

"I slipped getting in and now my cast is underwater," she said, frowning.

"Tell you what. Finish your bath and I'll drive you over to the hospital to get a new cast put on. We'll call them when you get out of the tub. Do you want some help?" I asked again.

"No, I can do it. I can't believe I managed to go this long without messing up, and now I get the damn thing soaking wet. Ugh!" she cried.

I just smiled and shook my head. I closed the door and got dressed in my room. I heard her moving around again and heard her bedroom door open. I took a chance and went into her room while she was trying to dress.

She had wrapped a towel around the cast since it was dripping, but the added weight was making it hard for her to move around. I told her to sit on the bed and I got her clothes for her and helped her dress. She pulled her hospital paperwork out of her nightstand and showed me the number to call.

I called the hospital and told them what had happened. They said they could see her in the cast room at 10:15 a.m. That only gave us 45 minutes to get there, so I hurried Stacy.

We stopped downstairs long enough to make to to-go cups of coffee, then headed for my truck. Which I didn't have. Shit. I'd forgotten.

I asked Murphy to drive us to the hospital. He was just finishing his breakfast and took his plate into the kitchen. We all walked out to his rental and climbed in.

The drive was quiet. I knew that Stacy was uncomfortable wearing a soaked cast. She seemed lost in thought so I let her be.

I talked in low voices with Murphy about upping my workout, and he gave me some suggestions of exercises I could add to my routine. He knew about my plan and why I wanted to increase my strength, but I hadn't filled Stacy in yet. Murphy said he would work out with me tonight if I wanted. I told him I would appreciate the guidance.

Stacy still hadn't said anything when we arrived at the hospital. Murphy dropped us off at the front door, and said he'd wait in the car for us unless we needed him. I felt relatively safe in the hospital, so I waved him on. I followed Stacy to the elevator and pushed the button for her. She looked up at me and smiled slightly. I wasn't sure exactly what was bothering her, but I figured she would let me know when she was ready.

We walked into the waiting room and checked in. I sat next to Stacy and took her hand in mine. She gripped my fingers tightly. I asked her what was wrong.

"The whole way here I was expecting something bad to happen," she started. "I couldn't get that out of my mind. On top of which, I'm still mad that I got my cast wet and we had to leave the house at all." She looked so forlorn, I leaned over and gave her a light kiss on the lips. She smiled at that.

"It's okay to be afraid. You've got good reason to expect the worst, but Murphy and I are here for you, and you're going to be okay. We'll get you a new cast and head home, and all will be good," I said with all the hope in my heart that I wasn't lying.

A young man in green scrubs opened the door to the back and called Stacy's name. I got up and went with her to the back. The man introduced himself as Maurice and walked us down a short hallway to a work room. He indicated an exam table that Stacy should sit on, and I helped her onto the table. Maurice stopped at another table and pulled on gloves and picked up what looked to be an saber saw.

He told Stacy that it would not hurt her, would only cut the plaster. I could sense Stacy's nervousness as she looked at the saw, and reached over to take her hand while I stood beside the table. Maurice turned on the saw and started cutting the cast. It had gotten so wet it was easy to cut and came off with no complications.

Stacy gasped when she saw her leg for the first time in several weeks. It was noticeably smaller than her other leg, and the hair had grown. There was also a wound from where the pins had been placed.

Maurice reached across his table for some wipes and began cleaning Stacy's leg. He checked the surgery site and said it looked good. He chuckled as he asked if she wanted to scratch anything while the cast was off, but Stacy was too shocked to answer. I told him to go ahead and put the new one on.

He had Stacy keep her leg out straight as he put on a stockingette. He then had her move down the table so her leg would hang over the side. He began wrapping the plaster tape around her leg and adding water as he went. It took about 30 minutes to make sure the cast was just so, and once it was done, I saw Stacy's shoulders relax. Maurice asked if she had any questions, but she did not. I handed her the crutches and helped her down off the table. I called Murphy to let him know that we were on our way out.

Murphy was waiting for us at the front of the hospital, and I helped Stacy into the back seat. I suggested she sit with her cast on the seat since it was still a little wet and she probably didn't want it to get stuck to the carpet on the floorboard. She turned and sat as I suggested.

Stacy didn't say much on the way back but did ask if we could pick up lunch from the diner on the way. I looked at Murphy for his input. He said that as long as I called it in and someone could bring it out to the car, it should be okay.

I called the diner and placed our orders and ordered some extra for those at home. When we pulled up to the curb, Mariah came out with two big bags of Styrofoam containers for us. I took the bags and set them in my lap. I thanked her and gave her a hefty tip. She waved and ran back into the diner. With as many diners as were watching out the front window, I wondered if we'd set a precedent for curbside pickup from now on. Geez, Mary would hate that!

Murphy stopped at the mailbox so I could get the mail, then pulled up in front of the house and came around to grab the bags from me. I got out and helped Stacy out of the car. I told her to grab her crutches so I could carry her up the stairs. I thought she'd had a rough enough morning not to have to climb the stairs on her knees. Or her butt.

Romi met us at the door. He had still been asleep when we left, and wanted to see for himself that Stacy was alright. She assured him that she was fine, and the cast was successfully replaced. He followed her into the dining room and sat down next to her. I went into the kitchen to help Murphy. We distributed the food containers around and saved one for Devon, who was patrolling outside. Barry said that once he ate, he would relieve Devon.

He told us that he had talked to Tom that morning and Tom was in negotiations with the company they were currently using to provide the security going forward. I liked the sound of that.

Stacy just nodded and ate quietly. I was getting worried. She had been quiet for so long and it wasn't like her.

After lunch, Stacy headed upstairs. I helped clear the table and get rid of all the trash. I took the trash out to the can and came back in. I hesitated for a moment, then went upstairs to see Stacy. I knocked on her door and she asked who it was.

I told her it was me, and she told me to come in. She was lying on her bed in her clothes, on her side. I sat down on the other side of the bed and laid on my side with my head in my hand.

I reached out with my other hand to rub it along her jaw. She opened her eyes and looked at me.

"I'm worried about you, sweetheart. You've been so quiet. It's not like you. What can I do?" I asked.

"I just didn't sleep well and had some nightmares that I can't get out of my head," she said with a sad sigh.

"Wanna talk about them?" I asked her.

"Not really. It's bad enough I keep thinking about them," she told me, looking down at the bed. "They're all about you getting hurt trying to protect me, and in one of them you died. I just can't get it out of my head."

"Hey," I said softly. I put a finger under her chin to pull her face up so I could look her in the eyes. "I'm not hurt, I'm right here. And I'm going to stay right here until you leave, then I just might go with you. They were just nightmares." I leaned over and pressed a kiss to the top of her head.

"This whole thing is a waking nightmare," she said softly as she lifted one hand to rest on mine.

"But we know it's gonna end soon, and then we'll have our whole lives together," I said with hope in my voice.

"It's the 'how' it's gonna end that worries me so much," she said, moving my hand so she could sit up.

"Can you just kiss me for a while?" she asked me.

"With pleasure," I said as I sat up against the headboard and pulled her into my lap. I started slowly with her lips, then moved along her jaw to her neck and up to her ear. I let my lips wander everywhere I could reach and just lived in the moment. I could feel Stacy relax and my lips moved over her skin, and after a while she began to take part in the kiss.

I don't know how long we kissed, but eventually we fell asleep lying on the bed in our clothes. We must have slept for hours because the next thing I knew, Romi was leaning over shaking my shoulder to wake me up.

"Your Gram's here, John. She's downstairs and I think there's something wrong."

I sat up and tried to carefully pull my arm out from under Stacy's head. I ran my hands through my hair and headed downstairs.

Gram was sitting in my armchair with her arms wrapped around her middle. This didn't look good. Not much bothered Gram.

"Hey, Gram. What's going on? Why didn't you call? I would have come to you," I said.

"There's someone at my house," she said, staring me in the eye.

"What do you mean, at your house? Are they inside? Did you see them?" I asked rapid-fire.

"I had just dropped off Bev and was pulling up to the house when I saw a guy with a shotgun walking around to the front of my house. I hit the gas and turned around and high-tailed it out of there. That's what I mean, kid," she stated firmly.

I pulled out my phone and called the office. I told the deputy on dispatch to get a unit to Gram's house ASAP and look for a guy with a shotgun. I hung up and grabbed Gram into a hug. Then I heard Stacy coming down the stairs.

"You'll stay here tonight. You can sleep in Stacy's room. I don't want you back at your house until we've cleared it, and not tonight," I told Gram.

Stacy asked what was going on and Gram told her. I stood up and went back upstairs to get a better look at my cameras. This guy had already targeted Gram once, and now he was doing it again. I didn't see anything on the cameras, but I kept looking. If he knew she'd come here, maybe he'd come here, too. I called back to the office to see if my new cruiser had been delivered there. I was told that it was in the back of the building and the keys were in dispatch.

I went back downstairs and told the guys to watch the camera app on their phones, that we might get a visitor. I asked Eduardo to drive me to the station so I could pick up my cruiser. I needed a vehicle now.

When we got back to the house, I was told that the cameras were still clear and no alarms had gone off, which I already knew.

After dinner, which Gram insisted on fixing for us, we all sat around and watched a movie that should have been funny, but there wasn't a lot of laughing going on in the house. After the movie, Stacy and I got Gram set up in Stacy's room and she followed me into my room.

It was the next morning when John remembered to look at the mail he had brought in yesterday. And I had another message.

This one was scarier and more gruesome.

> *I'll cut your heart out, bitch. I'll watch you bleed out and stomp on your dead body.*

I only saw the message because I was standing behind John when he opened it. He wasn't planning on showing it to me. I just stood there, my mouth hanging open. I couldn't understand the kind of hate this person had for me. it was just incomprehensible.

I sat in the dining room, just staring out the back door into the woods. I didn't hear anything anyone said, just sounds like talking underwater. My back was stick straight, my hands were shaking and my eyes wouldn't blink. I didn't feel it when John wrapped his arms around me from behind. I only noticed his hands in front of me in my peripheral vision. I didn't notice when he picked me up and carried me into the living room and set me on the couch and covered me with a blanket. I didn't feel the couch cushion sink when he sat on the edge next to me.

Once my eyes were able to blink, they blinked back tears. I could see the scene on the wall in front of me; myself, lying in a street with my chest torn open, bleeding to death, and John next to me, begging me to hang on. I started sobbing hysterically and John sat next to me and pulled me into his arms.

When I started feeling again, it was little things. The beat of John's heart. The wetness on his shirt from my tears, the feel of his breath against my hair. I was taking baby steps back to the land of the living.

Romi brought over a box of tissues and John gave me a handful. I blew my nose and wiped my eyes. He sat down next to John and me and rubbed my back. I felt John take his phone out of his pocket. I heard him call the station ordering a 24 watch on his mailbox so we could hopefully catch Doug in the act.

I didn't think it would work because the patrol car would be visible from any direction on the road, and Doug may be psychotic, but he wasn't stupid. He'd gone this long without being caught. He wasn't going to let himself be caught in an obvious stake out.

Once I was feeling a little stronger, I decided to head upstairs and get some work done. Romi offered to come with me, and I smiled and told John to stay downstairs with the guys. He smiled back and nodded his understanding. I needed some time alone with my friend.

He slowly followed me up the stairs to my room. I threw myself down in my favorite chair by the window. I pulled my guitar out of the case and started to strum random notes. I didn't really feel like doing any work, but playing my guitar was always soothing. He just stared at me like he was afraid I was going to lose my shit any minute. I wanted to reassure him, but I wasn't sure that he was wrong.

I started to play a song, one of the new ones the execs had sent. It was the somber one that I didn't like that much, but it seemed appropriate for my mood.

Then I started playing the song I had written for John. That one made me smile as I thought of him. When Romi saw that, he sat back in his seat and seemed to relax a little. I played the song again and kept smiling.

Then I moved into the faster songs for the album, and pretty soon he was moving with the beat and clapping his hands along with my singing. There was a knock on the door and Gram stuck her head in.

"Can anyone join this jam session?" she asked.

"Come on in, Gram. Romi, let her have the chair, would you?" I asked him.

"Here, Gram. I'll sit on the floor," he told her.

Gram sat in the chair and started clapping her hands along with the beat, same as Romi.

I sang the rest of the songs, and made my way back to the one I wrote for John. I was sure Gram hadn't heard it the first couple of times. She grinned and clapped like her life depended on it. Once I was done, I told her it would not be on the album, but that I might do it live a couple of times during the tour. She was delighted!

Suddenly the adrenaline of singing wore off and I felt very sleepy. I told them that I was going to lie down for a while, and they both headed out.

I slid out of my shorts and my bra and lied down in just my shirt and panties. I pulled the covers up to my head and closed my eyes. That same scene played on my eyelids, and I opened my eyes back up. I heard a soft knock on the door and knew instantly that it was John.

I called for him to come in. He walked over to the other side of the bed, kicked of his shoes and took off his jeans. He got into bed beside me and pulled me up to his side. I snuggled into the crook of his arm and closed my eyes again. This time the scene wasn't there, and soon I was asleep.

I woke up to John's even breathing, and my face cushioned by his chest. I desperately had to pee, so I got up as gently as I could and searched around for my crutches.

I was just coming out of the bathroom when there was a knock on the door. I went up to the door and asked who it was. It was Murphy, so I hid behind the door and opened it with only my top half showing.

"I was looking for John," he said.

"He's asleep right now, but I can wake him if it's important," I told him.

"No, it'll wait. Thanks, though." He turned and went back downstairs.

I looked at my watch. We had missed lunch. I hope Gram wasn't bored down there. Then again, she had all the big, strong men to herself, so I guessed she was happy.

I closed the door and turned back toward the bed. I found John's sleepy eyes on me. I walked back and sat down on the bed and looked at him.

"Who was that?" he asked me.

"Murphy. He said it would wait, whatever it was," I said.

"M-kay," was all he said as his eyes closed again. I was awake now, but knew I had to take my opportunities as they came. I laid back down and curled into John's body. I started thinking of a new song, this time the words came fast and easy. I kept saying them to myself so I would remember them, but knew I had to write them down. I crept out of bed as quietly as I could on crutches, and went to my chair. I found my pad and started writing madly. I wrote and scratched out, wrote some more, scratched out some more, turned the page, and wrote again. The juices were really flowing. Finally, I was satisfied and I tossed down the pen. John was starting to stir, and I was glad because I wanted to grab my guitar and start working on the music for this one. I felt better about this one than the other songs I had written.

Suddenly an alarm went off on John's phone. He was instantly awake and out of bed, pulling his phone out of his jeans on the floor. He looked at the phone, then laughed and brought the phone over for me to see.

Apparently, the bear had returned and brought some friends. There was a large bear near the back porch, and three smaller bears, maybe cubs, running all around, climbing trees and the porch railing. I laughed, too. They were fun to watch.

John was thoroughly awake, though, and reached down to put his jeans on. He sat on the bed to put his shoes on and tie them. I started strumming my guitar as I looked at the words I had written. John walked over to me and leaned down to kiss the top of my head. I looked up at him and kept strumming, smiling as I did so.

"I love you," I said as I strummed.

"Love you more," he said and grinned widely.

"Not possible," I retorted.

He just shook his head and headed out the door.

Hunger finally drove me out of my room about an hour later. I headed downstairs and went into the kitchen to find a snack. I located a box of crackers and some cheese from the fridge and set them on the breakfast bar.

I hoisted myself up onto a stool and started eating. I saw that Gram was still here. I guess she didn't feel safe going home. I wondered if anyone had found Doug over at her house. I supposed not, because there would have been a celebration if he had been caught. I called Gram over.

"Hey, Gram. How're things at your house? Have you heard anything?" I asked her.

"They didn't find him but found some tracks around the house. I don't trust that he won't come back, though. John went over there with Henry to install some kind of camera system around the house, kinda like his. I don't know about all that technical stuff. I think a good gun is all you need, but John insisted."

"I think the camera system is a good idea. You never know when it will come in handy. Like when bears pay a visit like they did here. It's good to be able to see what's going on," I said just as an alarm sounded from someone's phone. I was sitting up looking for where it came from when the gunshot sounded. I heard glass breaking upstairs and pulled Gram to the floor with me.

Romi came running down the stairs screaming that he'd almost been shot. Eduardo and Martin ran up the stairs into his room, but came back out saying there was no sign of a shot. They went into my room, and when they came out, I knew what they had found. Their faces said it all. Suddenly there was another shot through the back porch window. That one sent glass flying into the dining room. I did my best to cover Gram, but I couldn't move well. Romi crawled over and laid down next to me.

I heard Martin and Eduardo run down the stairs and Barry come flying down, too. Murphy was on the phone to John, then called 9-1-1. Another shot came through the back door and I screamed as heat hit me in the back. Romi screamed next to me, and one of the guys, I don't know which one, ran over to me and lifted me off Gram.

I was pulled into the kitchen and laid out on the floor as he checked my back. I could feel the burn as he lifted my shirt. I heard Romi sit down next to me, and Gram was beside him. Another shot rang out upstairs, probably in my room again. I heard the sound of sirens coming down the drive and the shooting stopped. Murphy took off after whoever was shooting, and probably to check on Kelvin, who was supposed to be on patrol outside.

I heard shouting outside, but couldn't tell who was doing it. The sirens stopped as the vehicles pulled to the front of the house. I heard Barry at the front door talking to someone, then two men with a stretcher came into the kitchen.

I was helped to my feet and placed on the stretcher face down. Gram reached up from the floor with her hand and gripped mine. Romi was still screaming so I screamed at him to stop. There was another EMT with him, so I knew he was being taken care of. I heard more yelling at the front door and heard John's voice. Oh, God.

John came running into the kitchen and stopped short at the sight of me on the stretcher. He knelt beside me and looked at me and then Gram.

I told him I was alright, and that Gram had not been hurt, but the look on his face said he didn't believe it. I tried to hold his hand, but he wouldn't let me. The EMTs said we had to go, and John stood as they wheeled me out to the ambulance. As we left the house, I saw another stretcher being wheeled inside for Romi.

I didn't remember much of the ride to the hospital. I must have zoned out. It didn't feel like I was in shock, but just not really present.

Once we got to the hospital, I was taken into a cubicle and my shirt was cut off, and my bra band was unhooked. The nurse told me the doctor would be in soon, and she pulled a sheet over me to my shoulders. I asked her what had happened to me, and she told me it looked like I had been grazed by a bullet.

Now the shock set in. I started shivering and felt like I was going to pass out.

I told the nurse and she added a blanket to the sheet, and raised my feet above my heart. I could hear my teeth chatter and the scene at the house started replaying in my head.

I was still shivering when the doctor, a young man with short, curly blond hair and blue scrubs, came in the cubicle. He introduced himself as Doctor Janssen, and moved the blanket and sheet to take a look at the wound. He poked and prodded around the wound and the pain was grounding me, helping me to stop shaking.

He stated that I was going to need stitches. I told him I was a performer and asked that he leave the smallest scar possible. He just laughed and said he'd call the cosmetic surgeon on call and see if they could help with that. I didn't think it was funny, but, oh, well.

An older woman in blue scrubs came in some time later. She introduced herself as Doctor Norton, the cosmetic surgeon on call. She said she could close the wound with minimal scarring and I thanked her. After she was done, she left me with a paper full of instructions to minimize further scarring and how to care for the wound. No baths for me for a while.

Romi walked in later and sat on the chair next to my bed.

"How are you? Were you hurt?" I asked him.

"Some flying glass caught me. Got a couple of stitches, that's it," he said with a sigh.

"I'm glad it wasn't serious," I told him.

"What happened to you," he asked. "Glass fragments?"

"No, bullet graze on the back," I said and immediately regretted it as Romi fainted and fell to the floor. I reached for the nurse call button. I told them my visitor had fainted and landed on the floor. Two nurses came into the room and brought him around gently. They got him back into the chair and asked if he was going to be okay. He propped his feet on the bed and leaned his head against the back of the chair and sighed dramatically.

"Yeah. My friend got grazed by a bullet, but I'm gonna be okay," he said. I swear he lived for this stuff.

The nurses left and Barry came in. He was here to take me home whenever I was released. Just as he sat down, a nurse I didn't recognize came in and told me I was being sent home, and handed me a bottle of pain pills with my discharge papers. I had a feeling the pills would come in handy tonight.

I thanked her and asked for a gown to wear home since my shirt had been cut and I couldn't wear my bra. She when to the cabinet in the corner of the room and got me a gown. After asking the guys to wait in the hall, she helped me on with the gown and tied it carefully in the back for me. I thanked her again and called for the guys. Good thing I had to go out in a wheelchair because I didn't have my crutches with me.

The nurse got me settled in the chair and we left the hospital. I asked Barry why John hadn't come, and he just said John was helping with the investigation. I knew what that meant. John was in his head again and needed space to reset. It really sucked that that he always seemed to need some space when I needed him most.

We got home about 40 minutes later, and there were still patrol cars in the driveway. I let Barry carry me inside the house and straight up to my room. I wasn't going to beg for John's attention. Besides, I was tired and my back hurt.

I asked Barry if he would bring my crutches upstairs, but just then Romi came in carrying them. I thanked Barry and asked Romi to get me a drink of water so I could take one of the pain pills.

He came out of the bathroom just as John came in my room. I didn't look at John, just shook a pill out of the bottle and downed it with the water Romi brought me. He sat on the bed with me, not leaving my side. I appreciated it. Yes, my feelings were hurt that John didn't come to the hospital, or let me hold his hand when I was hurt. I was sure I would get over it, but right now I didn't want to be over it. I had needed him with me, but he had stayed behind.

"I'm sorry I didn't come to the hospital. I had to stay here to help, and to make sure Gram was alright. How are you feeling?"

"I feel like I needed you with me, but you stayed here. I felt like holding your hand while I was lying on that stretcher in your kitchen, but you couldn't be bothered. And my back hurts. That's how I feel. Goodnight, John," I said as I lied down on the bed on my stomach. Romi took the hint and left, but John did not. He sat down on the bed.

"Again, I'm sorry. I needed time to process, but that could have been done later. I should have gone with you once I knew Gram was safe. I'm trying, here, Stace. I really am," he said.

"Fine, you're trying. Goodnight," I said again. As I said that, I noticed that there was plywood over my window. Tears started leaking out of my eyes into my pillowcase. I sniffled and tried to be quiet, but I couldn't. I saw a hand in front of my face holding tissues. John. He couldn't take a hint. I took the tissues and blew my nose as best I could while lying on my stomach.

I felt John get up from the bed and figured he had finally gotten the hint, but he appeared on the other side of the bed and laid down next to me on his side with his head in his hand.

He just watched me as I cried, pushing hair behind my ear to keep it out of my face. I tried to stop crying because every time I sobbed, it pulled on my back. John laid his hand on the back of my neck under my hair and just laid there.

The pill finally kicked in and I began to feel like I was floating as I drifted off to sleep.

I couldn't do this. I didn't know how to be in a relationship. I kept letting Stacy down when she needed me most. My need to be alone to process things was coming between us. I knew that eventually she would forgive me, but at what cost to her? How could she ever depend on me for anything if I kept it all to myself and left her to deal with stuff on her own?

I was glad she didn't know yet how much I had lost it when they found that bullet lodged in the wall of the breakfast bar, near where they said Gram had been standing when the shooting started. Stacy had saved Gram's life, that's for sure, but had gotten hurt in the process.

I couldn't believe she had been grazed by the bullet. I had punched a hole in my kitchen wall when the stretcher left with her on it. I had almost throttled Romi with all his screaming when he was barely hurt. I had damn near torn down the back porch with my two hands when they found footsteps only a hundred feet from the back of the house.

And then Kelvin. He had sat down on a bench near the side of the house and fallen asleep. He was supposed to be watching the house, but he'd taken a nap. How did I know? I'd rewound the tapes of the camera feeds. He had woken up disoriented and had been no help whatsoever. He had since been fired from his position and was on his way back to Bristol to look for a new job.

And then there was me. Screwing it all up because I 'needed time to process'. Of course I needed to process, just not when Stacy needed me. I felt like my love wasn't strong enough to make up for all my failures.

I went back downstairs to help Gram up. I told her she could sleep in my room and I'd stay with Stacy to check on her during the night. I could tell Gram was beat from all the excitement. She really wanted to talk to Stacy and thank her for what she did, but I told her that Stacy had taken a pain pill and fallen asleep. Talking would have to wait until tomorrow.

I got Gram settled in my room, grabbed a pair of pajama pants from a drawer, and wished her a good night. I stopped in the bathroom to change and went into Stacy's room. I stood by the bed for a few minutes just watching her sleep. She looked so uncomfortable on her stomach. I knew she was a side sleeper, though, so hopefully she would change positions soon.

I crawled into bed on the other side. I laid on my back with my hands behind my head and thought.

What a rotten night. I was glad it hadn't turned out as badly as it could have, but I wasn't sure how much more of this any of us could take. I knew Stacy's nerves were frayed, and Romi was a basket case.

I was worried that the company that Barry and the others worked for might pull out of being Stacy's go-to protection group. Gram could have been killed, just like Stacy could have been. I had never felt more impotent than I did now. Nothing I did was good enough to catch this guy. I felt like I had no power over the situation, and I wasn't setting a very good example for my deputies. Maybe this was a sign that I needed to step down.

I rolled over and laid on my side while I looked at Stacy. She was my world now. I had to find a way to make things better for her. To make her feel safe, to make her actually safe. I reached out and ran a hand down her arm and smiled when she sighed in her sleep. She turned over onto her side and grimaced a little. I waited to make sure she settled back down, then ran my hand down her arm again. I wasn't trying to wake her, just wanted to feel her, to know that she was alive and well.

THE SHERIFF'S STAR

I fell asleep with my hand on her arm. I woke a few hours later to find Stacy staring at me in the dark. In a voice raspy with sleep, she said, "I love you."

"I love you," I said, getting choked up. I moved my hand to rub it up her side, careful not to touch her back. She smiled and cupped a hand on my face.

I reached for her arm and tugged her over to straddle me as I switched to lay on my back. She laid down with her head on my chest and her legs on either side of me. I didn't try to move her or to do anything. I just let her lay there with her ear to my chest and her hands on my sides. I wanted desperately to be inside her right now but knew instinctively that this was not the time, that this was the time for just feeling one another, for warmth and love.

We fell back to sleep like that. I woke later to sunshine and Stacy asleep on top of me. I ran my hand down the hair that fell across her back, but stopped when I got to the bandage on her back. I ran my hands back up her hair, smoothing it away from the bandage. I felt Stacy shift her body to lay on her side, and let her slip gently off me onto the bed. I kept one arm wrapped around her and moved to my side to face her.

She moaned in her sleep. That sound made me immediately hard but I ignored it. Stacy needed her sleep, and I needed to get up and help clean up downstairs. I gently pulled my arm from under her head and got out of bed. I knew that Gram would already be up, but just in case I knocked on the bathroom door leading to my room. When I didn't get an answer, I slowly opened the door and peaked around the corner. The bed was made, and the room was empty. I grabbed some clothes and headed back into the bathroom to take a shower.

When I got downstairs, Gram had already fixed breakfast and everyone else was eating. I made a cup of coffee and sat down at the table. I looked over to the breakfast bar and saw the hole in the wall and the chalk circle around it. I looked out at the back porch at the ruined door and window. I shook my head to myself and said nothing. Gram handed me a plate of breakfast, but I wasn't hungry. I told her no thanks and just sipped my coffee.

I was just finishing my coffee when I heard the sound of Stacy's crutches upstairs, I leaned back in my chair to look up at the landing and saw her there.

"John, can you come help me, please?" she asked.

"Sure," I responded, and took my cup into the kitchen before heading upstairs. I found her in the bathroom.

"I want to wash up but can't get my wound wet. Can you use a washcloth to wash my back for me, please?" she asked me.

"Happy to help, Stace." I grabbed the washcloth she handed me and got it wet under the water faucet. I put some soap on it and ran it around her back, careful not to touch the bandage. I ran the cloth over her sides and under her arms, as well. I rinsed the washcloth and wiped all the soap off, then rinsed it once more to make one more pass to be sure I didn't miss anything. I wanted to take the bandage off to see how bad the wound was, but knew that wasn't appropriate. I handed the washcloth to Stacy and asked if she needed any more help.

"No, I've got it from here. Thanks, though. I feel better already," she said as she smiled at me. I leaned down and gave her a quick kiss. Then I headed back downstairs.

I got out my phone and called Charles at the hardware store. I needed to order supplies.

"Moore Hardware. Charles speaking. How can I help you?" he answered,

"Good morning, Charles. How are you?" I asked.

"I'm good, Sheriff. Heard you had some trouble last night. Those poachers are getting too brave out there!" he said.

"Yeah, they are. I need some supplies to get things back together. I need to order two windows, one for the guest bedroom, and one for the back porch. You should have the measurements on file, right?" I asked.

"Sure do from the time you got those new windows. What else do you need?" he asked.

"I need to patch two holes in drywall, so whatever you think I need for that. One's the size of my fist, the other is smaller. I'll also need a small can of the paint in the kitchen. That should be on file, too. Oh, and I need a roll of screen for the back porch door. That should do it, I think," I told him.

"Okay. The windows will take about a week, but I can have the other stuff sent over later today. Will that work?" he asked.

"Yeah, that's fine. Oh, hey. Has anyone strange been in the store lately?" I asked.

"Not that I've noticed," Charles said, "but my afternoon guy might have. I told him to be on the lookout, but he's in high-school and you can't tell him anything. I did notice recently that we've sold six, six-cell batteries, though. Don't usually sell those unless someone's clearing trees and needs to blast stumps. No one's doing that so's I've heard."

"Okay. Thanks, Charles," I said and hung up.

I went out onto the back porch and started tearing down the ruined screen from the door. I put on my heavy leather work gloves to remove the remaining glass from the window. Then I got a broom and swept up the glass and put it in the trashcan. Then I double bagged the trash to protect the garbage man from getting cut and took out the bag.

By the time I got back inside, Stacy was sitting at the table waiting for her coffee to brew. Romi was sitting beside her, holding her hand. I could understand his need to be so close to her. I wasn't jealous of him. I knew how close they were before I fell in love with her.

"I have to go back to Gram's and finish installing the camera system," I said as I walked up to Stacy. "I should only be a couple of hours. You'll have all the guys here with you. I've got one of my deputies helping me at Gram's," I finished. I ran my hand down her head to her shoulder and squeezed. She looked up at me and tried to smile.

"I understand," she said. "We should be fine. Will you be okay over there?" she asked.

"Yeah, we'll be fine. I want to leave everyone here today, just in case," I told her.

She motioned me to lower my head to hers.

"I love you," she whispered into my ear.

I kissed her ear and whispered back, "I love you, too, babe."

I left to meet the deputy over at Gram's, hurrying so I could get back sooner. I wanted Gram to feel safe in her own home, but I also wanted to get back to mine to be sure Stacy was safe.

I finished at Gram's in about two-and-a-half hours. I decided that since things seemed okay at home, I would go by the station and check in. I wanted to see how Rogetski was doing with her added responsibilities and how the other deputies were doing. I also needed to check in with Hastings. I had really dropped the ball there, with everything going on at my house.

I texted Stacy to let her know my plans. She texted back that she was working with Romi and they were fine.

I got to the station and it felt like it had been forever since I had been there. I stepped into my office and sat at my desk. I'd forgotten how squeaky the desk chair could be. I called Hastings to check in.

"Hello?" he answered.

"Hastings? This is Sheriff Leppard. How are you doing?" I asked.

"I'm okay, Sheriff. Probably better than you from the sounds of things. I hear you've had some trouble out at your place," he said.

"News travels fast around here, doesn't it?" I joked.

"Sure does. Have they caught the guy yet?" he asked me.

"Not yet, but we will. I'm determined. But I want to hear about you. How's your vision now that you've had some time to heal?" I asked.

"Still tunnel vision, unfortunately, but at least what I can see is clearer. The docs aren't sure how long the tunnel vision will last, and HR says I can't come back until I have full vision. I'm on short-term disability right now."

"I know. They told me. I'm sorry to hear that, but I want you to let us know whatever you need, you hear me?"

"Thanks, Sheriff. We're alright for now, but I'll let you know," he said.

"You be sure that you do. Don't make me hunt you down to find out," I told him.

He laughed, as I'd intended. "Will do, Sheriff. You take care, you hear?" he said.

"Will do, Hastings. Will do." I hung up the phone but smiled. I was glad to hear that he still had a good attitude.

I looked over some reports that had been left on my desk and filed them for the county. I went into the bull pen to see who was around, and found Rogetski looking over the report from the shooting at my house.

"How's it going?" I asked her.

"Good, Sheriff. It's good to see you in the office. How're things at your house this morning?" she asked.

"Messy, but I got it cleaned up and supplies are on the way for repairs. How does the report look to you?" I asked her.

"It looks good. I just wanted to go over a few things with you and Ms. Varner. I was going to head over to your place in a bit, but we can go over it now, if you have the time," she said.

"Let's do it." I pulled a chair over and straddled it next to her desk.

We spent 30 minutes going over the report. She asked if she could go to my house to talk to Stacy. I told her that would be fine. She said she'd make sure I got a copy to give to my homeowner's insurance people. I thanked her and got up. I put the chair back where I found it and headed out the back door for home.

I texted Stacy before I left that Deputy Rogestski would be by to talk with her, and that I was on my way home. She texted back that everything was still good, and Gram was itchy to get back home. I told her to tell Gram to wait for me since I had to show her how to use the new system and to download the app on her phone.

When I pulled up to my house, Gram was waiting by her car for me. I groaned. I wanted to be home for a while, but it looked like that wasn't happening. I got out of the cruiser and walked up to Gram.

"Do we have to do this now, Gram?" I asked.

"Yes. I've let that bastard chase me out of my house for two nights now, and that's long enough. I want to go home, kid," she said firmly with her hands on her hips.

"Alright, Gram. I'll follow you home now." I looked up at the house and saw Stacy standing in the doorway. I waved to let her know I saw her. She waved back and grinned.

I got back into the cruiser and waited for Gram to turn around before I followed. Once we got to her house, I loaded the app on Gram's phone and showed her how to use it. I walked her through the alarms and how to reset them as needed, and how to use the app to reach me in an emergency. I advised her that I had her cameras on my phone, now, too, so I could see what she saw.

I told her that the most important thing was to make sure the cameras were on, and not to turn them off. She said she understood, but I wasn't sure. She could be a stubborn one. I told her I wanted them on at all times, not just when she was away. She nodded but didn't say anything.

I had explained all I could and was ready to head home. I made sure the cameras were on and left the house. Gram stood in the doorway and waved as I drove off. I hoped she would be okay.

I was just glad to be headed home where there was no bad news waiting for me. I stopped by the mailbox on my way up the driveway. I looked through the mail and found a message for Stacy. I decided not to give it to her or let her know it had come at all. I folded the envelope in half and stuck it in my shirt pocket. I would put it in a baggie once I was in the house. This asshole was not going to scare Stacy again.

The next few days passed in relative silence. Romi tried to keep me focused on the music, and I tried to stay focused on John. I mean, I had done the recording and touring stuff twice already, but this love I had for John was a new experience, and one I wanted to fully embrace.

I worried every time John left the house, but he texted me when he got where he was going and when he was coming home. I wanted to go to Bingo with him and Gram, but everyone vetoed that idea.

Gram had been doing well at home. John said whenever he checked, her cameras were on, so that was a good thing. I think he expected her to turn them off out of sheer cussedness. And she still might.

The day for getting my cast off was drawing near, and the tension was building between John and me. We had to be touching all the time, no matter what we were doing or who was around. We didn't talk much but made love every chance we got. He started coming home from the office earlier and earlier, and everyone noticed.

Tom had even called to check in, and commented on how much time John and I were spending together. Romi had been a busy little spy. The two of them had been thick as thieves working on the tour prep and getting things ready to record in Nashville. My agent had even called to see how I was doing.

Apparently, Tom had called her with the recent updates and had spilled the beans about my real reason for being in Whirlwind so long. She had not been happy about being kept out of the loop.

I knew I was still getting messages from Doug, because nearly every time John came home in the evening, he had something folded up in his shirt pocket, and he never pulled it out in front of me, just went in the kitchen and put it in a baggie and put it in a drawer. I appreciated him keeping them from me because I knew how I'd react to reading them. I didn't know how many more times I could go into shock and survive.

I just played the songs and practiced lyrics. I played Rummy with Romi most days, and he kept his head down when John was around. I knew he didn't approve of my relationship with John because he felt I was going to get my heart broken. But what he didn't realize was that I was not going to let that happen. However I had to, I was going to be with John, whether it was on the road or at home in Nashville, John would be a part of my life.

The third day was different. Terribly different.

John had texted to say he was on his way home, later than usual so it was just getting dark. About 15 minutes later we all heard the first explosion down the driveway. Then there was another, another, another, and then another, then John spun into the parking area and stopped the cruiser. He didn't get out but looked behind him to see what had happened.

Once he finally got out of the truck, Martin and Eduardo went out to meet him. They stood by the truck, pointing down the driveway and shaking their heads. There weren't any more explosions, so they finally came into the house. I was standing in the window watching, and when they started toward the house, I hurried as best I could to meet them at the doorway. Martin and Eduardo came in first, followed by John. I leaped into his arms and my crutches fell to the floor. I wrapped my arms around his head and held on tight. John wobbled but managed to hang on to me.

I lowered my arms and my body so I was eye-level with him.

"What just happened, John?" I asked, shaking.

"There were some small explosions set along the driveway. I don't know if they were remotely controlled or if that asshole was out there, but they almost ran me off the road," John said.

"Oh, my God!" I cried.

"Shhh, it's okay, sweetheart," John whispered as he carried me into the living room and set me on the couch. He sat down next to me, and Romi sat on my other side. I didn't know where he had been during the excitement.

"Don't coddle me," I said as I turned to him. "John's the one who was almost hurt."

"I'm not coddling you," he insisted. He then asked how John was.

"I'm good," John told him grimly.

I looked at John. "We saved you some dinner, if you're hungry," I said as I laid my head on his shoulder.

"Starved, actually," he said as he settled into the couch.

"Romi, would you go get John's plate, please?" I asked.

He just nodded and got up. He returned a few minutes later with a plate on a hot pad and set it on the table in front of John. I lifted my head so John could sit up and eat. He grabbed the plate and hot pad together and set them in his lap and ate.

"Are you going to call this in?" I asked while he ate.

"Nope. I'm going out there tomorrow and collect any evidence on my own, then I'll file a report. I'm tired of calling in incidents at my own home," he said between bites.

I had to laugh at that.

He had just finished eating when an alarm went off on his phone. He pulled out his phone and looked at it and frowned. He turned to me and said, "It's at Gram's house. I've got to go!" He took off out the front door, and I half expected more explosions to sound as he went down the driveway, but they didn't. I knew it wasn't far to Gram's and expected to hear from him soon that all was good.

But 30 minutes later I still hadn't heard from him. I decided to text him.

Hey. Is everything okay at Gram's?

Ten minutes later I still hadn't gotten an answer.

I tried texting him again 15 minutes later. Still no response. I wanted to jump in a car and head over there but knew that wouldn't be happening.

Finally, about 45 minutes later I got a text.

Someone tried to break into Gram's. Called 9-1-1 and am here with deputies.Will be home with Gram soon.

I sank back against the couch cushions. Not again.

Thirty minutes later, an alarm sounded on the guys' phones. Barry pulled up the app and said the Sheriff was driving down the driveway. No explosions this time. When he pulled up, Barry went outside to help Gram out of the cruiser and up the stairs. John was carrying an overnight bag.

I stood up and greeted Gram and John at the door.

"What happened, Gram? Are you alright?" I asked her as I ran a hand down her arm.

"I'm good, Girlie, but that's more than I can say for him!" she cackled loudly.

"What do you mean, Gram? What did you do to him?" I asked nervously.

"I'm glad to hear you think I did something to him, not the other way around! I shot the little bastard is what I did! Winged him, too!" She was so pleased with herself.

"What?! You shot him? Gram!" I shouted. John came over and stood next to me and put his arm around me.

"Yep! He got the front door open, and I had my trusty .380 with me on the end table, so I picked it up and shot him. Got him in the leg. Left lots of blood behind. Gonna be hell trying to clean that rug," she said.

"Gram's house is now a crime scene, so she has to stay with us for another day or two until they're finished investigating. Fortunately, the cameras picked up the break-in, so Gram is in the clear. They just have to collect evidence and process the shooting," John said, smiling at his Gram.

"Yep. So I'm back!" Gram said loudly.

"Glad you're all right, Gram," I told her.

"Yeah. Glad you're all right, Gram," Romi said as he walked past us and up the stairs. I knew he wasn't handling this well. Gram just chuckled.

"I've got a call in to all the hospitals and clinics in the area. If he shows up for medical care, we'll be alerted and he'll be held," John said.

"Well, that sounds promising," I said as I looked up at John.

"It is, assuming he's smart enough to go for help," John replied.

Gram just rubbed her hands together gleefully and said, "Let's see what I can rustle up for dinner." She headed into the kitchen and I followed her.

She found some steaks in the fridge, and some large potatoes in the pantry. John didn't want anyone outside using the grill, so we decided to broil them in the oven. We wrapped the potatoes in foil and put them in the oven to cook first since they would take longer, then we put together a salad and got the steaks seasoned and ready to go.

Since it would take about an hour for the potatoes to cook, I played cards with John and Gram at the dining room table to pass the time. Once the potatoes were done, John took the pan out of the oven and put in the steaks. He also set the table.

Once everything was ready, we called everyone to the table. Romi didn't come down. John went up to try to get him to come eat, but he said the door was closed and he didn't answer. I knew that meant I'd have to go talk to him after dinner.

Everyone enjoyed dinner because Gram once again entertained us with stories from when John was a child. He had a very exciting childhood living in Whirlwind, and I was kind of jealous almost. While he was running and fishing and hunting and falling into ponds and catching things on fire, unintentionally, I was practicing and singing and entering shows. I'd been fortunate, but he was lucky.

After dinner I headed upstairs. I knocked on Romi's door then went in. He was just sitting on his bed with his back against the wall. His bed didn't have a headboard.

I sat down on the other side of the bed and just looked at him. He knew I could out-stare him, so he looked at me and shrugged.

"What's going on?" I asked.

"It's just all been too much, Stace," he said, looking down at his hands.

"It has been a lot, I agree," I said. "But it's bound to be over soon. Just need to be strong. Can you do that for me?" I asked him.

"I wish it was just about your safety, but part of me—don't hate me—thinks what will happen to me if something happens to you? This job, our friendship, is my whole world. I don't know what or who I'd be if I wasn't your friend and your assistant. And now all this drama, and then there's John, too. I just feel lost and I feel guilty about feeling lost," he said with a sob.

I climbed over closer to him and wrapped him in a hug. I could feel him shaking as he cried.

"You're always going to be my friend, and I hope you'll always be my assistant. But whatever happens with my career, you'll be taken care of. And if, God forbid, something happens to me, you're taken care of in my will. And regardless of my relationship with John, I will always need you and want you around. Do you understand me?" I asked as I rubbed his back.

I felt him shrug against me. Not good enough.

"Romi, do you understand what I said?" I asked again, wanting him to understand.

"Y-yes, I u-understand," he stuttered between his sobs. I pulled away from him and reached down to pull up the blanket to wipe the tears from his face. There was a large wet spot on my shirt now. I looked down at it, then back up at him.

"Drama queen," I joked.

"The best," he joked back.

"Okay. Now that we've cleared that up, what say you go down and eat your dinner? It was really good," I prodded.

"What did you have?" he asked.

"Cod fish, brussels sprouts and deviled eggs," I said with a grin.

"Funny," he said, "smelled like steak."

I grabbed a pillow behind me and smacked him with it. He hit me with his pillow in return.

I climbed off the bed and grabbed my crutches. He got off on his side and went into the bathroom to wash his face. When he came out we went downstairs together.

Romi sat down at the dining room table and Gram brought him a plate of food. He thanked her and smiled. I sat down with him to watch him as he ate. Gram brought me a glass of lemonade. I thanked her and she headed into the living room. John came in and sat down next to me.

"Everything okay here?" he asked.

I laid a hand on his leg and smiled at him. "Yep. Romi and I worked everything out. He's gonna b alright," I said.

He had his mouth full, so he just nodded.

Now that I knew why he had been so cold toward my relationship with John, I could work on making him feel included. I just hoped there would always be something to be included in.

Late the next day Gram's house was released back to her. She and John went over to look at the damage and see what needed to be done. When John came back, he was alone. He said Gram had insisted that she could stay in her own home, that the 'rat bastard' would be to afraid to try to get in again.

The front door hadn't sustained much damage and the lock had been replaced. The cameras were all intact, but the rug couldn't be salvaged. John said Gram moaned and groaned the most about that. I could tell that John was uncomfortable about Gram being home alone because he kept checking the app on his phone, making sure the cameras and alarms were on.

I sat next to him on the couch and tried to distract him with funny trivia I had picked up from one of the puzzle books Romi had brought me in the hospital. John was barely paying attention. I knew he was worried, but I didn't know what I could do, if anything, to help him. So I just sat back and put a hand on his knee and watched the TV. I wasn't paying much attention to the program until I heard my name mentioned. Or, rather, Darci's name. It was a TV magazine show, and apparently I was news for some reason.

The anchor said rumor was I was pregnant with a love child, and that was why I had been away from Nashville for so long. Rumor further had it that I would not be touring this year because of the baby. Even more rumors were flying about who could be the father. They named several medium level stars as possible fathers. Oh, brother. My phone started ringing. It was Tom.

"What the hell, Tom? What is going on and where did this story come from?" I asked instead of just saying 'hello'.

John must have finally zoned in on what was being said because he looked thunderous as he looked at the TV.

"I don't know, Stacy. This is so out of the blue. The recording label has already called me and wants proof that you're not pregnant, and assurances that you're going on tour. Anne has gotten a call from the studio wanting confirmation that your pregnancy won't interfere with filming! I'm trying to find out where the rumor came from, but it's going to take some time to run down.

"You need to make a full-body post immediately to staunch the rumors. I'll take care of things with the label and Anna will handle the studio. Sorry, kid," he said all in one breath.

Romi came over and handed me his phone. He had one of the gossip rags pulled up and the top story was my rumored pregnancy. John took his phone and read the story, getting angrier by the minute.

"John, unfortunately, this is par for the course in my line of work. Rumors start, and we can only play damage control. Don't let it bother you." I put my hand back on his leg and he handed Romi his phone back. He looked at me, eyes full of anger.

"I don't want people talking this way about you. It's all lies. They shouldn't be saying these things. And naming all those possible fathers! It makes you sound like a slut! I won't have it!" He stood and started pacing the living room. My phone rang again, it was Gram.

"Girlie, what are you doing over there? Did you forget to tell us somethin'?"

"No, Gram. I'm not pregnant, never have been, don't know most of those guys, either. It's just a rumor that we are going to quash. No story here," I told her. John just looked over at me and shook his head.

"Gram, I've got to go make a post. I'll talk to you later. Be safe, okay?" I told her and hung up. John was still pacing, but I couldn't do anything about that. I had to make a post ASAP. I got up and headed upstairs to put my face on and take out my contacts. Romi followed me to help.

I got my makeup on, and he picked my tightest shorts and a crop top to wear. John was going to hate this, but I had to show the world I wasn't pregnant. Romi grabbed the light ring and my ball cap and we headed back downstairs. I figured the back porch had enough light for a post, but was dim enough to cover up the color of my hair.

> *"Helloooo, Dorsetters! Well, I guess you've heard the rumor. No, I most certainly am NOT pregnant. I am simply on vacay restin' up for the tour that IWILL BE MAKIN' a few months from now. I have to shoot a film first. I've never been involved with any of the men mentioned in the article and I'm not pregnant. Take a look for yourselves.* (Romi walked around me 180° so they could see me from most angles) *As you can see, I'm my usual self, no baby bump. I hope y'all will all keep watchin' for updates on the album and the tour. Keep believin' and keep listenin'!"*

Romi nodded his head and hit 'Post'. After we finished I noticed John watching from the back door. He still did not look happy, but he no longer looked like he was ready to kill someone. I got my crutches and went back inside to clean the makeup off my face and put my contacts back in. And change clothes.

John followed me upstairs and Romi stayed downstairs, most likely to monitor the social media accounts following our post. I headed straight for the bathroom and John was right behind me. I reached for a makeup remover wipe, but he took it out of my hand and started wiping my face himself. It was good for him to see me made up so he could get used to it. I lived dolled up most of the time, but not in Whirlwind.

He gently cleaned the makeup off my face and threw the used wipe away. He got another one and kept working. After he finished with that one, he grabbed a washcloth and wet it with hot water and wiped my face with it. I felt very clean and very loved. No one had ever done something like that for me. I really liked it.

John took my hand and helped me stand up. He handed me my crutches and followed me into the bedroom. I sat on the bed and he sat down next to me. I could tell he had something to say.

"I like you better without the makeup," he said softly.

"I know. I like me better without it, too, but it's a tool of the trade, as they say."

"I know I have to get used to you looking like that, wearing clothes like that in front of people, but it's gonna take me some time, Stace. I've gotten used to you one way, and now have to get used to you another way. Remember that plan I told you I had?" I nodded my head.

"Well, once you leave, I'll be going to the training program for your new protection company, with the understanding that I will be on your security detail at all times. It's an eight-week program, so I'll be doing that while you're recording your album and filming your movie. Then I'll be with you all the time. They know we're involved, and it doesn't really meet their usual protocol. If they decide not to hire me, I'll just take their course and be your boyfriend/bouncer/security on my own. If you still want me, that is," John was looking down at his lap as he talked, not looking at me. I knew this took a lot of courage on his part and wanted him to know I appreciated it.

"I love the idea of you being on my security detail. That will give you something to do while I work. But what about Whirlwind? What will happen if you're not here?" I asked.

"I'm training Rogetski to take over for me. I figure I'll take an extended leave of absence so she can get used to the job, then they'll hold a special election and I have no doubt she'll win. She's my best deputy and will do a great job," John said.

"So we can be together? All the time?" I asked, too excited to sit still and started bouncing on the bed.

"Yes, all the time," John said, then he put his hand on my head as he settled his lips on mine. He leaned me back on the bed and continued to kiss me gently until I opened my mouth. Then he went all in.

Today was the day. The beginning of the end of Stacy's time here. She was getting her cast off today. I had taken the morning off so I could take her to the hospital for her appointment. Eduardo was following us in his rental.

We got to the hospital just in time to head to x-ray. They took pictures of Stacy's leg, then we went to an exam room to wait for the doctor. We had been waiting about 45 minutes when he finally came in. He was a tall man with salt and pepper hair. He introduced himself to me as Dr. Michaelson. Stacy already knew him.

"Hello, Ms. Varner. How are you doing?" he asked her.

"Good. Ready to get this thing off, though," she said with a laugh.

"Well, let's look at the x-rays and see how things are progressing," he said.

He put the x-rays up on a lighted board and looked at them. He um-hmm'd and nodded to himself several times, then turned to Stacy.

"So, here you see the plate we put on each of the bones, and the screws. Those will stay in place forever unless they have to be removed for some reason later. The bones seem to have healed very well. I am pleased with your progress. I think we can take the cast off and replace it with a removable boot, a big black thing with straps. You will be able to take it off to bathe and let your leg air out, but I want you to stay non-weight-bearing for another two weeks. You will need to do PT starting tomorrow, if possible, to get that leg back up to usable strength. Do you have any questions?" he asked.

"No. I understand. So will they give me this boot when they take the cast off?" she asked.

"Yes. I will put the instructions in the computer now. You can head down to the cast room now and they will be waiting for you. Have a good day, Ms. Varner. Sir," he said then left the room. I helped Stacy down from the table and we headed down one floor to the cast room.

Once there, things moved quickly. A technician used an electric saw to take off the cast. It took a little longer this time because the cast wasn't wet. Once it was off, Stacy's leg was cleaned, and a huge black boot in plastic wrapping was brought to her.

The tech unwrapped the boot and undid all the Velcro straps. He had Stacy scoot back on the table so her leg was up there and opened the inner lining of the boot and set Stacy's leg inside. He showed her how to secure the straps and made sure they were comfortable, then helped Stacy off the table. I handed her the crutches and we both thanked the tech for his help.

I called Eduardo and told him we were headed out to the cruiser. We walked slowly so Stacy could get used to the weight of the boot. I could tell she badly wanted to walk on her leg, but she was following orders.

I waved at Eduardo as we passed him, and I helped Stacy up into the cruiser and put her crutches in the back seat. I was just about to start the truck when an alarm sounded on my phone. I looked at the alert and saw that Gram's car was headed down my driveway. That was odd. She knew we were going to be gone. Well, she'd just have to wait for us to get back, the little snooper.

Eduardo was looking at me from his car and held up his phone with a questioning glance. I nodded and flashed him the okay sign and started the engine. We headed back to Whirlwind.

I had just rounded the curve into my parking area when the scene in front of me registered.

There was a man standing on the top step of my porch with his left hand gripping Gram's right arm and a gun to her head. He had some kind of fabric tied around his right leg. Devon was standing on the ground at the base of the steps with his feet apart and his hands behind his back.

I stopped the truck so suddenly Eduardo tapped my bumper. But I didn't care. I had to get to Gram. I reached back for my rifle, but the man on the steps shook his head and wiggled the gun he held to Gram's head. I brought my hands back in front of me, and slowly opened the door. I told Stacy to get down on the floorboard and stay put.

I stepped out of the truck with my hands held up around my ears.

"Gram, are you okay?" I asked, panicked.

"Yeah, I'm fine. This rat bastard here got the jump on me at home and made me drive him here in my car. He even stole my Bersa." She tilted her head toward the gun, which made me even more nervous. I walked slowly toward them until Meznu told me to stop.

"I want Stacy. I know she's in the truck, I saw her. Tell her to come out," Meznu yelled.

"No. Anything you want to say to her you can say to me. I'm not telling her to get out of the truck until you hand over that gun!" I yelled back.

"Tell her to come here, or Grandma here is gonna get it in the brain pan! I want to see Stacy." He pushed the gun harder into Gram's head. In my peripheral vision I could see Devon making slight movements. It looked like he was trying to get his hands free.

I heard the truck door open and the sound of crutches on the dirt. I turned and saw Stacy walking toward me slowly. I shook my head at her but she looked determined to be part of this.

She stopped just behind me. At least I was in front of her.

"What do you want, Doug? This has gone on long enough!" Stacy yelled at him.

"I want you dead! Just like I've been saying! You should have wanted to be with me, but you ignored me, and now no one gets to have you!" he yelled as he turned his gun in our direction. Stacy tried to step around me, but I was quicker without crutches and moved to the right so I was in front of her again. I could see Devon still wiggling subtly, and I suddenly heard a car pulling up behind me as an alarm went off on my phone. I didn't dare put my hands down to pull out the phone, but knew the alert was about this car. I didn't turn around to see who it was, but hoped they called 9-1-1.

Suddenly I saw Devon make his move. He headed for the steps, running with his head down to take a body shot at Meznu. At the same time, I saw Gram kick the side of Meznu's knee. His arm wobbled and there was a shot. I moved a little more in front of Stacy and felt the burning in my chest immediately.

I fell backward and landed on something soft. Stacy. The pain was radiating from my chest outward and it was getting hard to breath. I tried to move off Stacy but couldn't.

I heard shouting as someone behind me pulled me off Stacy and someone was yelling that Meznu was subdued. Everything started to get black around the edges, and I could barely hear someone talking, saying they needed a chopper immediately. Was that for me? Was someone else hurt? I hoped Stacy was okay after I fell on her. That was my last thought as the blackness swelled around me.

Eventually I woke up, but wished I hadn't. The pain was incredible. And there was something in my mouth and throat. Oh, no. I had the slightest hint of déjà vu. Stacy had been in this same position just weeks ago.

I tried to look around by just moving my eyes but couldn't see much. I could see an IV pole with several bags hanging on it, and a window, but that was about it.

It felt like one of my hands was trapped in something. I moved the hand and whatever was around it squeezed. I looked in that direction, and suddenly I could see Stacy's head pop up into my line of sight.

She smiled and squealed excitedly. She reached for something on the bed and I heard her say, "Mr. Leppard is awake." Someone answered but I couldn't tell what was said. I blinked several times as I looked at her. She seemed to have survived my landing on her. I couldn't believe she was here with me.

The door opened and I could just barely see a nurse come in. She was tall, with short dark hair and purple scrubs. She came around the bed to the IV pole and looked at the bags. Then she looked at the machines and made notations on a tablet. She looked down at me and smiled and introduced herself as Emily.

"Hello, Mr. Leppard. As you've probably deduced, you've been intubated. Please don't try to talk or remove the tube. You also have a chest tube, so please try not to move your left arm around since it might knock the tube loose. You have a nasogastric tube that we'll be using to feed you. I can bring you a pad of paper and a pen. In the meantime, blink once for 'yes' and twice for 'no', okay?"

I blinked once.

Stacy laughed. "Boy, that looks familiar," she said.

The nurse looked confused.

"Oh, I was in this same position just a few weeks ago," she told the nurse.

"Um, okay. That's a rather strange coincidence," Emily said. I wanted to nod but didn't dare.

"I'm going to head out," Emily said, "here's the remote. The big red button is for the nurse, and the TV and bed buttons are also on here, but don't try to adjust the bed just yet." She made a notation on the whiteboard by the door and left.

"Well, I'm sure glad you're awake," Stacy said. "The doctor was in here earlier, but you were out cold. I was beginning to wonder if you'd ever wake up. You've been out for two days."

I could feel my eyes grow big in astonishment. Two days! Good grief! I wanted to ask about Meznu, but couldn't. Stacy must have read my mind.

"That idiot Doug is in the hospital, too, under guard. He got an infection from Gram's gunshot when he tried to break in. He's handcuffed to his bed. It's awesome! I peaked in his room. Made me feel good. All the bad stuff is over now. You can just rest and get better. I'd like to stay at your house for the next couple of weeks, if that's okay?" I blinked once.

"Cool. Romi and I can get some work done and I can have Zoom sessions with my band. Once I can put weight on my leg I have to get back to Nashville to start rehearsing in person and recording, or I'll be late getting to LA. We've let the security guys go home to rest before starting their new duties. I'm sure there'll be a delay in you taking that training course, but Murphy said the offer's still open whenever you recover. I'm guessing this means you won't be able to join me right away, though. You need time to heal."

She leaned over and kissed my cheek. I felt a tear roll down the side of my face onto my pillow.

Stacy ran her hand down that side of my face to wipe away the tear. I wished so much I could talk to her. I had so much I wanted to say. I tried to say it with my eyes.

"I love you, too, big guy," she said, tears pooling in her eyes, too. I was able to give her a small smile. She could see my words in my eyes.

I heard a ding from her phone. She pulled the phone out and read the message.

"Okay. I have to head out. Romi got a new rental and he's ready to head home. To Whirlwind. I'll be back in the morning, alright?" I blinked once.

"Good. You get some more sleep and it won't be long until I'm back here with you. Sleep tight." She kissed my cheek again and left.

I laid there, moving my feet and legs for something to do. I lifted my right arm and flexed, but that made my chest hurt. I closed my eyes and thought of Stacy. I remembered our nights together. I remembered our date and the time in the park. I remembered watching movies with her and her falling asleep halfway through them. I could hear her voice singing the songs for her album. It was almost like she was with me. Finally, I fell asleep.

I felt a hand on my left shoulder shaking me awake. I slowly opened my eyes and saw a woman in a white coat standing next to my bed. The embroidery on her coat said 'Dr. Robechard'. I looked at her and blinked.

"Good morning, Mr. Leppard. I heard you woke up yesterday. That's very good news. How's your pain level this morning? Blink once for good, twice for bad."

I took stock of my pain and decided it wasn't bad. I blinked once.

"Good, glad to hear it. I know the nurse told you about the chest tube. That will be in for a few more days, as will the ventilator tube. There was considerable damage to your left lung, but based on your age, and apparent good health and workout regimen, I expect you to make a full recovery. You'll probably be in the hospital for two weeks or so while we monitor your breathing and the health of the damaged lung. I would ask if you have questions, but that wouldn't be fair. Do you understand all of this, though?" she asked. I blinked once.

"Great. I'll be back to check on you tomorrow. Try to stay calm and get all the rest you can. I believe you have a visitor, which should make you happy. Have a good day." She left the room, and the door opened again, and Stacy walked in.

"Good morning! Are you feeling okay?" she asked. I blinked once.

"Awesome! Guess what? I drove myself! Can you believe it? Romi was never an early riser, and I had to be here early since I have a Zoom call later this morning, so I drove. It felt so good to be able to go by myself!" she said excitedly. I blinked once.

"Oh, Gram came over last night. She wanted to come with me, but the doctor says she has to stay at home for a few more days to recover from all the excitement. She wasn't hurt, but she is up there in age, and the doc wants to err on the side of caution, I guess. Gram is hating it! She wants to come see you. She told me to give you her love. I think I might go sit with her tonight for a while if I get enough practice in today. She's so funny! She never runs out of stories about you!" I blinked once.

"I think I've finally got that first song 'commercially ready', as the execs would say. I tossed out the second one because it was too sad, but the third one is coming along. I think it'll be ready for the album soon. My band is happy to be back at work, too. They haven't heard the songs I wrote, so it'll be fun to surprise them."

"I bet I know what you would like. How about I give you a sponge bath?" I blinked once.

"Good, I'll call the nurse and get what we need," Stacy said.

"I knew that would sound good. Let me check the bathroom for a washcloth. If not, I'll get one from the nurses." She got up and headed around the bed to the bathroom. She picked up the remote and called the nurses' station.

"We need supplies for a sponge bath, but with my crutches, I can't get them. Can you help, please?" she asked. I heard a nurse respond that someone would be in in just a few minutes.

While we waited, Stacy pulled the right side of my gown down my arm and down to my waist. She smiled as she looked at my body, but frowned as she saw the large bandage on my chest and the chest tube for the first time. She looked angry, too. She ran her hand up and down my left arm until the nurse came with bath supplies. Stacy thanked her and got busy with my bath.

I had to admit, the warm water felt good, and I felt better being clean. She stroked gently around the bandage without getting it wet and stayed clear of the chest tube. She was very thorough around my abs and the left side of my chest. Then she washed my face, and I could feel the washcloth pull on my growing whiskers. She must have noticed because she said, "Tomorrow I'll bring your razor. Would you like that?" I blinked once. Anything she wanted to do was fine with me.

Stacy dried me with the towel and pulled my gown back up. She sat down in the chair and held my hand. She leaned down and kissed my knuckles. I squeezed her hand in response.

She told me she had called her parents and told them the whole story now that it was over. They had been aghast to hear what she had been through but sent their thanks to me and the protection detail for her safe delivery from the situation. I waved my hand at that. I didn't feel like I deserved their thanks, but I wasn't in a position to argue the point.

Stacy stood up and said she had to go. She had a Zoom meeting in an hour and didn't want to be late. I blinked once. She promised to be back tomorrow to shave me, and with news from home. I didn't know what kind of news to expect, but I blinked once anyway. She leaned down and kissed my cheek then left the room.

I felt around until I found the remote and held it up where I could see it. I could just see the TV on the wall in the corner of the room and decided to see what was on during the day. I flipped through channels until I found a reality show about building cars. I turned the sound down and just watched mindlessly for a while until I fell asleep.

I arranged to have my physical therapy at the hospital so I could save time by doing it when I went to visit John. I had so much practice time to make up for with the band that my days were taken up with that. I always made sure to visit John in the mornings, though.

He was on the ventilator for almost a week. I could relate to how happy he was to get those tubes out of his body. The chest tube had come out the day after the ventilator tube. He was moving his left arm like crazy to make up for having to keep it still for so long.

I'm ashamed to say that his voice after he got the tubes out was sexy in how raspy it was. I told him so, too. He laughed or tried to. Mostly he just coughed and smiled.

Now that he could raise his bed, we could see each other better. Sometimes we played word games on the phone, or did crossword puzzles out of the books we had used when I was in the hospital, or sometimes we just talked. He was still confined to the bed, so I kept up with his baths and his shaving, although he should have been able to shave himself. I think he just liked having me leaning over him so my boobs were at eye level. I told him that, too. He tried to laugh again. Cough. Cough.

My PT was coming along well. I was rebuilding some muscle in my leg and I had good range of motion. Only another week then I could put my leg on the ground, but that also meant I was leaving. I hoped John would be out of the hospital before I left, but it wasn't looking good. He was still in ICU.

I was there one morning when John's doctor came in. She seemed like a nice lady who enjoyed her work.

"John, do you mind if I speak in front of your visitor?" she asked.

"She's my girlfriend, so you can say anything you want in front of her, Doctor," he said.

"Well, John, I think we can move you to a regular room tomorrow. I want you to start OT for your lung capacity, as well. How has the pain been?" she asked.

"It's bearable. Mostly hurts if I turn too much or if I take too deep a breath," he said.

"All perfectly normal. I also suspect you have a higher pain tolerance than most, so I'll take what you say with a grain of salt. I'll get the move set up. I also think we can work on getting you out of bed today to sit in the chair and try going to the bathroom. I'll have one of the nurses come take out your catheter so we can see how you do. Any questions?" she asked.

"No, I think you've explained everything well. Thanks for all your help," John said.

"You're welcome. Now it's time to work on getting you home," she said as she left the room.

"Yay!" I squealed as quietly as I could. I was so excited for John.

"I'll be so glad to get out of this bed," he said with a sigh.

"I'm so happy you get to sit in the chair and go to a regular room! That's progress!" I said.

Suddenly the door swung open hard and we heard, "Hey, hey, hey, let's get this party started!" as Gram came barreling into the room.

I jumped up and gave her a fierce hug and led her to the right side of John's bed so she could hug him. She gave him a sweet one-armed hug and kissed his cheek.

"How ya doin', kid? They ready to spring ya yet?" she asked.

"They're springing me to a regular room tomorrow, and I finally get to get out of bed today," he said.

"You've been slacking long enough, kid! Time to get up and get moving!"

"I have a better idea. Let's hear what really happened the day I got shot. How did you wind up at my house and how did Devon get wire-tied?" John asked her.

"I was sittin' at home mindin' my own business when a truck drives up to my front porch. I opened the door to see who it was, and that rat bastard was standing there looking at me.

"Well, I remembered him and saw where I had hit him last time, so I turned back into the house to get my Bersa. He followed me in and wrestled the gun out of my hand. I slapped him and kicked him, but he got my arm behind me and put the gun to my head and made me walk out to my car. He forced me to get in, then got in the backseat with the gun on me.

"He told me to drive to your house. Guess he knew you wouldn't worry if you saw my car on the cameras. When we pulled up and no one came out of the house, he made me get out of the car and walk to the porch. About that time the big guy, what, Devon? Yeah, he came around the side of the house and RB trained the gun on him and handed me some wire ties. Told me to cuff the guy's hands. Not too, bright, RB, because he didn't check my handiwork. I left those things loose enough that the big guy could work his way out of them.

"Then RB told me to stand at the top of the steps. I guess no one was home because no one came out to help us. As soon as he heard your truck coming up the drive, he stuck the gun back to my head, and the rest is history. You were very brave, kid. And so was Girlie, getting out of that truck. And I'm glad I got to kick that RB right where I shot him. He had it comin'."

"RB?" John asked.

"Rat Bastard," Gram clarified.

"I know where everyone was," I said. "Romi had to go to the hotel to use their fax machine and the guys still at home went with him because he was afraid to drive himself. They all saw the alert when Gram drove up, and just like you,

John, they weren't worried when they saw it was her."

"And how is it you didn't know who was driving up to your house, Gram? Weren't the cameras on?" John asked with a perturbed look on his face.

Gram had the grace to look sheepish. "I turned them off since it was daytime, and I didn't figure he'd be stupid enough to come back for more. I mean, how stupid could he be?" she asked as she shrugged her shoulders up to her ears.

"Pretty stupid," John said. "Just like turning off the cameras was stupid. They're there for a reason, Gram. Please use them," he said with a soft look at her.

"I never needed them before. Don't see why I need them now that RB's been caught," Gram said defiantly.

I could see that John was getting upset and I knew he needed to stay calm, so I tried to change the subject.

"John, I forgot to tell you that the window guys came and replaced the one in my room and the one on the back porch. They look good as new," I told him.

"Good. One less thing to worry about," he said. I could tell he was still stewing over Gram's disregard of the cameras. I suggested we all play a word game together. Gram had never played before and beat us both. I was convinced she cheated but couldn't figure out how. We played two more games, and John and I each won one.

The door opened and a nurse wearing a gown and gloves came in.

"Hi, John. I'm your nurse, Tonya. I'm here to get you ready to get out of bed. Would you like me to come back later?" she asked.

"No, don't do that. I have PT and Gram was just leaving, too. We want you able to get out of bed now. I'll see you in the morning, babe." I leaned over and kissed him quickly. I stepped back and Gram gave him a one-armed hug, and we both left.

I walked Gram to the elevators. She was headed down and I was headed up. She hugged me before she got on her elevator and said she'd see me at home.

The whole time I was at PT I was thinking about how I had to leave soon and how much I didn't want to. Sure, I wanted to get back to work, but why did that have to mean leaving John? Life sucked sometimes.

As always happens when you're dreading something, the week flew by. John was getting stronger every day and doing well with his OT. He was even using a treadmill for short periods of time. He was anxious to be home, though. He didn't like either Gram or me making that long drive to see him, but neither of us was willing to leave him in the hospital alone.

The day finally came when I was able to put my foot on the floor. I had scheduled PT earlier that day so I could go before I saw John. I wanted to be walking when I saw him.

I knocked on his door and waited for him to call me in. I opened the door and walked in with both feet on the floor and no crutches. My boot made a loud thumping, but at least it was on the ground. John smiled so big and I walked over and sat on the edge of his bed.

"Congratulations, Stace! You're doing great! How's it feel to be a two-legged creature again?" he asked as he hugged me.

"It feels so good!" I told him. Then my face fell. He knew why.

"It won't be for long, you know. I'll be out of here before you know it, and taking that training, then I'll join you wherever you are. We'll do Facetime calls and maybe I'll even fly to Nashville to see you before you head to LA. This will work. You still want that, right?" he asked.

"Of course, I want that more than anything! I'm just going to be so busy and hard to get hold of. I don't want you to think for a minute that I've forgotten about you, even if you don't hear from me for a bit. Promise me that you won't think that," I practically cried.

"I promise. I know you'll be busy. And I've got a lot to do to get back to fighting strength, so I'll be busy, too. I'll be going to OT, too, once I get out of here, so plenty to keep me busy. I just want you to concentrate on your work, and I'll join you soon. Okay?" he asked.

"Okay. I'll try to focus, but it won't be easy. Romi and I are headed out tomorrow. I'm going to clean the house tonight so when you go home there won't be anything for you to do but rest and get stronger. Promise me you'll get better. And I'll call you every morning."

"I'll be looking forward to your calls. I can't wait to hear what the band thinks of your songs. And I want to know how the album is going and what the plans are for LA. You keep me in the loop, okay babe?" he said.

"Okay," I said. I looked at my watch. I only had an hour to get home for another Zoom call with the band. "I've got to go. Have a Zoom call soon with the band. I won't be able to be here tomorrow because we have an early flight, but I'll call you on the way to Blountville. I love you, John. Please remember that." I leaned over and kissed him as hard as I dared. I wanted to remember this kiss in the coming weeks.

He kissed me back just as hard. We kissed for so long he got winded and we had to stop. I gave him a huge hug and pressed kisses all over his face. He smiled and chuckled.

"Get going so you're not driving rushed. I'll talk to you in the morning. And feel free to pack one of my t-shirts if you want," he told me, and I could feel the tears welling on my lower lids. This was so hard! I shouldn't be leaving when he was still in the hospital, but I was committed to these things and I had to go.

I stood up and looked down at him. I loved him so much it hurt right now. But I had to be strong.

"Goodbye, John. I love you."

"See you soon. I love you, too."

I blew him a kiss and turned and walked out of the room. I made it to the car before the tears started to fall. I sat in the car and cried for what seemed like forever but was only about 15 minutes. Crap. I was gonna be late for my call. I called Romi and asked him to start the call without me and that I was on my way. I was still hiccupping as I started the long drive back to Whirlwind.

The night was both too long and too short. After my call, I cleaned the house top to bottom, even enlisting Romi's help despite his allergy to cleaning. I even made a couple of meals and froze them so John wouldn't have to worry about cooking when he got home. I went in his room and picked out my favorite t-shirt of his and packed it in my suitcase. Then I took it out and slept with it.

The morning came too soon. We had an early flight so I had to get him up and going. I made us both coffee and heated some blueberry muffins I had made a few days ago. We ate standing up and I cleaned up our mess. I put the mugs in the dishwasher. Then I wrote John a note.

John,

Sorry about the greeting, but I just couldn't write 'Dear' in front of your name. LOL. I already miss you more than I can say. I wish so hard that I didn't have these commitments that make it imperative that I leave now, or ever. I love being here in Whirlwind with you. I love the sound of your voice and your laughter, I love the way you smile just for me. I love the way you touch me and how you kiss me and make love to me. I would give anything to be staying here with you.

I can't wait to see you again in person, so please come visit soon. I love you so much and I want you to always know that. Not remember it, because I don't plan to give you time to remember, I plan to tell you every day as often as I can. When you listen to my songs please know I am singing them to you and for you. Again, I love you.

Always yours,

Stacy

I left the note on the breakfast bar so he'd see it easily. I cried the whole time I wrote it and the paper was wrinkled from my tears. Romi walked up behind me and gave me a hug.

I got up and grabbed my guitar case and my backpack and headed out to the car. I went back in for my suitcase while he carried out his two monster suitcases.

I went back one more time to lock the door. I swore I could feel eyes on me and knew that John was watching the cameras. I waved at the closest camera and blew a kiss. I walked down to the car and got in.

He looked at me and raised an eyebrow in silent question. I pointed forward and we were off.

I called John once we were on the highway headed to the airport. He was chuckling when he answered the phone.

"How'd you know I was watching you?" he asked.

"I felt you watching," I told him with a sniffle.

"Hey, none of that. I'll be seeing you soon. You've gotta go be a rock star, right?" he said.

"Something like that," I answered.

"Yeah, something like that. You're strong. You've got this. We've got this," he told me.

"I love you," I told him, still not tired of saying it. "I wrote you a letter and left it on the breakfast bar," I said.

"You're my life, Stace. I love you," he said.

"I've gotta go. I'm about to cry like a baby," I told him. "I'll try to call tonight, okay?"

"Okay, sweetheart. Have a safe trip and take care of that leg. I love you," he said once again.

"Love you." I hung up, crying like I'd promised. Like. A. Baby.

"God, Romi, this sucks."

I got out of the hospital six days after Stacy left.

The house felt empty without all those people around. There were no voices arguing sports, no Romi being dramatic. No Stacy. And even though Gram spent a couple of nights with me to make sure I was all right, I still felt lonely.

I found Stacy's letter on the breakfast bar and cried like a baby myself when I read it. I folded it up and put it in my nightstand to keep forever. I'm mushy. Sue me. I still take it out and read it once in a while.

Now, don't get me wrong, Facetime is a wonderful invention and has its place. But it can't take the place of in-person conversation. I lasted two weeks before I had to go visit. I was still out on medical leave, so I had the time. I told Stacy I was coming, and she screamed in my ear. She said Romi would meet me at the airport.

She wasn't kidding about her schedule. She was running from sunup to sundown. Between band practices, photo shoots for the album and recording sessions, we only got a few minutes together at a time. I went with her everywhere, though.

I met the band and sat in on practices. I went to photo shoots and was asked my opinion of the photos. I sat in the control booth for recording sessions and listened in awe as she sang her heart out.

She even recorded the funny little song she had written about me so I could have it.

I loved every minute of it, and hated it a little, too. She worked so hard, and I knew that most people would never know just how hard it was to be Darci Dorsette.

Stacy was also working hard on her PT and OT. She was walking better and had regained most of her muscle tone. She had taken to wearing long skirts and billowing pants to hide the boot but would soon be out of the boot and walking normally, just in time to film her movie.

I spent a week with her in Nashville, then had to head home. I had a follow-up appointment with my doctor I had to keep. It was almost harder saying goodbye this time than it had been last time. I told her I was working out my plan, and that I would see her soon. I knew we would miss each other, but if things went as I hoped, we'd both be too busy to notice in the next couple of weeks.

After my follow-up, I was given clearance for light duty at work. I called Invicta Security Services, the company now providing Stacy's protection, and asked about the next training session. I spoke with the head of the company, who told me their insurance would not permit them to have me in the training given my injury. That put an end to my big plans to join Stacy's security detail. Now how was I going to be with her?

I couldn't just mooch off her and follow her around. I needed to be doing something constructive and earning an income. I pulled up the recording of the song she wrote about me. I listened to the words and thought about my life here in Whirlwind, and about being the Sheriff. It hit me that this is where I was supposed to be, but maybe not all the time.

Rogetski and Long Cloud had become my workout buddies. I had noticed that Long Cloud had bulked up a lot in the last few months and asked him to help me rehab and build up some more muscle. I still wanted to be able to protect Stacy if needed. So, when Rogetski came over later that evening for a workout, I broached my idea with her.

I asked her if, for the next six to eight months, she would be willing to be acting Sheriff for a week a month. She thought about it all during our workout, I could see it on her face. When we were done, she told me that she was willing to do it for the experience, but that she would most likely take that experience somewhere else where she could be sheriff full-time. I told her I understood and that was fair.

Two days later we had a meeting with the county HR director and the town council. I told them that I was dating Darci Dorsette and needed time away to be with her on tour. Jaws dropped and there were gasps around the room as they recognized the name, but it took several minutes for what I said to really sink in.

I outlined the plan that I had come up with and explained that Rogetski was on board with it. I also told them about my training her for the last eight weeks and about how well she did as acting Sheriff while I was on medical leave.

The HR director had questions, of course, as did the Council. We hashed out the details and came to an agreement that everyone could live with.

I was feeling pretty lighthearted when I got back to my office. It was late morning, and I wanted to have a meeting with all my deputies about the changes coming. I stepped into my office and stopped short.

Stacy was here! She was sitting in the chair in front of my desk, her right leg jiggling a staccato beat.

"Stacy? What are you doing here?" I asked in shock.

She jumped up and turned around. She ran to me and grabbed my in a bear hug.

"Hey, is everything okay?" I asked her.

"It is now," she said, her voice muffled by my chest.

"Shhh, it's okay. Tell me what's wrong."

"Everything and nothing. I just missed you and I lost my focus and I had to see you. I can't stay long, but I had to see you," she said quietly.

I reached behind me to shut my office door. The meeting could wait.

I wrapped both my arms around her and just held her, swaying a little. She seemed content to stay like that, so we did. After a while, I pulled back gently to look at her face. There were tears there and her eyes were slightly puffy. And I noticed that she didn't have her contacts in, and her hair was red again. She wasn't hiding any more.

I pulled her gently over to my desk chair, where I sat down and pulled her down onto my lap. She wrapped one arm around my shoulders and sank into my chest. I leaned back slightly and heard the usual sound of squeaking.

"I'm glad you're here, because I have some news," I told her.

She lifted her head up to look at me. "News?" she asked. "About what?"

"My plan is finally in motion. I will be taking one week a month and flying to meet you wherever you are and staying with you. Anywhere in the world. Until your tour's over. How's that sound?" I asked.

She sat up fully and grabbed my head in her arms. "Oh, my God! Are you serious?" she cried.

"Yes," I mumbled from under her arms.

"Oh, sorry." She moved her arms so I could speak and breathe.

"No worries. Yes, it's all set up with the Town Council and Rogetski. In three weeks, I'll be flying to LA to be with you while you film your movie, then every three weeks after.

"Oh, John, that's wonderful!" she cried. "I mean, three weeks is a long time, but knowing you'll be coming for sure will help a lot!"

"I know it's not perfect, but it'll work for this tour. Then we will have some time off, I hope, to come up with a better plan for the next tour. Right?"

"Right. I've decided to take a year off after this tour. Three tours in as many years is too much. I want to have a good long time alone with you after this tour is over," she said as she snuggled back into my chest.

"When do you have to leave?" I asked her.

"First thing in the morning," she said.

"Well, then I'm taking the rest of the day off. Come on, let's go home."

I gently set her up on her feet and got out of my chair. I took her hand and pulled her out the front of the office. I stopped by dispatch and told Sandoff to call a meeting for all hands tomorrow morning at 10 a.m.

Stacy followed me home in her rental car. Once we got there and got out of our vehicles, we grabbed hands and walked up the steps together. We were just about to go inside when Gram's car came barreling around the curve and stopped in front of the porch. She slammed out of the car and climbed the stairs slowly. I just sighed and let out a long breath.

"Gram, what are you doing here?" I asked, frustrated.

"Just came by to say hi to the Girlie," she said. She wrapped Stacy in a big hug and kissed her cheek.

"Heard about the plan, kid. Glad you worked it out!" Gram said as she headed back down the stairs. I jumped into action to help her. I saw her to her car and smiled as she got in.

"I'll keep everyone away from here today. We'll talk after the girl leaves in the morning," Gram said.

I had no idea how she knew so much, but she did. I nodded and closed the car door. Gram spun around in the gravel and headed back down the driveway.

I raced back up the steps and unlocked the door. Once inside I locked it again. I didn't want to be disturbed. I took Stacy's hand and led her up the stairs. When we got to my room, Stacy immediately began to pull up my shirt to take it off. I pulled the neck from behind and whipped the shirt off. This was the first time Stacy was seeing the scar from the shooting. It was still red and puckered, like the wound from the chest tube, but it was closed and healing.

She ran gentle fingers over the scar, then placed a soft kiss on the spot. God, I loved this woman. She began placing little kisses all along my pecs, seeming to notice the extra work I was putting in. She ran her hands along my arms, noticing the increased biceps, too. I felt about 10 feet tall as she was loving me, and I knew that the rest of my life would not be enough time with this woman. She ran her hand back up to my left pec and her palm grazed my nipple, turning the peak into stone. I knew that every day was going to be a lifetime if I had anything to say about it.

EPILOGUE ONE

Stacy

Making a movie sucked. I mean, serious props to actors who do this all the time and do it well. As for me, no thanks. I didn't think I'd ever do one again. I appreciated the opportunity and all, but no.

I'd always thought that movies were made in the order we saw them, one scene following another. No. They filmed out of order, but you were still supposed to show the right emotion, or make the right moves, so that it made sense once the movie was done. Ugh. It was so hard! Especially the love scenes. Which just happened to be filmed the week John was in town. Geez.

He was a trooper, though. He got on well with my co-star, a fellow singer that I'd only met on set. John knew that I was thinking of him whenever I had a love scene, and he seemed to be okay with it all, but I wasn't. Especially when I was expected to suddenly have a love scene after shooting a car crash or some other scene that didn't make sense at the time. And the director. Ugh!

"Is the girl on set?"

"Why isn't the girl in makeup?"

"Has the girl been to wardrobe?"

I was just 'the girl'. He never addressed me directly and he never used my name. He didn't have that problem with my co-star. Just me.

"Two more weeks and you're done. Just remember that." John was rubbing my shoulders after a particularly difficult scene.

"I know. I just don't want to do this again. Remind me of that if anyone every asks me to, please?"

He chuckled. "I will, sweetheart. I will." He leaned down and kissed me gently on the lips.

"Get the girl! Let's do this again!" Mr. Hart yelled.

"Ugh. Again?" I asked no one in particular.

"You can do it, Angel," John said.

"I love you," I told him.

"Love you back," he said.

We finished filming two days early, so I hopped a flight to Nashville almost faster than my fingers could make the reservation. Romi wanted me to head home and do some work with him, but I was going to connect straight into Blountville and drive to Whirlwind to surprise John. He was due to leave on tour with me in two weeks, but I wanted to celebrate finishing the film with him.

I was driving up his driveway when I saw him standing on the porch waiting for me. He must have figured out who it was since he didn't recognize the car.

As I parked, he ran down the steps to my side and opened the door. He grabbed my hand and pulled me out and into his arms.

This was home.

THE SHERIFF'S STAR

EPILOGUE TWO

JOHN

It had been a long eight months. The tour had gotten extended twice, two weeks at a time. Stacy was playing to sold out audiences around the world. Tonight was her last show, though, and it was here in Nashville at Bridgestone Arena.

I had seen the rehearsals and knew that Stacy had the songs and choreography down pat, but it never failed to awe me just how wonderful she was on stage. I always had an up-front view from the wings, so maybe I was prejudiced, but I didn't think so. She was perfection. And soon she'd be on a one-year break.

This night was going to be extra special. I reached inside my pants pocket and felt the small box I had tucked there. I was going to wait until she had come off-stage and showered and calmed down from the adrenaline high, then I was going to ask her. In our hotel room. Just us. No paparazzi. No onlookers. Just us.

Suddenly my attention returned to the stage as a stagehand brought out a stool and Stacy's trusty Mathilda. This was new.

Stacy went back out on stage after a water break and sat on the stool. She picked up Mathilda and started strumming. The applause was deafening. She held up her hand to quiet the audience, no small feat given the size of the crowd.

"Shhh, everyone. I have something special I would like to dedicate to the man in my life, John. He's been with me this whole tour and is the greatest man I know. Let's give it up for John!" she said and the audience roared with applause. I could feel my face turn bright red as she looked over at me.

Then I noticed the tune she was strumming. I had heard it many times coming out of my phone. She was playing the song she wrote for me. I felt my ears heat up.

She sang like an angel, and even as I smiled, I fell a little more in love with her, as if that were possible. She finished the song and held out her hand in my direction. Romi was behind me, pushing me to move forward. I took off my old

Stetson and held it by my side as I slowly made my way toward Stacy on stage. I didn't dare look out at the audience for fear I'd throw up. I just looked at Stacy.

When I reached her I took her outstretched hand in mine. I stepped closer and dropped her hand to wrap mine around the back of her neck and I kissed her like I had never kissed her before. There, in front of tens of thousands of people, I kissed the love of my life.

Later that night, as we were laying in bed, I summoned up the courage to propose. I leaned down to get the box out of my pants that were lying on the floor by the bed. I pulled the box behind my back as I lay on my side.

I looked Stacy right in the eyes as I started.

"Stacy, I love you more than my own life. I've never been as happy or as fulfilled as I am right now, and I know you're the reason. It's been a tough several months, but we've gotten through it together, and now we get to spend some time alone and quiet, and I can't wait. I want to spend every night for the rest of our lives together. I don't want to go another day without waking up next to you. I want my every breath to be filled with your scent. And I want my every thought to be of you. Will you marry me?" I asked her.

"Oh, John," she said, tears filling her eyes. I pulled the box out from behind my back and opened it. She looked at the ring then at me.

"Before I say yes, there's something I have to tell you," she said solemnly.

"What is it, baby?" I asked.

"I'm pregnant," she said as she sobbed.

"Pregnant? Are you sure?" I asked, in shock.

"Yes. I found out when we were in Munich but didn't want to say anything until the tour was over. I'm just over two months along. Are you happy?" she asked, not looking at me anymore.

"Happy? I'm ecstatic! This is wonderful!" I sat up and pulled her up onto my lap and kissed her hard.

"So, what about an answer to my question?" I asked.

"Yes! So many times, yes!" she yelled. I slid the ring on her finger.

I wrapped my arms around her and squeezed. This was going to be the best year ever. Until the year after that. and the year after that.

I had the love of my life, and we had created a new life together. I was so excited for this new chapter of our lives and couldn't wait to get started.

I moved one of her legs so Stacy was straddling me, with her upper body lying on top of me and I kept my arms around her. I whispered silly, sweet nothings in her ear until she fell asleep, warm and secure in my arms.

THE SHERIFF'S STAR

THE PROTECTOR'S Heart

GUARD MY HEART 2 SERIES

JULIA MARTIN DARE

Candice just escaped her abusive husband with her young niece, but he wasn't letting her go so easily. He tried to kill her, and now he's terrorizing her at every turn. Finally, her brother sends a friend to keep Candice and her niece safe from their abuser.

Malcolm was trained to protect those weaker than him, but the moment he set eyes on Candice, she was more than just an assignment to him. Suddenly he was getting so caught up in the family that he felt getting out was the only way to save his sanity. But he couldn't just leave Candice alone to be victimized all over again.

What was going to happen to Candice if he left? What about the permanent reminder of her past that she carried? How could he hope to protect her when her abuser hid behind others? All he wanted to do was love her and make her family his, no matter the cost.

COMING JULY 2023

Made in the USA
Middletown, DE
19 June 2023